THE LAST TANGO OF SEÑOR MENENDEZ

THE LAST TANGO OF SEÑOR MENENDEZ

Reg Carr

Book Guild Publishing
Sussex, England

First published in Great Britain in 2008 by
The Book Guild Ltd
Pavilion View
19 New Road
Brighton, BN1 1UF

Typesetting in Meridien by
Acorn Bookwork Ltd, Salisbury, Wiltshire

Printed in Great Britain by
Biddles Ltd., King's Lynn

A catalogue record for this book is available from
The British Library

ISBN 978 1 84624 234 2

Dedication

This story is dedicated to all those British and Argentine servicemen, killed, wounded or mentally scarred during the short war over the Falkland Islands/Las Islas Malvinas. As someone once said, `War is the failure of diplomacy. Talk, talk is far better than war, war!'

Chapter One

June 1981 Islas Malvinas

The gale came roaring out of the southwest from south of Cape Horn, a violent, roaring monster throwing hail showers, shards of ice crystals and curtains of rain like chain mail at the small trawler fishing to the south of the Falkland Islands, or 'Islas Malvinas' as the Argentine crew called them. Her skipper quickly turned the ship into the steadily building grey seas and they dragged the trawl around. The bow cut heavily through the large waves climbing above the height of the bridge, rushing down upon the ship, hitting the sharp bow with a crash then parting to sweep swiftly along the ship's side before meeting again in the churning wake. The ship pitched and rolled violently in the rough southern seas, but she was designed to cope with the conditions out there and met every challenge confidently.

They were sailing outside the 12-mile limit claimed by the British and trawling in the rich fisheries around the islands in the traditional fishing grounds of generations of Patagonian fishermen. They would have a full fish hold when they hauled in this time. Their skipper was an old hand and also a member of the Argentine Naval Reserve. He had been keeping his eyes open and monitoring radio traffic and movements around the islands in the vicinity, as the Navy always wished to know what was happening around these islands long claimed by Argentina. They had

1

been sailing off the 700 islands of Islas Malvinas for the last two weeks. All seemed to be quiet and they hadn't seen any British warships.

Leaving the small ship behind, the storm moved on up Falkland Sound and over the main islands of West and East Falkland, battering the scattered settlements and lashing and soaking the hundreds of thousands of sheep grazing on the poor grass, and the penguins and black-browed Albatrosses feeding in the rich seas. Blasting the oldest suspension bridge in the southern hemisphere at Bodie Creek, it rattled on the corrugated walls and roofs of many of the houses and hammered the windows of the more substantial English style cottages in Stanley, the main town. In one of the grander residences there, although still no larger than a country house in the Lake District, the Governor looked up as the hail lashed the conservatory fixed solidly to the back of the building. 'What a god forsaken place this can be. Yet an hour from now the storm will pass and the sun will catch the retreating clouds and shine in the wet roofs and across the low-lying hills that fringe the coast, the wind will die down for a while and the wild beauty will hit you between the eyes. So like the moorlands of Britain, low glacial-eroded granite hills covered with sedge grass and peat except here there are few walkers to enjoy the views. But so beautiful when there is that wonderful watery light that comes in the aftermath of a storm.'

As the storm moved away to the northeast and the sun shone through gaps in the clouds, the trawler hauled in its nets, stowed the fish and began the long journey northwest across the Mar Argentino to its home port of Comodoro Rivadavia, rolling heavily across the oily grey ocean as the seas came in on the starboard quarter, with petrels skimming along in its wake, leaving Islas Malvinas to the depredations of the South Atlantic Ocean, and the men who jealously eyed the rich potential of the fisheries around the islands and the oil-bearing rocks beneath.

June 1981 Buenos Aires

At the eastern end of the Plaza de Mayo in Buenos Aires stands the Casa Rosada. Its pink façade is said to be an attempt in the 1870s to bring peace between the opposing political groups by mixing their colours of red and white. Others say it came from the historic practice of painting buildings with bovine blood. Whatever the cause the presidential palace looks a delicate shade of pink in the winter sunlight. Should anyone in the crowd in the Plaza de Mayo look up, they would see a portly grey-haired man in uniform looking out from the long windows behind the famous balcony where Eva Peron once addressed the crowds. In the Presidential Office in the Casa Rosada the group of senior Junta members watched the man gazing out of these long windows that look down on the Plaza de Mayo and the hundreds of people strolling in the winter sun. He was staring at the light blue national flag across the square moving gently in the breeze, and agonizing over the proposal presented to him a few minutes ago. Having been President for only a few short months, he didn't see how he could reject it because of the weakness of his personal position. His personal thoughts, although he kept them to himself, were, 'Is this really what it has come to, the only way we can save the Junta because of our economic ills is this risky military adventure?' Turning to his fellow Junta members, he said, 'So gentlemen, your proposal is that we should overcome our economic and political troubles by

3

focusing the country's energies on a national aim. It makes a lot of sense but clearly there are great risks. How do we know the British will not react?'

One of the Admirals present answered, 'Sir, the British have announced the withdrawal of their ice-patrol ship and there is much debate in their parliament about the costs of maintaining their remaining colonies. I doubt they'll lift a finger if we take action,' he added dismissively.

Another senior officer supported him, 'We also found an excuse to insist on the recall of their military attaché and have refused to let them appoint another one. So they have no expert here to monitor our build-up of forces.'

The air force general offered the President the final reassurance, 'We understand the United States will support our case should a protest be brought to the UN.'

The President turned from the window and looking steadily at the assembled group of senior officers uttered the fateful instruction. 'So be it. The presentation is clear and the objective is very attractive. The outline project is approved. Begin planning of Operation Rosario with implementation in February 1982. The glorious year 1982 will be when we reclaim Las Islas Malvinas from the British and restore our national pride.'

October 1981 Rokko Gyoen Hotel above Kobe

The two men, one Caucasian the other Japanese, were relaxing in a private hot spring bath whilst they were bathed and pampered by two young women. Mr Yamauchi, the Japanese, gave a pleasurable sigh, 'Well, John, isn't this the best way to relax after a hard day at the office. What about these girls? They are very pretty and skilled?'

John Ridley laughed, 'I'm not sure about relaxing. This girl has made me rock hard. I think it's time to dress and have some dinner as I sense we have much serious discussion ahead of us tonight. Your summons is an ominous portent.'

Yamauchi suggested, 'You can have her later if you wish, she will wait for you in your room after dinner.'

'No. I think a quiet night is required and anyway she is too young for me these days. In my job abstinence is by far the safest option.'

The two men splashed out of the hot tub and the two girls happily dried them with the all-enveloping hot towels and produced fresh clothes for them to wear at dinner. They made a strange pair, Mr Yamauchi (no-one ever used his first name) was a short and stocky grey-haired, middle-aged and very formal career diplomat. John Ridley was 31, tall, lean with fair hair, and currently International Personnel Manager for Nippon Health. However what brought them together had nothing to do with Japan or the pharmaceutical industry.

They moved through to the small, simply appointed private dining room and sat down on the tatami surrounding the low table. The girls now tastefully dressed in kimonos served them Kirin beer and some rice crackers then withdrew until dinner was required. John waited whilst Yamauchi enjoyed his beer and marshalled his thoughts.

As was his usual practice, Yamauchi opened the conversation obliquely and tentatively, 'John, we have known each other for some years and have become great friends, I think.' At these sentiments John nodded vigorously and made to reply but Yamauchi stopped him with a gentle movement of his hand. 'I think we are going to find our friendship and loyalty to each other is severely tested over the next year or so.'

'This sounds very serious, even for you,' smiled John. 'I guess I am correct about the portents. Obviously I'm getting more superstitious as I get older. Now you have whetted my interest perhaps you should explain further without delay.'

'We've been friends, have we not, since we first met when I was in the Japanese Defence Forces and you visited Japan on Royal Navy business in 1972, and then again when I spent a pleasurable secondment in your Ministry of Defence in London just before you resigned. I've always had a great respect for the British and as you know I am happy and honoured to help British Intelligence when the tasks do not affect Japan.'

Again Ridley tried to interrupt but at Yamauchi's wave of the hand sat back on the sofa.

'We also know you are still a member of British Naval Intelligence although you are believed to have resigned in 1975. You have a Canadian passport, live in Toronto and as a citizen of a small liberal western democracy you have ready access into most countries in the world should you wish to go there. Your personnel management and business development role provides an excellent rationale for all the travelling you do. But what of your home in the UK, don't you miss it?'

'I don't think much about my self-imposed exile these days and I like my place in Toronto. I think it is a great city and it is easy to keep in touch with developments through my contacts in the High Commission.'

'Can you ever go to London?' asked Yamauchi.

'Occasionally I pass through London and meet up with the Director in a secure room at Heathrow, but I have to keep away from Northumberland and Hexham in particular – they are not places a Canadian would visit. Hopefully some day when I give this work up I'll go back and walk the northern fells, particularly the Simonside Hills near Rothbury. It's a grand place and I remain very fond of it.'

'You have become a bit of a loner, my friend. That's not surprising, but it isn't good for you. You need to find someone you can trust.'

'I suppose you are right. I've always liked intelligence work right from the very beginning at university. I mean the real thing, the targeted gathering of information and the slow build up of the picture – not the James Bond image that people have! But you learn not to trust most people.'

Yamauchi changed the tone. 'You are correct in your earlier assumption that we have serious matters to discuss. Our boss believes there could be problems in the South Atlantic before too long and wants to have intelligence resources positioned there. Admiral Collingwood still has a good nose about these things, don't ask me where his information comes from: he seems to have contacts everywhere. Well, he wishes to put a watcher in place, although the political view at the moment is to discount the assessment that the Argentines mean trouble. Your political masters are much more anxious to reduce defence costs than hang on to a colony thousands of miles from the UK in the bleak southern ocean. Your boss suspects the Argentines may be planning some action against the Falklands. They refused the British Embassy permission to appoint another military attaché. Quoting some nonsense about the embassy being over the agreed size. So there is no one there capable of making an expert naval assessment.'

'Is there a plan?'

'I have managed to get myself appointed as cultural and business attaché in our embassy in Montevideo, Uruguay, and they want you to spend much of your time in Argentina and Uruguay. The Japanese Embassy serves both Argentina and Uruguay but my office will be in Montevideo. This will make it easier for you to contact me but in an emergency it will not be thought strange that I go across to Buenos Aires. They suggest you set up a Nippon Health subsidiary in Argentina. This would provide the rationale for the necessary visits. Your Spanish fluency will be important but so might your German given the heritage of many Argentines.'

'I suppose it would make sense', mused Ridley, 'we are under-represented in South America compared to other Japanese pharmaceutical companies.'

'They want you to continue to operate out of Toronto and on no account over the next twelve months are you to travel to or via London. A fresh contact will be activated in the High Commission in Canada. This is likely to be a woman so social contact through your friends at the High Commission will not look strange and after an interval she will be able to visit your apartment without comment. Your boss is also approaching a long-standing contact in Canadian Intelligence and we hope to have a Canadian to act as your courier in Argentina should this prove necessary. When you visit Uruguay as part of your fact-finding exercise I shall meet you, as I am also the business development official for Japanese companies in Montevideo.'

Pausing he smiled at his friend, 'Now shall we have some dinner?'

He moved to the doorway and sliding back the door spoke quickly to the girl kneeling outside. She rose elegantly, bowed deeply and then rushed to get their food. A short while later after a pleasurable silence the men heard the door slide back and the two girls entered carrying dishes that they placed on the low table. From the large bowl they gracefully served miso soup, and then a handsome meal of Oyako donburi, gyoza dumplings, mushrooms and pickles followed by some raw Maguro sashimi, yakitori, mixed tempura and thick udon noodles. After the plates were cleared away the girls returned bringing Sake and rice cakes and the conversation turned once more to Argentina.

'John, last week I happened to meet a director of your company and I took the opportunity to mention that our government would like Japanese companies to consider developing their businesses in South America in a more positive way than is possible through wholesalers. He seemed quite receptive to the idea and he recognizes that this is what their western competitors are doing. I am sure therefore a proposal from you to develop the business in Argentina and Uruguay will find favour. I suggest you put it to Nippon Health when you visit their headquarters tomorrow.'

Ridley smiled at the 'just happened to meet' comment but said nothing. He sat quietly for a while lost in his own thoughts, running his mind over the business implications and the intelligence challenges of what was proposed. 'I can see the plausibility of your suggestion and I think it could work. I will have to get up to flying speed pretty quickly as I don't have much knowledge of the Argentine and Uruguayan pharmaceutical industries and markets but that in itself gives me a good excuse for going there, meeting key authorities and visiting the main towns and ports. The main difficulty will be communications. I'm sure the local intelligence services will be monitoring all communications closely so during a period of tension it will be important to either get stuff to you or this courier for onward transmission. The alternative will be for me to bring it out to Toronto and then send it on by my secure link or this contact that is being set up. You said you would be in Montevideo from next January so before then if the assessments aren't urgent I can send them from Toronto. I presume we will continue to use the same system for setting up meetings?'

Seeing Yamauchi nod, he continued. 'As for the business proposition, I think I'm highly regarded by Nippon Health and my views are trusted not only about personnel matters but also business development ever since the work I did in Saudi a year ago. I think there is a case for setting up a subsidiary in Buenos Aires so I'm sure I will get approval to do the exploratory work and the necessary letters to show the Ministries of Health and the industry associations. Especially if your Foreign Ministry and MITI are encouraging,' he added with a smile. 'When do we think things might come to a head?'

Mr Yamauchi shrugged, 'It is not clear but we don't think they will wait beyond their autumn, that is April or May next year. It will be one of your jobs to try to put together a timeline if you can.'

After a further contemplative pause he looked seriously at his friend. 'This is likely to be one of your most difficult and dangerous missions. Don't underestimate Argentine military intelligence, they are sharp and professional and very ruthless. They have been operating in an internal security role for many years and since the Junta came to power they have ensured its survival. Have you heard of the *Desaparecidos*? These are their political opponents and their families, and they have literally disappeared off the face of the earth. So be very careful and keep a low profile. That won't be easy when you have to go into Patagonia but do your best. I trust nobody in Argentina knows you from your previous life?'

'No, I don't think so. OK, I hear you, Yamauchi-san, I will be very careful. As far as I know there is no one in Argentina who can challenge my present alias. Thank you for the briefing and *gochiso sama*. I wish long life to you and your family and, if not before, I shall see you in Montevideo in January.'

So saying he rose from the tatami, bowed low as custom demanded and strode across to the doorway. Sliding open the thin door he saw the young girl kneeling with downcast eyes. Taking her hands he raised her up and smiling gently kissed her on the cheek. He thanked her for her care and attention, and politely refused her offer to be his companion in the short Japanese bed in his room. In his room he took off his Japanese clothes and pulled on the wrap provided before sitting by the bed mulling over what his friend had said. This was going to be a daunting challenge but one that filled him with excitement. He had never been one to fear the unknown, for his approach was to prepare meticulously. He didn't know Argentina but new places always attracted him. It also sounded as though this could be a vital project and he always revelled in work that fitted into important global strategies. Anyway the next day's visit to Tokyo had now assumed more significance than the usual routine progress report, so he had better sketch out a business project on the plane from Osaka. With that he turned in and slept like a log.

In the morning refreshed he took a light breakfast of miso soup, gohan, nori, pickles and green tea in the hotel on Mount Rokko overlooking Kobe and Harima-nada Bay. He gazed out over the steep mountainside to the sprawling Osaka/Kobe conurbation and the frenetic bustle of a modern Japanese city below, and marvelled how peaceful it was at the top of the mountain. Drinking his tea he watched the large ships out at sea moving to and from the international port. Finishing his breakfast he took the ten-minute cable car to Rokko Station and caught a train to Osaka Airport for the flight to Tokyo Haneda. After the hour-long flight on a packed jet he disembarked in the flood of Japanese and headed for the taxi rank and the Head Office of Nippon Health close by the Imperial Palace and the Akasaka Tokyu Hotel. His meeting with the head of sales development was not until after lunch so he had time to develop his proposal and have it typed by the secretarial assistant allocated to him. His meeting with Mr Ishuro Tana went very well and he received approval to develop the proposal further and bring it to the February board meeting. A letter was prepared assuring the authorities in Argentina and Uruguay of the seriousness of the project. Mr Tana confided that he had received a request from MITI (Ministry of Industry, Technology and Information) to look for opportunities to develop in South America so Ridley's proposal was very attractive and opportune. Ridley made no comment.

After the meeting he headed back by the bullet train to the new Tokyo Narita airport for his flight to San Francisco via Anchorage, Alaska. Flying business class on the B747 was very relaxing and after a good meal he pushed back the seat and slept for a few hours waking refreshed as the plane touched down in Anchorage to refuel. A quick switch of planes in San Francisco and he was on the Air Canada flight to Toronto as usual feeling that rush of pleasure as the plane touched down in his adopted city.

Chapter Two

Toronto October 1981

Leaving the taxi that brought him from the airport he entered his apartment block at Victoria Square off Dupont Street. His tenth floor apartment had superb views over the city and the lake from the spacious sitting room furnished in the minimalist style of the bachelor. Painted white throughout with a warm terracotta-coloured carpet, the furniture Swedish 'designer', it was full of lights and glassware. On the walls were photos of country cottages and landscape prints by the Canadian artist Tom Thomson. The double bedroom was comfortable with a large bed and more photos, this time of British Columbia, but the most important room was the study next door with its extensive library of reference books where he did his serious thinking and planning.

Over the next few days he worked on his plans for the Argentine subsidiary and set up a trip to Buenos Aires, organized briefing meetings with the Ministry of Health, the pharmaceutical industry association and wholesalers. On Friday afternoon his phone rang. 'Hi Paul, long time no see. What, this evening? Yes, I guess I could make it even though it is rather short notice. I haven't got anything on. Who is this surprise party for anyway? Oh, a new colleague from the UK. OK I will be delighted to accept the invitation from you Brits, see you out in Mississauga about 9p.m. then.'

So everything was moving fast. Paul Gregory was from the British High Commission. A new member just arrived from UK based in the Trade team in the offices down near the lakeshore. His new contact. John had known Paul ever since he joined the High Commission about two years before, not long after John had set himself up in Toronto in his Nippon Health personnel role. He had received an invitation to a reception at the High Commission in Ottawa and once contact had been made, friendship had developed, and Paul had become John's conduit for information to the UK only used sparingly but necessary for really vital information.

Later John drove his car out of the underground garage and headed westwards from the city on the highway stretching ribbon-like across the flat countryside towards one of the new condominiums in Mississauga, and the large house Paul maintained in this developing town and business centre to the west of Toronto. The party was in full swing when he arrived and he slipped quietly into the house and grabbed a glass of white wine before talking to some acquaintances. He knew Paul would have spotted him and left it to him to engineer the meeting with the new contact.

'There you are then,' said a voice in his ear and he turned to see Paul Gregory standing next to him accompanied by the most gorgeous girl he had seen in a long time.

'Hi, Paul how are you doing?'

'Well I am doing OK, but I would like to introduce you to a new member of the High Commission who will be in charge of the Toronto Trade Office. Meet Andy James. Andy, this is John Ridley who is international personnel manager for Nippon Health. He is a Canadian based here in Toronto, but has global responsibilities including the UK so he will no doubt wish to pick your brains from time to time. He is also very knowledgeable about hiking and exploring in this part of Canada and can give you good advice about how to avoid being chased by a bear.'

Having made the contact, Paul wandered off leaving John and Andy together. They engaged in some natural and desultory small talk then joined up with another group before separating and moving off in different directions. Ridley felt strangely unsettled by the brief contact. Later on as the party quietened about midnight, they bumped into each other and sat down on a sofa and began to chat very generally and gently got to know each other. After a while they realized they were not acting, they really liked talking. John asked, 'Andy, where are you staying at the moment?'

'They've put me up in the Napier on the Esplanade not far from the office in Downtown.'

'Have you got a lift organized tonight or should I drop you off?'

'John, that would be great if it isn't too much trouble,' she replied. John got to his feet and holding out his hand pulled her upright. 'OK let's go then.'

When they were in the car and on the way back to Downtown on the 405 John asked, 'Are you SIS?'

'Yes, for about eight years since leaving university,' she answered.

'Have you been fully trained in tradecraft and have you operated as an agent's contact before?'

Andy replied, 'I see they are correct about you.' Seeing his quizzical look she continued, 'You are very precise and direct just as they said you would be. It will be a challenge working with you. I am fully trained and have operated as a back-up agent's contact. Until this posting I worked on

15

the South American Desk so I'm up to date with the intelligence assessments and still have all my contacts should we need them.'

'That's great', said John, 'I am sure you will be a great help and it is always reassuring to know there is someone you can rely on back at base. What else did they tell you about me?'

'That you are very straight and would never let me down.'

After this initial skirmish that left them both feeling privately elated, they got down to the serious business of how they would operate together. 'We need to gradually develop a friendship to the point where it wouldn't be surprising if you spent the night at my apartment', stated John.

Andy suggested, 'If things develop quickly in Argentina we may need our communication route soon. We also need our code so you can pass some information over an open phone line.' She smiled at him, 'You can ring me while you are away like a dutiful lover.'

'Right,' said John. 'Then my first task is to ask you out to dinner tomorrow evening. I know this fabulous Italian restaurant, Giovanni's, in King Street East that isn't far from your hotel. I shall make a reservation for 8 p.m. and look forward to our first date. It's quite formal by Toronto standards so a little black number would be ideal.' Soon they approached the Esplanade. 'Here is your hotel. Sleep well, I'll see you tomorrow evening. Goodnight Andy!'

With that he drove off to his apartment thinking that after all this might be a very pleasurable assignment. As Andy got ready for bed she felt strangely moved by the meeting. For someone who operated as an agent on the margins he was a nice guy. They seemed to hit it off from the first as equals but there was a dangerous frisson around that would have to be controlled. 'The manual says no emotional involvement,' she reminded herself.

The next morning Ridley was up early and had a good workout in the gym in the basement of the apartments. Then after a light breakfast he grappled with the challenge of fitting in the intelligence-gathering exercise around the pharmaceutical fact-finding process. Andy would provide a lot of the detail but he felt confident he could get to many places by locating a sales rep or using a pharmacy wholesaler to distribute there. The big problem would be getting into Patagonia if the balloon went up because the military would restrict movement. 'There are at least two airbases down there that I will have to assess,' he mused. 'And I must check the amphibious capability because without it there can be no threat to the Falkland Islands.'

Having established a clear way ahead and what information he needed from Andy James, he called up a friend to see if he had a spare ticket for that afternoon's Blue Jays baseball match at the Exhibition Stadium. After spending a pleasant afternoon watching the game and hanging out with the guys he returned to his apartment for an hour relaxing with a chilled glass of Chardonnay and some cool MJQ jazz.

At five minutes to eight, for like many naval officers he regarded not being five minutes early as being late, he was seated at his favourite corner table in the Ristorante Giovanni on King Street East. Just after eight Andy arrived and yet again she took his breath away. She was dressed simply in a slim black high-necked cocktail dress that stopped just above the knee with pearl earrings and a single strand pearl necklace. A fairly tall girl she was wearing heels and seemed to glide along as she was escorted to the table. He was very conscious of the envious stares from other diners as she came towards him. She had a wonderful smile on her face and looked really happy to see him, and he was aware that he had a stupid grin on his face.

Her gorgeous deep green eyes looked straight at him and she smiled again.

'John, this is fantastic. You could easily imagine you were in Tuscany. If the food is as good as the décor I am going to really enjoy this.'

'Andy, it is really good to see you. You look fantastic. Would you like a glass of Prosecco whilst you decide what to eat?'

'Mm,' said Andy with a satisfied look on her face.

The meal passed pleasantly as they shared their life histories, or at least the public versions. He learned about her career in the Department of Trade and Industry and he told her about his work as an international personnel manager and his plans for South America. After their single expresso however a silence fell between them and they both became intensely aware of each other. Inhibited by the thought that making a pass at a colleague is not the done thing, John agonized about the next step. Andy could see the thoughts flashing across his eyes as she looked at him, and so she took his hand in hers. 'John', she said softly, 'we can't fight this. We're not youngsters and we both know we're massively attracted to each other: it's like lightning flashing between us. We have to acknowledge it and handle it, not avoid it.' She smiled and looked at him with those gorgeous green eyes, 'I am happy to take the risk if you are.'

John sighed, 'Andy, you seem able to read my mind. Thank you, I feel exactly the same and want to be with you. Shall we go then?'

'Yes sir,' said Andy, 'I want to see this bachelor pad that you have described so exquisitely this evening. We had better stop off at my hotel so I can change into something more suitable, and ...', she grinned, 'get something suitable for tomorrow!'

As the taxi drew up outside the apartments in Victoria Square Andy looked around. 'What a beautiful neighbourhood, is there really a good view over the city?'

'Well come and see,' and with that he took her hand and led her through the smart foyer and into the lift. As the lift door closed she moved quickly to him and wrapping her arms around him and pressing her body against his, gave him a beautiful gentle kiss that wasn't virginal. 'Mm, I needed that,' said Andy.

As they left the lift and reached the door of his apartment John turned to her and gave her a quick kiss and said, 'Life is too short. So let's just take it as it comes and work out each step along the way.'

With that he led her into the apartment whose sheer simplicity and design excellence impressed her. John clearly was a sophisticated and complex man. He led her to the sitting room windows and she looked out over the lights of the city, the flashing lights and rotating restaurant on the CNN Tower and the ferries moving on Lake Ontario. Leaving her for a moment he opened a chilled bottle of Pinot Grigio and rejoined her with two glasses. They gazed out over the city sipping their wine for a while, then she turned to him with a smile and said, 'Well, what happens now?'

John answered her smile, 'Well, my lady I shall take you to bed and we shall make love, then in the morning I shall prepare a wonderful Canadian breakfast for you.' With that he took her hand and led her into the bedroom.

On Sunday morning, after lying for a while listening to her breathing gently beside him, he slipped quietly out of bed, and leaving a note to say where he was going, took his regular morning jog before calling in for fresh French bread from the boulangerie nearby. As he entered the flat he heard the shower running and called to her. Leaving a dressing gown for her he prepared breakfast. A few minutes later she entered the kitchen looking freshly scrubbed and very happy, and leant over to give him a gentle kiss. 'Well,' she said, 'that was a wonderful night, where do we go from here?'

'Breakfast!'

'You know what I mean,' she chided him.

John pointed out, 'Our plan was to develop an artificial friendship as our cover, that has happened and the feelings we have for each other mean it will be realistic. We must keep reminding ourselves that we are entering a dangerous game.'

Andy, looking steadfastly at him, a hint of tears in those beautiful green eyes replied, 'I don't want to lose you and I want to help you. You can trust me completely. I know it can be very difficult to trust anyone in this business.' With that she turned away and went out of the kitchen, turning in the doorway to smile that beautiful smile of hers.

He moved quickly across to her, 'We shall share the risks together and hopefully come through this safely. Now let's have some breakfast. Then I want to take you to the park.'

Later sitting in his study they reviewed the position and Andy briefed him on the military dispositions in Argentina. 'The main fleet base is at Puerto Belgrano near Bahia Blanca, the submarine base is at Mar del Plata, and there appear to be other naval bases in Patagonia at Puerto Deseado and Rio Gallegos. There is also a Marine Corps base near Rio Gallegos so an invasion force could sail from there as it is the closest to the Falklands.'

'What about airbases?'

'There are two air arms, the air force and the navy, and they are both well equipped. There are a number of airbases down the Atlantic coast and we will need to identify where the main strike aircraft might operate. A lot of the airbases are joint military and civil ones so this may make observation a bit easier. The navy operates from Buenos Aires international airport, Bahia Blanca, Rawson and Rio Gallegos in Patagonia, and Rio Grande on Tierra del Fuego. But we think it would be virtually impossible to get down there as you cannot justify it as a base for a pharmaceutical representative: not enough business. The air force operates out of airfields at Comodoro Rivadavia, San Julian and Rio Gallegos all in Patagonia. Your boss isn't too worried about army movements but it is vital we get a picture of fleet and air operations.'

'The problem will be moving around so as to not excite interest in Patagonia. It's very sparsely populated. If they decide to act against the Falklands they are bound to try to button up Patagonia tightly as that'll make it very difficult to obtain up-to-the-minute intelligence. We won't be able to suborn locals and anyway if I remember correctly there weren't many there anyway. I'll become part of the landscape so they don't see me as an outsider if it blows up. I need to get this pharmaceutical project moving.'

Andy said, 'We must establish our code. How about: the number of times you say "Love" means the number of escorts. If you say "Missing you" the carrier is there. "Warm day" means submarines are there. "Can't wait" means there are coastal patrol vessels there. "Toronto" means the Cruiser Belgrano. "Party" means A4 Skyhawks. "Quiet dinner" means Super Etendards. "Lovely day" means you have

21

met someone who poses a potential risk. If you think the risk is low say, "Also should be a lovely day tomorrow".

'This'll get the key information out quickly by phone if something happens. We're also hoping to get a courier into Buenos Aires. Can we call it BA like the locals do? It's such a mouthful? He can take things out for you but this can't be confirmed at the moment. I gather there will be someone in Uruguay who will provide close support but I don't know who it is. Anyway you shouldn't tell me.' And then she smiled, 'And I certainly don't want to compromize your safety now I've found you.'

'You have clearly thought this through. I'm very impressed.'

'The final topic we must address is the Americans. This is very much their sphere of influence and we believe they're giving tacit support to the Junta as they see them as a bulwark against communism, particularly after what happened in Chile some years ago. We're not confident they will support their NATO ally if Argentina decides to invade the Falklands. It's vital you steer clear of the US intelligence community. You aren't known to them?' she checked.

'No, I'm clean. I've never operated with the Americans and as a Canadian they'll despise me as the hick from up north.'

Andy sat back in her chair. 'What's the next step?'

'I've a flight booked to BA tomorrow via Miami,' said John, 'so by Tuesday morning I should be at the hotel. I've reserved a suite at the Hotel San Martin. I'll spend about ten days there and in Montevideo before flying back, so I should see you a week next Friday. Now after all this hard work let's go out and enjoy ourselves. I want to take you to a wonderful park not far from here where we can get a great sandwich. Tonight I'll cook a meal and then I think you should go back to your hotel as I hate early morning farewells and I shall have to be up at six.'

So they spent a quiet Sunday afternoon comfortably in each other's company, and later after dinner they made languid love in his big bed before he walked her back to her hotel. Andy gave him a quick kiss, turned and skipped up the steps at the hotel, giving him a bright smile from those green eyes just before she disappeared into the hotel foyer. He turned and strolled on down to the waterfront with joy in his heart before returning home to pack.

Gazing along the lakeside at the bright lights in the water he felt as he usually did at the start of a job, a mixture of anticipation, excitement and challenge and that adrenalin surge. There was something new though. He knew he was going to miss that girl, Yamauchi-san was right, he thought, 'I do need someone I can trust. But I have to put her out of my mind while I am away.'

Chapter Three

Buenos Aires October 1981

Tuesday morning Ridley walked out into the early spring morning at Ezeiza airport in Buenos Aires and raised his arm to attract a taxi. Soon he was on the thirty-minute journey to the Microcentro where the Hotel San Martin is located. Having checked in and quickly changed into a smart business suit, he picked up his briefcase and headed for the Ministry of Health offices and his first meeting with the senior official responsible for pharmaceutical business development. It was vital to convince the official of the seriousness of the project and the benefits for his country. Ridley was ushered into Señor Andres Roca's large office and after shaking hands they moved to the conference table where coffee was served. Roca was clearly a career civil servant as he had that urbane air recognizable across the world in public administrations, and probably knew his trade very well. He could be a very useful source of information provided he felt there was something to be gained by it.

'Señor Ridley, I am delighted to meet you', opened Roca, 'I am very interested in hearing how your company proposes to invest in my country. We certainly will welcome a development by a Japanese pharmaceutical company provided our country gains from it. So far most such companies have based their operations in Brazil. I understand you are Canadian. How long have you worked for Nippon Health?'

John realized he was being gently interrogated. 'Yes, I am Canadian and I live in Toronto. I've worked for Nippon Health for five years firstly as international personnel manager, and then a year ago, after I had been involved in business development projects in Mexico and Saudi Arabia, I was offered the additional portfolio of business development manager for Africa and the Americas. This will be my second major project.'

'Señor Roca, I have brought with me the initial project proposal and a letter from a Nippon Health board member confirming the commitment of the company for this project. Clearly we cannot make any firm business or financial commitment until we have evaluated the business opportunity here and in Uruguay, but I can say we really would like to make it work. I am also gratified by your comments. I am anxious to get your advice and as much information as possible so I may develop the project proposal quickly.'

'That is very reassuring,' replied Roca. 'We are certainly looking to broaden and diversify our pharmaceutical provision and from what I know of your products I think there are some which we would find very attractive. What are your plans?'

'Our plan is to set up a major subsidiary to market and sell throughout Argentina and probably Uruguay, and at a later stage perhaps coordinate further business development in South America from here. I don't know much about the country and would value help from some of your staff and the pharmaceutical business association. I'll then visit key centres across the country to talk to pharmacies and clinics. I have to work very fast as I'm expected to make a formal business report to the board meeting at the beginning of February. If the business proposition is accepted I estimate it will take twelve months to set up the operation provided the Argentine approvals are forthcoming. How long might this take?'

At this question Señor Roca smiled, 'I imagine these would take no more than a few months provided everyone has confidence in your company.'

Nodding agreement John replied, 'I think I shall be here until the end of next week on this first visit, and I wondered whether you and your minister would allow me to entertain you so I may brief you further in a more informal atmosphere. Perhaps you would discuss this with him and suggest a possible date and a suitable restaurant.'

'I think that would be very appropriate as in our culture we much prefer to gauge the measure of a person through such an occasion. I shall discuss with the minister and leave a message at your hotel. Did you say it was the San Martin?'

The two men rose and after the final pleasantries, Ridley left and headed for a café lunch. Later, after an initial meeting with the director of the Argentine Pharmaceutical Association he returned to the hotel to make some calls, set up further meetings and organize his travel plans. By the early evening he had made his arrangements for the rest of the week, heading south to Bahia Blanca then on to Comodoro Rivadavia, before flying down to Rio Gallegos in the south of Patagonia, and returning on the Friday evening flight.

Wednesday morning Ridley made the short journey to the Aeroparque Jorge Newberry to catch his domestic flight to Bahia Blanca. Argentina being only slightly smaller than India, flying was the only sensible way to travel about. It was a ninety-minute flight to Bahia Blanca but at least a four-hour flight to Rio Gallegos in the very south of Patagonia.

Soon his Boeing 727 was lifting off and he leant out of his business class seat to gaze down on the pampas passing below. As well as grazing beef cattle he saw large expanses of arable land beginning to turn green as the corn sprouted and pushed up through the earth. The plane began to descend and he had views over the naval port and the ships alongside, and was soon disembarking in front of the civilian terminal building on the Esposa Naval Base east of the city. It was clear from his brief aerial view that the aircraft carrier, 25 de Mayo, was undergoing a short refit, the cruiser General Belgrano was in port as were four of the six guided-missile destroyers. He didn't see much activity around the naval airbase. Soon he was heading into the centre of this stylish city with its grandiose buildings, attractive plazas, and boulevards lined with shade trees and palms. It was a cosmopolitan city in miniature with a population of around a quarter of a million. Checking in to the Hotel Santa Rosa, he quickly freshened up and then headed for the largest real estate agent in the city.

Soon he was being ushered into the office of the commercial real estate agent. 'Good morning, Señor Bosco, it is good of you to see me at such short notice. Here is my business card. I am the business development manager for Nippon Health currently evaluating the business opportunities in Argentina and we may wish to set up a subsidiary company down here. We obviously would have our headquarters in BA but a small regional office might be based here. I would therefore like to check potential properties and the likely cost structure. This is very much a tentative enquiry at this stage and it will probably be April next year before I am in a position to take up a lease on some offices however.'

'Señor Ridley, I welcome your interest in Bahia Blanca

which is very heartening,' responded Señor Bosco, 'I think we have many suitable offices here available on a regular basis. Bahia Blanca is not suffering the same economic problems as much of the north of the country. We have a major port here, also agrochemicals and petrochemicals manufacture, as well as the main naval base, so there is much economic vitality. So it would be an appropriate base for your company. We expect the city to grow and will get better hospitals and clinics, and the surrounding agricultural area is rich, so there should be good business here for you. Let me have a few minutes to prepare a list of some suitable offices that I think might meet your requirements.' Leaving Ridley with a coffee he rushed off. Returning a little later, he said 'Shall we go and view them?'

They spent the remainder of the morning and the first part of the afternoon viewing the properties and establishing the likely cost. Ridley then visited the director of the Bahia Hospital and the local pharmacy distributor and after excellent detailed discussions with them felt he had made a good start. He informed them he would visit again in a few weeks and they agreed to meet him then. He returned to his hotel and in his usual disciplined way wrote up his detailed business notes before dinner. He then called Andy at her hotel and whilst it was only a brief call, and they shared only brief endearments and what each had been doing in the short time since they parted, he felt wonderfully elated as he went down to the restaurant for dinner. At the bar and later over dinner he listened to the conversations that washed over him and from which he captured key information about the airbase and the main fleet base. He would not write down any of this whilst he was in Argentina but would memorize it until he was on the flight back to Toronto. He hadn't spotted anyone shadowing him but he was sure all the people he had visited would be quizzed about their new visitor from Canada and asked whether he appeared genuine. He would no doubt be interviewed back in BA at the end of the week should there be any suspicions.

Thursday morning he was back out at the airfield for the first flight from Bahia Blanca to Comodoro Rivadavia. Arriving after another ninety-minute flight he went through the same cover story there. 'I might base a sales representative here so I require information about the area that could be covered both by car and air.' The view was that air communications were good and likely to get even better over the next few years and it should be possible to cover the whole of south Patagonia from there. The large city was a very pleasant place nestling between the sea and some high rocky hills inland. There were high cliffs nearby but the port was large with significant jetties and was the major port on that part of the Atlantic coast. He noted the town was the centre of the oil industry so it would be important to monitor movements in the port. There were significant medical and pharmacy resources there so it would be sensible from a business point of view to have someone based there. He didn't see much military air activity at the airport, and there appeared to be no naval vessels of any kind in the port at that moment.

Ridley then flew to Rio Gallegos on the evening flight where he had reserved a room at the small Hotel Comercio in this medium-sized town at the southern tip of the Patagonian mainland. The land he had flown south over was a vast area of arid steppe-like plains rising towards the Andes in a series of abrupt terraces. The only cultivation seen was in the broad river valleys on the way south and there were herds of beef cattle grazing near Comodoro Rivadavia. As they flew further south the grazing appeared to get poorer and he spotted large flocks of sheep further inland just before arriving at his destination. As the turbo-prop commuter plane manoeuvred for landing he got a good view of the harbour and wide estuary and then the airbase just to the west of the town. This again was a joint military/civilian airfield and as the plane taxied to the small civilian terminal he observed some single-seat delta-wing Mirage 3s outside a hardened hangar and also a maritime reconnaissance Lockheed Neptune waiting to take-off. A small town with a strategic airbase, Ridley would have to be careful how he asked his questions. He hadn't seen a lot of security around the airfield but he was certain there would be some security surveillance around the area and he did not want to draw attention to himself. Anyway, he thought to himself as he settled down to his meal in a friendly local restaurant close to the hotel, 'I will soon be able to get back to the bright lights of BA.' As this thought entered his mind he realized that he would rather be in Toronto with the tall blonde girl with green eyes who made him feel so alive. 'I will have to watch this, I am turning into a moonstruck teenager: a sure way to make some mistake and get caught.'

Friday morning he walked briskly around this wind-pummelled provincial capital, thankful it was early spring. Most of the buildings were single-storey with red corrugated roofs so they were able to remain clinging to the earth when the gale-force winds blew out of the Antarctic. He had arranged to meet the director of the local hospital for lunch but decided before that to do some sightseeing. He visited the local museum in one of the original settler houses with wooden walls and a red corrugated roof, saw the modern business development near the port behind the long promenade and the position of the Prefecture Naval, a two-storey white building with brown, stained wooden doors and windows and a green low-pitched roof, close to the wide harbour that had broad piers and two small jetties. There was a small patrol vessel in the harbour and he reckoned it was based there. The Prefecture Naval had low-power radio aerials on the roof so it was probably not a main naval communications centre. More likely he suspected that to be on the airbase. He would see if he could check as his flight back took off.

Before leaving the port area he took a final glance into the inner harbour area and spotted a fishing vessel moored well into the inner harbour where it was hidden from prying eyes. He risked a second look. It certainly didn't look like an Argentine trawler, more like a British one. He glanced casually about him but there didn't seem to be anyone about and there was no one obviously keeping watch on the small naval vessel, so he decided to stroll casually along the jetty towards this interesting vessel. Getting close to it he could see the name *Seagull* on a board attached to the deckhouse and painted on the hull the designation 'SY5' indicating it was registered in the Falkland Islands, or at least that was its camouflage. 'What is it doing here?' he wondered. 'I don't think any Falklands trawlers have been arrested recently.'

As he was thinking about this he heard voices and slipped quickly into the warehouse behind him. Moving behind some packing cases he was hidden well enough but could still see the ship's gangway. The voices approaching were speaking Spanish and as they went up the gangway he could see that one was an Argentine naval officer and the other a senior rating. So his question was answered. This vessel was definitely being used for intelligence gathering around the Falklands. This was the first piece of evidence that the Argentines were up to something. Not wanting to risk meeting the naval personnel if he went back on to the jetty he searched the back of the warehouse and luckily found a badly secured door there. Opening it carefully he slipped quickly out and made his way unconcernedly towards the town although he would admit his heart was beating a bit faster than usual. 'Getting too old for this,' he thought.

Continuing his stroll he visited the small pink Catedral N.S. de Lujan before meeting the hospital director for traditional parrillas, salad and some excellent coffee. He learnt that the military used the town's hospital facilities and so the population served was not just the 90,000 in the town but sometimes could be as many as another 10,000 naval, marine and airforce personnel. The director also confided that he had been advised that for a few weeks early next year the military numbers might increase as a major military exercise was being planned.

Ridley then took the afternoon B737 flight back to BA from the airport. On the apron was an Aerolineas Argentinas B747 in the process of refuelling. B747s regularly stopped here to refuel before taking the polar route to Auckland in New Zealand. So the airfield had a long runway. 'It is also very clear the air force keeps a large number of offensive assets here,' he observed. As the plane took off he could see some Skyhawks parked as well as more Mirage 3s or the Israeli-manufactured version, the Dagger. He thought he spotted the communications centre but he couldn't be certain in the descending gloom. On the four-hour flight through the dark he mulled over all he had learnt. There was clearly intelligence-gathering going on around the Falklands and a major exercise was planned for early in 1982, according to the hospital director. A big challenge still remained and at the moment it seemed insoluble. He was certain the airbase at Rio Gallegos would play a pivotal role in any conflict about the Falklands given its location due west of them, but it would not be easy for him to get back down there after the action had started. He couldn't really see how he could hang around down in southern Patagonia, as there was no rationale for basing a medical representative there, and nowhere to go to ground. The SAS or SBS might have to be inserted off a submarine to monitor operations. He resolved on his next visit to identify a couple of observation points from which operations from the airbase might be monitored.

Back on the ground in BA he took a taxi to Hotel San Martin and ordered a meal from room service and while waiting for it to arrive he placed a call to Andy at her hotel. 'Hello,' said the voice he had grown to love, 'Andy James here.'

'Andy love, it's John, how are you?'

'Oh John, I am OK just missing you now the weekend has come. I keep thinking about last weekend and how wonderful it was.'

'Well, I shall be leaving BA next Friday morning for Miami and Toronto so I should arrive at Lester Pearson airport around six a.m. Why don't you come around for breakfast about eight but be prepared to stay for the weekend?'

Andy said, 'That's a date. I shall look forward to that. I don't want to go out on our first evening together again, will you let me cook you a meal in your precious kitchen?'

John smiled to himself. 'Of course you can. I promise to keep out of the way.'

'Oh no you don't', replied Andy, 'I'll require you to supply regular kisses to sustain the chef. How's the review going?'

'Quite successful I think, my love', reported John, 'I've been to Bahia Blanca, Comodoro Rivadavia and Rio Gallegos and obtained a lot of information. I love you and am missing you lots and can't wait to get back to Toronto. I have just flown back from Rio Gallegos so I should really go and have something to eat. By the way do you think we should have a party soon?'

With that they said their fond farewells and reluctantly hung up. John thought, 'Well it'll be interesting to see what information Andy gleams from that call, which seemed a bit clumsy but might just be taken as the confused ramblings of a man in love.' He sat in contemplative silence after the long call to Andy until his reverie was broken by the arrival of the room service waiter with his meal. After deciding he would spend the next couple of days sightseeing in BA he turned in for the night.

Chapter Four

After continental breakfast in his room at the Hotel San Martin on Saturday morning he set off for his sightseeing. He was alone in the lift as it descended from the eighth floor but it stopped on the third and as the doors opened he looked out to see who was joining and his heart nearly stopped! Standing there was a short and stocky dark-haired young woman who looked just as startled as he was. 'John', she started to say as he moved quickly to the door and placed his forefinger on her lips and hustled her into the lift. He whispered, 'Say nothing, just follow me at a distance when I leave the lift and the hotel.'

Ridley quickly left the lift on the ground floor and walked across the foyer, past the reception desk and out into the street, and then set off for a small café he'd spotted a few days ago in a quiet side street not far from the hotel near the Avenue Cordoba. Entering the dark interior he selected a table near the back of the room well away from the window, the bar and the telephone so they should not be seen by a casual observer or easily overheard. She entered rather hesitantly, looked around then walked slowly towards his table, didn't sit down but rather stood awkwardly beside him. 'For God's sake sit down Maria before everyone takes notice of you,' hissed John in Spanish, and she quickly and silently seated herself opposite him. 'Before we talk about anything I want you to realize I am a Canadian and I have a Canadian passport but my name is still John Ridley. What are you doing in BA? It is the last place on earth I expected to see you.'

'My husband is an Argentine and we live in the south of Patagonia inland of Rio Gallegos.' She said wryly, 'I am now Maria Santos Gomez. I teach at the college down there and I have just been on a specialist course in political science at the university here. I will be flying back on Sunday afternoon.' She looked fondly at him with those dark eyes. 'How are you?' she asked, 'It must be at least eight years since we met that last time in Madrid.'

Ridley stared intently at her and waited until their coffee and pastries were delivered before replying, 'I cannot explain but it is very important that you think of me as a Canadian you knew in Spain when I was on a Spanish language course and spent time with your family at La Toja in Galicia practising the language. You haven't heard from me for more than eight years until you met me in BA and I told you I work as the personnel/business development manager for a Japanese pharmaceutical company and that I live in Toronto. If you are ever asked about me it is vital for you and me both that you stick to this story.'

Maria's dark eyes were downcast as she listened to him, then when he was finished she looked up into that face she had always loved but thought she would never see again and assured him, 'I have always thought of you as the big brother I never had, and you have always been the dearest person to me outside of my immediate family. Of course I shall do as you ask without question. I am just so happy at meeting you again even if I am a little confused for I thought we would never meet again. We mustn't waste today arguing as there is so much I want to tell you and you must share with me all you have done.'

'I agree, I was going to do some sightseeing today so why

don't you show me all the sights. We can then have a meal together before you fly back.' Smiling happily she finished her coffee, picked up her handbag, and headed for the street with him following in her wake.

'You don't walk any more slowly then,' quipped John as they headed south on the Avenue San Martin towards the Plaza de Mayo and the presidential palace, the Casa Rosada. When they arrived in the square they gazed at the grand public buildings that surround it including the Cabillo, which was the town council building in the colonial era, and the solemn Catedral Metropolitana.

'The *Catedral* curiously enough contains the tomb of the man our hotel is named after, General San Martin, who died in France in exile and his body was later brought back.' Turning to him she smiled, 'The Argentines have a tradition of this, remember Eva Peron. This place is very much the centre of political activity in BA, no doubt before you leave you will see at least one demonstration here against the Junta and the despcrate economic situation the country is facing. If you are here on a Thursday afternoon you will see the *Madres de la Plaza de Mayo* marching around the square with photos of family members who have disappeared since the military came to power. They call them *Las Desaparecidos* and they claim thousands have disappeared presumably killed because of their opposition. It is very sad.'

'Are most people against the Junta then?'

'No, I don't think so. Sadly Argentina finds it difficult to live with democracy and freedom. It is thought more important to prevent socialism and communism and this approach certainly gains the Junta the support of the US Government and they are very rich.' Pointing across the square she said, 'The monument in the centre over there is the Pyrámide de Mayo which was erected to commemorate the first anniversary of independence from Spain.' After saying this she looked rather wistful and reflective and then without saying anything more she began to stroll along the Avenue de Mayo towards the Palacio de Congreso.

Ridley sensing the sadness suggested to Maria, 'Let's just stroll and talk. You seem rather sad today and we have lots to share with each other.' Turning to him quickly she put her arms around him and held him tightly to her. Shorter than him her dark hair nestled below his chin and he caught the brief, stifled sob and sensed rather than saw her tears. 'Little sister, are you so desperately unhappy?' he asked.

'Oh, not really unhappy but life isn't exactly what I hoped for when I went off to university in Madrid on that scholarship. I did well there and you know from the last time we met that I was really enjoying my life. Just before our last meeting I met a young man who was studying business management and finance and I was quite attracted to him. Perhaps he attracted me because he came from Argentina, and to the Spanish the old colonies have a sense of allure and mystique as though we wish to recreate the adventures of Cortés and Pizarro. His family is quite rich which is why he went to Madrid to study. Anyway we fell in love, or at least,' she said cynically, 'I fell in love with him or what I thought he was and represented. I am not sure whether he really loved me then: he doesn't now.'

Ridley squeezed her hand in sympathy but didn't interrupt her.

'He was a year ahead of me and worked in Madrid for a merchant bank. After I finished my course we got married and I became the grand Señora Santos Gomez with an estancia in southern Patagonia and an apartment in BA.

My family were very proud I had made such a good catch. It was so wonderful at first. After we came here he joined a merchant bank and we lived in the apartment we took in the Recoleta district and I did some work at the university. It all seemed very idyllic to begin with but after a couple of years he suggested we should go to live on the ranch. That was so different from what I had been used to even in Galicia and that wasn't the most sophisticated part of the world. I was so bored there that I finally obtained a teaching post at the local college in Rio Gallegos which is only an hour's drive from the ranch. It really is a most desolate part of the world and I take every opportunity to escape to BA or Bahia Blanca for a bit of civilization.'

'Yes, I know', said John, 'I came back from there last night. I have been down on a fact-finding trip for my company. I visited Bahia, Comodoro Rivadavia and Rio Gallegos and you certainly know you are far south when you reach Rio Gallegos. I was glad I wasn't there in winter.'

'Sometimes it can be wonderful but often it is bleak and the wind howls incessantly: you come to hate it.'

'How are your parents?'

'They say they are well but I haven't seen them since I left Spain. My father was unsure of Rafael but went along with the marriage because I was so much in love with him. But they were very sad I was moving so far away.'

Maria attempted to change the subject as they reached the end of the avenue and stared at the bulky Palacio del Congreso. 'Tell me what you have done since we last met.'

Taking her arm he turned her back down the avenue and as they headed for the busy Avenue Florida shopping street he outlined his life since they last met. 'The great plans we shared when on La Toja did not work out. You remember I thought I might join the Royal Navy after university?

Well, I got a very good offer from a pharmaceutical company that promised to sponsor me on a personnel management course and offered a job afterwards. So I took it and did well. I then got a more senior job with Nippon Health, a Japanese company that was looking for a westerner to help it grow the business outside of Japan. I have done well with them and they decided my Spanish would make me a useful business development manager for the Americas. The company decided to establish a subsidiary here and I am preparing a report. I've lived in Canada since I finished university and I now have a nice apartment in Toronto. I felt there was nothing to keep me in UK so I decided to take Canadian citizenship.'

'I would love to see it', sighed Maria, 'I am sure it will be beautiful and Toronto is supposed to be a very lively city. Don't you miss your parents?' Then she gasped and put her fist to her mouth in anguish. 'John, I am sorry I forgot you were orphaned as a baby.'

He squeezed her arm. 'Don't feel bad, it's a natural mistake. Anyway as I never knew them it is difficult to miss them. Like any child I would have liked a set of parents but as I haven't I have had to get along on my own.' He added wryly, 'It makes one perhaps too self-reliant but that cannot be helped.'

'Do you have a girl?'

'A week ago my answer would have been no,' grinned John, 'but just before I came down here I met someone who I think might be the one. It is still early days but I feel I want to spend my life with her.'

'Is she young?' asked Maria.

'She is about your age, with blonde hair, green eyes, she is quite tall and slim and very determined and brave.'

She laughed, 'Ah, quite different from me then!'

'I thought sons are supposed to look for something like their mothers not their surrogate sisters,' riposted John, 'you haven't carried a torch for me have you?'

'Oh, no I never wanted you as my lover and husband, but you will always be my brother and part of the family and I am glad we have met again. I don't want us to not see each other from now on.'

'How will your husband react?'

'I am not proposing to say anything about you at the moment. In fact I see so little of him these days so the need may never arise.'

John explained, 'The project means I will be spending a week or so here every month, maybe longer, until the middle of next year. I am planning to take a small apartment for six months from the beginning of the year so if you like you can visit me there. It will be much more private and we can just be together. It will have two bedrooms so it will be perfectly respectable.'

'I would like that. It will be an opportunity for us to redevelop our friendship. By the way I trust you completely so have no concerns about being alone with you at night.'

Turning to look at him she added, 'After all this serious talk I am feeling famished. Let's find somewhere to eat but not meat, the Argentine cuisine is worse than the Basques, meat, meat and more meat!'

'How about that Italian restaurant over there, we could get some pasta and salad or a pizza?' She nodded her agreement and soon they were settled at a nice table sipping a glass of local Merlot and anticipating their pasta dishes, not saying much but sitting together in companionable silence, occasionally smiling at each other and both thinking of adventures together a decade ago and thousands of miles away.

'It's like it was a different life,' thought Maria. 'How young and naïve we both were, but we were optimistic and so full of promise. John was always so caring and strong, so different from all the Spanish boys I knew: a real big brother.'

Spain was just escaping from the Franco era and young people were getting to know the world but he seemed so worldly wise. He'd shared so much of his knowledge and experience with her and always supported her when she was uncertain. She didn't really understand why he had gone away and failed to contact her for so long nor why he now had Canadian nationality, but she was content to leave these questions unanswered for now. She was just happy again to re-discover him.

Ridley's thoughts were going along parallel lines. He was trying to make sense of Maria's story. Thinking back to the time in La Toja and also that last time in Madrid, he struggled to recall what motivated her. As he recalled from a letter from her parents she achieved a good degree. There was no mention of her marriage or her moving to Argentina, but that might have been to avoid hurting him, as they knew he was fond of her and did not have any family of his own. Now he wondered whether perhaps they did not like her husband or they were uncomfortable with his family's wealth? He would proceed cautiously until he knew her better. If he decided to trust her he might have found his entry route and bolt-hole near Rio Gallegos but that decision could wait a month or so as he felt sure nothing would happen for at least a couple of months.

After lunch John took Maria shopping on Avenue Florida and they went into Galerias Pacifico, the very large and classy Parisian-style department store. Maria seemed to shed the years and many of her cares as she excitedly searched through the designer clothes and tried on outfits for his opinion. 'I haven't felt so good for so long,' she breathlessly said after trying on the tenth outfit. 'Rafael just isn't interested in shopping, he spends all his time with his cronies.' By the time they finished shopping she had an armful of designer shopping bags and they decided to drop them back at the hotel.

'I could do with a shower and putting my feet up for a few hours and I am sure your feet are probably killing you,' suggested John. 'Should we meet later for dinner? Do you happen to know a good restaurant?'

'Yes, let's eat together later. Shall we aim for around eight? The Cordoba in the Plaza Dorrego in San Telmo district is good if we can get a table at short notice. I ate there last time with a girl friend. We should take a taxi from the hotel as it is a bit far to walk and by the looks of it, it may rain this evening.'

Leaving John to organize the reservation through the hotel concierge, she wandered into the lift and up to her room. A short while later as she was slipping out of her clothes before taking a shower, the extension rang and John said he had been able to book a table. She agreed to meet him later in the foyer.

Ridley then put a call through to Andy in Toronto. 'Hello love, how are things with you? I have had a lovely day sightseeing today. I think the forecast is for a lovely day tomorrow so I shall do some more sightseeing before going over to Montevideo on the ferry on Monday morning.'

After hearing the first phrase 'lovely day' Andy's heart was in her mouth and she had to fight hard not to make any comment. As he repeated 'lovely day' she thought, 'Blast the man, he made me wait in agony before signalling he thought it was low risk. I guess this is the pressure and anguish my boss lectured me about a few days ago. I am not going to give John up though, and I am better working with him and knowing what he is doing than living in an ignorant void and worrying just as much until he returns.'

John had clearly worked out what was going through her head because he just waited in silence. Eventually she said in a calm voice, 'I am glad it is all going well for you. Usually you tell me you don't have any time for sightseeing so make the most of it. Some day I would like to see South America especially Buenos Aires, Rio de Janiero and the Andes and those big birds which fly there and carry off sheep. Do they call them condors?'

'Yes, I think they do. BA is a very smart city with great shops, cafes and restaurants, although they serve too much meat for my taste. I am hoping to have a fish dish tonight and that will make a change. The plan for next week is still the same. I am going over to Montevideo on Monday, coming back on Tuesday. On Wednesday I will then look at some possible offices in Downtown here before meeting some business analysts to get an independent view of the economy. On Thursday I have a meeting with one of the recruitment agencies and in the evening I am hosting a dinner for the Minister of Health and his top officials at some very expensive restaurant. So take care until then my love. I can't wait to see you. Bye!'

'Take care, John, all my love, bye!'

Ridley reluctantly broke the connection thinking what a brave girl she was. She knew he was potentially at risk but she stayed calm and recovered well later in the conversation. She acted very professionally. If he had needed any further proof of her feelings for him then her love had just been demonstrated many times over. He just hoped she understood that he loved her just as much as she did him.

Now it was time to concentrate on his problematical female nearby. From what she had let slip he guessed her marriage had broken down and her husband probably had a mistress somewhere, which is why he was often away. They would have to be careful if this mistress was in BA, because if he spotted Maria and himself together he probably would be jealous of another man apparently sharing his wife's favours, even if he had apparently discarded them. Ridley concluded he must find out more about Rafael Gomez that evening if at all possible. With that he stripped off his clothes and took a long hot relaxing shower, humming quietly to himself one of his favourite folk tunes.

Just before quarter to eight, John was waiting in the foyer for Maria. The lift opened and she appeared in one of the outfits bought that afternoon. A short, stocky, bosomy girl she was wearing a long Gypsy skirt with a pattern of subdued colours, a loose linen top and with short black leather boots beneath. After a brief peck on each cheek they took the waiting taxi for the short drive to Plaza Dorrego and stepped through the open door of Restaurant Cordoba to be greeted by the patron. Escorted to their table to the accompaniment of tango music, Maria said, 'Later there will probably be a tango demonstration. This is a popular restaurant with the tourists but it is still a good one and not too expensive by BA standards. There will be some good fish on the menu and they cook it very well. The wines here are also excellent.'

They ordered their meal then Ridley asked her about her job at the college in Rio Gallegos. 'I teach history and politics to students of sixteen to eighteen years and who are trying for university. It isn't very challenging but it does keep my mind active and I value the special courses I am able to attend here at the university three times a year. I

45

will be attending one in January so hopefully I will be able to meet you then.'

'I should certainly be here the second and third week in January as I shall have to finalize everything before going to Tokyo to make the business presentation to the board.' He probed a bit further, 'So you are quite busy but what does your husband do? Is he fully occupied by the ranch business?'

Maria grimaced, 'I have to say I don't honestly know these days. When we were first married he worked for a merchant bank in BA and seemed to be doing well, although he didn't need the money as his allowance from his family is substantial. Suddenly after the Junta came to power he announced he wished to spend more time on our estancia and we sold the apartment and moved down there. Before that his ranch manager had run everything pretty expertly as far as I can judge. The manager is still there and seems to be in charge so I don't know what Rafael does. He used to spend a lot of time at the bank in Rio Gallegos and out at the airbase, then a couple of years ago he started coming back to BA, and spending about two weeks here every month. Recently he's spent most of his time away.'

She added, 'I suspect he has a mistress somewhere in BA but that doesn't account for all the time he spends here. I think he has some links with the Finance Ministry and I think he is close to the Junta but that is just a suspicion. Perhaps he is advising them on how to overcome the present problems with the economy.'

'If he is,' said John, 'I hope he is successful because I want to set up a subsidiary in a thriving not a declining economy!'

Following the antipasti, the trout from the Patagonian Lake District was excellently cooked with almonds and mustard dressing accompanied by a wonderful selection of vegetables. After an excellent dessert John complimented Maria. 'You made a good choice for us this evening and all the dishes were delicious. I had been told about this famed trout dish and its reputation is well deserved. What time do you have to leave tomorrow?'

'I have to be out at the airport by nine in the morning. The flight leaves at ten and as it is a direct flight I should arrive about two-thirty in the afternoon. I leave the four-wheel drive station wagon at the airport so I should get back to the ranch before it is completely dark.'

John asked, 'Is the ranch inland from Rio Gallegos then?'

'Yes, it is about one hour west just off the road that goes to Rio Turbio and then on across the Andes into Chile. It is very good sheep grazing country.'

After numerous cups of coffee John reluctantly requested the bill and then they took a taxi back to the Hotel San Martin. In the foyer Maria whispered, 'Goodbye my big brother. Thank you for a wonderful day. I am very glad to have found you again. I shall see you in January when you visit. Leave a message here for me and I will call you at your apartment after I arrive. Give my love to your girl and wish her much happiness from me. I hope some day we shall be able to meet.'

'Goodbye Maria, take care. I hope we can meet in January. Have a good journey back to Rio Gallegos. I shall not forget you my little sister. All my love.' With that he hugged her and then she went up to her room.

Chapter Five

Back in his room Ridley resolved to check out some military installations on Sunday in the BA area along the Rio de la Plata, and possibly down to Mar del Plata. The international airport at Ezeiza was also a naval airbase but he did not spot much stationed there and he doubted they would operate combat aircraft there in full view of the prying eyes of the press. The naval training airbase Punta Indo was south east of BA down the estuary so he could pass there on the way to La Plata, and then either take the RN2 direct to Mar del Plata or the RP11 down the Atlantic coast. On reflection he decided he would negotiate a taxi for the day, although it would be a long drive, for he would see more that way than going by train. He would go first to La Plata and then straight down the RN2 to Mar del Plata so he could check out what was supposed to be the submarine force base. Calling down to the reception desk he asked them to enquire about a taxi for the day and a little while later he was booking a car to meet him after breakfast.

Sunday

'Señor Ridley?' enquired the man when Ridley descended to the foyer. '*Si, Ilamo Señor Ridley,*' John replied. They went out to the splendid, gleaming black Mercedes 230, and after a brief discussion about the route and plan for the day the driver headed off south out of the city towards La Plata keeping up a running commentary of sights along the way. Not knowing whether the intelligence services employed taxi drivers as watchers of foreigners as happened in communist-bloc countries, John was careful not to show undue interest in military establishments. Luckily near the Punta Indo airbase there was a national nature reserve on the salt flats along the estuary coast, and he was able to surreptitiously observe the set-up there and establish the layout as they viewed it. After returning to the car, he read the sign at the main entrance as they went past, confirming this was indeed the headquarters of naval air training. Security at the main gate appeared to be very lax for he had not seen any checks made on any of the cars entering the base.

Passing on they soon arrived in La Plata, a bustling city with a well-planned centre and some fine buildings. Parking close to the Plaza Moreno his keen guide led him efficiently around the main sites and he observed the Piedra Fundacional, the founding stone at the precise original geographical centre, the neo-gothic cathedral and various Palacios in a range of styles from Spanish through German Renaissance to French Classical. After a welcome coffee and croissant they were soon backtracking slightly to get on to the main route to Mar del Plata, the RN2. This took them across the pampas now often cultivated as arable rather than as good grazing land for beef cattle, although at this time of the year there was little sign of the wonderful golden fields to come later in the summer when the corn had ripened and the ears were waving in the breeze. Travelling along a road completely flat across featureless countryside was incredibly boring, and the trip reminded Ridley of a journey he once took on the Canadian Pacific railway from Toronto to Calgary. For two days on the train the prairie did not change and the monotony finally became oppressive.

'It's no wonder that most of the tourists going to Mar del Plata's beaches either fly or go by train,' he thought. From La Plata it was a three-hour fast drive so they arrived in time for a late lunch near the beach. Being sunny but chilly there weren't that many people about and although it was a Sunday some of the restaurants weren't open. However they did find a suitable place and had a decent meal. After lunch Ridley told the driver he was going to explore the town and agreed to meet him by the Central Casino on the Playa de los Pescadores at five o'clock.

Leaving the taxi driver in a small café to have a well-earned smoke and coffee, Ridley set off south around the coast past Cabo Corrientes and down along the Playa Grande towards the main port. Part way along the road, he stopped to check unobtrusively that the taxi driver wasn't following him. Not seeing him, he found a road that climbed above the port before turning back towards the coast and by walking in this direction he was able to overlook the jetties. Strangely, close by was the naval base and beyond that the fishing port and then the commercial port. He would have guessed the naval base would have been further away and harder to observe. Casually gazing over the harbour he was able to see there was a submarine support ship and four submarines in the base. There didn't appear to be any activity, it was all very quiet, in fact a typical Sunday afternoon in port. He knew he wasn't up to date on Argentine submarines and made a mental note to ask Andy to provide him with a full briefing before his next trip. At least there were four units there and he doubted whether they possessed any more. They were also clearly visible from his current observation point so it should be possible to check on their movements in future without too much difficulty.

Not wanting to excite any interest he retraced his track along that road then along another that turned north past the Parque Primavesi, went through the Los Troncos district and finally reached the neo-gothic Stella Maris Church on the hill near the coast, whose virgin is the patron saint of local fisherman. He then strolled north along the road fringing the coast and the famous beaches until he reached the casino. Finding a café next to the beach he settled down to watch the strollers on the beach whilst enjoying a coffee and an excellent cake. He didn't spot any navy men in uniform as he watched.

Keeping an eye on the front of the casino, Ridley saw his driver wander up and went across to meet him. The drive back was completed without conversation with the driver and his passenger listening to a music channel. Around ten o'clock Ridley arrived back and after tipping his driver well, retired to his room well satisfied with the results of his expedition. He called down to request room service and to inform the hotel he would be away for one night but wished to retain his room and then turned in.

Monday morning, carrying a small overnight bag and his briefcase, he arrived at the Darsena ferry terminal for the Montevideo ferry and, after a cursory check by passport control, he bought his ticket and moved into the ship and out on to the upper passenger deck as it was a fine morning. He marvelled that so long after being on HMS Bronton he still enjoyed being on the sea, for the river estuary was as broad as the sea and it was just possible to make out the tall buildings beyond the low river banks on the far shore that is Uruguay. The crossing took three hours so it would be lunchtime when he arrived. His first appointment was at two o'clock at the Ministry of Health but he wanted to call at the Japanese Embassy first, so he decided it would be better to get a meal onboard. It would save him time ashore.

As the ferry went astern to clear the ferry terminal he looked back to the vast sprawl of Buenos Aires, home to about three million *porteños* or port city dwellers, and more than double that number in the extensive suburbs. As well as speaking a form of Italian Spanish, they use a local vernacular slang known as *lunfardo* that sometimes makes them difficult to understand. He found this with Roberto his taxi driver of the day before but not in the shops or in his hotel. He had been surprised how cosmopolitan a city it was, refined and stylish and its people were just the same. 'If circumstances allow, I will certainly bring Andy down here, we can come on our honeymoon,' he thought. Realizing the truth of that thought he resolved not to rush things but to let the relationship develop until this operation was finished, but he was certain he wanted Andy to be his wife forever.

After all these unprofessional thoughts he realized the far bank had come a lot closer and if he wasn't quick he would be disembarking without any lunch. Ridley was just finishing his coffee and sandwich as the ferry came alongside and grabbing his bags he joined the flood of passengers rushing up to Immigration Control. As was the case with mass transit border crossings everywhere in the world there really wasn't any scrutiny, but he was certain this would be tightened considerably if there was trouble with Britain. He would need an assessment on the likely reaction of the Uruguayans. He knew the country had done very well over the last twenty years, and the people were quite well off, even the poor, but the economy was now being affected by the latest global economic woes, not least those being experienced by Japan, and the predominantly agricultural economy here was beginning to suffer. Uruguay had a complex relationship with its large neighbour across the river. They may have felt the need to side with Argentina as it provided them with much of their oil supplies, on the other hand they also had strong economic ties with Brazil and they were more likely to unofficially side with Britain in any trouble. So who knew which way Uruguay would go? Maybe they would just stay neutral which would be excellent, as it had to be his escape route if the balloon went up.

From the ferry terminal he took a taxi to the Japanese Embassy in the Boulevard Artigas. Going up to the fifth floor he introduced himself to the elegant young Japanese woman at reception and handed over his business card, holding it with both hands in the correct manner and bowing at the same time. The card had English printed on one side and Japanese on the other and she was so surprised to see this that she automatically answered in Japanese. Quickly, after they exchanged formal greetings in her language, he switched to English because his Japanese was extremely limited. He explained his business and asked to make an appointment to see the cultural and business attaché tomorrow before he returned to Buenos Aires. This was regarded as correct behaviour in Japan where there would be a series of short formal visits to exchange pleasantries before getting down to business. It is a vital process in a culture where people do not like to refuse a request and it allows a compromize to be gradually arrived at without either side losing face. Taking the name of his hotel she promised to leave a message for him there confirming the next day's appointment.

She then looked in her tray under the desk and brought out a small envelope which she handed delicately to him.

Smiling politely and bowing respectfully she said, 'This was left for you Mr Ridley and is I think a message from Tokyo, perhaps it is from your company.' Ridley guessed it was more likely to have come in the diplomatic bag from Mr Yamauchi but kept up the pretence, 'Yes, I expect it is from my boss in Nippon Health.'

With that he made his departure with much formal bowing and descended to the ground floor, and out onto the street to find a taxi to take him to the Ministry of Health. He would be a little early but it would allow him to get the feel of the place. He expected the meeting would take no more than an hour as this was not important business for the country would not benefit directly, other than through the employment of one medical representative based in Montevideo. The later meeting with the pharmacy distributor and tomorrow with the main hospital were much more important, as about half of the country's small population lived in Montevideo.

Late afternoon Ridley arrived at the Hotel London overlooking the Plaza Caganchi in the Microcentro, checked in without difficulty, and refusing the porter's assistance, headed for the lift and his fourth floor room. He entered, quickly threw his bag onto the bed and moved across to the elegant desk, switching on the French classical style lamp. He opened the envelope he was given at the Japanese Embassy. It was indeed from Mr Yamauchi.

Dear Mr Ridley

I hope your business research is going well. I just wanted to let you know that your business development director has approached the Head of MITI and as a consequence it has been decided that I should start my next posting a little earlier so I

54

may be of more assistance to you. This is because I know your company well and have experience of the pharmaceutical business.

The Japanese Government also regards the proposed investment in South America as a very important one for the economy. I have been instructed therefore to provide you with full assistance.

I will be joining the Embassy in Montevideo in the middle of November and will be very happy to provide you with whatever assistance you may require from that date. I suggest you telephone me at the Embassy after that date so I may confirm when you plan to visit.

I have the honour to be your servant,

Mr T Yamauchi

Reading between the lines Ridley was comforted that his friend would be down here sooner. He would value having another mind to help analyse the complex, confusing, and often downright contradictory information that he might unearth. Somebody had clearly pulled some strings because Yamauchi couldn't organize this on his own. Someone very senior had persuaded MITI and the Foreign Service to approve this urgent posting. He saw the unofficial machinations of his boss behind this. It was strange though that the Japanese appeared so keen to help the British down here in South America. Perhaps they thought they might get future business opportunities because of it. Of course there was a big Japanese population in Brazil and it might have something to do with that, he supposed. Andy might be able to find out. He must add it to the long list of things he wanted from her. An image of her beautiful body and warm mouth slipped across his mind but he banished it as quickly as he could, albeit reluctantly. 'This won't do at all,' he thought.

Putting the letter into his business file he spent some time planning for the meetings the next day. Very conveniently the Japanese business attaché had suggested a meeting mid-afternoon before he caught the ferry back to BA, so Ridley would be able to report his initial conclusions. Then he went down for his lonely dinner in the hotel. The Hotel London was a small but elegant hotel built in the 1920s, and its first floor restaurant was small but warmly decorated. He was seated at a small table in the window and had a good view out over the Plaza and the surrounding buildings but, as he glanced out after finishing his first course, he caught a movement to his left and glimpsed a man standing partially in the shadows. He thought there was something about him that was familiar. He resembled a man he had seen a couple of times during the day, as he came out of the Japanese Embassy and also the Ministry of Health. Did this mean the Uruguayans were also curious about him or was it the Argentinians checking up on him? he wondered. After these thoughts he got on with his dinner and also decided to treat himself to a small glass of Remy Martin with his coffee. Reminded by the watcher that he must continually be on his guard, he returned to his room and started, in the solitariness of his room, the first poem he had written for years. The words didn't come easily and eventually he gave up and went to bed. 'At least my emotions are much awakened if I feel the need to write,' he thought. 'Oh, Andy, what a powerful effect you have on me, woman.'

56

Tuesday passed quickly in a succession of meetings and as Ridley moved between locations he felt sure he had spotted his watcher on a number of occasions. If he saw him at the ferry terminal in BA then it was fairly likely he was from Argentine security. Did this mean that Maria had reported him or just them checking as part of a broader review of Nippon Health's viability? Mid-afternoon found him back at the Japanese Embassy and being shown into the business attaché's office and going through the traditional ritual of a first meeting. Over Japanese tea they engaged in polite conversation about the country and his business, and he gave a brief report on his researches to date, carefully avoiding giving any conclusions. Smiling, he reminded the attaché that this, of course, would breach commercial confidence. Having given sufficient information to satisfy the attaché, Ridley took his leave and headed back to the ferry terminal for the five o'clock ferry to BA.

Going once more onto the upper passenger deck he took a seat where he could observe other passengers coming up the ladder and soon spotted the watcher who had been with him all day. The man withdrew having assured himself that Ridley could not move without being spotted. At the end of the crossing Ridley slowly left the ferry amongst the crowd and, whilst he was waiting in line in the taxi queue, he noticed the same chap hovering at the corner of the bus terminal trying to look as though he was waiting for a bus. 'He seems to be on his own,' thought Ridley. 'That's why I've been able to spot him, so they clearly haven't allocated many resources to this. I reckon they are just curious and want to assure themselves I am doing what I claim to be doing. Should be no problem there then. In fact, much better to check me out now rather than later, if things go critical.' Heading back to the Hotel San Martin he remembered he had only three more lonely nights here before he would be back with Andy, although because of flight times it would be Saturday morning before he could see her.

Wednesday morning he viewed a series of medium-sized offices near the Microcentro with the real estate agent. After going around a number of them they discussed probable cost of leases and agreed on the likely requirements. The agent assured him there were always offices similar to these on the market and there should be no problem finding somewhere in six months' time. After this useful beginning he set off on a hectic round of meetings at hospitals, pharmacy distribution companies and a major recruitment agency after which he concluded the proposal was deliverable. Before he knew it, Thursday lunchtime came around and he reminded himself he must prepare for the business dinner he was hosting that evening at the Il Presidente restaurant in San Telmo. Señor Roca had left a message at the hotel to say he had taken the liberty of making a reservation of a private room at this restaurant on Ridley's behalf for seven-thirty on the Thursday evening. He also informed Ridley that in addition to himself, the Minister of Health and also a representative from the Ministry of Information would attend. At least, thought Ridley, they don't seem to be freeloading massively on this first occasion. Perhaps they want to limit any generosity to themselves.

Twenty-past seven saw Ridley attired in a smart, freshly-pressed dark suit, entering the entrance of the finest restaurant in BA. The maître d' quickly moved over to him and when he gave his name guided him to the back of the large opulent main restaurant towards a set of mirrored doors. Pushing open one of these he led him into the room that had a small bar at one end and a medium-sized dining table set comfortably for four people. The walls were covered in large mirrors and there was a large candelabra hanging above the table. Informing him about the arrangements for drinks and the meal, the maître d' told him that Señor Roca had also taken the liberty of ordering the meal and the wine, and he hoped Ridley had no objections. Ridley, mildly piqued by this presumption, smiled and agreed there was no problem.

Around seven-forty the door opened and the waiter ushered in his guests and Ridley quickly crossed the room to greet them. Señor Roca smiled at him and shaking his hand said, 'Good evening Señor Ridley. May I present my Minister of Health, Señor Lopez, and also General Coro from the Ministry of Information who is also very interested in your business project.' Smiling, Ridley thought, 'I bet he is. He is certainly after information but he is either head of intelligence or security here so I had better be very careful this evening. Make sure they drink plenty but watch the consumption yourself, lad,' he reminded himself.

'Gentlemen thank you for accepting my invitation this evening. It provides me with the opportunity to tell you more about my company's planned business project and my conclusions at the end of my preliminary visit. Thanks also to you Señor Roca for obtaining this private room and organising the meal for me, it relieved me of one last minute task when I returned from Montevideo on Tuesday afternoon. Shall we have a drink before we talk? What might I get you to drink?' So saying he turned to the waiter who mixed their drinks for them, pouring for Ridley a glass of chilled Argentine Chardonnay.

'Ah, I see you have discovered one of our secrets,' said the Minister of Health. Looking at General Coro he added quickly, 'I mean of course our wine.'

'Yes, I really like it,' replied Ridley, 'however I don't think much of your wine can be exported as I haven't seen any in Canada. We tend to get American or French wines there. The best of your white and red wines are clearly of the highest quality, and would stand up well in comparison to these Australian wines now coming on the market that make the French wines seem so old-fashioned.'

'I think you are a wine-lover,' suggested General Coro.

'Yes, I think I am,' agreed Ridley, 'I much prefer wine to beer or that European lager that is becoming very popular. You cannot beat relaxing with a wonderful glass of wine whilst listening to some classical music. Shall we take our places and I will signal for them to start serving dinner. I suggest we talk generally until we reach coffee and then I will be delighted to brief you on my initial conclusions and answer any questions you may have.'

They all agreed this was a good plan and the four educated men spent a pleasant two hours over a delicious meal savouring the wonderful Chardonnay and Merlot wines from the district of Mendoza. Ridley asked them about the development of the economy and its current challenges and received very bland replies assuring him of its current vitality. They reminded him that the country had vast natural resources of oil and coal and that the land was very fertile. He was left wondering therefore why the economy was struggling so much and there was so much resentment amongst the population.

General Coro was sitting to the left of him, and every so often Ridley saw him staring at him through the mirror opposite as though he was trying to bore into his brain to find out who he really was. Ridley wondered, 'Or is it he is trying to place me from somewhere? I don't think I have ever met him before.' Eventually turning to him, he asked, 'General, what role do you have in the Ministry of Information?'

Coro replied, 'I am responsible to the Junta for the publicity that the ministry puts out and I check on its appropriateness. However, I leave most of the day to day activities to the professionals. I have come this evening because I think your initiative could be a very important one for Argentina, and I wished to be able to report personally about it to the Junta.'

'I am very gratified to hear this,' answered Ridley, 'perhaps I should begin my presentation as I see the coffee and liqueurs are about to be served.

'Gentlemen, I appreciate being given the opportunity to make this presentation to you this evening on behalf of my company, Nippon Health. I am sure there could be a fruitful partnership of benefit both to your country and my company. Our initial set-up would be a small head office based here in BA with general, marketing, sales and finance managers and probably two medical representatives to cover the north of the country and Uruguay. I envisage a couple of reps based down in Comodoro Rivadavia initially to cover the south of the country. So to begin with we would probably recruit around fifteen people including support staff. My researches indicate there are quite a few experienced pharmaceutical industry people here so I imagine we would only need to second the general manager, probably from our company in Mexico. I need to do more research into the likely sales of our products but early indications are hopeful, and there appears to be interest in our newer compounds that have just been approved in Japan. I would hope we could get these quickly approved here so I have some new products to launch when we establish the new company. As for the next steps...' Ridley went over his plans

61

for developing the business proposal. He explained that he would be spending more time in Argentina in December, and also in January, to finalize the proposal before the February board meeting in Tokyo. Then he would return to start seeking the necessary approvals from the Ministry of Health.

As John ended his presentation, Señor Roca looked at Lopez and Coro and seeing their nods of agreement told Ridley, 'That has been an excellent presentation, very clear, and we are convinced your proposal will be of benefit to our country. We are happy to support your company in this. It would of course be better if we knew more about Nippon Health.'

'Yes,' agreed Ridley, 'that makes much sense. I would suggest we arrange some visits for you and your wives to Tokyo so you may see more of the Japanese culture. I am sure the Board will want to show you Kyoto and the many beautiful temples there and express their gratitude with much hospitality.' They looked delighted with this response and Ridley quickly followed this up with another suggestion. 'I think we should also plan for you to visit Mexico City once the necessary approvals are in place so you may see the Nippon Health production site near there.'

'Very satisfactory suggestions,' replied Señor Roca looking very pleased, 'we look forward to a fruitful relationship with you. Thank you for an excellent meal; the whole evening has been very enlightening. May we drop you at your hotel?' So Ridley quickly settled the outrageous bill with his American Express card and joined them outside the restaurant. There waited a gleaming black Mercedes 500 that soon sped him back to his hotel.

'Adiós, Señor Ridley,' said Roca just before the car drove off, 'please call me before you arrive in December so I may make time available for you.' With that Ridley waved them off and turned into his hotel.

'That is as close to an order as it could be,' he thought.

Sinking into the comfortable chair in his bedroom he ran carefully through the evening's discussion. He was certain he had not made any mistakes and in fact he was sure they really believed him. From previous experience he knew the benefit of a real activity when working under cover. The challenge was to be subtle with the intelligence gathering so they could never separate it from the business project. 'I am surprised that security is so interested in me, however. What is making them nervous?' he wondered. Rousing himself he sat at the desk to make some notes about the discussion, being careful to limit this to the pharmaceutical evaluation. Then having called down to reception to ensure they would have his account ready first thing in the morning, he packed and went to bed with happy thoughts of the girl awaiting him in Toronto.

Chapter Six

Friday nine o'clock Ridley's Boeing 747 lifted off from Ezeiza airport en route for Sao Paulo and then Miami, and as soon as the seat belt sign was switched off he pushed back his seat and dropped off to sleep only waking for lunch and dinner. He had always had the annoying facility, as far as any companions were concerned, of easily going to sleep once a plane was in the air. Twelve hours later the plane touched down at Miami and without too long a stopover he was soon on the American Airlines jet, bound for Toronto's Lester Pearson airport.

Just before six a.m. they landed. He quickly collected his baggage and cleared immigration and customs. Grabbing a taxi he was soon back in his apartment and having a wonderful hot, invigorating shower. He then quickly prepared breakfast as he expected Andy to arrive about eight. He was therefore rather surprised when the doorbell rang around seven-thirty. He checked through the spy hole and when he saw Andy standing there, quickly opened the door. The next moment she was in his arms and saying breathlessly as though she had run up the stairs, 'I couldn't wait any longer. You don't think I can wait until after breakfast, do you?'

With that she walked away from him and shedding clothes headed for the bedroom. John followed the trail that ended just before his king-size bed with a bra and a pair of knickers and saw her head poking out from his duvet. 'I know you're probably exhausted but I need to be held by you and hold you tight,' pleaded Andy. 'Get your clothes off and get in here now!' John stripped and slipped into the bed to hold this wonderful girl who appeared from nowhere and now meant so much to him.

'I have missed you, love', he said. 'Thinking of you kept me going.'

'It has been the same for me', agreed Andy. 'I was a bit worried by that call you made. You must tell me all later.' After this John found he wasn't as tired as he thought and before long they were gently making love and bringing each other to wonderful climaxes. It was lunchtime before they reluctantly roused themselves and showered together, then wandered around the apartment hand in hand.

Sitting down in the sitting room John smiled at her, 'I love you and I'm pretty sure I want to spend my life with you. Once this is all over I will have a very serious question to ask you. It wouldn't be fair to ask it now but in a few months it'll be different.'

With a trace of tears in her eyes Andy whispered, 'I shall look forward to it and I don't think you should have any doubt what my answer will be. I would die for you', she said fiercely. 'It seems to have hit us both completely.' John just held her tight and stroked her blonde hair affectionately.

Pulling herself together she attempted to become the professional intelligence officer but with little success as she kept staring at him, smiling and touching him as though to reassure herself that he was really there. 'This is hopeless,' she said, 'I can't concentrate on anything. I should really debrief you but I can't concentrate.'

John smiled, 'Well I thought you had debriefed me very effectively a couple of hours ago.'

'Be serious,' she protested. 'We must plan your debrief.'

'I suggest', said John, 'that we have today to ourselves and then spend Sunday here doing the formal debrief. This will be better for me as usually the jumble of facts takes about a day to sort themselves out in my mind and I find I can make a better appraisal and summary after that. We can then agree all the follow-up actions for you and I am afraid I think there is a lot for you to do before I return to BA in early December.'

'OK, I'll go with that but you must assuage my curiosity about one thing. What was it that caused you such concern that you felt you should report it?'

'Yes, that was a real shock. Last Saturday I was coming down in the lift to go sightseeing and a girl came in who I had last seen in Madrid more than eight years ago. I managed to stop her making a great fuss and I persuaded her I was a Canadian these days and had never joined the navy. I took her to a café and explained this and my assessment is that she will go along with this story. When I was at university and already in naval intelligence, I was sent on an intensive language course at the University of Madrid and stayed with a family. I went to Galicia in the west for language practice, to a family that owned a house on the Isla La Toja just off the coast. This girl, Maria, was the daughter and she is a year or two younger than you. Well, I spent a couple of holidays there and she sort of adopted me as a big brother and I thought of her as my little sister as I have no family of my own.' John paused and Andy made a mental note to ask him about his family.

John continued, 'I saw her once after that, then my work prevented me from visiting the family and I suppose we drifted apart. Having met her again I find I am still fond of her.' Seeing Andy's strained look he held up his hands palm upwards and protested, 'Now hang on, Andy! I mean

I am fond of her as a little sister not as a lover. She feels the same about me, she says she has always thought of me as her big brother and still feels that now. You certainly don't have to feel jealous of her and you can stop looking sceptical. She asked whether I had a girl and when I described you, she said I was to give you her best wishes and she hopes you both may meet one of these days.'

Somewhat mollified, Andy queried, 'So what is the problem? She clearly trusts you and is happy to have met you again.'

'There may not be a problem but the main uncertainty is she is married to an Argentine and the marriage is pretty rocky. I suspect her husband has some links with the Junta but she doesn't really know what. We will need to find out more. On the plus side she and her husband own an estancia about an hour's drive inland from Rio Gallegos. Before I met her I was racking my brains about how I could get down there in a period of tension. The more I think about it the more certain I am that the airbase there will play a big role in any operations against the Falklands. It might be possible now, if we think the risk is minimal, for me to hide out at the estancia for a few days and observe the base. I could set up an OP near the base on a low hill I think I spotted as the plane took off. I need to check it on a map. This would be OK if the husband is not around and I think there is little risk of this as he seems to have a mistress in BA who keeps him occupied.'

Nodding, Andy agreed, 'I see this is a risk you might have to take. If you are there for only a couple of days it is unlikely you will meet him. You are clearly not a hundred per cent confident of Maria?'

'No. How can you be after eight years? But I feel she can probably be trusted. I will just have to proceed cautiously.'

She nodded. 'I hope we can minimize risk as much as possible by working up a good biography on the husband. We should also check on Maria with the Spanish authorities. I can get the South American Desk on to this on Monday. Let's work it all through tomorrow. Now I'm famished. Take me out for lunch then I want to go shopping.' Grinning at him she said, 'You aren't the only one with news. I've found an apartment to rent about two blocks from here and I can move in next week. It's furnished but I would like to get some ornaments to personalize it and I thought you might like to buy me a present.'

'Whatever you would like, my love.'

'Well, I would like a very sexy nightie that I can go to sleep in when you are away. It will enfold me like your arms do. I know I won't need it when you are here.'

'That's a wonderfully romantic thought', said John, 'why don't I buy you half a dozen?' So they put the affairs of the world to one side and concentrated on the affairs of the heart.

Toronto November 1981

Sunday morning they rose early and relaxed after their day together and she organized the debrief as Control should.

'Right, we do this by the book and I'll tape the discussion so I can go through again later in case there's something we miss. They'll then be sent in the diplomatic bag to SIS and DNI so they can do an evaluation.'

'OK, fire away,' agreed John, impressed by the business-like way she was taking charge.

'Let's start generally then. What are your conclusions from your discussions with government officials?'

'At very senior levels there is an awareness that something of great importance is about to happen. Nobody said anything specifically but there's excitement in the way they acted and I don't think it's just their culture and personality. The minds of the Ministry of Health people just weren't focused on my project. I felt they were going through the motions as a smoke screen. Not having been to Argentina before I can't be sure, but the level of interest the security service took in me supports this contention. None of this is substantive but normally I wouldn't have thought a business development manager of a Japanese company would merit a personal scrutiny by a high-ranking member from the intelligence community. My cover is rock solid at the moment essentially because I am conducting a business evaluation, and I hope they may relax their monitoring of me now they have given me the once over. The problem will come when I have to stick my head above the parapet. But let's not worry about that now.'

'OK, let's move on to military installations. What evidence of military preparation did you see?'

John gathered his thoughts for a moment then began, 'There was little evidence of any military preparations taking place. I think what we now have is a good benchmark against which to assess any changes in the future. At the airbases I observed, there was little activity and there didn't appear to be more training flights at Punta Indo. Also there was little going on at Comodoro Rivadavia and Rio Gallegos. However, I suspect the Rio Gallegos airbase, and Rio Grande on Tierra del Fuego, will be pivotal to any air operations as they're directly opposite the Falklands. It will be impossible to observe Rio Grande other than by an SAS or SBS spotting team inserted by submarine. Rio Gallegos will also be difficult although it is alongside the estuary, and we may be able to use a similar force there, however we should investigate the possibility of me using Maria and her estancia at least for an initial observation at the start of any Argentine operation. I couldn't find a reason to go past the San Julian airbase so I have no information for there. When I landed at Bahia Blanca I got a good view of the military side of the airfield but it was just the same. There are Skyhawks at Comodoro Rivadia and Rio Gallegos, and I also saw Mirage 3s or the Israeli copy the Dagger at all three. Maritime patrol aircraft Neptunes are based at Bahia and Rio Gallegos – I saw one waiting to take off there. I didn't see any sign of those blasted Super Etendards though', he exclaimed in exasperation. 'Rio Gallegos has a very long runway.'

Pausing to marshal his thoughts he continued, 'Most of the surface ships were in the Puerto Belgrano naval base. Only two of the Type 42 guided-missile destroyers were absent and I guess they were on patrol. Some of the vessels looked to be on assisted maintenance so I don't think action is imminent but that could mean they are preparing for it. I managed to get down to Mar del Plata sightseeing, all four submarines were there and a support ship. By the way, we need some recognition manuals so I can get up to date on the Argentine Airforce and Navy. Best if they are left at the High Commission and I visit you, just in case someone decides to search my apartment.'

'Do you think that is likely?'

'No, but it is possible, if they are still curious about me. Remember they can probably call on the CIA to check me out.'

He continued, 'As for embarkation ports my guess would be that they will use Puerto Belgrano, with Comodoro Rivadavia as the back up. The marine battalion from

Rio Gallegos might be used and I suppose they could pick them up from there but the port installations are limited. They may fly them in of course if their special forces overwhelmed our token force and secured the airport.'

'That's fine,' decided Andy, 'let's turn to some of the personalities you met. Now Maria ... what's her married name?'

'She's Maria Santos Gomez and her husband is Rafael Gomez. Maria was a Spanish citizen but I don't know whether she took Argentine nationality when she married or whether she has dual nationality. He's an Argentine from a wealthy family and gets a substantial allowance. They gave him the estancia near Rio Gallegos when he married. He did a business management degree at Madrid University and finished about a year before Maria, then worked for some merchant bank in Madrid. I guess when they returned to Argentina he continued to work for the same firm. They lived in BA then he dropped out and retreated to the ranch. After six months or so he started going to BA for weeks at a time and she suspects he has a mistress there. She also suspects he's doing some work for the Junta.'

Andy nodded, 'He's clearly a potential risk to you so must be investigated. He may also be an interesting link with the Junta that might allow us to peel back a few layers of their organisation and objectives.'

'One other interesting character is General Coro who wished me to believe he worked for the Ministry of Information. I guess he's a member of Argentine military intelligence. We should check him out as soon as possible. I don't think the Ministry of Health officials are anything other than what they claim to be so I don't think we need to worry about them.'

'I suggest I get on with things tomorrow and despatch the

tapes to London on the Monday evening flight. I'll probably have to go up to Ottawa on Tuesday as Paul will be anxious for an update, so I will come round on Wednesday evening if I can. I'll call you from Ottawa on Tuesday evening to let you know. I'd hope to have the first information back from the South American Desk by Wednesday at the latest and I'll bring it back with me. If I get it we can go through the material on Thursday. After that we begin planning for your next visit in December. What about you?'

'I know I can't see you all the time but I plan to wine and dine you at least three times each week and share your bed at least as many times. How about cottage country next weekend for some walking?'

'Great. It sounds fantastic. But what about work?'

'I'll have plenty to do for the project, and I need to see some business analysts in Toronto, so I'll spend some time with them this coming week. I must send an initial report to Tokyo and that will be a long fax plus one or two phone calls. Plus of course I'll be at your apartment warming party!'

'I suppose I should have one as the High Commission staff have been very good to me since I arrived, and Paul's been a great support while you were in Argentina. But as I'm not planning to move in until Thursday that will have to wait for a while.'

With that they ended the debriefing and went out for a meal on the lake side after stopping at the High Commission offices to put the tapes and papers in the safe. Eventually John took her hand and led her slowly back to her hotel. In the foyer he kissed her hand in a very old-fashioned manner, turned towards the entrance and with a final wave to her, he went out into the street and strolled slowly back to Victoria Park and his apartment that now felt strangely empty without her presence.

When Andy reported her attachment to John, that it was for real, not make-believe, her boss pointed out over the secure line from the UK that it might bring pain as well as happiness. Her boss was a senior woman who had married someone in the Service and her advice had been, 'Act professionally and objectively as his Control,' she said, ' and do your best to keep him safe. I know John and he'll trust and respect you so much more if he knows you're able to do this for him.' With a smile in her voice she added, 'And from my experience the homecomings will be utterly fantastic.'

Andy climbed into bed and for the first time in a long time she said a prayer, 'Dear God please keep him safe and help me to be good so that you let me keep him for ever.' With that and a gentle sigh she turned over and slept the sleep of the untroubled soul.

Monday morning they were both up and busy at their appointed tasks. As soon as Andy was in the office she made long calls on the secure line to SIS requesting information searches on the key persons, and for the recognition manuals. Then she arranged to go up to Ottawa on the Tuesday morning plane and stay over in the High Commission guesthouse. After this she decided to play through the tapes again and marvelled at how matter-of-fact John seemed as he described the dangerous work he was doing, a few small slips and he could be picked up by Argentine security, and it would more convenient for them that he just disappeared.

John meanwhile worked on his report for Nippon Health. Late morning as he finished off the fax for his business development director, his phone rang and he was surprised to hear Señor Roca on the line. 'Good morning, Señor Ridley, I am just calling to thank you for the dinner last Thursday. Both my minister and General Coro were very pleased. I just wished to confirm to you that the resources of the Ministry of Health are at your service should you require them. I have also spoken with my Uruguayan friends and they also welcome your company's interest. I know you haven't been back long in your office but do you know yet when you will be returning here?'

'It is very good of you to call, Señor Roca,' replied John, 'I don't know definitely yet as I have to speak with my boss this evening but I would expect to fit in another trip at the beginning of December. It is never a good idea to try to do business just before Christmas so I expect it will be a short trip to clarify some points in December, and then a longer visit in January before I have to finalize the report for the February board meeting.'

'Very well, Mr Ridley', said Roca, 'my diary is fairly clear then. Please let me know the exact dates when you can so I may ensure some of my advisers are available. *Adiós* for now.'

'Well,' thought John as Roca rang off, 'what a turn up for the books. Are they just desperate to have this investment or are they checking my address and movements again? I assume they're uneasy about me moving round the coastal region. I must spend some time north of BA and in the inland pampas zone well away from the coast and the south. I should go there anyway for the benefit of the business evaluation. I'd better tell Andy.' With that he picked up the phone again and told Andy about the call from Roca. He then despatched the fax so his boss would have it when Ridley rang at seven o'clock which was 9 a.m. in Tokyo. He suspected it would be a long conference call as his boss would wish to know every detail.

After arranging to see Analysts Inc the next morning out in Meadowvale, Mississauga, he dialled Nippon Health in Tokyo and asked for Mr Tana. Tana expressed satisfaction with the detailed fax John sent, but had a large number of further queries. Tana also wished to be reassured that he could still meet the tight timetable. Having received Ridley's assurance on this matter and after being informed of and approving his next visit to Argentina, Tana passed him on to the personnel director who wished to discuss some issues in other parts of world that local general managers had raised with him recently. Adding these to his already long action list, Ridley promised to deal with them before his next trip to Argentina. Putting the phone down he shook his head thinking, 'If I am doing one job it would be incredibly demanding, and here I am trying to hold down two roles both of which are unreasonable masters. Something will have to give some time soon. It may be, anyway, that after this episode I will no longer be persona grata in South America and if the project fails because of this I would have to resign anyway.' His fervent hope was that he wouldn't have to leave Canada.

Chapter Seven

Tuesday found him in Mississauga with his friends at Analysts Inc going over the economic situation in Argentina and Uruguay which didn't sound too promising. James Lockyer, the director explained: 'As you know for a long time they relied on agriculture, then Peron encouraged the development of an industrial base to try to revive the economy. This was state-led but, as in many countries, after providing a useful stimulus it outlived its usefulness, became moribund and many of the state enterprises are very corrupt. They have vast oil and coal reserves and the pampas retains its fertility, but agricultural exports depend on other countries having the wealth to purchase them. Transport costs are high from down there and there are cheaper products available and in surplus from other parts of the world. Western economies are currently experiencing economic downturn caused by the oil crisis in 1973, so there is a lot of deflation around, and inflation is set to take off. This doesn't help the Argentines. This is the downside. The upside is that both Uruguay and Argentina are affluent countries with strong state social services, especially health services, so there is a good market for pharmaceutical products. Our assessment of Nippon Health's pipeline indicates that the new compounds will be attractive to these countries and you are likely to be able to receive a good reimbursement price for them.'

'That sounds more reassuring, I think,' commented John, 'except for this concern about their economy. How are they going to get out of the large debt burden and the flood of imports you mention that has continued during the last four years of military rule? It seems to me the economy is in chaos going from mini-crisis to crisis.'

'Yes, that is the nub of the problem,' replied Lockyer, 'but don't be too pessimistic. Many countries may seem to be going bankrupt but they don't because the major economies can't afford to let them. I dare say the IMF will step in before too long and bale them out, after demanding they take some severe action to restrain imports and lower the debt burden just like they did for the UK in the 1960s.'

After this overview they dived into the detail and Ridley enjoyed the day's debate and analytical challenge completely forgetting the real reason for him going down there. On the return journey down the 405 to the apartment he mulled over what he had learnt that day. He realized there was another short-term strategy to avoid trouble with the general public over the economic problems. That was the well-tried strategy of many dictators in the past – start a war and harness the latent opposition into the national fervour in the battle for the country's honour. The Junta might be tempted to use such a strategy with the Falklands as the excuse.

Wednesday found him working hard on the multitude of personnel management issues that crawled out of the woodwork since he went to Argentina. The phone and fax lines were engaged much of the day. Andy had called to tell him that she would be landing around 8 p.m. from Ottawa, so he headed for the airport to the west of Toronto.

Not long after eight he spotted her blonde hair between the passengers coming down the ramp and she was soon in his arms, and after a long kiss she hooked her arm through his and they headed out to the car.

'Did you have a useful trip,' he asked as they headed for the apartment.

'Yes, London has worked very fast and we have a lot of information to digest tomorrow. Unfortunately there are also a number of gaps so I am afraid some of the assessments are a bit iffy, the probability may only be around 70%.'

'I am not surprised, that is often the case,' observed John. 'I sometimes get nervous when the intelligence is 100% as I just don't believe you can ever be that sure.'

'On another matter,' said Andy looking excited, 'will you help me move into the flat tomorrow afternoon and stay over? I want to cook for you in my own place. I love your apartment but I am really excited to be getting one of my own.'

'Of course. In fact I am so besotted with you I believe a shack in the woods would seem like the Hilton.' With that he turned into the underground garage and they quickly made their way up to his apartment, and the lovely meal he had already in the oven. Afterwards grinning at him and stretching out her long legs so that her skirt rode higher on her thighs, Andy suggested, 'You will certainly make some girl a good husband if you keep cooking like that.'

His quick-fire reply while looking at her legs was, 'It's a good job I didn't see your beautiful thighs before we ate, then all you would have got is my desire, not food.'

'You do say the nicest lusty things', she purred and took him to bed.

The next day he woke to find her sitting cross-legged and straight-backed on the floor in his sitting room with papers spread out around her. 'I woke quite early and my mind was racing over all this information so I thought I would get up and sort through it to see if I could spot any patterns.

Let's shower and have some breakfast and then we can look at it together. I love problem-solving with you.'

After breakfast they sat down in his study and she relayed to him the reports she had received. 'You have clearly interested someone down there,' she said. 'SIS informed me that Canadian Intelligence received an enquiry about you on Monday from the CIA. This clearly must have come from Argentine Military Intelligence. You must have very deep cover, and my security clearance doesn't get me anywhere near it, but I am instructed to tell you that the request was, in accordance with instructions, forwarded to the Director CanIntel who informed them that you were just a Canadian citizen working for Nippon Health and based in Toronto.'

As she said this John nodded thoughtfully and grimaced, 'It's not a good sign. At least their current approach has been rebuffed. The possible involvement of the CIA means I shall have to be careful about travelling through the US if things go critical otherwise I might find myself picked up by them. My situation isn't all that complicated and now isn't the time to go through it. Let's leave it until we get up to the cottage on Friday evening.'

'You managed to organize it,' she exclaimed excitedly, 'you are wonderful.' And at that she leant over and planted a quick kiss on his cheek.

Returning to business she added, 'The recognition manuals will be in the office here by the end of the week so next week you can come down and go through them. I can then test you on them. Now, the personalities you queried. General Coro is a very interesting person. It is thought he was a colonel in 1974. There was a report in the files from the then military attaché suggesting he was in intelligence and close to the general staff. He probably supported the first military president and was rewarded with promotion. He is often seen with the Junta so he is fairly senior in the pecking order, and the assessment is that he is Head of Military Intelligence, but they give that only an 85% probability.'

'I am duly flattered,' drawled John. 'It's a good job my cover is watertight at the moment. It must be because I am going to places along the Atlantic coast and they are anxious I shall see what I am not supposed to, and if I am intelligence gathering I will report it. This does seem to support the contention that they are planning something. Has there been any rhetoric about the Falklands recently?'

'No, and that is considered significant in itself. The DNI assessment, via SIS, is that the silence is because they are planning something against the islands. SIS doesn't support this view yet and your boss says it is up to you to bring him the information to back up his supposition.'

She added, 'The good news is that nothing is known about Maria other than what she told you, and a check with NATO Spanish section confirmed this so you can probably trust her. The news is not so good about her husband though, by all accounts he seems to be a nasty piece of work. Why she married him I can't understand. He seems to have been an ultranationalist at university and a strong supporter of Franco. Very rich, arrogant but tall and handsome. Perhaps he provided a taste of the high life.'

'That's probably it,' agreed John. 'She was always the country girl from Galicia before she went to Madrid. She still strikes me as being like that, except there is now a brittle veneer because she has found out the world is not necessarily a nice place.'

Checking the file Andy added, 'Gomez did work for a merchant bank both in Spain and back in Argentina and is now suspected of being very close to the Junta. We also think we have found out why he went to ground in Patagonia a few years ago. We think his family exiled him after they saved him from a nasty scandal. He was about to be accused of raping his personal assistant at the bank, and his family got it hushed up by paying off the girl and her parents. Anyway he seems to be rehabilitated now and spends a lot of time in the capital. He's thought to be a senior adviser to the general overseeing the Economic Ministry. It isn't known whether he has a mistress,' she smiled. 'Our Embassy seems very prudish in this respect. You'll need to be very careful if you are with Maria as I think her husband could be a very jealous man.'

She looked steadily at him with those gorgeous green eyes and he felt moved to assure her. 'Don't worry darling I shall be very, very careful in my dealings with her. I don't intend to be seen out with her in hotels or restaurants. I suggested she should stay over at the apartment I am leasing from the beginning of January.'

'My, you are a quick worker,' she retorted.

He hastened to reassure her again. 'I said as we regard ourselves as a surrogate brother and sister we could stay together but sleep in separate rooms. She feels the same about it as I do,' he added defensively.

He asked, 'Do you think we might get more of a clue about any timetable or even what is contemplated by concentrating more on Gomez?'

'It's certainly worth considering,' she mused, 'let's think about it for the next week or so. Perhaps via Maria or another contact in BA. I understand from your boss, by the way my service has authorized me to report directly to him when necessary, that they are considering other support for you if things look like going critical, such as a courier. This is all to be set up around Christmas. Your boss is a nice man isn't he, but he grilled me like a father checking up on his future daughter-in-law. What is your relationship with him? You are obviously close.'

'Ah,' laughed John, 'that is another story for cottage country. I think we've about exhausted this topic for the moment. Are you going to show me this new flat of yours?'

They set off the two blocks east to her new apartment and after going up in the lift to the third floor she opened the door and proudly led him into her cosy home. Not as large as John's palatial apartment but with a good size lounge. There was one double bedroom, a reasonable size modern kitchen, and a nice bathroom with a bath, a shower and also a bidet. 'I can tell yours is a bachelor pad. There are two things missing for a woman: a bath and a bidet,' she pointed out. 'I think the owner must be from Quebec as there's a French influence here.'

'The only place I have seen a bidet was in France', agreed John. 'I didn't know you could get them over here. Anyway it proves I haven't had many girlfriends if this essential piece of information about women has slipped past me. Should we go get your luggage?'

Later he helped her to unpack her things and the various ornaments and lights they had bought the previous Saturday. Soon the place looked Andy's, especially when it got dark and she switched on the table lamps and a soft glow spread across the lounge. Rummaging in the last bag she pulled out a bottle of Robert Modavi Merlot and said, 'Open that, will you, John,' and they drank to her new home and another place where they may be comfortable together. Later she cooked him a wonderful trout dish that he enjoyed, but which unknown to her reminded him of the link with Maria and the Cordoba restaurant in San Telmo. 'It never leaves you,' he thought wryly.

Friday afternoon he collected Andy at her apartment and they drove the two hours northwards to cottage country. She marvelled at the straightness of the road. John joked, 'There are only two sharp bends along this whole length of road and believe it or not someone manages to miss one or other of them every week!'

Just after it got dark they went through the town of Owen Sound on Lake Huron and reached the Sauble River, and soon after he pulled up alongside a dwelling near to some others. 'Not sure I would call this a cottage,' said Andy, 'it looks more like a mansion.'

John grabbed the bags and led the way up to the front door shining a flashlight to show their way. He opened the front door and went over to a cabinet on the wall. Opening it with one of the keys he had, he switched on the power supply. Then he turned on the lights and she saw in front of her a lovely cosy room with a rug-covered wooden floor and panelled walls with examples of Canadian quilting hanging on them. Taking her hand he led her through the cottage showing her the large kitchen and the dining room, and then opened the door from there on to the deck which, bounded by a rail, extended out over the river bank. Switching on the outside light she was able to see the river and the outline of other cottages on the far bank and realized there were boats moored by most of them. 'Do we have a boat?' she queried. 'Yes, I want to take you out on Owen Sound and into Georgian Bay tomorrow. Perhaps we may have a picnic on Sauble beach then a barbecue back here if the weather is warm enough.'

'Who owns this cottage?' she asked him.

'A business friend of mine bought it a few years ago. He is married now and I still see them occasionally. He and I usually come up here together on two or three weekends each year to do some walking and scuba diving in Georgian Bay where there is a National Marine Park.'

She couldn't resist asking, 'Have you brought any other girls here?'

He took her hand and gently answered, 'No, my love, until I met you I hadn't had a girlfriend in Canada. We may have had blokes and girls here for weekends but no girls who were special to me. I didn't think I could handle a girlfriend in my job. However, I have changed my mind now.'

After they had settled in, eaten their meal and sat down with another glass of wine she returned to the two questions she posed earlier in the week. 'John, I understand that security may mean you are unable to tell me everything, but I feel I am close to agreeing quite happily to spend the rest of my life with you. I trust you implicitly, yet I know virtually nothing about you or your family. Please tell me what you can.'

He smiled at her with that lovely smile of his, then sighed, 'I see I am not going to escape the inquisition. I was born in Northumberland but my parents were killed when I was very young: I know few details except it was a car crash. There were no other relatives and I spent the first thirteen years of my life in the Dr Barnardo's Home in Hexham. I was never adopted for some reason, but I was very well looked after, and all the people there were very kind. I don't think I ever felt lonely for I didn't know any different. When I was thirteen I was told I had a guardian and he was sending me to Pangbourne, which you may know is a public school with a nautical emphasis on the River Thames near Maidenhead. Before that I didn't know I had a guardian. I went from there to university and early on I was recruited into naval intelligence. I studied modern languages and geography at Bristol University, and as you know I met Maria at La Toja when I was doing intensive language practice in Spain. I also speak German quite well. I subsequently did basic naval training but have primarily operated under cover since university assuming a Canadian nationality courtesy of Canadian Intelligence.'

'How were you recruited so quickly?' wondered Andy.

'This all hinges on the identity of my guardian,' explained John. 'You will be surprised when I tell you, but he won't be surprised I am breaching security to tell you. He will see it as a demonstration of how much I trust you.'

'This is all very mysterious,' whispered Andy, 'I love a secret!'

'Quiet, woman or I won't tell you,' chided John. 'My esteemed guardian is none other than Rear Admiral Andrew Collingwood who as you will recall is my boss.'

'What! I don't believe it, you're having me on,' she exclaimed.

'No it's true. Apparently for many years he was unable to take a direct interest in my welfare other than by providing funds when required. This may be why I was never adopted. Later on, as a bachelor, he didn't think it was best for me to live with him so I was sent to Pangbourne, but I stayed with him during the holidays at his home in Northumberland. Needless to say I was well trained in tradecraft before I went to university and at that time he recruited me into DNI and subsequently set me up in Canada. He is a very complex man and I wouldn't say I understand him but I am very fond of him. Perhaps one day he will explain. He can also be very determined and ruthless so don't look to him for sympathy if I get into trouble. You know the naval expression: if you cannot stand the pace you shouldn't have joined!'

He added, 'I think you can now understand why you got interrogated by him. The old romantic rogue, he was indeed checking you out as a future daughter-in-law or whatever you call it if one has a guardian.'

Andy shook her head exasperatedly, 'After that tale I need another drink. May I have another glass of Merlot please. Blast it, the pair of you have entrapped me completely and, you know what, I'm so happy.' With that the tears ran down her face and he wrapped her in his arms and rocked her gently as all the tension eased out of her. 'I don't want to lose you ever,' she sobbed. 'I'm so sorry you never knew your parents.'

'I'm used to it now. I don't feel there is a void in my life and I have learnt to get on with my life. I worry about the here and now, not what might have been!'

On Saturday morning they woke early, both wanting not to waste any of the short daylight at this time of the year. By the time it was getting light they had finished breakfast, John was fuelling the boat and Andy was busy in the kitchen making the picnic and filling the flasks. Soon all was loaded into the motorboat and John handed her a lifejacket to put on over her anorak, and gave her a blue peaked cap embroidered with the word 'Captain' to keep her head warm.

The weather was set fair and it looked as though it would be a bright day, but in the late autumn there was always a sharp chill in the air and it wouldn't take much for snow to appear. John steered the boat slowly down the river and out into the wide expanse of Owen Sound, past all the houses set in the trees on the banks each with its own boathouse, and then the large grain elevator at the mouth of the sound. Reaching the entrance he gunned the engine and they sped out into Georgian Bay, heading for a cluster of small islands on the horizon where they spent the morning exploring the coves.

Then he turned the boat back towards a long sandy beach near Owen Sound. Pointing ahead he said, 'That's Sauble Beach where we'll have lunch. The beach shelves gently so I can put the boat safely on the sand but you should take off your shoes and socks so they don't get soaked. I packed a towel just in case.' Soon the boat was gently nosing on to the beach and they found they had the whole beach to themselves. Not a soul in sight for at least a couple of miles in either direction. Securing the boat in the sand with the anchor they had their picnic then spent the afternoon exploring along the beach and in the pine forest behind.

Then as the light began to fade it was time to return and he pushed off the boat. Motoring steadily up the Sound they were soon at the mooring by the cottage. Coming to the front door they saw a note pinned there. It said:

Hi, we shall be having a barbecue at 6 p.m. this evening and we hope you will come. Everybody up here has been invited. Bring some barbecue provisions and some drink.

Janie and Bill

'Luckily I know where they live. It's only three cottages up river on this side. Shall we go?'

'Yes, please, it will be nice to meet some other Canadians. I want to find out as much as possible about this wonderful country.'

They arrived promptly at 6 pm, for in Canada it is impolite to arrive late at barbecues. Everyone is expected to help with the barbecue and once the food is cooking, the guests may pour themselves copious amounts of wine or beer and set about partying. John and Andy found themselves in the centre of a crowd of jolly people and had a great evening. Andy found out little about Canada but a lot about Canadians.

After large amounts of steak the guests settled down on the deck and someone produced a guitar, and suddenly everyone was heartily singing folk songs including a number she thought she had heard John humming in his apartment. About midnight they sang their way back to the cottage and crawled sleepily into the cosy bed and were soon asleep in each other's arms.

Sunday morning they woke late and after breakfast decided to just stroll along the Sauble River to the Sauble Falls where they stood on the bridge above the Falls and watched the rushing water below, then they wandered back through the forest. After lunch they set off back to civilization. On the return journey Andy wondered whether they had got it wrong, and they were in fact leaving civilization. John dropped her at the apartment after agreeing to meet her in her office Monday morning.

As she got ready for bed she remembered all the wonderful experiences of the weekend. More and more she was convinced that John was the man for her. He was such a wonderful companion and friend, as well a good lover, and a brave man, and she didn't think a woman could hope for anything more when she married. 'He really is my best friend,' she thought. 'Without any family he must have been so lonely at times. No wonder he is so self-reliant. But now he has me as well.'

Monday morning he arrived at her office at 10 a.m. and was shown in by a smiling secretary who clearly knew of their relationship. After coffee was served she pulled out the current Jane's recognition manuals for navies and air forces. Turning to the Argentine Navy she took him through all the types and tested him until he was able to recognize all of them with only a brief glance. They then turned to aircraft and ran through the various types of Skyhawk ground attack aircraft and Mirage 3 delta-wing fighters. They concentrated on the differences between the Mirage 3 and the Dassault Super Etendard so he would be able to make a confident identification if he came across them. The Super Etendard's Exocet missiles were considered a major threat to the Royal Navy's surface ships. By lunchtime his excellent memory had retained all this essential information and he took her out for lunch. Later he returned to his study to continue his Nippon Health tasks during the afternoon.

For the rest of the week they were very busy with their essential tasks, seeing each other for a short while most evenings, but in an unspoken agreement of allowing a breathing space in their relationship, each going back to their own place to sleep.

Chapter Eight

Stanley Harbour East Falkland late November 1981

The Chilean trawler moved slowly past Cape Pembroke into Port William Bay then through the narrow strait, between low lying hills, that joined it to Stanley Harbour. Ahead they could see the small town of Stanley: the capital of the Falkland Islands Dependencies and Britain's only territorial possession in South America. To the west were the highest hills, flattered by their description as mountains, providing a protective ring around the anchorage from the strong gales that blow in from the Antarctic.

The ship limped into harbour and tied up alongside the main jetty. Fishing to the west of the Falklands outside of the territorial limit it experienced a main generator failure and requested permission to enter Stanley Harbour for urgent repairs. The harbour master was waiting on the jetty as the ship arrived and was soon on the bridge examining the skipper's papers and hearing about the problem.

Luckily the skipper spoke quite good English for the harbour master's Spanish was virtually non-existent. There was a policy here to completely ignore the continent two hundred miles to the west.

'Thank you, skipper, your papers are all in order. We're happy for you to remain here until your repairs are completed. You have to pay harbour dues for the duration of your stay. I'll let you know how much. You'll have to pay in English pounds as there is no possibility of a bank transfer from Chile. The bank here will change your Chilean pesos.'

'Thank you', replied the skipper. 'I radioed Moody's about the problem before we came in and they say they have the part in stock and promise to do the work tomorrow. Hopefully there won't be any problems when we restart the generator. I expect we'll leave early Wednesday as I'm anxious to get fishing. Each day's delay costs us a lot of money.'

Completely satisfied the harbour master left the ship and headed home for his tea.

The skipper went down to the deckhouse where the crew were waiting. 'OK, the harbour master seems happy we are a Chilean trawler. We're confident that the fault we have looks genuine?'

'Yes', replied the engineer with a grin. 'I isolated the part then put a massive charge through it to burn out the bushes. It looks like a major problem on a main generator but it isn't a difficult job to replace it so they will complete the task tomorrow. We checked they carry spares here before we began the operation.'

'Good. Let me remind you of our objective for the next 24 hours. Remember we are not navy men but fishermen so I don't want any shaving while we're here and, for God's sake, don't splash on any aftershave. You're supposed to be hairy fishermen. We're here to watch and listen. If you're not helping with the repair get out and about in Stanley. Check the lie of the land round the harbour, especially Cape Pembroke. Talk to people but don't question them in case they get suspicious. Find out what the military presence is and when they expect a British warship.'

Turning to the cook he ordered, 'Now let's have something to eat. Then we split into two groups and go down to the pubs. Don't drink too much. I'm afraid you'll have to drink that stinking beer the English drink!'

Later in the pubs the visitors were soon the centre of attention, for visitors were a bit of a rarity. To the Argentines the Falklanders were extremely gullible, content with their isolation two hundred miles out in the southern ocean wastes. Everyone was very talkative and the Argentines were soon in possession of much useful information about military preparedness on the islands: in a word 'negligible'. The British RAF had no aircraft permanently stationed there and there had been no British warship in the area for months.

Back on board they pooled their information and the skipper made detailed notes that he then locked safely away from prying eyes in the ship's strongbox.

The next morning the maintenance crew from Moody's arrived with the spare part for the main generator. They examined the damage and agree the spare part should sort the problem. So leaving the engineer to supervise the work, the rest of the crew set out intelligence gathering around Stanley glad that the weather had stayed fine. A couple of them walked east towards Cape Pembroke and checked out the eastern side of Stanley and the entrance to Port William Bay. Another pair climbed up Sapper Hill to the south of Stanley and scanned the surrounding area towards the airport to the west. The rest spent the morning wandering around the town getting to know every inch in case their troops had to fight their way in.

By mid-afternoon the repair was complete, the generator was run up and worked correctly and the skipper announced they would sail with the tide at 0700 the next morning. That evening the skipper contacted the harbour master and informed him they would be leaving the next day. They met for a farewell drink in the pub then the skipper returned to his ship.

0700 the trawler slipped and made its way steadily across the harbour, through the narrow strait and was soon lost in the thin veil of rain drifting across Port William Bay for although it was summer the weather could change dramatically in a couple of hours. Clear of the islands the trawler continued to head north until they slipped below the horizon. As there was no fear of being tracked on radar, the skipper then turned the ship to port and set course northwest for Comodoro Rivadavia, their home port. Before long the crew would disperse to their units and he would be back in the Naval Intelligence Headquarters in BA. Another successful intelligence gathering operation; another piece in the jigsaw so vital before the final invasion plan was completed. Though he couldn't understand why anyone would want to own these islands.

Toronto late November 1981

On the Monday before Ridley's departure for BA, Andy appeared at his apartment with a full briefcase and told him it was time to plan his next trip. 'John, I've been recalled to London tomorrow for a further briefing and planning meetings in SIS and DNI. I won't be coming back until Saturday. When are you setting off for Buenos Aires?'

'I've booked on a late evening American Airlines flight to Miami on Saturday which links with the Miami–Buenos Aires service so I will be arriving there late Sunday evening.'

'Well, I'm not planning to see you when I get back on

Saturday. Call me superstitious if you like, but not seeing you the night before your departure last trip seemed to keep you safe so I plan to keep the same routine this time.' With that she looked defiantly at him. 'If anything new crops up when I'm in London I'll call you immediately. I'll call you anyway Friday evening before I leave London to wish you luck.'

Having delivered this *faît accompli* she became business-like once more and threw a pack of papers at him from the enormous briefcase she brought with her. 'These are the latest intelligence and economic assessments that came in the bag a couple of days ago. They reached me here yesterday afternoon and I spent last evening going over them. I haven't spotted anything but you look through them while I make coffee.'

John took the pack of papers and without thinking moved off into his study and sitting in his leather Swedish office chair began to work through the intelligence assessments and propositions. As he came to the end of the papers, she appeared with two cups of strong steaming coffee, his black the way he really liked it. 'There isn't very much here,' he said disappointedly, 'the main evidence that they're up to something is that we can't find any evidence of it.' With an exasperated shake of his hand he pointed out, rather obviously it seemed to Andy, 'No politician will act on this basis.'

'True,' agreed Andy, 'but we have identified a couple of people in Argentina you could approach who seem to be able to pick up whispers at the edge of government and might pass on some information. One is Tony Marini, a journalist on the La Nación national newspaper, and we think it would be perfectly appropriate for you to brief him on your company's plans. He is known to challenge the

Junta, although cautiously, and we think he is a closet liberal. His home number is on that list and I suggest you note it down with your business contacts. The other is more difficult. She is Elena Mantovani, from an Anglo-Argentine family, though her husband as you'll have guessed is of Italian ancestry. She is a section head in the Foreign Ministry but is thought to be unhappy at the stance being taken against Britain. We are sending out someone on a visit masquerading as the new business attaché for South America, and have requested the embassy organize a small reception next week for him to meet local people. You know, the usual thing, fact-finding etc etc. We'll be inviting her, as well as other officials and some government ministers, and we think she'll attend, as she's a regular at British Embassy functions. You'll also find an invitation awaiting you when you get down there. We suggested they invite any businessmen that are around, especially any from Japanese companies as our government is anxious to encourage Japanese investment in the UK. Our man will make sure this happens when he arrives later this week.'

'You've all been busy these last couple of weeks,' observed John. 'Given the interest I elicited last trip I thought I'd avoid the Atlantic coast this time and focus much more on BA and the north and west of the country. I should go up-river to Rosario and Santa Fe, and visit the pampas west of BA just to see what business opportunities are there. As far as I can tell there are no air or army bases in these areas that would play a part in any action around the Falklands. I also have to continue my set up planning and meet with the recruitment people, and I must organize my apartment for next year. If I can get an opportunity to speak to Marini and Mantovani that may provide us with the substance we lack.'

'You must be very careful though,' she warned him. 'Your boss spoke to me yesterday and told me the Canadians received a request about me from the CIA last week so they're following up all your associates. It seems that we must be under surveillance from the Argentine Embassy in Ottawa. The Canadians confirmed I was accredited as a member of the British High Commission business section and they had no reason to doubt my role.'

She went on, 'At the end of this discussion your boss asked me outright whether you'd told me your life history. I confirmed you had and, do you know what he said? He said well done! Then he said, "take care of him".'

'I told you he was a sentimental and romantic rogue. Don't jump to the conclusion that he would hesitate to order me into a dangerous situation if the circumstances demanded it. I understand this and could never criticize him if he did. You mustn't hate him if he does.'

Without replying, she pulled the papers together and grabbing her coat said she had to get back to the office, but he should come around at about six and she would cook a meal for him. 'Bring your PJs and a spare shirt cos I would like you to stay the night, then you can see me off to the airport in the morning.' Giving him a quick peck on the cheek she dashed off into the lift.

Buenos Aires December 1981

On a very warm Mediterranean style evening Ridley stepped off the plane at Ezeiza and headed for the Hotel San Martin. Being early summer it was still quite light and he could look across the Rio de la Plata and see the many small boats and yachts making the most of the last hours of the weekend.

The forecast seemed to promise good weather for the week so he hoped that was a good omen for his trip. The Friday before he had called Señor Roca and arranged an appointment for Monday morning to go over the objectives of the present trip. He had mentioned that he thought he should go to Rosario and Santa Fe, and Roca had offered to provide him with a guide to accompany him. He had also suggested they make some appointments at the local medical authorities and hospitals for him. Ridley would find out what had been arranged and hoped to go up there on Tuesday. Soon the taxi pulled up outside the hotel and the clerk on reception greeted him as an old friend. Quickly he registered, handed over his passport and received some letters left for him. The bellboy whisked his bags up to his room, placed them neatly on the shelf, and left after receiving his tip. Going over to the desk by the window John switched on the lamp and examined the letters. One of them he noted as he turned it over bore the crest of the British Embassy. The letters didn't seem to have been tampered with, but he presumed that the Argentines also had some people skilled in opening and re-sealing envelopes without leaving any obvious traces.

Opening the envelope from the embassy first it was, as he suspected, the invitation to a reception in honour of James Grant who had the splendid job title of 'Business Attaché South America'. 'I must try not to smile when I'm introduced to him,' he thought. The reception was at 6 p.m. the next day so that was very convenient and it shouldn't get in the way of his other plans.

Monday morning he was being ushered into Señor Roca's office. He was surprised to find Roca wasn't alone. A very attractive, elegantly dressed dark-haired young woman sat on one side of the conference table and he presumed she was his secretary.

Roca greeted him pleasantly. 'Good morning, Señor Ridley, it is a great pleasure to see you again. I hope you had a pleasant flight, that is, if any flight can be pleasant these days; they get longer and longer. I much preferred it when one landed every two hours and had the opportunity to stretch one's legs on the ground.' Turning to look at the girl sitting at the table he introduced Ridley, 'May I present Señora Sabato from my personal office. I thought it might be a good idea for her to act as your liaison officer and accompany you to Rosario and Santa Fe.'

'I wonder if this is going to be a honey-trap set-up. Mind you, I won't object to her as my guide as I am sure she will be very pleasant and attentive,' he thought, reverting to a true arrogant male.

'*Buenos días*, Señora Sabato, I am pleased to meet you,' said Ridley, and she smiled her greeting showing a perfect set of white teeth. Ridley thought, 'At least she will be a pleasant jailer but she will be disappointed that I don't express any interest in her personally. I don't want her hanging around on my trips next year so I must accept gratefully now but on a limited basis, so there's no expectation that I will require her "services" on future occasions.'

Looking at her he said, 'I would be very grateful for your assistance on this trip. However, when I return in January I will be putting together my final business proposal and the information then will be highly confidential.' As a parting shot he added looking across at Roca, 'I'm sure your government wouldn't want there to be any suspicion of complicity between my company and your ministry.'

Roca agreed and looked pleased at how easily Ridley had accepted his 'minder'. He then became very helpful when Ridley produced his list of information needs. After a while he suggested that Señora Sabato would be able to deal with most of his requests and so she took him to her office. As he followed her along the corridor he had a perfect view of her excellent figure encased in a long pencil skirt, and on high heels he had to admit that her bottom moved very sexily. Hidden in the information list he had given her was a request for information about the military medical services, so it would be interesting to see if it got through. If it did, he would get a current list of military medical locations and that could be useful. They agreed that Tuesday would be a good day to visit the towns north of BA and that she would set up a number of meetings for him. She also offered to drive him, saying it would be better than going on the train as they would be able to talk more easily and confidentially. She managed to imply with this latter statement a sensuous promise and he guessed she was really trying to get him into her bed. Just before lunch, having agreed that she would pick him up at his hotel at 7 a.m. the next morning, he made his departure and headed off to prepare for his afternoon meeting at the recruitment agency.

Over lunch at a nearby café Ridley reviewed the morning's revelations. He believed he had signalled a finite period for Señora Sabato being his minder and the reason was plausible and probably would be taken at face value. He hoped to get more information from her than she could squeeze out of him. After all, he was the skilled interrogator. He hoped the intelligence services were just being cautious and didn't have anything on him. Provided he stuck to the plan for this trip their fears should be allayed and he should have no problem during the visit in January, as they would be used to him by then. 'Staying away from the Atlantic coast should reassure them,' he hoped.

His meeting with the recruitment agency went well. He went through the outline job profiles he had drafted and described the main qualities and experience he needed for the marketing, sales and finance manager positions. They suggested six candidates who met the specification and might be approached for the positions. Ridley was very satisfied with this response as this was exactly what he would have expected. In fact it appeared that a couple of the possible candidates also had international experience with US companies and that would be a bonus.

As Ridley left the recruitment agency offices he was intercepted by two men who looked very much like Argentine security. One of them, in a very snappy suit, displayed his ID card and told him, 'Señor Ridley, General Coro would like to see you. Would you please come with us now and we will take you to his office.'

Assuming they were armed, he saw he really had no choice, that to refuse would make them even more suspicious. Anyway it might not mean discovery, just something innocuous and that Coro had sent his henchmen because he was impatient; that was how he always was. Or that Coro was fishing, trying to startle him into some fatal mistake.

Ridley tried to smile at them in a relaxed way, although the adrenalin was beginning to pump around his body. 'Of course,' he replied, 'I will be delighted to see General Coro. Is it some query about the business project do you know?'

They shrugged, turned and led him to the parking area where he saw a large black Mercedes parked illegally. As the rear door was opened for him he slid in, followed by one of the security men. The other one got into the front next to the driver who then quickly drove off. As they drove along Ridley scanned over his actions on this trip and couldn't think of anything that might have betrayed him. 'I'll just have to see how it develops,' he thought.

As he suspected, Coro didn't work for the Ministry of

Information, for the car headed into the city centre. He spotted the Casa Rosada as they headed up the Avenue San Martin towards the Plaza de Mayo. He guessed they were heading for Army Headquarters situated close by. He was taken up to Coro's office in Military Intelligence on the top floor of the building. Opening the door they indicated he should enter. Coro was sitting behind his desk in the palatial office and looked up as Ridley entered. 'Ah, Señor Ridley do please come in and take a seat.' Smiling broadly at him he added, 'Thank you for agreeing to come to see me at such short notice, but given your busy schedule I thought I had better catch you when I could.'

Ridley looking closely at him wondered whether there was a deliberate inflexion on the word 'catch'. 'Oh, that's OK. You caught me between appointments, so that was fortuitous.' As he said this, he wondered whether it was. Perhaps they had been monitoring his calls and had kept a very close eye on him. Now why would they do that?

'I have an engagement to attend at the British Embassy this evening but until then I am at your disposal. Before that I was only planning to write up my business notes on today's discussions.' Having hopefully sounded totally unconcerned, Ridley sat back and waited for Coro's opening challenge.

For a while Coro remained silent, swinging around on his swivel chair, occasionally glancing out of the tall window and then looking back at Ridley. He was clearly trying to raise the tension using the old trick of saying nothing until the suspect began to talk to relieve the tension he was feeling. Ridley resisted the urge to speak, continued looking at Coro, and waited patiently for him to begin.

Coro's first question was very oblique indeed. 'Mr Ridley what is your view on Communism?'

'I prefer Capitalism and Western democracy to the totalitarian states created by the Soviets and their communist satellites. I know capitalism has its failings but at least people have freedom and that is clearly not the case in USSR. I don't think communist economies can ever compete with capitalism.'

Coro nodded. 'We are very concerned about communists here. We saw what happened in Chile and we do not wish our country to go the same way. In Chile the army had to reassert control and we have done the same to ensure that communists and their left-wing political supporters are not able to take over the country. Nicaragua, Guatemala, Panama and Colombia have all suffered at the hands of the communists and look what continues to happen in Cuba!'

Looking hard at Ridley he warned, 'We don't want any ultra-liberal ideas here.'

Ridley looked confused. 'I understand your message but I am not sure why you are warning me. I work for a Japanese pharmaceutical company, I am a Canadian, I live in a western democracy and I am not a member of the Communist Party. In fact I am not a member of any political party!'

Coro didn't answer him but posed another question. 'How is it a person claiming to be a Canadian does not have a North American accent?'

'That is easily answered. I was born in the UK but after my time at university I decided to emigrate to Canada. I also got a job with Nippon Health and they helped me move to Canada. I have been a Canadian citizen and have lived in Canada for seven years. This is quite common practice amongst young British people for there are much better job opportunities over there compared to UK where unemployment is very high.'

'Does Canada still have very close ties with the UK? Don't they both have the same ruler, this Queen Elizabeth? I do think it is very old-fashioned not to be a republic.'

'No. Canada is a separate country and it makes its own decisions. It is a parliamentary democracy like many countries including the UK, and its monarch is Queen Elizabeth, along with many countries of the British Commonwealth, but the Canadian Prime Minister and his Cabinet are the real rulers of Canada. Canada often doesn't agree with the actions of the UK. Canadians see themselves as independent although many of them have great affection for Great Britain, or France,' he added with a smile.

'So Canada is in the pocket of the USA?'

'No I don't think that is the case either. The USA has massive economic power and is Canada's biggest customer, but Canadians are different and have different aspirations and want to do things their way. The Americans are often uncomplimentary about us Canadians, but we like the way we are – different to them!'

'You appear to know a lot of people down here. Why have you been invited to the British Embassy reception this evening? You also seem to know the new Japanese business attaché.'

Ridley shrugged. 'I don't know why I have been invited to the reception this evening, but I don't usually pass up an opportunity to make more business contacts or promote my company. I am the business development manager for the Americas after all and some of my major competitors are British pharmaceutical companies. The British seem to be making a specific push to re-develop business in Latin America and certainly need to do so to kick start their export business and help their economy. I don't know this James Grant chap, it will be interesting to hear what he has to say. Mr Yamauchi is an old friend. Before being appointed here he worked in Tokyo and I came into contact with him during my visits to my company's head office there. He was very helpful on many occasions and we became friendly, although there is a wide age gap between us. I have even been invited to his house.'

Coro continued to look at him impassively. Ridley decided it was time to do a bit of challenging himself.

'General Coro, l am very happy to engage in a discussion with you if it is helpful to my business project and my company's ultimate success in Argentina, but I cannot see what the purpose is of these oblique questions. If you have a specific accusation to make against me perhaps you would please inform me of it now.'

Coro smiled at him. 'No, l don't have any specific allegations to put to you, Señor Ridley. I am just curious about you and your project. I keep thinking, why now? Permit me one last question if I may?'

Ridley waved his hand in acceptance and waited to see what Coro would throw at him next.

'I am sure you know that Argentina disputes Britain's possession of Islas Malvinas. What is your view?'

'Where and what are the Malvinas?'

'Las Islas Malvinas are what the British call the Falkland Islands. They lie about 200 miles off the east coast of Argentina across the Mar Argentino.'

'Why don't they belong to you then? We wouldn't stand for this in Canada if Newfoundland or the other islands off Canada did not belong to us. How is it that the UN hasn't pressurized the UK to give up these Islas Malvinas?'

'The British stole them from us during the revolutionary phase in Argentina and have always refused to return them. They populated them with their own people and ejected the Patagonian fishermen who had lived there. We have argued for their return at the UN but up to now the USA has always supported the UK. We have hopes that the USA may change its position in the near future.'

Ridley looked quizzically at Coro who responded, 'I just wanted a further discussion with you before your project is too far advanced. We have to be very watchful to ensure that the right type of development is being encouraged in Argentina and the right people are coming here to work amongst us. I feel I know you a little better and am more relaxed about your company's business project here. I will be very interested to watch its progress.'

With that he stood up and came around the desk to shake Ridley's hand. The outer door opened and an aide escorted him out of the building, telling him there were usually taxis waiting on the corner of the Plaza de Mayo. Ridley walked steadily away from the entrance knowing a number of eyes would be assessing his behaviour. Reaching the square he found there were plenty of taxis there. He was soon back in his hotel.

Standing still in the centre of his bedroom he reviewed the discussion with Coro. It was full of threat, implication and innuendo but nothing concrete. He had been with Coro for about an hour and he thought he had held his own well and reacted quite naturally to the interrogation. He hadn't been too calm or too twitchy so Coro probably thought he was fairly innocent. The questions were interesting; quite wide-ranging and potentially could make up a threatening picture for him if they ever fitted the jigsaw pieces together. Interesting he mentioned the Malvinas. He must avoid the British Embassy after this evening. He must pass that on to James Grant when he met him.

Returning to his hotel, he wrote up his business notes

then took a shower and changed, before heading just after six o'clock to the British Embassy. After showing his invitation to the guard on the gate he walked up the steps at the imposing entrance to the colonial *palacio* that forms the embassy. Showing his invitation once more he was directed to a large reception room on the first floor. Here he was greeted by the short receiving line of the ambassador, his wife and James Grant 'Business Attaché for South America'. After being announced and formally greeted by them he moved through to join the throng and grabbing a glass of champagne from a passing waiter looked around to see if there was anyone here he recognized. Just as he reached the end of his scan around the room he spotted a short person at the far end in conversation with an elderly woman and he realized it was Mr Yamauchi. 'Somehow he must have wangled an invitation, perhaps it is because I am a representative of a Japanese company. I'll leave it to him to engineer a meeting later. Now where is Señora Mantovani?'

Just at that moment he felt a hand on his arm and turning he looked around at James Grant. 'Mr Ridley, thank you for coming this evening,' he said. 'I gather you are considering investing in Argentina and have experience of business developments elsewhere in the world. I would certainly like to learn from your experience, as I am sure this could be of use to those British companies who plan to invest down here. I gather you have some responsibilities for your company in the UK so I'd also value your views on the UK business environment at the moment. Should we find a quiet corner where we can talk?' He led John to a small anteroom but left the door open so people wouldn't suspect this was a secret meeting.

Leaning forward Grant said, 'Your target is the red-haired

lady in her forties who is wearing a knee length green dress with a matching coat. We have primed her that you are here to consider a major pharmaceutical development and suggested that you were very influential and thought to have potential to make the main board.' He grinned, 'These diplomats are always susceptible to people with power and influence.' They talked on generally for a few minutes then raising his voice he thanked Ridley, 'That has been very enlightening. I wish you every success with your present project.'

Returning to the main room, they parted company and Ridley began to circulate, nodding politely to people he passed until he was close to Señora Mantovani. As he was about to pass, the man she was talking to turned and said, 'If I am not mistaken you are John Ridley, business development manager for Nippon Health. Have you met Señora Mantovani from the Foreign Ministry?'

Marvelling at this very smooth introduction to the target, Ridley smiled at them both and introduced himself, '*Buenas tardes*, Señora. Yes I work for Nippon Health. I am very pleased to meet you. What is your role in the Foreign Ministry?'

As they began to converse the embassy official excused himself and Ridley, followed by her, moved a little out of the main crowd towards one of the corners. Explaining 'It was rather noisy over there,' he looked expectantly at her and she answered his initial question.

'I am responsible for the section that deals with Britain and the rest of the European Community. That is why I am here this evening.'

Gallantly he replied, 'What a pity you don't deal with Canada or Japan as I would enjoy dealing with such a charming official.'

As she smiled at his compliment, he asked her about the main challenges in her job and how the relationship might develop with Europe, before steering the discussion around to the UK. He suggested that the view from Canada was that Britain and Argentina were spoiling for a fight over the Falklands. He asked her, 'If this happens is it likely to affect the economy? That wouldn't be good for my business project.' Glancing cautiously around the room she replied in her quiet voice, 'I am afraid this concerns me a lot at the moment. I believe it's in our best interests to maintain good relations with Britain but there are more senior people in the Foreign Ministry who believe that a challenge to Britain about Las Islas Malvinas will be good for the national spirit.' She smiled. 'They believe it'll take the people's minds off rampant inflation. I'm afraid the balance of power has shifted in the Junta since the appointment of the new president. We also seem to be picking a fight again with Chile over the islands in the Beagle Channel and I hope we won't do anything stupid. The more liberal members have lost influence.'

Realizing she had revealed more than she should have she looked worried, 'I fear I have been less than diplomatic. You must forgive me and please don't quote me as I'm afraid I would be forced to deny it.'

'Have no fear, Señora Mantovani,' promised Ridley, 'I am just grateful for such an honest personal assessment and I certainly won't put it in my report.' Looking at her watch she excused herself, saying something about a dinner appointment and he was left standing alone in the corner of the room. But not for long, for the official was soon hovering nearby bringing with him Mr Yamauchi whom he introduced, and after some small talk left them alone. After the charade of introductions, Yamauchi said, 'So you have met La Mantovani. She is thought to be very influential in the Foreign Ministry so any comments made by her should be carefully listened to and evaluated.'

In case they were being overheard they stuck to the script and John explained that he would not be able to visit Uruguay this trip but they agreed to meet on his next trip in January. John would call Yamauchi from Toronto to arrange a meeting. In the meantime Yamauchi would see the Minister of Health to promote the case of Nippon Health. They then went their separate ways, Ridley being caught up in an embassy group, including James Grant, that was going out for a meal at a nearby restaurant. So it was gone midnight when he got back to his hotel. 'It's a good job I don't have to drive tomorrow,' he thought, 'I really need a good night's sleep.'

Chapter Nine

Tuesday morning as he reached the hotel entrance Señora Sabato pulled up sharply in her red Alfa Sud Sprint. She leant over, opened the passenger door and after he climbed in she quickly drove off explaining it would take about three hours to get to Rosario on the RN 9 which luckily was a good road. Continuing to look out of the windscreen she then suggested neutrally that they should stop for dinner on the way back although it would mean a very late return. Looking at her as she drove competently and quickly, leaning slightly forward over the steering wheel and weaving easily between the traffic in the Latin way, he knew it would be a very pleasant day. He thought, 'I know I should but I don't feel even slightly guilty about this.' She had clearly dressed carefully for him. She was wearing a short grey skirt, that rode up very attractively as she drove showing off her good legs, and her blouse had been chosen carefully to show off her figure. She seemed sophisticated and in her early thirties and Ridley had always enjoyed being with women; he both liked working and socialising with them, although, until he met Andy, he had always avoided getting too involved.

On the long journey they shared information about each other but Ridley reckoned he got more information about her than she did about him. Although she was married, it seemed her husband worked overseas and Ridley guessed she was Roca's mistress. She had more assurance and authority than he would expect of a personal assistant.

They moved swiftly alongside the estuary and soon the flat land changed to the delta around Tigre and they began to cross the succession of watercourses that form the Delta del Paraná. The banks of these waterways were densely wooded but between the trees he could see many small houses. 'Another version of cottage country,' he thought. Then on northwards along the RN 9 across the flat and fairly empty pampas, following the Rio Paraná towards Rosario. She certainly knew her stuff however, so by the time they arrived at the hospital in Rosario he had obtained a lot of information about the health services in this part of Argentina.

She briefed him about Rosario, a city of just under a million people at the southern end of the fertile pampas region known as Mesopotamia. It is a fine nineteenth century city, laid out in the usual grid pattern alongside the Rio Paraná, with all the facilities of a provincial capital. Large seagoing vessels can come up river so there is also a substantial port. With its major hospitals and other significant medical facilities she said that in her opinion it would be a good place to base a medical rep to cover the north east of the country. She added, 'Santa Fe, 167 kilometres north, has about half the population of Rosario and is older. It was established early in the colonial period. It's the centre of the fertile pampas but there's a smaller population in the hinterland. Market potential is likely to be less although there's a good hospital there.' She smiled proudly as she gave him this information that she researched earlier. He thanked her warmly, reassuring her it would be very helpful background for the business proposal. When they arrived they didn't have much time for the sights of Rosario, but she showed him the large art deco monument to the national flag and some other art deco architecture in the centre before they went to their first meeting.

All the meetings went well in both Rosario and Santa Fe and at about six o'clock they set off on what would be a four-hour return journey as there was virtually no traffic on the road. About nine thirty on the outskirts of BA, she pulled into a small roadside restaurant and they shared a pleasant meal of *bife de chorizo*, a wonderfully cooked sirloin steak with vegetables. She was very friendly over the meal and moved her legs against his under the table but he was careful not to respond, although he had to admit it was a very pleasant sensation. To slow her down he mentioned he had a girl in Toronto and to her credit she did seem to be uncomfortable on hearing this. A little later he paid the bill and she drove him back to his hotel where she made no suggestion about joining him. Thanking her for her assistance, he assured her that he would tell Señor Roca she had made a useful contribution to his review and that he had personally enjoyed the day out with her. Then giving her swift kisses on each cheek he quickly got out of the car and with a cheery wave went into the hotel thinking, 'I think I did quite well to extricate myself from that minefield. She really is an alluring woman!'

Wednesday morning he called Señor Roca as he had promised Señora Sabato, and then left a message for Tony Marini at La Nación newspaper offices. He then spent the morning writing up a report of Tuesday's meetings and just before lunch his room extension rang. It was the journalist returning his call. After explaining why he would like to brief him they agreed to meet for dinner on the Thursday evening before Ridley returned to Toronto.

That set up, Ridley got on with all the other actions to complete before the end of Thursday. Early Wednes-

day evening he returned to his hotel after more successful meetings to find Señora Sabato waiting for him in the
lobby clutching an envelope. Standing up, as he crossed
the lobby, she greeted him, 'Señor Ridley, I thought I might
drop this information off for you when I left the office.
Everything you requested is here,' she said glancing down
at the envelope. A little hesitantly and shyly she asked, 'I
know you are on your own here and I did wonder whether
you would like some company this evening if you haven't
got anything arranged.'

Ridley smiled at her, 'Who could resist such a charming
offer? I would be delighted. Might I just have time for a
quick shower and shave as it has been a long day?' Nodding she handed him the envelope and sat down again in
the lobby. He headed for the lift thinking, 'Well, they're
still after more information about me. It would've looked
suspicious to refuse her offer, as I probably wouldn't have
said no to the real estate people had they offered. Anyway
she's very attractive and I enjoy dining with sexy women.'
He had a refreshing shower and shaved then slipped into
a smart brown check jacket and grey trousers, with cream
shirt and tie with a discreet flower design, before opening the envelope and discovering that all the information
requested was there, even the military medical locations.
'So they aren't scrutinizing my information requests,' he
noted. 'Is it me personally they are worried about?' he
mused.

Returning to the lobby she informed him that during his
absence she had arranged a reservation for them at a quiet
restaurant just off the Avenue Cordoba in easy walking distance of the hotel. He looked at her shoes and she smiled,
'Oh yes, Señor Ridley I can walk OK in these shoes!'

'If we're going to have a friendly dinner I don't think we

should be on such formal terms,' replied Ridley. 'My name is John.' Nodding she reciprocated, 'My favourite name is Cristina, although in the way of families here I have a number of grand names.' As he helped her on with the light silk jacket that she was wearing over a plain white blouse and a long single strand pearl necklace, he could feel her delicate shoulders through the material. Yet again she was wearing high heels and a pencil skirt that stopped just above the knee, and he observed her good figure. Hooking her arm through his they headed out into the street, and walked the short distance to a small and very quiet restaurant patronized by a couple of couples fully engrossed in each other. He had not spotted any surveillance as they strolled along but he reasoned, 'Well, they wouldn't need to with her accompanying me all the time and reporting back.'

As they settled at their table and the waiter handed the menus to them she said, 'John, I know it is not feminine for the woman to choose the dishes and the wine, but if you will allow me to do so on this occasion I promise you will find you have some interesting regional specialties to taste.' Seeing his nod of agreement she continued, 'Argentina is not famed for its cuisine. Perhaps in time its wines will be, but we do have some interesting dishes other than the ubiquitous beef. Here they serve venison and wild boar Patagonian style and some delicious river fish from Mesopotamia where we were yesterday.' Looking at the short *carte* that the waiter had handed to her she suggested, 'Perhaps a venison paté salad to start followed by grilled fish with some lightly sautéed potatoes and some fresh vegetables in butter. I know you North Americans will say that is unhealthy, but I do think the butter brings out the flavour. With this I would suggest a glass of Merlot followed by perhaps a Chardonnay with the fish.'

'That sounds excellent Cristina. I do like a woman who enjoys her food. I don't like women who have bird-like appetites.'

Looking at him she queried, 'I take it that doesn't apply to your girlfriend?'

'No, she's like you, she enjoys her life and her food,' he replied.

After the waiter left she looked directly at him, 'I think I can guess what you have been thinking but I am not trying to get you into bed with me,' she said in her very forthright manner. 'Nor has anyone asked me to, just in case you are wondering. They did suggest I should be very nice to you but nothing more. As I find you very attractive that hasn't been difficult!'

'Well, I would be lying if I said the thought hadn't crossed my mind. I don't know why anyone would want to organize this, but there again I am not the arrogant male who thinks he has only to smile and every woman wants to have him.'

'Oh, how little you know,' thought Cristina, 'you are so gorgeous and the way you look at me with those gentle blue eyes, I should hate this girl in Canada. I have to try to get information about you but it would be so easy to become your friend and then fall heavily in love with you. You make me feel so alive.'

Frantically trying to regain her composure for she could feel her nipples hardening as she thought about him, she signalled to the waiter and ordered. Soon the wine arrived. They silently toasted each other, gently touching their glasses together, and she asked him about his early life. He told her of his time in the UK, how he had come to learn Spanish (but passing over the link with Maria), then after university emigrated to Canada. Satisfied about

115

his early life, she quizzed him about his work for Nippon Health and he fascinated her with his amusing description of Japanese culture. She felt he really enjoyed his work and that he was genuine about what he did. She couldn't see why people were suspicious of him. He just seemed a very nice man.

Soon the main course arrived on two very large oval stainless steel platters. Each had set out on it a large portion of grilled fish, a wonderful selection of vegetables and a small pot of chilli sauce. The Argentine Chardonnay arrived well chilled and complemented the grilled fish perfectly. Ridley thanked her for her excellent choice then asked, 'Cristina, we have talked a lot about me this evening but what about you? You told me you were married but if I may be so bold, you don't ever talk about him.'

'I'm estranged from my husband and have been for a couple of years. Of course, here it is not possible to divorce so we go our own ways discreetly. I had to go back to work again, and as I'd been a secretary, I took this up again. I managed to get a job in the Ministry of Health through my family and as I was efficient I soon caught the eye of Señor Roca. He made me his personal assistant.' She smiled wryly, 'Of course, from time to time I am required to provide additional services for him out of hours but it would be wrong to think of me as his mistress. It is more that sometimes he needs comforting and I spend the night with him, rather than a passionate affair. I don't really think he is usually desperate for sex with me on most occasions.'

She looked sharply at him, 'Not like you would be. I can see it in your eyes so don't try to deny it. Unfortunately, I can also see it is very well controlled and for that,' she added, 'I should quietly damn your girl. Soon you are going to say that you like me and want to be my friend, but to someone strongly attracted to another this is like cold steel into the heart.' There were tears in her eyes, and feeling for her he took her hand.

'Cristina, we haven't known each other for long but I do like you and it would be good to have a friend here. I find you attractive and fun to be with, but I do not desire you and I don't love you. I don't know how we got on to this topic, but I would like to know more about you and spend some time with you as a friend on future visits.'

Smiling through her tears she said, 'I am just being silly. I've just turned thirty, I meet a great man and just my luck he's already taken! I couldn't keep it penned up any more. It's probably best I said it out loud. At least we know where we are. Let's have some coffee before I get a taxi. Are you still going back on Friday?'

'Yes. I'll be back in January and I'll fax Señor Roca my dates. I'll be taking a suite here for six months as it'll be more convenient. I hope we can meet then.'

Saying farewell as the friends they had become he saw her into her taxi and with a cheery wave he wandered back to his hotel. 'I do have the knack of collecting women,' he thought. 'Andy will never believe I am the passive player in this! Cristina was clearly put up to get more information on me but she was also anxious to signal that she wished to be my friend and more if I wanted it. She may prove useful next year as long as she doesn't find out about Maria.'

On Thursday he continued his discussions and with a sense of satisfaction returned to his room at the end of the afternoon. But then he realized with a sinking feeling he had forgotten to call Andy. 'Andy, sorry my love for not calling earlier but things have been very hectic; meetings, a reception at the British Embassy, a Ministry of Health official came with me to Rosario and Santa Fe, and the last couple of days have just been wall-to-wall meetings. I'm still planning to leave tomorrow so I'll be back in Toronto around 6 a.m. Can I see you in the morning?'

'Get here for breakfast at eight,' she commanded, 'but have a shower first. I don't want to hug and kiss a sweaty man.'

With that he got ready for his meeting with Tony Marini. The journalist had suggested a small restaurant up in the Recoleta district in the north of BA so Ridley had to take a taxi to get there. He suspected it was a place the journalist used away from too many prying eyes, and if it was it would suit Ridley's purpose also. He preferred not to be seen talking to the liberal press at the moment. He thought his surveillance might have been withdrawn, as he hadn't spotted anyone during the last couple of days but he would remain cautious.

Marini turned out to be a tall, lean, slightly stooped man and a heavy smoker.

Ridley went through the motions of briefing the journalist about his business plans and promised to keep him in touch with progress, so a story might be published at the time Nippon Health made a formal application to the Ministry of Health. It transpired that Marini was far more interested in political stories than business ones, but he promised to write a couple of paragraphs at the appropriate time for the business section of the paper.

Over dinner Marini told a story he was following up. 'Did you realize we are arguing with Chile about some islands in the Beagle Channel at the moment? In fact I wouldn't be surprised if we come to blows down there. I really cannot understand this nationalist fervour. I know we Argentines are very emotional and chauvinistic, but to argue over a few islands in the icy seas off Tierra del Fuego does seem

118

a bit crazy as there's no economic value, nor does it affect our jurisdiction over a slice of Antarctica.'

By this stage of the meal they had consumed the best part of a couple of bottles of wine or at least Marini had, and when the coffee was brought he ordered whiskey for them both. As Marini lit his tenth cigarette of the meal, Ridley asked him, 'What is the Junta going to do next?'

After a long pause during which Ridley wondered whether Marini had heard the question, the journalist leant forward and quietly stated, 'They will invade Las Malvinas of course. The people would like that better than a fight with Chile.' Having dropped this bombshell he sank back in his seat with glazed eyes.

'Surely not,' suggested Ridley, 'what makes you think this is in their minds?'

'I have a source in the Navy Department and he tells me there is logistic planning going on at the moment. Nobody knows when it might happen but they are considering it seriously.' By this stage he was virtually asleep in his chair so Ridley paid the bill, and finding out from the restaurant owner where the journalist lived put him in a taxi. Returning to his hotel and mulling over what the journalist had said, he very pensively prepared for his departure the next day.

Chapter Ten

Toronto December 1981

John returned to his apartment, unpacked his bags and chucked his dirty washing in the washing machine. He had a long relaxing shower and then dressed in a Ralph Lauren shirt, cord trousers and a Burberry sweater. Finding his thick parka jacket, for it was beginning to snow, he went back out into the street and walked the two blocks to Andy's apartment with his briefcase over his shoulder. Reaching Andy's apartment he rang the bell and the door was wrenched open. 'Darling, I love you, let me hug you, I've missed you so much!' All these expressions of endearment spilt out from her like shaken lemonade when the cap is removed. Grabbing his arm she pulled him into the apartment, and, slamming the door, planted a long, lingering kiss on his lips. Unable to stop touching him she led him into her sitting room and sat down holding both his hands in hers and gazing affectionately at him with those lovely green eyes.

'She looks so blissful,' he observed.

'Andy, it's so good to be back. My love seems to get stronger all the time and the more I get to know you the better it is. Anyway I shall be here for about four weeks now so we can really get to know each other like normal people.'

Smiling at him she agreed, 'It has been rather strange hasn't it. All a rush and very intense, perhaps it's our age.

120

Like you I haven't had any second thoughts, but it would be good to go steadily for a while. We need to know we can live with each other in normal circumstances.'

Getting a grip on her emotions, she took him into the kitchen and served him up a splendid Canadian breakfast of eggs over easy with Czech bacon, waffles and muffins accompanied by copious amounts of strong coffee. 'Wow, you have been doing your research,' remarked John.

After she had fed her man, she asked him about the trip. So he produced the notes he had written on the flight to Miami. Passing these to her he got on with drinking his coffee while she read quickly through his neat handwriting.

Reaching his calm statement of the interrogation by General Coro she stopped still and hardly seemed to be breathing as she realized that at that moment she might have lost him. Looking at him she put out her hand to touch his arm, smiled bravely and commented 'It is a good job you didn't report this over the phone in our code, for I'm not sure whether I could have coped.'

'I think you would,' he reassured her.

'This isn't usual behaviour is it, even in Argentina?'

'I can't say, for I don't know enough about the behaviour of the security services, but it did seem strange. I think he was just acting intuitively. Something about the project is worrying him. Whether it's the timing or the funny mix of nationalities, you know, Japanese company and Canadian project leader. I don't really know. He seemed to accept my answers and I didn't notice more surveillance during the visit. I'll just have to be very careful.'

'They seemed reasonably satisfied with your identity at least by the end of your visit,' concluded Andy. 'That's good news because once they're used to you they won't see you when you move around. It was a good plan to just do business on this trip. It was interesting they decided to give you a minder. Was she attractive?'

'I would say so,' grinned John, 'she has a very good figure and a very sexy wiggle when she walks. She would have jumped into my bed if I had given her the least encouragement, which, for the record, I didn't do. I found the opportunity to tell her I had a girl in Toronto, and to her eternal credit at that point she backed off. I guess she is Roca's mistress and she does his bidding.'

Andy shook her fist at him, 'You're a beast to describe her like that. I suppose I should be flattered you can look at a woman, find her sexy and available, and turn her down because of me.'

She went on, 'At least the discussions with the two contacts have produced a bit more information. I would say the embassy managed the contact with Señora Mantovani very well. Do you think she saw through your alias or did she just relax her guard on this occasion?'

'I think she just relaxed her guard but I don't know enough about her to say positively: she may wish to put out a few feelers to see what is the likely support. The statement Marini made about the Falklands was definitely unguarded because he was three-quarters drunk by then. Unfortunately he doesn't have any details of when it might happen.'

John added, 'Both Mantovani and Marini mentioned a dispute that is blowing up between Argentina and Chile over some islands in the Beagle Strait. This is off Tierra del Fuego and I gather it has been a sensitive area for years. They both seemed to fear that some armed confrontation might occur. Now whether this might divert the Argentines' attention from the Falklands, or is just a smokescreen for the action they're planning, we don't know. It may however make it more difficult to judge what any military activity is for.'

He added, 'I nearly forgot! Mantovani also mentioned that she believed the liberals in the Junta were being side-lined and had lost influence.'

'OK, I'll report all this to London. I gather you also met Mr Yamauchi from the Japanese Embassy at the same reception. By the way, I was informed during my briefings in London that my security clearance had been increased and so I now have access to everything to do with you. They also told me about your friend, Mr Yamauchi, and that he would be in Montevideo. I am authorized to contact him directly in an emergency and he is being informed that I am your control.'

'That's good. That reassures me now you'll be working with my good friend to help me see this through,' he assured her.

After running comprehensively over all the other points he wished to make, John summarized their discussion, 'We now have two independent sources plus circumstantial evidence suggesting the Argentine military is planning an adventure against the Falkland Islands to divert the Argentines from their domestic problems. However we don't have any hard evidence so we need to be very precise in the way we draft our report otherwise it will be pigeon holed as unsupported. I think we should leave it until Monday when we've had time to digest all the information and see what gaps still remain. Let's go down to the Eaton Centre now.'

Leaving Andy's apartment they walked the short distance to the junction of Younge and Queen Streets where the Eaton Centre was located. This large four-storey shopping mall was brand new, having opened only a couple of years before. 'Its inspiration is the Galleria in Milan and it has a glass-domed ceiling running the full length of the shopping centre,' explained John.

'I think this is a fabulous place,' said Andy as they went inside.

'Have you seen the large mobile sculpture?' queried John.

'No, I must have bypassed that.'

'It's quite easy to be sidetracked by the piazzas and fountains and escalators and miss it. Come on let me take you there.' Grabbing Andy by the hand he walked her quickly to the centre of the building where looking up she saw a flock of Canadian geese silhouetted against the glass ceiling.

'This is fantastic,' she cried, 'how could someone imagine this?'

'This mobile was created by an artist called Michael Snow. It's called Flight Stop,' explained John. 'What he did apparently was photograph geese coming in to land and then modelled one for each phase of flight and landing. So now you get a large flock coming in to land.'

'I think it's the most beautiful creation I have ever seen,' exclaimed Andy, 'Canada is such a marvellous place. Let's do some shopping. I need a new dress for my party. I forgot to tell you we're hosting a flat-warming party next Saturday so we're officially an item.' Turning, she looked coyly at him saying, 'I hope you approve?'

'Rather. I need some new shirts as well.'

So they spent a pleasant afternoon in the Eaton Centre. He watched her affectionately as she shopped, liking the way she pursed her lips as she concentrated. The way she moved swiftly across to a rail of clothes that had taken her eye, then quickly flicking the hangers along the rail dismissed those that didn't appeal, then lingered over one or two items that perhaps took her fancy. Occasionally she picked up one and held it against herself in front of a full-length mirror. If the garment might possibly be suitable she turned towards him with a quick smile, her eyes asking the question, 'How do I look?' Eventually she had her formal cocktail dress, some casual trousers and a lovely chunky jumper suitable for the Canadian winter, so she turned her attention to him. He wanted a new jacket and fancied a Ralph Lauren country-style but she persuaded him that an Italian style Armani would make a change and that he looked fabulous in it. Some shirts and ties to go with it and then he would be suitably attired for the party. That evening they ate in and then spent a quiet evening together before retiring to bed.

Sunday dawned a bright crisp day so they decided to go to Niagara Falls. They walked across to John's apartment block and got his station wagon out of the underground garage. 'This is an enormous car,' said Andy. 'No, this Buick Century is only medium-sized by American standards,' replied John. 'Admittedly it has a 3.8 litre V6 engine but you need that because the car is so heavy. We didn't take much to the cottage the other weekend but imagine going for two or three weeks and taking bedding and food. You need a big load carrying capacity for that.'

Soon they were heading westwards along the side of Lake Ontario and passing through Oakville and Burlington on the way to Niagara. Before reaching their destination they crossed the Welland Canal with its large locks providing the passage for seagoing steamers from Lake Ontario into Lake Erie, and on to the other lakes in the system. When they stop to see a large ship in one of the locks, Andy marvelled at the size of ship that can make it all the way to Sault Ste

Marie and Lake Superior. Soon they were entering Niagara-on-the-Lake with its quaint weather-boarded buildings, nowadays a tourist enclave. They stopped to see the apothecary shop and the first parliament building of Upper Canada, and then visited Fort George and looked out across the lake at its American rival, Fort Niagara, before sitting down to lunch in one of the many restaurants there.

Later they passed through tacky Niagara Falls town and its border crossing and finally reached the falls themselves. The weather had been very cold for the last few weeks so all the trees around were ice-covered. The surface of the Niagara River and the tops of the Horseshoe and American Falls were ice-bound but below this the water still roared and tumbled dramatically over the high drop. They donned waterproofs, went through one of the many tunnels cut in the side walls and stood looking out at the solid wall of water rushing past in front of them. They were completely deafened by the sound made by millions of tons of water dropping down the falls. After this experience, they walked a little way from the falls and took the dramatic Spanish aerial car over the whirlpool. Andy looked down fearfully, and John laughed at her affectionately and held her arm, as the cable-car hanging suspended from just two cables made its way above the maelstrom below.

When it began to get dark they returned to the car for the journey back to Toronto and as agreed, their separate apartments for the week. On the drive back John found out more about the girl he loved.

'Nothing particularly interesting in my life history,' she declaimed. 'I have a younger sister and we grew up in West Sussex in the village of West Stoke. I went to school in Chichester and was quite sporty as well as academic. I played hockey and tennis and did some dinghy sailing.

I've had a number of boyfriends over the years but nothing serious, until now that is,' she added smiling. 'My father's a doctor, a GP, but I never fancied that. My mother never worked: she supports him and brought up the children and we were all very happy.

'I went to Southampton University to study Modern History and got a good degree. I was sounded out there about the service and decided it seemed an interesting opportunity. I was always interested in world affairs and I guess I hoped I could make a bit of a difference with what I did. Studying history is so enlightening and frightening. The number of times history seems to repeat itself is scary. How is it that politicians don't recognize this? So I joined eight years ago and since then I have followed the standard career training. As you know my last posting was as an analyst on the South American desk and there I supported the control on one operation. You are my first fully independent operation.'

Looking sideways at him as he drove she said tentatively, 'John, regarding the report to SIS and DNI, I've been thinking about this. If it's OK with you I think I should do the report myself so they can't claim it isn't fully objective. As you pointed out, it will be difficult enough to persuade the politicians to take it seriously but we may stand a better chance if we follow procedure.'

'That's fine with me. Just call me at the apartment tomorrow if you need any further clarification. I'll drop you outside your apartment. See you next Friday after work. Are you coming to my place?'

'Yes, I'll come to you on Friday then Saturday we can prepare my place for the party. See you then.' With that she was out of the car and quickly opened the door to her apartment block.

The next week passed quickly for John and Andy both engrossed in their separate but intimately linked activities. John's information was seriously debated in London and the Joint Intelligence Committee (JIC) assessed the information as highly probable, but the Foreign Office listening to the view of their American cousins regarded it as highly improbable. The Argentines wouldn't dare to challenge Britain! So the report was filed and forgotten.

John got on with his Nippon Health tasks and inevitably there were plenty of problems to keep him busy. He had always had the ability to focus on a particular problem and forget about others until later, so he thought little about Argentina. He was content to wait until Andy came back with news. He was not however content to wait for Andy. His romance there was developing fast and he knew Andy felt the same. He hoped this operation would end soon because if not the two of them would instantaneously combust with love and lust. They would need to formalize this relationship very soon: it couldn't stay in its present state for much longer. He resolved to discuss it with her next Sunday after the party.

Friday morning he sent a fax to Roca at the Ministry of Health in BA informing him that he was planning to return in January, and would like an appointment with him on Monday 11th January to update him on progress. He also informed him that he would like to test the outline proposal with him prior to presentation to the board of Nippon Health. He contacted the recruitment agency and the real estate company to give them his more detailed requirements, and requested meetings with them during his first week in Argentina. He also told the real estate agent in Bahia Blanca, and was assured by them they would be happy to see him at fairly short notice as they knew when he would be visiting. He hoped these plans would reassure Argentine Security should they check up!

Late afternoon his fax machine chuntered into life and began to spew out a succession of messages. The first one was on Argentine Ministry of Health stationery:

Dear Señor Ridley,

I am delighted to learn that your project is proceeding satisfactorily.

We shall of course be delighted to see you to hear your conclusions.

Might I suggest we meet at 12 noon so we may continue our discussion over lunch? Assuming this will be satisfactory, I shall arrange for Señora Sabato to pick you up. Please confirm this will be convenient for you and let us know where you will be staying.

Yours sincerely,
Andres Roca
For Minister of Health

Thinking, 'This is a neat way to get my new address,' Ridley drafted a quick reply, confirming the time and date would be convenient and a lift from Señora Sabato would be helpful. He informed him that he would have a suite at Esmeralda Suites in Recoleta on Avenue Puyrredón.

Friday evening soon came around and Andy arrived at John's apartment. He showed her the various faxes that had arrived and then they spent a quiet evening together. John realized she was a bit fidgety and asked her what was troubling her.

'I have two things on my mind. One is personal involving you and me, and the other is business.'

'Well, let's have the personal one, then,' smiled John.

'John, we like being with each other and are very much in love with each other aren't we?' asked Andy. Without waiting for a reply she rushed on, 'And we want to be with each other for ever don't we?' She tailed off, smiling yet tearful and a little fearful.

'Andy, dear, are you trying to propose to me?'

'Yes, yes, yes,' she cried, 'but I ran out of courage.'

'Dearest love, I would very much like to marry you and be your husband. Had you not got in first I would've asked you to be my wife on Sunday after the party. Do you want to make it an engagement party tomorrow or keep it secret for a while?'

Taking his hands she said happily, 'Yes, let's make it an engagement party. I told my parents this week and I mentioned to my boss that I was going to ask you so that is OK. Now don't be angry but I also mentioned it to your guardian and he wishes us the best of luck.'

John burst out laughing, 'You asked Admiral Collingwood for my hand? How ever did he take that?'

'He muttered something like this was all very strange. It wouldn't have occurred like this in his day but if it turned us on then why should he stand in the way of young people today. I think he said something about you having your hands full by the sound of it.'

'I'm very flattered that you want me so much to do this, but I think he's correct I will have my hands full and I'll have to keep you under tight control sometimes.' However, John couldn't keep up his air of mock seriousness and soon they were both kissing and laughing and hugging and kissing so much that they nearly forgot to eat. But a quick call to the local pizza delivery shop soon corrected that. As they were tucking in and realizing how famished they were Andy said, 'There is one other thing you should know, although you aren't allowed to change your mind. My full name is Adrienne Susanah James, which is why I call myself Andy.'

As he sought to reassure her that he loved the name Andy the outstanding business question just evaporated!

So Saturday turned into rather a rush. In the morning they headed back to the Eaton Centre and soon Andy was scrutinizing trays of engagement rings and eventually decided on a diamond solitaire in a gold band. As they left the shopping centre Andy proudly waved her ring around and was so happy that John was certain everyone there knew that they had just become engaged.

Then it was back to Andy's apartment to take delivery of the wine and food, and get down to the preparation for the party. Andy had asked a couple of girls to help and they arrived about 5 p.m. and, of course, for a while work stopped because of the excitement caused by her surprise engagement.

Eventually they were ready for the first guests to arrive at seven and soon the party was in full swing. Everyone was having a good time and even Paul Gregory seemed happy about the engagement. Later on John asked him to send a private message to Admiral Collingwood confirming the situation, and asking him to take care of Andy should anything untoward happen.

Paul also quietly mentioned that John and Andy would be invited for the Christmas holiday as members of a house party at a large place just outside Ottawa that he had booked. He said Andy would tell him more about it. Clearly this was the major planning session for 1982 operations.

Chapter Eleven

Christmas 1981 Ottawa

Early on Christmas Eve Andy and John loaded up John's station wagon and headed up the Trans-Canada Highway through Peterborough to Ottawa, to a house in Gatineau on the other side of the capital. There had been some snow but the highway being clear they made good time and arrived before it was dark. Pulling up, and announcing themselves on the intercom, the gates swung open and they went up the drive and parked near the house. Getting their bags they headed towards the front door that opened as they arrived, and they were welcomed, then escorted to their room. They were pleased to see that they were given one large bedroom so there wouldn't need to be any creeping around in the night. After freshening up they were informed they would be welcome in the sitting room downstairs.

Coming downstairs they headed towards the sound of voices and pushing open the door they found the Gregorys in conversation with a thin tall grey-haired man who they both instantly recognized as Andrew Collingwood. Seeing them he quickly came across and took Andy's hands in his. 'My dear, please accept my congratulations on your engagement. I'm sure you'll both be very happy. You clearly have something very special,' he suggested with a twinkle in his eye, 'for him to fall so quickly and so completely for you.' Changing the subject he told them that a briefing and planning meeting would take place on Boxing Day. 'So tonight and tomorrow there's to be no talk about Argentina.'

The Gregorys then briefed them about the other guests who would arrive later. Everyone was associated with the intelligence services so they could be relaxed, and there were even a couple coming from Canadian intelligence. As everyone started arriving the party began to get into the festive spirit. John and Andy excused themselves for a while and walked hand in hand in the snow in the grounds, occasionally stopping to throw snowballs at each other, dodging behind trees to avoid them and marking the pristine snow with their footprints. Andrew Collingwood, watching them from the window, turned to Paul Gregory and another guest. 'It is good to see them so happy. I'm so glad her boss agreed with me that it is better they got engaged. She'll worry for him all the time he's away but she would do that anyway. Now we can at least give her support when he is away. You'll insist that a girlfriend stays with her?'

Gregory agreed, 'Yes, we have that organized just in case anyone tries to have a go at her. We don't know whether the cousins might try something. She has been briefed and she agrees but insists he should not be told.'

Jim Graham, Head of Canadian Intelligence nodded, 'I think that's best. We are tracking all the CIA agents around Ontario so we can warn Paul if necessary. Are you going to tell him who I am?'

'I really think I have to, but nothing more as it might endanger him. I'll tell him you are his godfather but nothing more. 'He'll have to remain curious for now. When will your guy come?'

'I've arranged for him to get here on Boxing Day afternoon so they'll have time to meet. He takes up his appointment in Buenos Aires on New Year's Day so he'll be in place before John gets there.'

Looking out at them again Collingwood exclaimed, 'She really is a plucky girl. John is very lucky. No, I am wrong, it's good judgement on both their parts. They didn't let the grass grow under their feet. They just grabbed the opportunity with both hands. I feel sure they'll be OK but there's sadness for someone along the way. I feel it in my bones and don't say it's my age,' he snapped.

As the cold started to cut through their warm clothing Andy and John turned and hurried back to the welcoming bright lights they could see shining out of the windows of the house. Stamping the snow off their boots and slipping on some indoor shoes they headed for the sitting room that seemed to have filled up in their absence. Paul introduced them to the new arrivals then brought them over to Collingwood who was standing talking quietly with a man of similar age and height. 'Ah, there you are. I would like you both to meet Jim Graham who is head of Canadian intelligence. We have something to tell you both so we shall take over Paul's study for a little while.'

So saying Collingwood hooked his arm through Andy's and steered her through a doorway at the far end of the room. They then all sat down cosily around the blazing log fire except for Collingwood who took up the traditional pose of someone about to announce a revelation.

'John, I have something to tell to you and it involves Jim here. I'm afraid at the moment this is an incomplete piece of information but I've a very good reason for not telling you more, and I'm afraid you will both just have to trust me about that. What I have to tell you is that Jim Graham happens to be your godfather and his wife is your godmother. Like me, Jim has watched over you since your parents died and we felt it is time to tell you this. It may now help you understand why I wished you to be based in Toronto and how you came to have a Canadian passport.'

'Hi John,' said Jim, smiling, in a wonderful deep Canadian accent. 'All I am allowed to add in explanation is that we were all dear friends of your parents and when they were killed we undertook to watch over you. Now we're very happy you've fallen in love with Andy, and some time soon we'll want you both to visit us so we can really get to know each other.' With that he shook John's hand and gave Andy a hug and a kiss, and then he and Collingwood left them alone in the study looking very bemused.

'Well, there's a turn up for the book,' said John taking Andy's hand. 'I wonder what those two lovable rogues are up to? I don't doubt the story, it had the unmistakable ring of truth about it, but there's a hell of a lot more to this. However, I'm not to worry away at it, he said. From my guardian that means put it out of my mind because worrying about it might make it dangerous for me. You seem to be doing rather well here, Andy. You have gained a guardian and now a godfather and godmother. I wonder who I shall inherit next?'

'Don't you have any family at all?' asked Andy.

'Not as far as I know. I do have one very good friend who I have known for years. He is a captain in the Royal Marines Special Boat Service, the SBS, you probably have heard they're the navy's version of the SAS. I've known James Sandison since Dartmouth and we have been close friends since then, although we don't see each other much and he doesn't know I am working for Naval Intelligence. In fact I must write to tell him we're engaged. You should try to meet up with him if you go to the UK. I think he's based near Chivenor in North Devon these days but I'm sure your contacts would be able to pin him down pretty quickly.'

'Is he married?'

'No. A bit like me he always said he enjoyed his soldiering and that and a wife didn't mix. I agree with him which is why I'll get out of this work after this current job.'

At this Andy leant over and hugged him tightly, whispering, 'Thank you.'

The evening meal was excellent and the company friendly and they found themselves very much caught up in the house party. It was as though everyone had set out to make it a happy time for them. As Andy prepared for bed, while John had a brandy with Andrew, she looked back over the day and how good it was to be there with John as a couple and about to go to bed like husband and wife. A dark cloud briefly passed across her heart as she thought of the dangers ahead but she banished it with a smile. 'I shall not be unhappy. I shall enjoy his love and he'll have mine for as long as we have together.'

Christmas Day was another joy. In the morning they explored the grounds and found the estate was much larger than they thought. The house was built in the French *chateau* style with wonderful turrets, gable windows and green roof tiles, and the grounds had lawns and formal beds near the house as well as woods on the periphery of the estate. More snow had fallen overnight so there was a wonderful pristine nature to it and it seemed a shame to spoil it. They wandered through the snow-laden trees with a clear blue sky above and with the bright sun beginning to melt some of the snow, and were very happy with themselves and the world. It would be wrong to say they did not have a care in the world, for responsible mature adults take a more realistic view of life, but they were as carefree as they might be in the circumstances.

All too soon Boxing Day dawned and the mood of the house party sharpened. After breakfast a more formal meeting took place, and it was clear that Canadian Intelligence had more than a watching brief. Ridley was the focus for the briefing and planning discussions, and Andy's role had sharply shifted to that of his director from that of his lover. To her credit everyone present, including Ridley, thought she achieved this very professionally. This girl was very good.

The nub of the discussions was how to insert Ridley safely into the area of the main naval, sea and air bases during a period of tension when security would inevitably be tighter. Whilst it might be not too difficult to achieve this around Bahia Blanca and Comodoro Rivadavia, it seemed impossible to get at the two airbases likely to play an important role, San Julian and Rio Gallegos. For part of the morning the team thought round and round the issue without getting any nearer to a solution. Eventually Andy suggested, 'Really the only solution we have has to be to use Maria Gomez. There is a considerable risk but hopefully we could test her out on the next trip in a low risk way, and if there is no problem and the balloon goes up, then John will have to just play the card and hope for the best.'

They had all privately come to this view but were reluctant to voice it in Andy's presence until they had tested all other possible options exhaustively. She had recognized this and so she articulated their thoughts and they could move on. Passing to get a fresh cup of coffee Andrew Collingwood acknowledged this fact by gently squeezing her shoulder as he passed. After this impasse was resolved they made good progress and by lunchtime they had agreed an outline plan for Ridley's January trip. John and Andy would work this up into a detailed plan that she would discuss with Paul

Gregory, and he would then communicate it to SIS and DNI for final approval, and then on to Yamauchi in Montevideo.

As the session came to the end, Andrew Collingwood rose slowly and turned to face them all. 'You have all made excellent contributions this morning and we have the best plan given the circumstances. Thank you especially to our Canadian friends because we know how difficult this is for you. We all know that the Argentines are planning some operation against the Falklands, but we haven't obtained sufficient details to persuade our political masters. It is likely the operation, if it goes ahead, will take place before the winter so February or March must be the most likely months. John Ridley is our only viable option and we may have to ask him to attempt a swift high profile incursion to check out fleet movements and force readiness.' Looking directly at Andy he added, 'Should that be necessary, and I won't authorize it unless I think it might save many lives, I will expect everyone here to use his or her best endeavours to extricate him safely with the information.' After this they went into lunch and afterwards most of the key players dispersed.

Jim Graham was still there and about 2.30 p.m. he brought in a man of about Ridley's age and introduced him as Arthur Dean who was about to take up the post of reporter for the Toronto Star in Buenos Aires. Dean was a member of Canadian Intelligence and was being loaned as a courier for Ridley. He would be responsible for picking up information from Ridley at dead letter drops and getting it to Yamauchi either in Buenos Aires or Montevideo for onward transmission to London. Ridley and Dean would not be in contact with each other and Yamauchi would inform Dean of Ridley's itinerary. They spent the afternoon getting to know each other, going over the contact arrangements and how the dead letter drop would operate. When the arrangements were clear Dean departed with Jim Graham. Andy and John felt they wanted to be on their own, so they decided to head back to Toronto although it would be late when they got there. They said their farewells to Collingwood and the Gregorys, and set off on the long journey back down the Trans-Canada Highway.

'Come January, John,' commented Andy, 'we won't have any time for ourselves so I want to spend all the time with you until after New Year's Day. I think I should move into your apartment until then, as it feels so good to be a normal couple. Is there any chance we could get up to that cottage for a couple of days at New Year?'

'They keep the road to Owen Sound clear unless there's been a blizzard. I need to check whether anyone else is using it as I presume you want us to be on our own?'

'Yes, I would prefer that but it was such a dear place that I would share it with another couple if we had to.' With that she tipped the passenger seat back and dropped off to sleep leaving John to drive steadily on towards Toronto.

Sauble River Cottage New Year 1981/2

They loaded up the station wagon on Wednesday 30th December and headed north out of Toronto but this time taking a road further to the east as John wished to show Andy another favourite place of his, Lake Simcoe. Usually he went there in the summer but it would be nice to see the flocks of birds that still lived there even when the lake was frozen solid. They drove along another very straight

139

highway but wider than the more direct route through Mississauga. After a couple of hours of steady driving they arrived at the small town of Barrie on the shores of the lake and then the nearby resort of Oro Station. Here they parked the car in a cleared parking lot, and wandered down to the lake's edge marvelling at the multitude of wildfowl grazing on the vegetation sticking through the thin layer of snow. As the biting cold started to get to them despite their thick parkas, hats and gloves, they went to a small roadhouse nearby and got ham and eggs and potato waffles and enjoyed a mug of steaming coffee whilst gazing out across the icy expanse of the lake. 'I can see why you like it here,' she said. 'It appeals to the solitary, outdoor side of your nature. You're a very complex and interesting man, John Ridley. However, I think the reason I fell for you is that you are just so caring and loving, and so gentle with me in bed.'

'Come on,' he chided, 'we still have a way to go this afternoon. Plenty of that stuff later, even though we won't be alone.' Setting off he turned northwest from Barrie and soon they reached the shore of Nottawasaga Bay on Lake Huron. After passing through the small settlements of Collingwood and Meaford, they soon arrived at the cottage by the Sauble River, to find that the others had arrived ahead of them. As they got the bags out of the car the front door of the cottage opened and two young children looked out and ran excitedly to hug John around the legs. As he picked them up in turn and hugged them, Andy murmured, 'Is there something you haven't told me?'

Turning and smiling at her he took the hands of the chattering children and led the way indoors. Inside the front door stood a tall, blonde-haired smiling woman who Andy judged to be a few years older than her. She gave John a quick hug and then turned to welcome Andy. 'My dear, I am very pleased to meet you. Congratulations on capturing this dishy man. If I hadn't got my own by now I think you might have competition for him. I am Angie – Angela for long,' and at that she made a moue and Andy just knew they would be great friends. They hugged then she took Andy up to the smaller of the two bedrooms upstairs. 'Ross is out back somewhere, so when you have freshened up come down to the kitchen and have a cup of tea. We tend to be very informal here, so casual dressing and just chill out if you wish.' She smiled, 'Or if you want to sneak off with John for a while we shan't mind. We won't play gooseberry. Isn't that what you say in the UK?'

The holiday passed quickly and the four of them and the children got on well. A couple of times Andy and John took the children out with them and found they really enjoyed it. Another day they took the skidoo and explored the surrounding countryside with Andy screaming excitedly as they sped across the snow. After a while he let Andy take the handlebars and it was John's turn to feel the exhilaration as she headed deliberately for a snow drift then at the last minute flicked them to slip past it safely. 'You've done this before,' accused John. 'Yes,' she cried, 'I had a holiday in Lapland a few years ago and we had a trip on one of these.'

New Year's Eve they got together with residents of the other cottages for a quiet party to see in the New Year, but all too soon it was Sunday and time to pack up and head back to Toronto and John's apartment. As they said their farewells Andy and Angie agreed to meet while John was in Argentina. Angie insisted that if Andy was lonely she should come out to Burlington on Lake Ontario for the weekend.

January 1982 Toronto

Monday 4th January Andy spent the morning in her office then returned to see John in the apartment for lunch. Afterwards they moved into his study and she told him about the latest updates. 'Mr Yamauchi reports no apparent action by the military anywhere. They seem to be following the usual government and military inaction over the main holiday period so the view is nothing's planned for January. We judge a fleet operation could take place fairly quickly but we think they'll need at least two months to set up an operation involving army or marines and heavy equipment. You'll be in Argentina for two weeks so if something is to happen during February there'll probably be some signs that you'll be able to spot. If not we have to hope you'll be able to identify some activity during March. If nothing's happened by then it's likely nothing'll happen till September or October this year.'

'Let's get on with the detailed planning then.'

'The main problem,' confirmed Andy, 'is still how to get you to Rio Gallegos without suspicion. Maria Gomez is the best chance we have. You must inform her that you're at Esmeralda Suites so you can get a good chance to talk to her in private. It's critical you find out whether you can trust her. I don't need to tell you how to do that. If you think you can trust her you need to ensure you see her on each trip you make down there. You also have to attempt to recruit her so she'll be willing to drive you into southern Patagonia and let you stay at her estancia.'

'I told her I'd leave a message for her at the Hotel San Martin,' John reminded her. 'She knew I'd probably be arriving on the 11th and she thought she would be coming to BA around then for another course so she should get the message quite quickly. I won't sign it in case it's opened. When she calls I'll get her to stay the weekend at the flat. We can talk over old times and I'm sure by the end of the time I'll have a good idea of her views and whether I trust her. Don't worry there are two bedrooms.'

'It isn't Maria I worry about. It's that she-devil Cristina Sabato who worries me. She's clearly set up as your attractive minder and would like you in her bed.'

'Well you don't need to worry about that. I like her but I'm not attracted to her. If I wasn't attracted to her before I am certainly not going to be now that I'm engaged to you. In fact I'll tell her so, then she'll have to buy me a drink to celebrate.'

'Seriously though, if she becomes fond of you she may help you if things get difficult. Let her drive you about if it's suggested. She won't be as observant as a professional intelligence officer so you have little to fear from her. I want you back here safe so if sleeping with her helps you escape I won't criticize you or love you any the less. I may hurt for a while but I would rather have you back in one piece.'

John reached out and put his arm around her shoulders protectively. 'No, Andy, don't worry. It won't come to that. I'll do my best to keep safe and get back to you. Cristina Sabato certainly has an entré into the Argentine ruling group and probably has her ear close to the ground for she has more poise and confidence than I'd expect in a personal assistant, so it'll be sensible to cultivate her, but no funny business because that leads to complications and possible blackmail threats.'

Andy looked down her list. 'The next one to discuss is your tame journalist, Tony Marini of La Nación. We feel he has more information to offer if he begins to trust you. By the sound of it, he has a bit of a drink problem so why not just invite him for a drink at your suites, and perhaps also take him out to a club where it's quite noisy and you probably won't be overheard. He may just let something slip provided you fill him up with drink and he may be moved to confide in you.'

Seeing him nod she moved on to consider the next target. 'The most difficult one to approach is Elena Mantovani. My intuition, based on her remarks last time, tells me she is uncomfortable with the way things are going and is offended by the consideration of possible action against the Falklands. I wonder whether it would be possible for Mr Yamauchi to host a small dinner at the Japanese Embassy in BA for some Japanese businessmen including you. He could make sure she gets an invite on behalf of the Foreign Ministry, and perhaps one or two others could also be invited from the Argentine Social Welfare Ministry so they don't think she is being singled out?'

'That's a bloody good idea,' exclaimed John. 'You really are functioning on top line today. I'm sure that would work. Get SIS to signal him and ask for the dinner to be set for either the 19th or 20th. He can send the invitation to the Esmeralda Suites. That would give me an opportunity to talk with her again after dinner.'

'Now we also need an update on the fleet dispositions so you'll have to visit Bahia Blanca and Comodoro Rivadavia. We don't think the submarines present much of a threat so, at the moment, ignore them. Try also to get an update on the naval air bases you see especially Comodoro Rivadavia, Bahia Blanca and Ezeiza. Keep your eyes open if you pass the Punta Indo base on the way down to Bahia to see if there appears to be more training activity or perimeter security. While you're in Argentina also think hard about your insertion into southern Patagonia. Have a good look at the maps I've brought and memorize them. Don't take them with you and don't buy any there. It's just too dangerous to be caught with a detailed map in your possession.'

'Yes ma'am,' agreed John giving a mock naval salute.

She rounded on him eyes blazing, 'And don't you ever do that again, John Ridley. You're not in the navy now. Doing that down there would completely jeopardize your safety! Do you understand?'

Much chastened and surprised at the violence of her response he replied, 'Yes, Andy, I am sorry. You are perfectly correct. I shall never again let my guard drop.'

Seeing his hangdog expression and hearing the contrition in his voice, she walked over and enfolded him in her arms and kissed him gently on his mouth. 'I know, my love, but you are just too precious to me, I cannot afford to lose you.

'Your main objective must be to come back with hard evidence that an invasion is in the final planning stages. Supposition doesn't take us forward. Many small facts that build up into a partial picture might convince the politicians but ideally we need a piece of really conclusive evidence. I think we've done sufficient for today. Let's just decide what remains to be covered and then get out in the fresh air.'

John commented, 'We need to work through my detailed timetable and inform both Arthur Dean and Mr Yamauchi so they can shadow as appropriate. I may need a dead letter drop in BA on this trip. I then need to set up my meetings. Do you need to get on to SIS about the request for Yamauchi to arrange a dinner?'

'Yes, I'd better set that in train,' said Andy. 'Let's walk down to my office and I will get on the secure phone to London. You can stretch your legs along the waterfront and watch the ferry going across to Toronto Islands. I shouldn't be more than half an hour and then we can go for a walk in the park. Alternatively if you like we can walk along Lakeshore towards Ontario Place and then go to a restaurant near Exhibition Road.'

Wrapping up warm because it was early January and there was some wet snow drifting steadily down in the way it did there, snowing for hours but never seeming very much, yet at the end of the day a foot or more had accumulated and the sidewalk cleaning machines would be out again overnight. Slipping and sliding they made their way towards the lake and Andy went in through the swing doors of the High Commission offices. John continued to head for Lakeshore and stopped by the ferry landing to look at the small ferries that made the regular but short trips out to the islands. Some people actually lived out there so there was a service all year, but it was a fairly limited one as there were no tourists likely to venture across in this weather. Luckily the water between the ferry landing and the islands wasn't frozen so the ferries could operate at the moment. If it froze they had to call in a small icebreaker.

Just opposite the ferry landing was a small café that they had used on a number of occasions near the offices of the local radio station, so he decided to have a coffee there while he waited. He knew she would come in this direction when she had finished talking to London. Looking out at the islands he thought he had never felt so happy or alive. He had everything to thank Andy for. Luckily she seemed to feel the same about him. Not really being superstitious he still crossed his fingers as he waited.

Before long Andy appeared and eventually, after another coffee, they set off along Lakeshore towards Ontario Place, but as the snow seemed to be getting heavier they decided to head back to his apartment and eat in. Curling up on the settee after their meal they watched some TV then went to bed.

Tuesday 5th January they worked through John's detailed programme so they were both clear when he would be in BA, Bahia Blanca and Comodoro Rivadavia. They also discussed in detail every possible contingency so she had a good idea where he was likely to be morning, afternoon and evening for every day. 'I hope it won't be like this when we are married,' quipped John.

'Oh yes, I shall want to know where you are every minute of every day in case I need your body,' responded Andy striking a very sexy pose that completely distracted him from the matters in hand.

Eventually they concentrated on business once more. 'Arthur Dean,' queried John, 'how are we going to get messages to him?'

'He will keep in touch with Yamauchi so if you contact him a message can be passed on. I am also authorized to contact him via Jim Graham. We've given some thought to the dead letter drop in BA. It's easier in the hotels where we'll do the newspaper under the door routine, with the envelope inside. In BA we think the simplest plan is not to do a true dead letter drop. You should go into the Hotel Phoenix at 6 p.m. and head for the gents. Dean usually goes to this hotel for a drink after work. He'll be in the toilet ahead of you and as you go in he will start to come out and you should just slip the envelope into his pocket before the door's really open again.'

'OK, that sounds good and simple. Let's adopt that as the plan. I need to agree an emergency code with Yamauchi in case I have to get across to Uruguay secretly but I can do that with him when I see him. I'll ask him for an appointment on the 14th and tell him I shall be staying over in Uruguay until the afternoon of the 15th. I'll also get him to set up an appointment with the Minister of Health there.'

'Right, I think we have covered everything on the list,' said Andy. 'I'll get back to my office as there's plenty to do to make sure everything's set up before you arrive. I may have to go up to Ottawa tomorrow but I'll be back Friday afternoon at the latest. I'll be here this evening though. On Saturday can we go to Giovanni's in King Street East again?'

'A good idea. I will ring and make a reservation for 8pm. See you later then.' She went off into the bedroom and in a little while appeared in a lovely frilly blouse, long rusty-coloured skirt and sheepskin boots. 'Suddenly I find I have been entertaining a Gypsy. Is that why I am so bewitched?' asked John. He hugged her, planted a light kiss on her cheek not her mouth so she couldn't complain he'd smudge her lipstick, then shrugging on her thick coat, and grabbing her briefcase and cavernous shoulder bag, she headed for the door. He thought she had suddenly become very business-like and the essence of the modern professional woman.

John also switched roles and assumed the mantle of personnel and business development manager. Soon he was dealing with the myriad of issues referred to him, as well as trying to set up the various meetings he required for his next trip to Argentina. He also called up the local travel company he used and requested a business class flight booking to BA starting on the 10th returning on the 22nd. He also got an open return ticket for his trip from BA to Comodoro Rivadavia on the 18th. They promised to send them around the next day when the full flight schedule had been confirmed.

Friday 8th January around 4 p.m. he heard the key being

put in the Yale lock and coming out of the study he saw Andy stagger in with her arms full of parcels. 'You had time to shop in Ottawa then,' said John.

'That is a rather obvious statement even for you,' retorted Andy. 'In fact three of these packages are for you with my love, darling.'

Giving her a long hug and lingering kiss, he finally turned to the packages she had put on the settee and began to open them. 'He's like a little boy with his presents,' she thought. 'It makes me feel so good to see him so happy and excited.' By now he had carefully unpeeled the first package in his meticulous way and found it was a lovely red sweater. 'I thought it would be ideal for cottage country,' stated Andy. 'It should be the correct size as I checked through some of your other sweaters.' Opening his other presents he found a smart silk tie and a Timberland casual shirt.

'Great minds think alike,' he said, 'I have a small present for you.' Going into the study he returned with a thin rectangular package beautifully gift-wrapped. Handing it to her he pointed out, 'It's three months since we met and one month since we got engaged.'

She removed the paper excitedly and opening the dark blue box carefully she found a beautiful gold chain lying on the velvet base. Taking it out she held it up to the light and then with shining eyes fastened it around her neck. As she settled it comfortably John remarked, 'I knew it would look good on your neck.'

'You are an old romantic John, you treat me too well,' she sighed happily.

Needless to say the evening proceeded rather chaotically as the evenings of lovers often do. Eventually their minds returned to more mundane matters and they shared what they had done over the last couple of days. 'Tomorrow morning I must do your final briefing then the rest of the day is ours. What time is your flight on Sunday?'

'I need to be out at the airport by 9 a.m. so I have booked a taxi for 8 a.m.'

'John, I hope you don't mind but I won't stay here tomorrow night. I've become very superstitious about this and not being here the night before you leave seems to keep you safe. So I'm not going to change the routine now.'

'I don't like early morning farewells anyway,' added John. 'I want you to have one of my music tapes while I'm away; it's the one by Peter, Paul and Mary. It has a track called "Leaving on a Jet Plane" which I think is very appropriate. If you play it you'll know what I am thinking as the plane takes off.'

Saturday 9th January they were up early, and while having breakfast she updated him on the latest assessments and confirmed all the arrangements had been made. Arthur Dean was in his new role in BA and reports no suspicion apparent on the part of the Argentines. 'No meetings with General Coro,' she emphasized. 'There is obviously something about you that worries them. I just hope they don't work it out, whatever it is, before you are able to finally get out.'

They then spent the rest of the day quietly together, strolling in the park in the afternoon and having a quiet romantic dinner at Giovanni's. Then he walked her back to her apartment, and after a long kiss and hug in the foyer he left his tearful love and headed back to his place to finish his packing. Slipping into his bed that seemed so cold and empty without Andy, he thought, 'Right, I've got to focus on the challenges ahead,' feeling a surge in anticipation and excitement.

Chapter Twelve

January 1982 Buenos Aires

6 a.m. found Ridley stepping out of the airport terminal at Ezeiza into what was going to be a very warm summer's day. Grabbing a taxi he headed into town to the Esmeralda Suites in Recoleta and checking in at reception was soon being shown into the suite he had leased for six months. The receptionist outlined the services provided including the location of the fax machine and how to operate it. She gave him a full set of keys for the suite and also the main front door that, as she pointed out, was locked when the reception desk was closed, between 8 p.m. and 8 a.m. She said she was only in early this morning because she knew he was arriving before 8 a.m. She also pointed out the two sets of emergency exits on the ground floor and Ridley noted they were bar-operated and didn't seem to be alarmed.

She departed and he settled in to his comfortable suite with its sitting room, kitchen, two bedrooms and a bath-room. His only disappointment was that it didn't have a shower but perhaps Argentines preferred baths. Apparently the maid attended daily and would make the bed, dust and clear up generally including anything left unwashed in the kitchen. It was also possible to order food in if booked through reception earlier during the day. 'I could get rather spoiled by this,' he thought.

Opening his briefcase on the desk in the sitting room he

took out his papers and referred to the schedule of meetings. Glancing up he looked out of the long window and realized he had a good view over to one of the parks for which that part of the city was famed. In the distance he could also glimpse the sea. Taking out a writing pad he wrote the letter to Maria, giving his address and suggested she visited him on 16th January. As he promised Andy he didn't sign it but suggested they might reminisce about La Toja so she knew who had sent it.

A little later his phone went and he heard Cristina Sabato's bright voice asking, 'John, I hope you had a good flight and are getting settled in. Would it be convenient for me to pick you up about 11.30?' Hearing his agreement to this suggestion she quickly rang off.

11.30 her red Alfa Sud Sprint was outside the front entrance and he found her chatting away to the receptionist. That day her slim figure was encased in a smart blue trouser suit with slightly flared trousers and a short jacket that emphasized the slimness of her hips and her legs. Seeing him she smiled and walked across to him and kissed him on both cheeks. 'John, it is really good to see you. How are you, did you have a good holiday?'

They chatted for a while then she looked at her watch, said goodbye to the receptionist and led the way to her car. After they got in she turned to him and kissed him hard on the mouth hugging him tightly around the neck. 'I needed that. I have missed you. Don't worry, I shall try to be your friend not your lover, but occasionally I may need to kiss you.' With that this exciting woman switched on the engine, put the car in gear and sped out into the traffic. Before long they reached the Ministry of Health offices and she parked in a reserved space at the rear of the building. She then led him through the warren of corridors in the old building to Señor Roca's office, where with a very brief knock, she threw open the door so he might enter. Seeing them both, Roca rose and coming around his grand desk welcomed Ridley and ushered him to the conference table where there was a tray of coffee and cakes.

Over coffee Ridley summarized the progress he had made and reassured Roca that the project was very much on track, and that this trip was just to finalize the detail before he presented the proposal in Tokyo at the beginning of February. As he ran through his schedule Roca made a few notes, and when Ridley came to his trips to Bahia Blanca and Comodoro Rivadavia, quickly suggested that Cristina should accompany him to ensure there were no difficulties. So it was agreed that she would fly with him to Bahia Blanca on the 13th and also to Comodoro Rivadavia on the 18th. She said she would book the Bahia flight and took his ticket to Comodoro Rivadavia saying that she would ensure they sat together and see whether she could get them an upgrade to business class.

A little later an excellent, if rather too large, lunch was served although before long Ridley had to excuse himself so he wasn't late for his next appointment. Cristina accompanied him to the exit and asked him whether he would like to have dinner with her this evening. They could go dancing afterwards at a not too noisy disco she knew. 'Cristina I would like that but I just would like to say I don't think it would be a good idea for you to come back to the suites. I think we would both regret it. Should I meet you at the restaurant?'

'The restaurant isn't far from the Hotel San Martin, perhaps we could meet there in the bar at 8 p.m.'

Leaving her, Ridley hailed a passing taxi and headed for an initial meeting with his tax advisers. He had agreed to take them through the proposal so they would have some time to analyse it in detail before the review meeting the following week. After the meeting he walked across the Microcentro to the Hotel San Martin and left the envelope for Señora Maria Gomez who he believed would be staying there later in the week. The reception clerk was very helpful and confirmed that in fact she would be arriving the next day for the rest of the week. He assured Ridley she would receive his message as soon as she arrived.

Coming out of the hotel he decided to walk back to his apartment, as it was such a lovely day. It was very warm and he was glad he was wearing a lightweight suit and a short-sleeve shirt. He just wished he didn't have to wear a tie but unfortunately, unlike Canada, business dress in Argentina was still very formal. Heading up through Retiro he strolled along the Avenue Quintada and soon arrived at the large cemetery in Recoleta. Fringed by tall buildings and trees, he saw the cemetery was packed full of funereal memorials of every imaginable shape and size, some of which resembled small churches and public buildings: spires, domes and towers with statues, angels, eagles or crosses embellishing them all. He then went through the Plaza Intendente Alvear and past the grand Palais de Glace, a former ice rink, and into the Parque Thays, where he enjoyed the heady scents of the flowering plants before going out on to his street.

Back in his apartment he called Tony Marini and invited him round for a drink on Tuesday evening. Marini was free so they agreed to meet up about 6 p.m. as Marini had a dinner date later in the evening. 'Ideal,' thought Ridley, 'I can be very hospitable and friendly but I won't have the problem of getting him home if he drinks too much.'

Ridley was conscious time was moving on and he didn't

want to be late for Cristina. So he had a quick cool bath, shaved then changed into a casual jacket and trousers. As he was going to be late he quickly walked down the road to a nearby hotel where he had observed that taxis waited. Luckily there was one there and soon he was heading back to the Hotel San Martin. On the drive he reminded himself that he must not rendezvous there any more with Cristina, as being spotted in her company by Maria would really upset things.

Walking into the bar a few minutes before eight he found Cristina had beaten him to it. Stopping alongside her he smiled a greeting, 'That's a fantastic dress and you look wonderful in it. I don't know why you haven't got all the dishy men in BA at your beck and call. I won't apologize for being late as I am still early for our date.'

'I'm sorry I'm acting like a young girl on her first date, not a mature, married woman. Would you like a glass of wine?'

They found they were very easy with each other and were becoming firm friends, if for her this was tinged with sadness that she couldn't have more of him. This enjoyment continued during the meal as she was such an attractive companion. Sitting opposite him in a simple black cocktail dress adorned with a single diamond brooch and wearing diamond earrings set off by her long dark hair, she looked fantastic. As dinner progressed he pressed her about her life.

'I have had a very happy life apart from the last three years,' she said. 'My family is very well off and my father is a senior official in the civil service. That is how I got my job in the Ministry of Health. They have a large house here and a small estancia near Mendoza that has a vineyard. I'm an only child and have always been independent. I went to a good school then I thought I might like to become a doctor. However I decided I would do some work first and I joined the civil service in the Foreign Ministry.' She smiled sadly, 'There I met a young, handsome diplomat who swept me off my feet and we got married. But I don't think it was really true love for either of us and gradually we realized this. I think he wanted a wife from a rich family who would help his career. It was perfectly amicable but we decided we would lead separate lives although we could not divorce. So here I am working in the Ministry of Health, on my own though I have my friend Roca, and now I've met you.' As her eyes begin to shine Ridley reassured her, 'Cristina we shall always be friends. We must find you a great guy to love. It's something you really deserve.'

After more desultory conversation she smiled bravely, 'I promised you some dancing this evening and I would really like to dance with you. I haven't been out dancing for years. There's a disco nearby that I'm told plays the pops and some jazz, but not too loudly so it's possible to talk. Shall we go there?'

After insisting on paying for dinner she collected her wrap, and they walked arm in arm a short distance towards a flashing light and a floodlit sign of a black cat. Entering Ridley was surprised to see it looked very nice and the people here were of a similar age to them. Couples were sitting drinking at small tables or dancing on the dance floor beneath spotlights in one corner. The lights were low but it was not a gloomy atmosphere. The music was mainstream pop and he recognized the current hits by Electric Light Orchestra, Chaka Chan and The Pretenders as they settled at a table and ordered drinks. As she promised the music was not booming out and he didn't feel as though he was going to lose his eardrums. Soon their drinks arrived and after listening to the music for a while, she took his hand and led him onto the dance floor.

She slid close to him and they danced with his arms about her to "You've Lost That Lovin' Feeling", and she felt a great peace in her. 'It's so nice to have a good friend and a man friend at that. It's a pity he doesn't want me sexually because I haven't had sex for a long time and I instinctively know it will be good with him. However just having a man to care for me feels so good.' They danced close through songs by Kenny Rogers and George Benson then the tempo changed and the music of Queen, The Rolling Stones, McCartney and Rod Stewart filled the air and they disco danced.

After a while they were both feeling the pace and they sat down again at their table. 'That is the first dancing I've done for three years,' she said. 'You really are good for me. I'm glad I met you, John Ridley, and that you like me.' Taking his hand she kissed it, 'I want to be your friend.'

Looking carefully around she lowered her voice and whispered, 'But why are they so interested in you? Security has been asking about you and I have to tell them everything we do together and what you say. I don't want to know any secrets you may have. I only want you to know that if you're ever in trouble and you turn to me for help, I will help all I can.'

'Cristina, I don't know why they're asking about me. Perhaps they always check up in these circumstances so they're sure the business propositions are genuine.'

'No, it can't be that. They've never checked up like this before for other business ventures. No, it's something about you personally, I think. Not your project or your company.'

Shrugging John responded smiling, 'Well I have nothing to hide so no doubt in time they'll forget about me.'

As midnight approached they collected their coats and left the club, and John found a taxi for her. Kissing her gently goodnight they agreed she would call for him at 8a.m. on Wednesday for the trip to Bahia Blanca. He then walked on a short distance in the stillness of the warm BA night until he spotted another taxi. Soon he was settled in bed thinking that everything had gone well and that Cristina Sabato was a very interesting woman. She deserved to find love and happiness.

Tuesday 12th Ridley spent most of the day viewing more offices in central BA until about 4 p.m. when he returned to the apartment. That morning he'd organized a small buffet to be delivered just before 6 p.m. along with a couple of bottles of wine and he checked with the receptionist it was all organized. He went up to his apartment and kicking off his shoes put his feet up on the settee. A little while later the phone rang and it was Maria saying she had received his message, confirming she would come over on Saturday, and asked shyly whether she might stay with him over the weekend. Apparently her course at the university was a short one, just three days, so she was planning to return to Rio Gallegos on Monday morning. John told her this was fine and she said she would check out early on Saturday morning and be with him by 10 a.m.

Marini arrived promptly just after six, in fact he nearly beat the food and wine, which thought Ridley would have been embarrassing. He looked little different from the last time Ridley saw him. Clearly the drink and cigarettes were taking their toll. Pouring out two glasses of red Malbec wine from Mendoza, Ridley updated him on his business project and the likely timetable. Realizing that the journalist's glass was already empty he quickly refilled it before sipping his own wine. Ridley then expressed the hope that the journalist would be able to provide some publicity when the formal application was made after Easter.

At this statement the journalist laughed, 'I just hope nothing spoils your plans.'

Refilling his glass again Ridley queried, 'Why? Is there some bad news about the economy about to break?'

'No, there is nothing new there. The economy is only as bad as it has been for the last couple of years. No, I was meaning that our glorious leaders are likely to do something stupid quite soon. I hear they've decided that some action against Islas Malvinas will take the people's minds off the state of the economy and the rising unemployment.'

'Do you have any hard facts about this?' challenged Ridley.

'No, it's all rumour and I don't know when it'll happen. There doesn't seem to be any unusual military activity at the moment according to my contact. I'm working on this quietly as it'll be a major scoop if I can get it.'

'Well, you are correct,' mused Ridley. 'If this occurs my company won't be happy to invest until the situation settles down again. They would be generous for any early warning you can give us about this.'

Having made this offer, Ridley refilled Marini's glass for the third time and he lit one of his foul-smelling cigarettes. They talked generally about his newspaper and life in BA, then, once the bottle was empty, the journalist prepared to leave and Ridley suggested they meet for a drink the next week.

Opening all the windows to get rid of the smell of cigarette smoke, Ridley thought, 'I had better go out to eat.' He decided to test whether he was still being observed. So he set a trap with some fluff placed on top of his closed briefcase. Should anyone enter and open the case the fluff would fall off. Having set this up he set off for the small restaurant down the road where he had a tasty pizza and salad and a couple of glasses of wine before returning. Sure enough, someone had been in the room because the fluff had gone and when he opened the case some of the papers weren't in the same order as he'd left them. Checking around the apartment very carefully and dismantling the phone he concluded that it wasn't bugged, they'd just wanted to look for incriminating evidence or some facts after Marini's visit. 'Cristina might be correct,' he thought, 'it may be me personally they're curious about, not whether I am an intelligence agent. I better tell Andy about this when I get back.'

Wednesday 13th Cristina as usual was very punctual and she was waiting for him when he came down to the foyer. She was dressed very casually in a tight top and shorts and was wearing trainers. Turning to him she grinned at him and said, 'It is such a great day I decided to bring my bikini. Why don't you take your swimming things? You do need to relax sometime.'

She drove them to the domestic airport and soon they were in the air on the ninety-minute flight to Bahia Blanca, and she was chattering to him happily like a girl friend. As they came into the circuit for landing Ridley again got a good view of Puerto Belgrano and he had no difficulty in seeing that virtually all the fleet units were alongside. After landing, the plane taxied across the airfield to the civil terminal and looking out he got a good view of the aircraft there. There seemed to be few combat planes on view.

Cristina quickly got them a taxi into the city, and in true Argentine style insisted they needed a coffee and a cake before getting down to business. She had arranged a meeting for him with the director of the Regional Health Board for 11 a.m. so they had time to sit at one of the cafés on the palm-lined boulevard. After the meeting with the regional director, Ridley called on the real estate company to get current figures for an office lease then they headed for some lunch. 'I find this all very interesting,' she remarked. 'I am glad I came with you. It's very interesting to see how you work. I'm also getting the view from the opposite angle to that of the ministry. Making pharmaceuticals isn't just a licence to print money, is it? There's a lot of skill required to run the business and a lot of cost associated with it.'

'Those are very perceptive comments, Cristina,' remarked John, 'but not ones that find much favour in social economies where pharmaceutical companies struggle to get a fair return for their investment.'

After lunch they called at the recruitment agency to see what skilled sales people they had registered at the moment and John updated them on his likely recruitment timetable. As the discussions went very well and they found they finished sooner than they expected, Cristina suggested they might relax for a while. So she hailed a taxi that she instructed to take them to a small cove a few miles south of the city, where she assured Ridley there was a lovely secluded beach. As they drove along he realized this cove must just be across from the fleet base and so he would be able to check out the locality without difficulty. It might prove to be a good OP for an SBS team. Arriving at the cove it was just as she promised, a lovely silver beach and a blue sea that looked very inviting on such a hot afternoon. The cove was quite narrow and was surrounded by low sandstone cliffs and the water looked quite deep, just shelving steeply close to the beach. 'An ideal place for landing a boat,' he thought. She negotiated with the taxi driver and John then gave him a quarter of the fare, the remainder being given to him when he returned in a couple of hours.

As the taxi drove off she ran down on to the deserted beach and had soon stripped off without any embarrassment and was slipping on the pants of her bikini. Clearly she intended to be topless and he could see why. She had beautiful breasts, not large but with big nipples which were clearly aroused by him looking at her. 'Come on, you shy boy, get your clothes off and let's swim!' So chucking his clothes on the sand and pulling on his shorts he ran after her and they were soon splashing happily in the water. Then they swam side by side in the warm sea out into the cove and a little way beyond the entrance before returning to sunbathe on the beach. 'You really are a water pixy,' he said. 'I have to be careful or you will drag me off to your watery lair.'

She turned to look at him with sand sticking to her damp breasts and a damp patch on her pants and he was struck by her vibrancy. She put a hand out to him and then he hugged her tight feeling a surge of emotion but trying to resist it. 'Thank you Cristina,' he said after a while, 'I think our friendship will always be very intimate but I am not going to make love to you. So I think we should get dressed and act in a more demure manner with each other.'

She looked through her long eyelashes at him and smiled for she knew she could have had him then if she had insisted, and he knew it. So she turned over, grabbed a towel and was soon dressed in her shorts and top and watching him as he got dressed. A little while later the taxi returned to find them sitting by the track looking down into the cove and enjoying the late afternoon sun. Before the taxi arrived John had time to stroll along the top of the low cliffs to check out the feasibility of the location as an observation post and he thought it would do well. The area was virtually deserted, was some distance from the road and down a rough track, and there was a good view across the water to the naval base on the far shore. Someone watching from here properly camouflaged would be unlikely to be disturbed, and would have a good view of the ships coming to and going from the fleet base.

They had time before the flight back for a meal in the city, and John judged it was a good moment to ask an important question given their recent intimacy. 'Cristina, if I needed to hide out somewhere for a few hours one day would you be able to help me?'

She turned her head to look at him questioningly then said seriously, 'Yes, I said I would help you. I have a key to a small holiday place in the delta that I could use. If you call me and say you need help I will take you there. Don't worry, you can trust me. You'd better have my home phone number.' Taking out a piece of paper she wrote her number on it and gave it to him. She didn't ask him any more but he knew she had worked it out, and it wasn't a problem for her because she was his friend and she trusted him.

Thursday 14th January he caught an early ferry across to Montevideo and was pleased the good weather was holding so he had such good views on the crossing. He watched for a shadower but he didn't spot anyone so perhaps they were happy to just have reports from Cristina. She no doubt had told them he was going across to Uruguay for a couple of days. When the ferry arrived he walked quickly to the Japanese Embassy and presenting his Japanese visitor card formally to the receptionist, asked to see Mr Yamauchi with whom he had an appointment. A few minutes later he was ushered into the office and his friend was greeting him profusely. A young girl assistant brought in some tea and small Japanese cakes, and once she had left Yamauchi beamed, 'Ridley-san, I understand congratulations are in order. She seems to be a very nice English girl and very professional in her work, I should add. I hope you will both be very happy.'

'How are things, Yamauchi-san?'

His friend shrugged, 'It is quite interesting here although of course it lacks the sophistication of Tokyo. There are quite a few rich Japanese living in Argentina and Uruguay so that makes life bearable. There are also a few single Japanese women looking for companionship so I do not lack company here.' He went on, 'Though I must say Japanese girls have a long way to go to catch up with the superb girls down here that you see sunning themselves on the beaches.'

Smiling at Ridley and sighing at his last comment he continued, 'Anyway back to business. In case there is a watcher on your tail I thought we should stay in a hotel at Piriápolis about a hundred kilometres from here. The classy resort is further on and many Argentines go to Punta del Este to spend their *plata negra*, their unreported income, so I thought we should avoid it. The Argentino Hotel in Piriápolis is four-star and very elegant so we will be very comfortable there. I suggest we leave after lunch so we will be there in time to watch the girls on the beach.'

'You remain a lecher I see, Yamauchi-san,' commented Ridley smiling conspiratorily. 'That sounds an excellent arrangement. Is my meeting with the Minister of Health this morning?'

'No, it is tomorrow at 11 a.m. followed by an early lunch. This lunchtime we're meeting the First Secretary here for sushi so you can impress him with your plans for Nippon Health and I can bask in the reflected glory! I've also arranged the meeting with the tax advisers here in Montevideo for early afternoon tomorrow, and I thought a short discussion with our embassy finance guy might be useful before you leave. He has dual representation so if you need more advice you can see him next week in BA as well. I suggest we use the remaining time before lunch to discuss any highly confidential matters as this room is fully secure and is checked regularly.'

Ridley checked with Yamauchi, 'You know I have a Canadian courier assigned called Arthur Dean?' As Yamauchi nodded he continued, 'I have a system arranged for dead letter drops and you'll need to contact him to arrange collection of the messages. I don't need to know what it is but it must be able to work quickly. We may only have a few hours' warning of something happening. I may also need to get out quickly. Where is the best place to cross secretly?'

'The only place to do it is the delta. It is patrolled but the smugglers easily find their way through and I've tested a route already. I have a trusted boatman who lives near Carmelo and he would be able to pick you up near Tigre. He keeps close to the Argentine shore then cuts across to Uruguay where it narrows. I would be able to pick you up from Carmelo but it will take me about three hours to drive there.'

'As it happens my safe house will be somewhere in the delta so that probably would work well. A friend has access to it so I could hide up there for a few hours. It would be helpful for me to have the detailed pick-up location so I can go there without any trouble. What is your telephone number here? If I say "London" to you you know I want out that night.'

'Take this, it's my business card and it has the embassy telephone exchange number. Call that and ask for me or leave an urgent message with the operator.'

Changing the subject slightly, John asked, 'What's your current assessment about this dispute between Argentina and Chile? The newspapers do seem to be inflaming the situation. There doesn't seem to be much love between these two countries at the moment.'

'We believe the situation is quite serious. There has been some mobilisation of army units and we think they have moved another squadron of Mirage 3s to Rio Gallegos. The army has been moving into southern Patagonia and westwards closer to the border. Nothing too obvious but the army is now looking westwards. We don't believe Chile will do anything. It is being stirred up by Argentina. There's a rumour that the Vatican is trying to arbitrate between them so it may all cool down. Remember the church in Argentina is very powerful and if they say don't fight then they won't! Now we really must see the First Secretary.'

He stood up and Ridley followed him out of the office and down the corridor to the plush office of the First Secretary, a small grey-haired man in his sixties. Mr Tanaka was a time-served diplomat who would become an ambassador on his last posting so they both bowed deeply as they entered his office. Ridley formally presented his card Japanese side upwards, holding it at the corners with both hands and pushing it forward as he bowed deeply again for Tanaka to take. Mr Tanaka's English was not as good as Yamauchi's but they were able to hold a good conversation and Ridley had no difficulty summarizing the project for him. It was clear Tanaka was very pleased and wished him good luck when he presented the paper next month. Ridley was left with a strong impression that the Foreign Ministry and MITI would be making strong representations to Nippon Health on his behalf. This was very flattering but he didn't really understand why. Must be 'wheels within wheels' he surmised.

Lunch was served and Ridley congratulated Tanaka on the quality of the sushi. Tanaka proudly stated that the embassy chef who he brought from Tokyo had prepared this. Ridley also said how good it was to drink Kirin beer again. Mr Tanaka complimented Ridley on his understanding and sensitivity to Japanese culture and after a barrage of mutual compliments they took their leave of Mr Tanaka.

Yamauchi closed up his office and told his assistant where he would be should there be any urgent messages, and then headed for the car park at the rear of the building. Yamauchi drove the new Honda Accord and to Ridley, now used to American cars, it seemed so small but he had to admit that it was fairly roomy inside. If what Yamauchi said was true then it was much less thirsty than his Buick Century, which of course was an advantage down here where fuel was much more expensive. It only took them about ninety minutes to reach the small resort of Piriápolis lying on a long stretch of sandy beach on the Atlantic coast and soon they were pulling up in front of the Argentino Hotel on the Rambla de los Argentinos. Once they had their bags out of the car, Yamauchi gave the car key to an attendant who drove it off into the hotel garage. As they checked in he suggested that they should change then stroll along the beach to see the 'sights' as he termed it.

So twenty minutes later they came out of the hotel and strolled along the boulevard at the beach edge, stopping at a beach side café for a coffee and enjoying the views of tanned bikini-clad female bodies. 'I always think,' suggested Yamauchi, 'that the female body is far more alluring when it tempts because some of the body is still covered rather than when there is full-frontal nakedness. I do think

167

South American women really understand this. Just think about Copacabana Beach in Rio.'

Becoming serious once more he said, 'The real reason I brought you here is I think somewhere along this coast will be a good base to operate from if anything develops, and you have to get out of Argentina but not the region. It is not far from Montevideo but far enough to be off Argentine radar. It will be easy for me as I have a guesthouse near Atlántida that is about fifty kilometres from both Montevideo and here. There is also an airport just to the east of here near Maldonado from which flights operate to Sao Paulo a couple of times each day. So it will be fairly easy to get in and out without attracting too much attention.'

'Yamauchi-san you have clearly done your homework very well as usual. I am so lucky to have such a wonderful back-up team in both you and Andy. You should know that I hope to recruit two other people to help me. One is a girl I knew in Spain many years ago who I met here.'

'This is Maria Gomez I think,' interjected Yamauchi.

'Yes, that is correct,' answered Ridley. 'I'm seeing her this weekend and I hope to recruit her as I think she's my only hope for getting down to Rio Gallegos and I am sure the airbase there will be pivotal in any crisis that develops. The other woman is Cristina Sabato who works in the Ministry of Health. She's in love with me but she knows about Andy, and she's become a friend, and has promised me help should I need it. She is the one who has access to this holiday cottage in the delta. I think I can trust her.'

'I shall remember them in case they contact me,' Yamauchi promised, 'and help them if I can,' he added. 'I think we should stroll back now as I'm starting to get hungry and I wish to show you the architectural delights of the hotel. Shall we meet at eight in the bar?'

They enjoyed a wonderful dinner together reminiscing about beautiful places in Japan they knew: the Zen Temple at Kyoto and the older temples at Nara both created when the south of Japan was the leading part of the country. Yamauchi started to talk about where he was born, the small town of Arita in the beautiful hills of the island of Kyushu that he left as a young man to go to university and then join the Japanese defence force. Ridley had been there and understood how his friend felt about the dark green steep-sided hills, and the narrow rocky valleys with the fast-rushing streams. Eventually the conversation petered out and they said goodnight with formal bows to each other.

Friday 15th January they were both up early and after a pleasant continental breakfast on the hotel patio overlooking the beach and enjoying the sun, they set off for the drive back to Montevideo. At the embassy Ridley parted company with Yamauchi and took a taxi to the Ministry of Health where he had a satisfactory progress meeting with the minister and his staff followed by a light lunch and a glass of champagne. He then moved on to his meeting with the Uruguayan tax advisers and after this headed back to the embassy to meet the finance officer. He was very helpful and provided some useful insights into the workings of both the Argentine and the Uruguayan tax authorities and suggested some ways to minimize tax payments that Nippon Health's finance department might consider. He also made some useful comments about grants possibly available through the Japanese Foreign Ministry/MITI Overseas Development Fund. Thanking him Ridley suggested that it would be useful for them to have a further meeting the following week before he departed for Toronto and they agreed to meet in BA.

Saying farewell to Yamauchi before he left the embassy, Ridley walked back to the ferry and was soon onboard and seated on the upper deck enjoying the late afternoon sun. As the ferry began to leave the jetty he moved to the rail and watched as Montevideo slipped astern, enjoying the slight breeze as the ship moved steadily across the estuary.

He was so lost in his reverie that he was quite startled when the man standing near him suddenly spoke.

'Did you have a successful business trip to Montevideo, Señor Ridley?'

Turning his head sharply to his left, he saw the speaker was a smartly-suited middle-aged man with short hair and a neatly trimmed moustache.

'I'm sorry! don't think I know you.'

'I am Colonel Lupo from the Ministry of Information. I work for General Coro', he added with a smile. 'We are very anxious to safeguard our interests and wouldn't want you to experience any difficulties.'

By now Ridley had the measure of him. He had been sent by Coro to keep him under pressure, to see if he would betray himself through some mistake or panic reaction. If you're from the Ministry of Information then I am a Dutchman!

'What is your precise role, Colonel?'

Lupo waved his hand dismissively. 'Oh, just a subordinate role advising General Coro as to whether some business developments might be against Argentina's interests. I keep an eye on projects involving foreigners.'

'Well, I am sure you understand I cannot divulge my business discussions for that would be a breach of commercial secrecy, and I am sure your government would not wish to be accused of colluding with one pharmaceutical company to the detriment of others, particularly US companies!'

'Of course we understand that,' Lupo snapped back at him. 'What we cannot understand is why your company has decided to invest in Argentina at this precise moment.'

Ridley stared at him and shook his head as though he was considerably frustrated and irritated by him. 'I would have thought that is pretty obvious. We judge that Argentina's economy will grow and with its increased wealth there will be business opportunities in many sectors, especially the pharmaceutical sector, for a richer economy tends to spend more on healthcare. My company believes it has the medical products you will want and we want to be well established here to take advantage of this. If you find this difficult to understand I suggest you contact Señor Roca in the Ministry of Health, because he certainly has no difficulty with this strategy! Most countries are usually only too anxious to get our business,' he added.

Changing tack Lupo leered at him. 'I understand you are engaged to a woman in Canada. Does she know you are screwing Señora Sabato? We have seen how you look at her. Is she fantastic in bed? I imagine she knows many tricks to satisfy a man!'

Ridley stayed calm and didn't leap to Cristina's defence, thus revealing his affection for her, a weakness that Argentine Security might exploit. 'I really don't know who has invented these fantasies Señor Lupo. In Canada it is the sort of story printed by the "gutter press", usually completely fictitious and invented by some desperate journalist. Is this what the Argentine Ministry of Information does these days? For the record I will tell you once and for all that I have not had sexual relations with Señora Sabato nor do I intend to. I am happily engaged to a girl in Canada. Señora Sabato has provided valuable assistance to me that has helped progress the project quickly and I shall certainly

171

be able to put my recommendations to the February board meeting as planned. Now, if I hear any more allegations of this sort I shall complain to the Japanese Embassy and I would expect a strong complaint to be made to your government. I don't think you would enjoy that, Colonel!'

Lupo looked totally unconcerned at this threat and this convinced Ridley that he had a powerful position in the Junta. He must be very careful and not over-antagonize this man.

'Perhaps you prefer men, Señor Ridley, is that why you have been meeting Tony Marini clandestinely? You never know what decadent behaviour goes on in some places these days. I would have thought you could have found someone less dissipated and rather younger, or do the older ones turn you on?'

Ridley shook his head again. 'You really do have a sick mind. My discussions with Marini are solely to get publicity for my company when the project is agreed. I don't know anything about his sexual inclination and I must say he has never hinted at anything like that. I would have to say I would be very shocked if he propositioned me for I don't go in for that sort of thing.'

Totally annoyed by this obnoxious creep he turned to leave the upper deck, but Lupo put out an arm to restrain him. He hissed, 'I wouldn't want to have to call my friends for support. Let me just give you a clear message, Señor Ridley. Stick to your business project and don't attempt to meddle in our politics. If you do you will find we can turn very nasty!'

After uttering this threat he released Ridley's arm and strolled off towards the gangway, leaving Ridley to consider the incident. He hadn't noticed any surveillance in Uruguay and he didn't think that both he and Yamauchi

172

would have missed shadowers, especially at Piriàpolis. Clearly they had been keeping an eye on him but he thought they were just guessing about the relationship with Cristina. She wouldn't have embroidered the story for she had her self-respect and wouldn't want to be thought to be prostituting herself for her country. They were still uncertain about him, but after thinking hard for the rest of the ferry trip he couldn't think what was causing their concern. He would just have to be very careful. It really did support the view that they were up to something, but unfortunately provided no more concrete information. He must be very careful with Maria this weekend.

Saturday 16th January he was up early and took a taxi to a local supermarket and returned laden with food and drink just before Maria arrived at 10 a.m. As he was packing everything away the phone rang and it was reception saying he had a visitor and she was on her way up. Just then he heard the buzzer and when he opened the door Maria was standing there clutching her leather bag and carrying her light coat. 'Maria, come in. It's good to see you. How has your course been this time?'

'It was very good, John, thank you. It was about the end of the colonial period in South America, with a detailed review of what happened and why in Argentina. I knew a bit about this from my previous studies but this course provided a lot more detail which will be useful for the courses I teach.'

'Let me show you around the apartment then you should unpack your bag before we do anything else,' suggested John. 'I have two bedrooms, this sitting room, a bathroom and quite a large kitchen. I have some food in so we can eat in tonight if you like. I am not a bad cook. You will have the spare bedroom and I hope the bed is comfortable. Mine is but I haven't tried yours. While you unpack I shall make some coffee, then we can talk.'

Picking up her bag he led her to the spare bedroom and after pointing out the door to the bathroom he headed for the kitchen and set up the coffee percolator. As the percolator was finishing hissing and puffing she reappeared. Today she was dressed very casually in a red t-shirt top and original Levi's that suited her. John thought how young she looked and rather vulnerable.

Pouring the coffee they moved back into the sitting room and he asked her how she had spent the last few weeks and whether she had had a happy Christmas.

'It's been very quiet since I met you,' she replied. 'I have been at the estancia and the classes went on up to the week before Christmas. Christmas was quite quiet although we always have a big meal on Christmas Day for all the staff and there's dancing in the evening. So it is always a good party. Rafael was home for Christmas but I didn't see much of him because he spent a lot of time with the ranch manager and also went down to the airbase a few times. After a few days he went back to BA saying he had some important financial task to complete for the government. I haven't seen him since.' Tears began to roll down her face as she sobbed, 'I'm so lonely and unhappy. I wish I'd never come to Argentina. I don't feel at home with the Argentines; they are not like Spaniards. I would like to go back to Spain if I could.' He went over and hugged her tight, stroking her dark hair as she sobbed brokenly.

'Couldn't you tell Rafael you need a holiday in Spain?' suggested John. 'I think you are a little depressed. What you need is a good holiday. Surely Rafael would not prevent you going. When you are there you can decide if you want to come back.'

'What you say makes a lot of sense,' admitted Maria, 'but my family would not forgive me if I did this. They are very religious and strict about such things. I would hate it if I could not go home to them. It is probably better to stay here now,' she said resignedly.

'Maria, it is your life and happiness we are discussing, not how Rafael or your parents will feel about it. If you are unhappy you should put yourself first.'

'John, please leave it now. Let us talk about more pleasant things for the rest of the weekend. I've been looking forward to it since Christmas. What I'd like to do today is go for a cruise on the Rio de la Plata. They run them regularly from Darsena at this time of the year and we can probably get one that goes to the delta. If we take a ferry around noon, we can lunch on board and get back early evening. It would be nice to eat here I think, if you don't mind. I will help cook, I'm quite good these days you know. What I want to do is talk and talk and just share our thoughts. We have so much catching up to do.'

Smiling John nodded his agreement and they prepared to go out for the day. At the ferry terminal they found the cruise they wanted and purchased tickets. About 11.30 the cruise departed and headed at a reasonable speed northwest up the Rio de la Plata close to the Argentine shore, and eventually the vast suburbs of the city thinned out and they saw flat pampas with vast reed beds at the riverside. Ridley thought, 'This is a lucky break for this cruise will allow me to reconnoitre the area up to the delta and it would be useful to know the lie of the land.' Later they approached the suburb of Tigre and the delta where the city dwellers, *porteños* as they are called, fled at weekends to enjoy river life around the many channels of the Paraná. Soon the cruise boat was nosing into the Estación Fluvial at Tigre and they had a short stop there to visit the Puerto de Frutos, a large and very colourful fruit market. Today there was also a large craft market in the square and the market abounded with many stalls selling leather and wicker products of all shapes and sizes. Hand in hand and very carefree they explored the market and John bought her a small leather purse that had taken her eye. They also had time to visit a restaurant nearby for a light lunch and a glass of Argentine Sauvignon Blanc before they returned to the cruise boat.

When the boat left Tigre it took an inland channel that cut across the main channels, firstly of the Rio Paraná de las Palmas and then, at the Paraná Guazú, it turned to starboard and followed this channel out into the Rio de la Plata. It then set course for the Isla Martin Garcia just off the Uruguay coast.

Turning to John as they stood on the upper deck leaning against the rail Maria said, 'This is brilliant. I've wanted to do this trip for a long time. I loved the fruit market and the trip through the delta was so different. It's so densely forested. It was fascinating to see so much wildlife and there are so many more birds than I expected. I hope it won't be too affected by tourism in the future.' Breathing in the warm salty breeze and looking across the water to the islands she said, 'It's a beautiful afternoon to be on the water.'

John observed, 'We seem to be heading for those islands near the far coast.'

Maria replied, 'The large one is the Isla San Martin, I think we stop there before heading back to BA. There used to be a prison here for Argentine political prisoners but now it's a nature reserve with some historic buildings. We can take a walk through the reserve and explore a bit.'

Soon the cruise boat came alongside the landing stage and they strolled through the small village with its old buildings. The north end of the island was densely wooded and this was where the nature trails were. Getting a map from a guide they set off along the trail to follow the green-coloured posts with numbers at intervals matching the descriptions on the map. Maria pointed excitedly upwards as a flock of small green parrots cackled past overhead. Luckily, she observed, the mosquitoes were not too troublesome because she had forgotten the repellent.

Then they returned to the boat and it soon headed out into the estuary and they saw the lights of BA begin to twinkle in the distance. John went down to the bar for a couple of glasses of wine and they stayed leaning over the rail watching the fluorescence in the boat's wake and occasionally making an observation to each other. The sun set leaving a lovely rosy hue along the horizon and everything was still apart for the steady low thudding of the engine. A little later they sat on a bench, John put his arms around her and she rested her head against his shoulder, and was soon gently asleep. From time to time she stirred slightly and made little noises, but mostly they sat close together protectively like brother and sister with John remembering the happy times on Isla La Toja.

Back in the apartment, they decided it was simplest to have pasta with beef accompanied by a nice salad since it was still so warm. Maria reckoned the temperature might have reached 30°C this afternoon. Soon they were sitting at the small dining table with their meal and a glass each of Malbec.

'I do like this wine,' commented John, 'I wish I could get

it in Canada. You can certainly live well down here and the Argentines certainly seem to have a passion for living.'

'They certainly do but I think they are more irresponsible and selfish than Spaniards,' she replied. 'They have a country with vast natural resources yet the economy is in difficulties and they show no sign of taking up democracy. I know Spain only became a formal democracy in 1975 but in the last years of Generalisso Franco he allowed it to develop. The Spanish people will never now turn their backs on democracy. I wish the Argentines felt the same.'

John asked, 'Is life really bad for the people then? Being a visitor and living in hotels it is difficult to assess this personally.'

Maria nodded, 'Having studied political science I suppose I am sensitized to the political nuances, and I see how the poorer people live both in BA and also down in Patagonia. I think life is hard. It is also likely to get harder because the difficulty with the world economy, that is causing so much unemployment in Europe, is starting to hit us. Inflation is increasing here, and we know that it is the poor who suffer during periods of high inflation, not the rich.

'What concerns me much more though,' added Maria forcefully, 'is the military government we have. Their *raison d'être* seems to be to prevent communism taking over but that means we have a form of Fascism here, not democracy. They retain their power through fear and repression. I told you about the Disappeared? Well every month you hear of someone or other who has been taken away by the police or security, and no one seems to hear of them again. We should have democratic processes in this country so that if the people are dissatisfied with the government they may dismiss them at the next election.'

They continued debating generally for a while and Ridley formed the impression that she was passionately against the undemocratic aims of the Junta. Later glancing at the clock they realized it was nearly midnight and the time had flown by, and they decided they had better go to bed. Undressing Ridley evaluated all she had told him during the day and concluded she may be trusted. 'She is still the Maria I knew,' he was pleased to find.

Sunday 17th January John woke to find Maria at his bedside with a cup of coffee. Still in her nightdress and wearing a wrap she smiled at him, 'You looked so sweet lying there asleep. Have some coffee while I have a bath. Then I shall prepare breakfast. Don't be too long.'

After breakfast John suggested they visited the Reserva Ecologica Castenera Sur on the shore in BA near the Plaza de Mayo. They could stroll down to the Avenue de Mayo and then go through the plaza across the canal and into the reserve. It was a nice park with good sea views and was very popular. After that, lunch in the centre and a stroll back. He suggested there was a little restaurant he had used near the apartment where they would be able to get a simple evening meal. They could talk again in private back at the apartment. Looking at Maria he could see she agreed this was a good plan for the day.

So off they walked hand in hand, chatting animatedly to each other as things they saw or did prompted their memories, and brought back shared moments when they were so young. By the time they reached the little restaurant it seemed the years had slipped away and they were the boy and girl on the shores of the Isla La Toja in Pontevedra, Galicia. They were old friends again.

Back at the apartment, slumping down into the settee and kicking off her shoes, she curled her legs under her as girls the world over do, and seriously asked him, 'John,

I know you asked me to think of you as a Canadian and of course I will do so, but what is the real reason for this secrecy? Surely you can trust me?'

John sat down opposite her and looked straight at her for a long while, staring deep into her eyes as though he was trying to see right into her mind. She sat still and left him to his inner debate and finally he relaxed and she knew he was going to tell her. 'There are two very good reasons for not explaining. Firstly it could affect your safety and secondly it could affect mine, and I don't say this lightly. If after considering this you still want me to tell you then I will do so but I won't think badly of you if you change your mind.'

'No. John, I think I already suspect but I want you to explain. There should be no secrets between us.'

'OK. Everything I told you when we last met is true and you must stick to that information if anyone asks you. I have a Canadian passport and I am here preparing a business proposal for Nippon Health. However I am still in the British Royal Navy and a member of Naval Intelligence, and I am trying to find out whether the Argentines are planning to attack the Falkland Islands or Islas Malvinas as you know them. I need to find out information to prevent it, not plan an attack on the Argentine people. We know from at least a couple of sources that something is being planned but we don't know what and when. On every trip I need to check the main naval bases and also the airbases to try to spot any unusual activity so I can warn my people. The problem I have is that the airbase at Rio Gallegos is likely to be very important if there is an invasion of the Falklands. There is also an airbase at San Julian further north I need to check. The other important one is on Tierra del Fuego but I have no chance of getting there. However if there is a period of tension I don't think I would be allowed to fly into Rio Gallegos.'

'I think you may be correct about something being planned,' agreed Maria. 'I don't have any concrete information but I think Rafael is involved somehow. He mentioned over Christmas that he was working to ensure that the country's finances would be supported by the US banks, if Argentina flexed its muscles, as he described it. I assumed he meant with Chile or Uruguay but it could be Britain. There is certainly a steady raising of tension about "the injustice of Las Malvinas" in the popular press and most people would support such a move. If Rafael appears at the estancia I shall pay particular attention to what he says in case he gives some clues. However, I don't think I would be any use observing aircraft. I have difficulty telling one type from another.'

John hastened to reassure her, 'When something begins to happen I will just have to throw caution to the winds and this means I would have to go quickly down the coast to check. I should be able to reach Bahia Blanca and Comodoro Rivadavia without difficulty. From there it may be easier to go by road. I can probably hire a car in Comodoro and then I can check out San Julian and drive on down to Rio Gallegos. I would think the road should be virtually empty so I wouldn't expect security checks. What I'd like you to think about before we next meet, is whether you would be able to pick me up at Rio Gallegos airport after I've ditched the car. I'd need to hide out at the estancia for one night and then I'd like you to drop me off in the country near the town on your way to work so I can observe operations at the airbase. Does Rafael have a waterproof jacket I might use, as I don't think I can risk carrying one? Also some binoculars if he has them. You'd need to pick me after work and hide me overnight and then I have to get to Comodoro again. There would probably be no problem with a flight from there.'

'That sounds very dangerous for you, John. Is there no other option?' Seeing him shake his head she continued resolutely, 'In that case then of course I will help you all I can. I believe somehow democracy must be returned to this country even if I feel more Spanish than Argentine. If doing this might bring that about, then of course I will assist you any way I can.' She rummaged in her bag, 'Here are both my phone numbers. The top one is the estancia and the other is the switchboard at Rio Gallegos College. I'm usually at the college from nine-thirty to four in the afternoon Monday to Friday.'

Looking fondly at this brave young woman, it was difficult to see her as the young nervous girl at la Toja. He felt he must stress the dangerous nature of the proposition. But as he started she held up her hand to stop him and said calmly, 'I know what you are about to say. I understand the dangers and I also believe it must be important if you're here risking your life. I've lectured many students about peaceful coexistence and the value of democracy, now it's time I actually acted on some of my statements even if it's dangerous for me. My self respect as a Spanish woman demands it.'

Terminating the discussion and smiling affectionately at him she ordered, 'Now give me a cuddle big brother and remind me of La Toja before we go off to bed. By the way, when do you arrive for your next visit?'

So John gave her the dates and agreed she could stay for the weekend, then they talked again of more memories of the beautiful summers they spent on La Toja. They remembered sitting by the water watching the fishermen standing in the channel between the island and the mainland with their nets spread out on poles to catch the fish as the tide went out, and talked of climbing the hills or sun bathing on the beach and watching the rich people come to the small casino at the hotel on the island.

Monday 18th January Maria and John were up early and after breakfast they said their farewells before reception rang to say the taxi had arrived to whisk her to the Aeroparque for her flight to Rio Gallegos.

'Goodbye my brother,' she whispered giving him a kiss and a hug.

'Goodbye Maria, please take care. See you soon.' With a happy smile she picked up her bag and they descended into the foyer and he waved her off. 'She is a brave girl,' he thought, 'however I really do think she should go back to Spain then tell her husband she has left him. I cannot see anything good coming from it otherwise.'

John then quickly packed a bag for his trip to Comodoro Rivadavia thinking, 'I feel like a real Lothario. Seeing one girl off and an hour later greeting another one. I shall be getting quite a reputation with the young receptionist here.' About 10 a.m. Cristina picked him up as usual in her little red car and they quickly weaved through the Monday morning traffic the short distance northeast to the Aeroparque. An hour later they were in the air sitting, true to Cristina's promise, in comfortable business class seats and she was chatting to him excitedly. He thought, 'You never have any problem getting an Argentine to talk. The problem is to get them to listen.' Anyway, supplied regularly with coffee and served a passable lunch just before landing they passed the three-hour flight very pleasurably.

As they came into land he could see oil wells on the flat cliff tops and the modern city spreading along the coast pinned in by higher hills north and south and inland. The coast seemed to be quite rocky and there were high sandstone sea cliffs. There didn't appear to be any military aircraft parked here at that moment. The airport was north of the city but it was only a short drive into the city. Cristina had organized a series of meetings for him and he marvelled that he was getting this much access to people. Without the support of the Ministry of Health he would not have managed to see half of the people on the current itinerary. So they moved swiftly between helpful meetings with the regional health director, the medical director of the main hospital and even the local senior military doctor as there was a unit for treating the armed forces attached to the hospital there. By 6 p.m. however they had covered all the appointments and Cristina turned to him, 'John, you deserve another coffee after all these discussions.'

'No, Cristina, I couldn't touch another drop for a few hours. I think I have caffeine overload. I'm not as used to it as you. What I'd like to do is stretch my legs and do some exploring before it gets dark. I think we should register at the hotel and we can change into something more casual and comfortable. I feel the need to walk a few miles if you're up to it.'

She looked down at her very chic outfit and inevitable high heels and smiled, 'I think that'll be best!'

So they headed for the Austral Hotel where he found she had reserved a fancy business suite for him and an adjoining room for herself. Sensing his unease she grinned, 'I like being your personal assistant and this is how businessmen travel in Argentina.' She smiled very sexily, 'They like to have all the services to hand when they travel. Don't worry, I remember my promise to you, but if she ever gives you up you will have to fight me off.'

184

A short while later as he was pulling on a light sweater, for the evening could be cool down there at this time of the year, there was a light knock on the connecting door and she came in dressed in a colourful print summer dress with a wrap over her shoulders, and with sensible low heeled shoes on her feet. Walking over to him she hugged him lightly and then kissed him voraciously and he found himself responding and kissing her back. Breaking off she laughed, 'I have needed that all day. I thought I had better kiss you here so at least I can repair my lipstick before we go out.' Looking at him, 'And I'd better clean you up also!'

Having once been the centre of the agricultural region, for the last seventy years Comodoro Rivadavia had been an oil town and even down there, there was a hint of Dallas in the major buildings, its airport and the large port that developed. The hotel was situated not far from the sea, so as they left it they walked east along the Avenida Rivadavia and soon they were looking over the ocean near the port. The commercial port appeared to be enclosed and he could see looking down on it that there were good facilities there. The fishing harbour was open to the public and they joined other couples strolling along the jetties looking at the fishing boats with romantic eyes that completely failed to see much of the rust and decay. For like many other places around the world the fishermen here were suffering the effects of over-fishing. 'No doubt they would like to get their hands on the rich fishing grounds of the Falklands,' he thought. He didn't see any naval vessels in the commercial port but at the end of one of the jetties in the fishing harbour there was a small lightly armed patrol boat. He presumed its role was fishery protection. There would be no problem embarking troops and equipment needed for an invasion force through the commercial port. Wandering back happily arm in arm he spotted the local naval headquarters but it didn't seem any larger than the one at Rio Gallegos, so he concluded the naval control was very centralized and usually the fleet operated directly out of the bases at Bahia Blanca and Mar del Plata.

Turning south onto the Avenida Ingeniero Ducos they strolled along the pleasant promenade that overlooked the Golfo San Jorge to the long flat sandy beach that stretched to the high headland of grey rock that cut off the city in the south. They could see the lighthouse, the Faro San Jorge, in the distance and then decided to turn north back to the city centre. Ahead and looming above the city was the mountain, the Cerro Chenque. 'It must be nearly a thousand feet high,' thought John. 'It certainly compresses the buildings into the coastal strip.' Strolling on past the cathedral John said, 'I feel much better now after this walk. I hope I haven't taken you too far?'

'No, I've enjoyed it. It's so good just being out with you especially as I think we enjoy similar things. We don't need to go back to the hotel before we eat,' suggested Cristina. 'Let's just walk more or perhaps sit for a while in that park over there before it gets too dark.'

So they headed for what turned out to be quite a large park with a pleasant mixture of lawn, a pond and fountain, some pretty trees and lovely flower beds. There were plenty of the ubiquitous palm trees but they sat on a bench near some ornamental trees and a bed of colourful flowers, and although they couldn't recognize the plants, they enjoyed the heady perfume coming off them in the warm stillness of the evening as the sun set. They also heard the crickets chirping and, although it was illusionary, the sound of traffic also seemed to fade away. So they felt they were alone in a small clearing in the country surrounded by beautiful flowers.

'Cristina, if I may say so, your life seems to be in a bit of a limbo,' remarked John. 'Do you think you will ever get back together with your husband?'

'No, I don't think so. I feel trapped in the relationship but that's the problem with the strict society we have in Argentina and the strong religious influence. Some of my friends have gone to Europe or the States and have divorced their husbands there. The trouble is they can't come back to live here and at the moment I don't want to leave Argentina. I really love it here, especially BA.

'I'd like to be happily married and possibly have children.' Turning to him she grinned wickedly, 'But I also like my independence. I like men and enjoy being with them, but I also have a number of girlfriends I spend time with. I'm not certain whether I want children more than this. I'd like to be married to a good man before I get too old.'

Keeping the tone light, John rejoined, 'We must try our best to find that good man for you.'

The few people passing them, if they thought about it at all, thought how lucky these lovers were. Little dreaming the woman couldn't have what she desperately wanted and the man was dreaming of his girl back home.

After each enjoyed their peaceful reverie John apologized, 'I'm sorry, I was thinking of Andy. That it's a very ungallant thing to do, when you're accompanying a beautiful and very sexy woman. You've become a good friend to me and it's great having you as a companion on these trips. It's often so lonely when you travel on your own.'

'It's OK, John, I really do understand,' she reassured him. 'You know how I feel about you but I shan't take advantage of you. I hope we'll remain firm friends and I'd like to meet your Andy some time. There's something else I want to reassure you about. Just hear what I say. I don't need an answer from you. You asked me before whether I'd help you. I just want to tell you I'd do anything to help you no matter how dangerous it might be for me.' With that she kissed him gently on both cheeks and taking his arm pulled him upright. As he got up he saw the tears on her cheeks and taking out his handkerchief he gave it to her and she dried her eyes. He hugged her tightly until she calmed down and then, taking her hand, led her out of the park in the gathering gloom.

Later they stopped at a small fish restaurant on the brightly lit Avenida San Martin and enjoyed a delicious cod dish before heading back to the hotel and bed. 'Lock the door between us if you want,' she said.

'No, I don't think that will be necessary,' he replied. 'You've given your word and Cristina Sabato is very honourable no matter how painful that might be.'

'*Gracias Señor, buenas noches,*' and then she went to bed.

John was anxious to speak with Andy. Although it was quite late he knew it was two hours earlier in Toronto so he put a call through to Toronto and eventually he heard her on the other end of the phone. As soon as he said, 'Andy, I love you,' he heard her sigh.

'Oh John, I am missing you. I love you too. How's it going?'

'It's going very well. The Ministry of Health is being very helpful and Señora Sabato has arranged a number of meetings for me and accompanied me on a couple of trips. I also had a visitor for the weekend and all the other things I planned to do I've managed to fit in. I'm still planning to leave on Friday afternoon so I'll see you Saturday morning.'

'Where are you calling from,' asked Andy.

'I am in Comodoro Rivadavia and we are flying back to BA tomorrow lunchtime.'

'She is with you there then. I am jealous.'

'Seriously, Andy, you have no cause to be.' After a pause John added, 'With either of them.'

'You're an arrogant pig, John Ridley, but I still love you. Take care, my love, bye.'

With, 'See you soon, Andy, all my love,' John ended the call and went to bed.

Chapter Thirteen

Tuesday 19th January they had a light breakfast in his suite and then they headed off for the offices of the main pharmaceutical distributor, for the company wished to present a case to Ridley that would use the distributor's sales force to sell Nippon Health's products across the whole of Patagonia. There could be a lot of advantages in this proposal, if – and it was a big if – the local sales force was sufficiently competent. During the meeting the managers impressed him and, having met two of their sales representatives, he felt more confident about this company's proposal. Promising to include the option in the proposal to the board of Nippon Health, they left and headed back to the airport for the late morning flight to BA. Ridley found himself asking her, 'Cristina what did you think of that presentation?'

She answered him very seriously, 'Well, I think they're very keen to get your business. So presumably they think they can sell plenty of your products across Patagonia. I'm no expert but I think they're a professional organisation. At least they didn't keep staring at my legs all the time.'

'Well, I did wonder whether you had an ulterior motive in wearing such a short skirt today. I couldn't keep my eyes off your legs.'

'Oh, that's OK in Argentina. They'd have me marked down as your mistress. That's usually what personal assistants are. I could see from your reaction to the answers you got from the reps, that you thought they seem competent, so I think overall you could gain quite a lot by using them. Would it be a much cheaper option?'

'Not a lot cheaper on a day-to-day basis but we wouldn't be building in a lot of overheads and inflexibility such as staff and an office. I agree they seem OK. In fact I'm pleasantly surprised.'

After they landed back in BA, Cristina drove him to the offices of the international firm of management accountants where he would be spending the rest of the afternoon. On the way he told her he didn't think he would have any more time to meet up on this trip, but that he would be back in March and he would let her know when. She smiled bravely, gave him her love, told him to take care and kissed him hard. Then with a brief wave of the arm she drove off with a squeal of tyres in her little Alfa Sud and was soon lost in the traffic.

During a break in the discussions he got a chance to call Marini and surprisingly found him at the newspaper. Muttering something about following up a lead he offhandedly confirmed he was still planning to meet Ridley that evening. 'Nine o'clock at the Dublin bar in San Telmo,' he said and rang off.

A little after the appointed time – Argentines are notorious for their lack of timekeeping – Ridley arrived at the dingy entrance and gained entry by mentioning he was here to meet Marini. The interior was surprisingly smart and bright and decorated in art deco style with shiny metal and glass everywhere but with muted furnishings. The waiter led Ridley to Marini who he could see sitting on a bar stool, his tall frame hunched over the bar and with the inevitable cigarette in his mouth and glass of whiskey in his hand. As he saw Ridley arriving he slid off the stool and walked over to a corner table with a reserved sign on it, and sitting down ahead of him asked, 'What would you like to drink?'

Ridley asked for a glass of red wine and Marini suggested they should have a bottle which duly arrived with two glasses. 'I think you mentioned you liked jazz last week so I thought you'd like this place. In a little while a combo will play and this club'll get packed out because they're very good and very popular. They play a mixture of modern and mainstream mixed with a bit of Brazilian like Gilberto, so you should like it.'

John described his recent travels. 'Well, I've seen a little more of the country since we last met. I've been back to Bahia and then down to Comodoro Rivadavia yesterday. I like the spirit of Bahia. Not sure about Comodoro, I think it's a bit too remote for me.'

Marini grunted, 'I am a true *porteño*. I need the sustenance of BA otherwise I will die. Did La Sabato look after you?' he queried with a leer.

'Your sources are very good,' remarked John. 'She proved very helpful and no I haven't bedded her, not because she isn't attractive and sexy but because I am engaged to a girl in Canada. I think I have all the information I need for my board paper and I will be returning to Toronto this Friday. How is your scoop developing?'

'Oh, I mentioned that did I? It's very difficult but I've cultivated a number of contacts at junior officer level in the armed forces and they don't realize it but each provided me with snippets of information. Surprisingly these fit together quite well. It's a bit like doing a jigsaw puzzle: eventually you have enough of the picture to allow you to fill in the rest. I understand operational planning is nearly complete for a major exercise in the Atlantic. This exercise has an amphibious phase and they will be embarking army units with air defence capability. This doesn't sound like the usual naval exercises that use the marines. I think they plan to land on Las Malvinas before winter comes and they wish to defend the airfield at Stanley so they'll be able to bring in more troops. To regain Las Malvinas would be a tremendous coup for the Junta and everyone would support them, even La Nación.'

As Ridley listened to him he realized how much the desire to regain the Falklands burned in the heart of every Argentine. 'Probably Cristina feels the same,' he thought. Trying not to be too obvious, he probed a little more, hoping fervently that Marini's senses were sufficiently blunted by the alcohol so he didn't realize he was being pumped for information. 'Do your informants give any indication when this may occur?'

'No, only that it will happen before winter. So, to me that means they have to invade by May at the latest. Perhaps they are delaying to ensure the United States and Latin American states are on our side. I understand the United States will support Argentina because they wish to remain the main influence in the Americas. They don't want any more left-wing governments developing like Chile's in the 1970s.'

As they had been talking and drinking, without them realizing it, the place had filled up, the room was dense with cigarette smoke and there was a hubbub. Then a sense of anticipation began to pervade the room and a hush descended, broken by loud applause as the jazz combo appeared, led on by the saxophonist, followed by the drummer, trumpet player and double bass. Without any delay once they had settled, the bass player began a complicated rhythm that was picked up by the drums, the trumpet wove the first variation, followed by the saxophonist taking it on in a style very reminiscent of John Coltrane at his best. In Ridley's judgement this was one of the best jazz groups he had heard in a long time. There was a raw earthiness there, in the way they attacked the notes, but overlaid with a thin veneer of sophistication. They listened more or less in silence for more than an hour just commenting occasionally about the music until the group took a break, then Ridley asked, 'Señor Marini would you be able to keep me in touch with the developments you referred to earlier? It concerns me that this might occur and I wouldn't want to be investing here until this was resolved. I am not asking you to compromise your country's security but some warning would allow me to delay. Perhaps you could just mention your scoop has come off or some such words as soon as you hear it is about to happen.'

Marini thought about Ridley's request for a while then he nodded, 'I can't see any problem with that.' He laughed, 'Even if you're a British spy it would be too late for the British to prevent it by that stage as they have no forces worth considering down here.'

They listened to another fantastic jazz set and then Ridley thanked Marini for inviting him and began to say his farewells. It was after midnight when Ridley finally set a glass of whiskey down in front of Marini who looked as though he would stay all night. Ridley departed pleading an early appointment tomorrow.

The next morning he was back with the management accountants. By the end of the day they had run through every possible business scenario and tax model, and he was confident he had all the information he needed. Heading back to his apartment he dressed for the dinner at the Japanese Embassy in honour of the businessmen from Japanese companies currently in Argentina, thinking, 'I really hope

194

Elena Mantovani from the Foreign Ministry will attend. Hopefully she will provide some clues to Argentine thinking.'

Promptly at seven-thirty his taxi drew up outside the entrance to the embassy on the Plaza Roma in the Microcentro and he presented his invitation at the door. Escorted by the attendant to a main reception room, he found the reception line waiting and introduced himself to the ambassador and his wife, renewed his acquaintance with Mr Tanaka and then greeted Yamauchi warmly. Moving on he accepted a glass of champagne from the waiter and looked around the room. As he expected all the businessmen had already arrived, as it would be impolite for Japanese to arrive later than the stated time for drinks. He couldn't see Señora Mantovani so assuming she came, she was clearly going to be 'Latin' and arrive late. He wandered over to someone he recognized from another Japanese pharmaceutical company and they shared business experiences for a while. Then there was a flurry at the door and he saw Señora Mantovani arrive accompanied by a younger man who presumably was an aide. Other than the ambassador's wife she was the only woman present in this male-dominated gathering but she didn't seem daunted by this. She moved with poise into the room escorted by Yamauchi. 'The smooth bastard,' thought Ridley. Again she was dressed in a smart knee-length suit, but in a lighter shade of green than last time. 'She clearly knows that green complements her red hair,' he observed. The Japanese attaché quickly got her a glass of champagne, and steered her into the opposite corner of the room from Ridley where another group of Japanese businessmen had congregated.

After a decent interval Ridley found an attendant at his shoulder and with a formal bow he was led to his seat at a very long, wide table. As he approached he found he was seated next to her in the centre of the table with the ambassador and his wife directly opposite. As everyone sat down he could indeed see that the young man must be an aide because he had been seated at one end of the table, and that Yamauchi was slipping into the seat on the other side of her. Ridley observed that the table was so wide that those on the opposite side would not overhear the conversations on this side, and with Yamauchi next to her little of any conversation would be overheard. 'These diplomats are very skilled in these things,' he thought admiringly.

The meal followed traditional Japanese lines and Yamauchi, and occasionally Ridley, gallantly explained the courses to her. It was clear she was enjoying the meal and the attention she was receiving. About half way through the meal Yamauchi suggested that the next dishes should be accompanied by saki and asked if she would like to try this drink. 'The old devil is trying to get her tipsy,' thought Ridley. She said she would like to try it so a glass of the heady rice wine was served and it was clear it quickly had some effect as her cheeks became slightly flushed. Yamauchi then asked her quietly whether there was any truth in the rumour that her government might invade Las Malvinas and Ridley held his breath.

'As you know, Mr Yamauchi, like you I am a career diplomat and I was trained to think that resorting to war was a failure of diplomacy. I feel sure that my colleagues and I could achieve a compromise with Britain about Las Malvinas, leading to joint sovereignty in a few years. Unfortunately, the Foreign Ministry is being excluded from the discussions and I hear some military expedition is being considered. Whether or not this is just to be used as a bargaining chip I cannot say.'

To keep her talking Ridley asked, 'Do you have no influence on the Junta then?'

'No, I don't think we do. Since the new president was appointed the liberal members of the Junta seem to have either lost influence or been replaced by hardliners. There is still a more liberal force in Argentina but it has gone to ground to survive. Some day we may be able to exert more influence but not at present. '

Noting her use of 'we' he gently moved the conversation on to safer ground and told her about the progress he was making with his business project and then Yamauchi steered her away to meet some other people over coffee. Ridley got down to the serious business of drinking Suntory whiskey with the other guests. After she had left Yamauchi came over to Ridley and they sat in a corner and reviewed what she had said. After agreeing to meet for lunch tomorrow in Montevideo Ridley departed for his apartment.

Thursday 21st January John was on the first ferry to Montevideo and soon in the office of the embassy finance adviser. At lunchtime Yamauchi popped his head around the office door and suggested they go to lunch. He took him to a restaurant near the Plaza Independencia saying Ridley could probably do with a break from meat. This restaurant, La Vegetariana, served some of the best vegetarian dishes in Uruguay and as John knew the Japanese appreciate vegetarian cooking. It also turned out to be fairly quiet so they found a remote corner where they might talk privately and John briefed his friend on the outcome of his trip. He described Marini's revelation and they also reviewed Elena Mantovani's comments. Yamauchi made some notes for the brief message he would send to SIS that evening.

Business over, John told him when he would be visiting Tokyo and how the business presentation process worked in Nippon Health. In a splendid Japanese non-confrontational way business proposals were presented to the board on a Tuesday and the board then reviewed them individually and in various interest groups. There was another board meeting three days later when the decisions were communicated and plans confirmed. In fact of course only those to be approved were on the agenda for the second meeting. If your project wasn't listed then it had been rejected but you didn't lose face by having to attend the meeting. So John would be in Tokyo on Monday 1st February when the papers would be typed in Japanese. Tuesday he would present the paper then he had to wait until Friday 5th to hear the result.

'I shall also be in Japan then, Ridley-san,' remarked Yamauchi. 'I am due some leave and have decided to go to my family home for a week. I'll be at Arita on Kyushu for the whole of the first week in February. I'd be honoured if you would visit me and my family for a few days. You can fly down to Osaka then catch the plane to Nagasaki on Tuesday evening and could return to Tokyo on the Thursday afternoon. We can spend some time in the hills and we can also visit the porcelain factory. On your last visit did you visit the house where Puccini wrote the opera Madame Butterfly?'

'No, but I would be interested in seeing that,' said John. 'May I check the itinerary and then let you know?' Seeing his friend nod his acceptance John thanked him for the lunch and they headed back to the embassy. Soon afterwards Ridley was back at the Darsena Fluvial as the next ferry completed disembarkation and the first passengers began moving onboard.

Friday 22nd January 10 a.m. saw Ridley being ushered into Señor Roca's office at the Ministry of Health, surprised to find him on his own.

Seeing his glance Roca explained, 'Señora Sabata is on leave today. She's having a long weekend away with some girl friends. I gather they've gone down to Mar del Plata for some sun. Señor Ridley, you promised to give me a progress report before you go to Japan. Should we sit at the conference table?'

'Señor Roca, I must start by thanking you for the assistance both you and Señora Sabato have provided on this trip. It's made it so much easier to complete my proposal. I've also received a lot of help from the Japanese Embassy here. I feel very confident I have a good business case and I am hopeful that the board will feel the same. The only difference from my previous plan is that I may use the sales force of the pharmaceutical distributor in Comodoro Rivadavia to sell our products in southern Patagonia rather than our own sales representative. I think this is a more cost-effective option.'

After Roca had asked a few more questions and the inevitable coffee had been consumed, Ridley took his leave saying he would not be back until around mid-March when he would prepare the formal business application. Back at the apartment he tidied up his papers and made sure all his clothes were stowed away neatly then packed his bags. Having told reception when he was likely to return, he waited for the taxi to arrive and then descended into the foyer, said *adiós* to the receptionist and kissed her on both cheeks, before jumping into the taxi that headed southeast to the international airport out at Ezeiza.

Following his usual route he landed in Miami and after a couple of hours his American Airlines connecting flight to Toronto was called. Before long it was taxiing out and after take off, he had a quick meal and then went off to sleep as usual. He slept soundly and only woke as breakfast

199

was served and just before 6 a.m. Saturday 23rd January the flight landed. It had been a full flight with vacationers returning after a spell in Florida as a break from the Canadian winter, and he was glad he was in business class.

Toronto January 1982

The bags took quite a time to appear and he wondered whether they were still in Miami or on the ground at Ezeiza, but then he saw them at the end of the conveyor. Walking out through customs and into the arrivals hall he was suddenly assailed by this sweet-smelling creature hugging him tightly, crying 'John, I have missed you.'

Pushing his trolley to one side he took her in his arms and calmed her, gently kissed her and stroked her hair and whispered endearments to her. Thinking with wonderment how much she loved him, and guiltily about how little he has thought of her. Making a promise to both of them that if he got out of this current business alive he wouldn't put her through it ever again.

Eventually disentangling himself from her embrace but holding her hand tightly he moved towards the underground car park where she had parked the car. Collecting herself she led the way and soon they were heading into town to his apartment. She swung competently into the underground garage and a different numbered space. As he looked quizzically at her she explained, 'I asked your leasing company if there was a spare place as I'd be spending a lot of time at your place. They told me it was OK for us to have two spaces.'

Going up to the flat Andy rather nervously admitted, 'John, I needed something to do while you were away. I hope you don't mind but I decided I would make the spare bedroom mine and I've chosen some things to make it special for me. You know bed linen, some ornaments and pictures just to make it feel like mine.'

Sensing her nervousness he quickly reassured her, 'Andy, this place is as much yours as mine. We are engaged and you know the vows we'll make when we get married, so I have no problem with what you've done. In fact I'm delighted.'

Referring to business Andy proposed, 'I suggest we follow our usual routine regarding the debriefing as I don't think there is real urgency. Better for you to be fully rested. So we'll do it Monday. I've seen a synopsis of the report Yamauchi sent through based on your report I think we should delve more into the background on Monday.

'However,' she added very forcefully, 'I want a private debrief now about these women you have been wining and dining and dragging about the country.'

John sighed, 'I know I won't get any peace until I give you the low down on this so here goes. Maria came on Saturday morning and left on Monday morning. I must have a fantastic reputation with the young receptionist at the suites because one hour later Cristina Sabato arrived to whisk me off to the airport.' At this male chauvinism Andy pouted. 'Anyway it's clear Maria is desperately unhappy and wishes she'd never married Gomez who she hardly sees at all. She sees me as family, as her big brother, and that's how we spent the weekend. In a way it's all so sad. She doesn't identify with the Argentines and hates southern Patagonia. She says she'll help me if I need her to because she thinks of me as family. She also said she believes it's time she stood up for democracy in Argentina. So after thinking hard I've decided I can trust her.'

Looking directly at Andy, John said very sincerely, 'Cristina Sabato is clearly in love with me but understands I'm engaged. She's stopped trying to get me into her bed but is still very fond of me and wants to be a friend. I asked her whether she could help me if I needed to find a bolthole and she said she would whatever the risk. She's a very straight person and won't let me down if it is in her power. I think she's guessed what I am doing but hasn't asked me directly.'

'OK that reassures me,' said Andy. 'It's not that I distrusted you, John. It's just the uncertainty caused by not knowing the details. You must tell me more about them so I can know them as women.'

Changing the subject she said, 'I thought it might be good for you to relax this weekend. I've seen Angie while you've been away and we've been invited to spend a quiet weekend with her, Ross and the children. We're planning to eat in this evening, but before then do lots of walking in the cold bright air this afternoon and then tomorrow because you probably need the exercise. We're expected for lunch today so we'll have to get ourselves organized. I hope that is OK?'

'That sounds a great plan,' agreed John. 'It'll be nice just to relax with friends and not have to stay on top line all the time. You're right about exercise. I really must get in the gym next week. Do you really like their children?'

She smiled brightly, 'Yes I do. They're so full of optimism and vitality. I was so lonely last weekend that I rang Angie and asked if I might stay. They were both most kind and Angie and the kids really made me feel part of the family.' Blushing slightly she added, 'I would like children like that.'

'Me too,' agreed John affectionately. 'Once we're married you tell me when you want to start and I'll do my best to oblige.'

So having laid another building block for their life together they happily packed bags and headed along the lakeshore to Burlington, where they spent a lovely weekend with their friends.

Monday 25th January found Andy and John seated in his study each with a fresh cup of coffee to hand. John waited for Andy to collect her thoughts and then to lead the debriefing. 'It might be best if I summarize what we have from Yamauchi and then check you agree with the assessment. Then add other points afterwards. This might save time.' Then she corrected herself, 'No that would be wrong because it'll influence what you say. We'd better follow standard procedure. You go over the key points for every day in Argentina and I'll capture them and then we can look at what it tells us. I have a deadline of 4 p.m. today as I have a 5 p.m. call booked on the secure line to SIS and I'm told Andrew Collingwood will be present also.'

So John began to give an economical but precise account of all his actions since he arrived in Argentina on the 11th January. He described the helpful stance of Roca of the Ministry of Health and the provision of Cristina Sabato as his aide and more if he had wanted it. She had told him she had to report on his doings and she felt it must be something about him personally that concerned them, not some economic security concern related to the business initiative, as the security service had never shown this level of interest in any other pharmaceutical project. 'I also had a run in with an obnoxious little shit from either Argentine Military Intelligence or Internal Security. His name was Colonel Lupo. His background should be investigated. He accosted me on the ferry back from Montevideo on Friday fifteenth. It was a 'fishing expedition' and an attempt to panic me to see whether I would betray myself. Without having any evidence he suggested my project might be a cover for some other activities. He wasn't explicit.' Keeping his tone light he added, 'He also suggested I got up to all sorts of sexual antics with Cristina Sabato. I rejected his innuendos firmly but I don't think I gave him any hint of a weakness to exploit. It was easy to deny his suggestion, for it wasn't true,' he added looking directly at her. 'Even more laughable was his suggestion that I was meeting Tony Marini for homosexual sessions!'

'He really sounds horrible! This took place on the upper deck of the ferry in earshot of other people?'

Ridley shook his head. 'No, they are cleverer than that. His henchmen kept other passengers off the upper deck so it was deserted except for the two of us. They did it to increase the tension.'

As John recounted this, Andy frowned and made a note in capitals on her notepad, but made no comment to him.

He moved on to describe the two meetings with Marini. 'He clearly felt the current tension with Chile would be defused and was more excited about a possible operation against the Falklands. Until I heard him talk I hadn't realized how strongly the Argentines feel about recovering them from the British. I can understand the temptation for the Junta as the national chauvism of the Argentines means the people will be right behind them. The telling point is the amphibious exercise he described that involved army and air defence equipment suitable for airfield defence. I agree with him that this indicates a test of an amphibious operation against an island with an airfield. The only one likely is Stanley airfield on East Falkland. You must emphasize this national feeling about Las Malvinas because

I think it's important, and the significance of this amphibious exercise.'

Moving on he described his two trips with Cristina Sabato to Bahia Blanca and Comodoro Rivadavia, ignoring the slight bristling in Andy. Given the tension with Chile he suggested, 'It was quite strange there was no real activity at the fleet base. Yamauchi's view that the only action being taken involves the army and air force is probably correct.' He told her Yamauchi reckoned the army had reinforced west along the border and that a squadron of Mirage 3s had moved to Rio Gallegos. He described the cove south of Bahia that could be a good OP on the Puerto Belgrano base and they got out the map and pinpointed it for the report. Andy resisted the temptation to ask what John and Cristina did there.

'What about Comodoro Rivadavia?' queried Andy, 'It's their main oil producing centre. Would it be vulnerable to attack?'

'No,' replied John, 'like most oilfields attack from the air is a waste of time. You need to get the oil running out of the pipelines and then ignite it. The wells look fairly dispersed and they have those nodding donkey pumps that are pretty robust. You might attack them using SBS but I'd've thought it would be a dramatic escalation to do this. I doubt whether the politicians would ever sanction it.

'No, the main learning point about Comodoro Rivadavia is that the commercial port could easily handle the embarkation of an invasion force. The distance to the Falklands is much shorter from there than from Bahia Blanca. There's only a limited naval presence for fishery protection I guess, with all the fleet operations controlled from fleet base at Puerto Belgrano at Bahia. So we need to keep an eye on it as a possible transport base.'

205

He went on to describe Yamauchi's planning and the selection of Piriápolis as a good base in Uruguay with good access from Brazil via the nearby airport at Moldanado. He also reassured Andy that they had a good escape route and described the possible safe house in the delta near Tigre, and Yamauchi's boatman from Carmelo who could come through the delta waterways and secretly pick him up near Tigre to get him back to Uruguay.

Finally he described his discussion with Elena Mantovani. 'She's clearly very concerned by the Junta's plans and I would judge she is privy to much secret information. She did say Las Malvinas specifically at one stage, so we can be clear about the focus of her concerns. Apart from that I think the most important information she imparted was the fact that the Junta had lurched to the right following the appointment of the new president, and the liberal members had either lost influence or been replaced by hardliners. She was keen to get across the point that there are still some liberals out there who believe in diplomacy and might be willing to work with us at some stage. She also identified herself with them.'

Pausing to collect his final thoughts John said to her, 'Andy, please make it clear in the report that I believe: the Argentines are planning to invade the Falkland Islands before winter comes down there; that such a move will be supported by the Argentine people; they believe the USA will be sympathetic; that the Junta are only contemplating it because of our weakness in the South Atlantic; that an increased temporary naval presence in the South Atlantic, for example an extended task group exercise centred on the Falklands, would probably deter them.'

As he stopped and opened his arms to imply that was all he had, she looked through her notes and began to probe and query his statements, and this continued during lunch, a hastily assembled salad taken in the study. Eventually she indicated she had had enough and giving him a brief affectionate kiss on the lips, she headed off into her new room to work on her report. He decided he was too tired to turn to Nippon Health matters that afternoon. So he opened a bottle of chilled Chablis Premier Cru and sat in his sitting room enjoying the view over the city while the sounds of Dave Brubeck's jazz came gently from the hi-fi. Later Andy put on her outdoor clothes and headed off to her office, and John promised to have a meal ready for them on her return.

Chapter Fourteen

Buenos Aires 26th January 1982

As the late summer sun streamed in through his office window General Alfredo Coro sat at his large desk in Argentine Military Intelligence located in army headquarters close to the Plaza de Mayo, and listened attentively to the report his aide, Colonel Johnson, was presenting. Also present at the meeting were Colonel Lupo from Internal Security and Coro's personal assistant.

'Sir, we have maintained a surveillance on John Ridley for the whole of his present business trip and I have to say we can find no evidence of any intelligence-gathering activities by him. He hasn't met any opposition agitators or politicians. He did meet Tony Marini of La Nación but we think it was to get some publicity for his company and its new business development. He accepted the assistance of Señora Sabato readily enough, but not her sexual advances, and she reports that on all her visits with him she judged he was working on his business project and nothing else. That is the proposal to set up this pharmaceutical subsidiary here for Nippon Health that he told you about on his first trip. She reports that he is engaged to a woman in Canada and seems very much in love with her, and very loyal to her. Our request for information from the CIA brought a negative report on both of them from the CIA and the Canadians.

'There was one strange incident however. The maid at his

208

apartment in the Esmeralda Suites reported that a woman was staying there over the weekend of the 16 to 17th January but it wasn't Sabato. She reckoned the woman was sleeping in the second bedroom, not in Ridley's bed. We managed to get a photographer down there early on the Monday morning and got a shot of her and Ridley as she left. We think she is Maria Gomez, the wife of that financial expert helping the Junta at the moment. As she left they kissed more as friends than lovers.'

'Is Rafael Gomez still playing around with that Alfonso woman?'

'Yes, he is like a dog on heat with her. Making a bit of a spectacle with her. I think he has established her as his mistress in an apartment somewhere in the Palermo district.'

Colonel Johnson continued his report, 'We don't know how Ridley met the Gomez woman but she was born in Spain so perhaps they know each other from there. Ridley speaks Spanish very well so it's possible he met her when he was studying the language. Interestingly she has dual nationality as she retained her Spanish citizenship after marrying Gomez.'

Coro decided, 'We won't say anything to Rafael Gomez about this. You know what these dogs are like. They go after every woman in sight but as soon as one of their women looks at another man it is all about their honour being besmirched. Ridley is probably OK but there is something about him that makes me uneasy. I just can't place it. Something at the back of my memory that I can't quite get hold of. As he isn't expected back here before the middle of March, let's shelve it for the moment. When he returns we should keep an eye on him so he doesn't find out anything embarrassing. Although by then it'll probably be too late.'

Buenos Aires February 1982

Monday 1st February was a wonderfully warm, sunny, late summer day with a cloudless blue sky, and people making the most of it strolling around the city and across the Plaza de Mayo. Gazing out from his office the president thought, 'This is a great day for Argentina, I'm glad I'm making this momentous decision on such a beautiful day. It really might come off. Before too long, this country will be celebrating Las Malvinas Day annually.'

Turning to the assembled senior officers the president said, 'So gentlemen, I see from your final operation report for Operation Rosario that you are satisfied we can re-take Las Islas Malvinas quite easily. The exercises to practice our amphibious capability have gone well and it seems the British have no idea of our plans. I am told by the Foreign Ministry, our American friends are willing to remain on the sidelines and the British diplomats believe we're just posturing in our threats about the islands. It's lucky their diplomats are asleep. So provided you can achieve complete surprise, and we can build up our invasion force quickly, the British will find us impossible to remove and Las Islas Malvinas will be ours for ever. There's still no indication that the British plan to reinforce their marines on the island or station more naval vessels there?'

'No sir,' replied the Fleet Admiral. 'They seem very arrogant and complacent. We are now equipped with some of their guided-missile destroyers, and we have our aircraft carrier and the cruiser General Belgrano, so we are a powerful force these days. Our ships are well maintained and at a high state of readiness and the British know it. Given the closeness of the islands to the mainland they would have difficulty operating there without air cover. We assess they will just very reluctantly give up possession. No doubt they'll complain to the UN Security Council but we can ignore that and make counter claims in New York ourselves. We have plenty of friends there these days. After all, they did steal the islands from us originally,' he added defiantly.

'All that remains to be decided then is the start date for the operation,' suggested the president. 'I think we should bring the forces to readiness on 1st March. This gives time for more diplomacy and at the beginning of March we will set the final date for the invasion. If we haven't begun by the end of April this year it'll be too late in the year because of the winter storms. In that case we'll have to delay until 1983.' Looking at the assembled admirals, army and air force generals he uttered the fateful words, 'Please issue the necessary orders with immediate effect for Operation Rosario, the invasion of Las Islas Malvinas.'

Having been given the orders the Junta members and other senior officers from the three military services burst into spontaneous ecstatic applause for the president and the expected glory for Argentina.

Ezeiza February 1982

The aircrew climbed into the back of the unmarked white van that swiftly carried them to the airliner with civilian markings parked out near the maintenance hangars on the far side of the airport. The aircraft was painted in the colours of a small private Chilean airline that operated out of Punta Arenas in Chilean Patagonia. However, this was no civilian passenger jet but an Argentine secret reconnaissance jet. The navy crew slipped out of their civilian uniforms, donned aircrew overalls and completed the final checks. Then the engines were started and the plane taxied quickly out to the main runway where the flight was given takeoff priority and was soon climbing clear of the airfield. When it was out of sight of the airfield the plane banked to port and steadied on a course that took it out over the South Atlantic. Eventually it would turn south and fly directly over Islas Malvinas before heading southwest towards the Argentine coast and the plane's destination, Rio Gallegos.

Closing the islands from the north some of the crew took up their positions at the electronic monitoring stations and the aerial cameras in the fuselage, while others stood by to carry out a visual scrutiny of the harbours and surrounding seas. Coming in over Berkeley Sound the chief pilot slowed the aircraft and they checked Stanley town and the airfield as they passed over them. Then as they reached 52°S 59°W at Lively Island they banked to starboard and flew over the Bay of Islands to West Falkland Island then headed southwest for Rio Gallegos.

The Captain hadn't spotted anything unusual and checked whether the crew had spotted anything. All was apparently quiet: no British warships anywhere near the islands, no strange electronic emissions and no unusual activity at Stanley airfield. As one of the crew joked, 'Just thousands of sheep.'

The high command had ordered that these flights would take place every two or three days until the invasion took place, using a number of different planes and flight plans so that the British remained unsuspecting until the invasion force arrived. Should any British aircraft or navy ships arrive they would be quickly spotted. The Argentines were leaving nothing to chance.

Japan February 1982

Monday 1st February, as the fateful decision was being made in Buenos Aires, Ridley was landing in Tokyo after his flight from Toronto via a refuelling stop in Anchorage. Picked up by a company chauffeur at Narita, Tokyo's international airport, he was driven into the company's headquarters and an immediate meeting with Mr Tana, the business development director. After explaining the key proposals to him and gaining his support he went to the office that had been made available for him. There he met the secretary allocated to him who he found spoke excellent English and seemed very efficient. In fact he soon realized the importance the company was placing on his proposal for she had as her assistant a young woman graduate trainee who also spoke English. They assured Ridley-san that the paper would be completed and circulated to all the directors before the end of the working day. Once this was achieved they would help him with his presentation slides. He learnt he was first on the agenda at the meeting the next day so his presentation would begin at 10 a.m. and he had one hour, followed by a period of questions. Nippon Health followed the principle adopted by the computer company Hewlett Packard: 'If a proposal is well worked through it is possible to summarize the key points on one sheet of paper.' Whilst not adopted rigorously it was seen as an excellent test of a project's validity and so brevity was highly valued.

So with little to do for the rest of the day except answer the queries of his staff as they prepared the documents, he roughed out the main points he wished to put over during the presentation and drafted a few slides that summarized the key business parameters. He then had time to think through some of the next steps and what he would have to do on his next trip to Argentina. At midday Mr Tana's secretary knocked on his door and, after bowing low, invited Ridley to lunch in Mr Tana's office. Following her into Tana's office he found laid out on the table the neat boxes of sushi and a flask of Japanese tea. Over lunch Tana explained that both the company and the Japanese government were expressing satisfaction with the way his project was being conducted in South America. He said the embassy in Argentina had received favourable comments from the Ministries of Health in both Argentina and Uruguay. ('If only they really knew,' thought Ridley.)

Tana also passed on the thanks of the personnel director, and then to Ridley's surprise, because it was completely out of the company culture, presented him with a large box as an engagement present. Ridley thought, 'Wheels within wheels, for the only Japanese who knew I was engaged was Yamauchi-san.' Remembering that in Japanese society it was impolite to open a present in the presence of the giver, he bowed very deeply as befitted the junior to a senior and thanked him and the company for their kind gift. Returning to his office and, with the two young women crowding round excitedly, he opened the beautifully wrapped package. Inside the large box he found a wonderful lacquer vase about eighteen inches high, beautifully curved and proportioned and in that deep lustrous red that he had long admired. Inside the vase there was a beautiful little card saying both in English and Japanese, 'With best wishes to Ridley-san and his lady from his friends at Nippon Health'. Ridley was overcome at this expression of friendship from his Japanese colleagues although he roused himself as the ladies badgered him for information about his fiancée, what did she look like, what did she wear, did she cook, did she work etc? 'I really will have to tell Andy all about this,' he thought and resolved to call her Tuesday morning before he made his presentation. Sitting down at his desk he wrote a formal handwritten note as convention demanded to thank Mr Tana and the company for the kind gift.

When all the preparations were completed he went across to the Akasaka Tokyu Hotel and after having some delicious Kobe beef in the restaurant, spent a quiet evening watching the regular samurai film on TV. He couldn't understand much of the dialogue but the action was good.

Tuesday 2nd he rang Andy early and she said she couldn't wait to see the gift. He then walked over to the Nippon Health offices in good time to collect his slides and run through his presentation. After this he went along to the board room to await his summons by the chairman's secretary. When it came, he entered the room and bowed very low twice to the assembled directors of the company then he made his presentation in English for, unusually for a Japanese company, he knew that they all spoke good English. His slides however were in Japanese and he had a crib of each one in English for himself. His presentation seemed to go well for he saw a number of them nodding in agreement as he moved through the recommendations. At question time he felt even more comfortable for the questions raised were very perceptive and clearly based on the paper circulated yesterday afternoon. So most of them had at least read it. Finally the chairman brought the proceedings to an end. 'Ridley-san, thank you for an excellent paper and the presentation today. I think we fully understand the proposal. We will now consider it in more detail over the next few days and let you know our decision on Friday.' Bowing deeply once more Ridley backed out of the room and went back to his temporary office for a well-earned cup of coffee.

Early afternoon, after thanking his ladies profusely for their work on his behalf and giving them little presents, he took the chauffeur car to the domestic airport at Haneda, and firstly the commuter jet to Osaka then the twin-engine turbojet to Nagasaki. Flying across the edge of the Inland Sea then over the north of Kyushu Island he was reminded of his last visit down there some ten years ago. He went there to take a look at a Russian Krivak destroyer that had run aground off Kagoshima. 'The Russians never had any luck down here,' he thought. 'In 1905 the Japanese Navy decimated the Russian Black Sea Fleet off Kagoshima. Then a modern Russian guided missile destroyer goes aground close inshore where it's easy to check all its weapons and surveillance systems.'

The plane came in across the city of Nagasaki and then flew across the harbour to the airport. Nagasaki was infamous as the first city destroyed by an atomic bomb. Completely rebuilt afterwards it still retained a sad air as though the very hills echo to the desperate cries of the burned and the irradiated. It was a city where people were still dying from the effects of the bomb. True to his word Yamauchi was there to greet him and quickly they drove north into the hills to the small town of Arita and its porcelain works. Arita along with its rival Noritake were the two famous Japanese porcelain manufacturers known the world over for the quality of their imperial porcelain.

They drove steadily up the narrow valley clothed in dense green vegetation past smallholdings, with each house sporting outside an inflatable fish on a pole for good luck. Eventually they arrived in the small town and stopped outside a house faced entirely in dark wood. Taking Ridley's bag Yamauchi led the way into the house, both slipping off their shoes in the doorway, where they met a smartly dressed modern young lady who turned out to be his daughter. Looking at his friend Ridley knew it wasn't the time to ask about it, but there was clearly some sadness here for he knew Yamauchi had never mentioned a wife.

The short break passed all to quickly. Yamauchi and his daughter were excellent hosts and they all had a happy time. They visited Yamauchi's parents who still lived in Arita, and they visited the guesthouse museum in the old international compound at Nagasaki where Puccini wrote his opera *Madame Butterfly*. There was a good view over the harbour, lovely gardens and a poignant sculpture of the heroine of the opera: the Japanese girl who loved and was deserted by her handsome American naval officer.

Seeing Yamauchi's daughter emotionally affected by the place, Ridley said gently, 'It is very sad isn't it that love doesn't always work out.'

She smiled sadly at him, 'Ridley-san you are very kind. I was thinking of my mother who died when I was only ten. Unfortunately she had cancer, perhaps caused by the bomb, perhaps not. My father and his family brought me up but sometimes I still miss her and feel very sad.'

Realising something was amiss Yamauchi came across and put his arm around his daughter. 'I am afraid we both get rather emotional here because it is a place she liked and she was very fond of western opera. Please forgive us, Ridley-san.'

'There's nothing to forgive,' Ridley assured them. 'I just hope you will both find happiness again in your lives.'

All too soon it was time for Ridley to leave and catch his plane back to Tokyo.

Friday morning 5th February he was again waiting outside the board room. At his hotel when he arrived there was a message to say his project was on the agenda this morning so he knew it was to be approved. Those whose projects had been turned down did not lose face by having to attend to hear their proposals had been rejected. He was gratified to find that all his recommendations were to be adopted. The necessary funding would be approved at the March board meeting provided the finance function agreed it. He was authorized to begin the application process in both Argentina and Uruguay to win approval to set up a subsidiary company in Argentina. Letters would be prepared and sent to the two ministries of health and also the Japanese Embassy confirming this decision.

As he was receiving their thanks and preparing to leave, the secretary handed him two envelopes. Returning to his office he discovered the first one contained an invitation to dinner that evening with the board at one of the best restaurants in Tokyo and he was requested to arrive at 7 p.m. The second contained an even greater surprise as it announced that he had been promoted to senior manager level and this was unheard of at his age. He was also awarded a bonus of C$ 5000, something that was quite strange, as this company didn't usually award bonuses.

As he knew the dinner would go on until late Ridley packed his luggage and made sure the lacquer vase was very safely packed. As he expected the dinner started in the bath and soon all the directors were in the hot water tubs enjoying a relaxing soak and chatting happily to each other. After drying off, they dressed in robes and slid sandals on to their feet, then sat on the tatami sofas for the formal Japanese meal. Ridley had to admit it was superb. A feast for the palate and the eyes, for the creations were fantastic. After much beer and saki the restaurant produced a videodisc player and a karaoke session ensued. Everyone sang including Ridley and they all laughed when he failed to remember the words. For Ridley, unlike the rest, was unable to read the captions at the bottom of the film. So ended a happy evening and after congratulating him on his promotion they said farewell.

Next morning February 6th Ridley travelled out to Narita to catch the Japanese Airlines flight to Toronto via Anchorage. He managed to save a day going back as he crossed the International Date Line. So he finally arrived in Toronto on Friday evening to be met by a happier-looking and more relaxed Andy James.

Arriving at his apartment he gave her the package. Opening it she carefully removed the vase from its wrappings. 'The only time I've ever seen anything like this it was in the V&A Museum in London,' she exclaimed. 'It's so beautiful. It must have cost a fortune. I love the colour, such a deep red! How nice of them to give us such a gift!'

John agreed, 'It is very good of them. I did write a formal note of thanks but I think it would be nice if you write a short note and I'll send it to Mr Tana. I presume Yamauchi-san must have mentioned my engagement to Tana because I hadn't informed him. By the way, I've also been promoted to senior manager and received a bonus so if you like you can have an expensive meal out this weekend.'

'Well done, darling, it is well deserved.' She hugged him affectionately and proudly. 'Mind, if they really knew what you're up to I doubt whether you'd get the bonus. I'd like to go out somewhere fancy tomorrow. I bought an outrageously expensive short dress this week and I'd like to show it off.' So they had a lovely weekend together happy because his next trip to Argentina was some weeks away.

Monday 8th February before going to work and leaving John to his Nippon Health personnel tasks, she updated him on London's reaction to his report. 'DNI and SIS – South American Desk – were delighted with your information. They believe it was high value and consistent with information from other sources outside Argentina. Unfortunately the Foreign Office continues to listen to messages from the US State Department, and the Secretary of State for Defence is too new to take any independent initiative. So they will not consider a movement of some fleet units, say for an exercise off the Falklands. So we're stymied. No one disputes the information but no one is prepared to take any action on it. It is the usual political mantra: 'doing nothing is safest'. So all we can do is try to give the navy sufficient warning, so they may reinforce the islands and present a show of force in the theatre before the Argentines get there.'

February passed quickly with both of them fully engrossed in their cover jobs. Occasionally Andy updated John on the current intelligence view but really there seemed to be little change evident. They braced themselves for the instruction to John to fit in another visit to Argentina but it never came. It seemed diplomatic efforts may be bearing fruit and the Foreign Office didn't want any complications stirred up by SIS or DNI. So they were allowed to live peacefully with each other. Steadily getting to know each other and themselves better, and falling more and more deeply in love. Heavy snow fell during the month and they were able to go skiing just outside of the city. Neither of them was an expert skier but they had fun in the snow, panting with the exertion of walking sideways up the low hills and then if they were lucky staying upright down the short slope, and laughing with pleasure if they succeeded. Throughout the afternoon they laughed and hugged each other with happiness.

John worked steadily on all the details of the business start-up. He spent hours on the phone to Nippon Health headquarters in Tokyo talking to the marketing, sales and finance experts until he was sure he had the best arrangements possible. The cost/profit projections were re-calculated weekly it seemed, but eventually everyone was satisfied, and he got the final approval to go ahead and commit Nippon Health's money for this development. So he communicated his final requirements to the real estate agents, the tax consultants and the recruitment agency.

He also forwarded Nippon Health's letter to the two health ministries and informed them he would be returning to begin the approval process on 15th March. He asked for early appointments with each of them and took the liberty of suggesting dates that would be convenient for him.

Toronto March 1982

Andy was very quiet over the whole of the first weekend in March. She was rather introspective and slow to smile, unusual for her. John recognized the signs though. 'We're a week away from my next trip and she's steeling herself for it,' he thought.

Monday 8th March she announced at breakfast, 'It's time to begin the detailed planning for your next trip. The last few weeks have been fantastic. The problem is it makes the next trip much harder to handle but I'm not going to give up my role. That would be even worse,' she added tersely. 'I've decided I should spend more time at my own flat this week and the night before you leave I'll certainly sleep there. I'm not doing anything different to break the good luck that's stayed with you so far.

'Today I have a series of conference calls with London so by the end of the day I should have an up-to-date intelligence assessment of the situation in Argentina. Mr Yamauchi should also provide an additional view so there'll be plenty of information to mull over. I suggest you come over to my place for breakfast tomorrow and we can spend the day working on this, and then you can take me to dinner. If you're a good boy I may even let you share my bed,' she ended lightly.

Tuesday 9th March it decided to snow heavily in Toronto. 'I hope this doesn't go on for too long as sometimes happens with March snows in Ontario,' worried John. 'It'd be very inconvenient to be unable to fly off this Sunday.' By the time he arrived at Andy's flat he resembled a walking snowman and had to spend time outside the entrance beating off the snow, and removing the rubber overshoes that protect the shoes and give good grip in the snow. Leaving them in the wet clothes area in the foyer he took the lift up to Andy's flat.

'Isn't the snow beautiful today?' she said as she opened the door. Looking out of her sitting room window he saw that in fact the sun was starting to shine through so perhaps the snow was easing. It was just a heavy flurry, not the storm he had feared. He remarked, 'I did hope this wasn't the start of a big snowstorm. We can get them here at this time of the year and all transport grinds to a halt including the airports.'

'Come and have some breakfast,' she encouraged, 'before we get started. I made a lot of progress yesterday so we should be able to finalize the planning today. This will allow you to make your travel arrangements and set up your appointments tomorrow.'

After breakfast she sat him down at her dining table where papers we neatly laid out. Picking up a folder she began to outline the present situation in Argentina. 'The British Government is beginning to become concerned at the attitude being taken by the Argentines, but they still see it as sabre rattling and a diplomatic bargaining ploy, rather than a real threat. The political and economic situation is deteriorating rapidly, and daily there are demonstrations against the Junta in Buenos Aires and the north of the country. Rampant inflation is developing and economic depression is extending. Unemployment has increased dramatically over the last few months and the Junta doesn't seem to have any policies to alleviate it. In fact all they do is crack down ever more severely on opponents.'

She added, 'As I know from my history studies the classic way that dictators have always persuaded people to support them in dire economic situations is to have a small successful war. The national fervour always diverts the thoughts of the people away from their own plight. As Argentina has a military dictatorship it would be surprising if they were not contemplating this. We believe they are and the heads of SIS and DNI support this assessment. Unfortunately the Government won't grasp the nettle. Your boss has persuaded the Admiralty – not the MOD. So covert planning is going on. Your information may be used quickly if they do invade. SBS are working on OPs for the fleet and airbases based on your information so far, but they'd like some more detail about the airbase at Rio Gallegos. CinC Fleet is also reviewing fleet dispositions and has quietly brought ships back for quick Assisted Maintenance Periods in case they are needed. They are also updating the list of merchant ships that can be brought under naval control at short notice. But that is as far as the navy can go without ministerial support.'

'That sounds a comprehensive assessment,' remarked John. 'I'm glad someone has listened,' he added drily. 'I am glad the navy is at least making some preparations. So I definitely have to get down to Rio Gallegos. I'll have to see how it works out, but early on I should go to Bahia Blanca and Mar del Plata and check on the fleet movements from there. Also see what's happening at the airbases down there. He smiled, 'I can use Cristina Sabato as cover.'

'Mind that is all you use her for,' she retorted.

John continued, 'I have to see the two ministries in BA and Montevideo early on otherwise my trip might excite suspicion. I think I should also try to have an early drink with Tony Marini to see if he has any new facts. If nothing looks like happening I'll proceed with the business set-up actions but leave the meeting with the pharmaceutical distributor in Comodoro Rivadavia as late as possible, as it provides me with the cover for getting into central Patagonia. I also feel they'll use this good port to ship back-up equipment and troops as it's much closer to the Falklands than the fleet base at Puerto Belgrano.'

Turning to face her and looking very serious he pointed out, 'You do realize that should the balloon go up, I will have to dispense with my cover. My best chance of avoiding arrest will be to move quickly and change my behaviour. So far I've flown everywhere and not avoided my "minders". I'll still have to fly to Comodoro Rivadavia but that's necessary for speed. I'll lose any shadow I may have then pick up a car and drive south. I can check the airbase at Puerto San Julian on the way then drive on to Rio Gallegos. It's a long drive but the country should be empty and the main road, RN 3 is very good, so I should make good time. I'll be gambling they won't expect anyone to travel in by road and they won't have security checks set up. Anyway, at some stage they'll close these southern airbases to civilian flights.'

He added, 'If I can make this rapid trip down the coast I might avoid detection, but I won't be able to get information back because they're bound to control international phone calls from down there. You'd better inform Arthur Dean that he should let it be known he intends to make a number of visits over the next couple of weeks. The places he might visit will be my itinerary. Tell him I'll confirm my trip plans at our contacts in the gents in the BA hotel. By the way, I think we should vary the meeting points and times in BA. How about using the Phoenix and San Martin Hotels? They are fairly close together. I would suggest he should be in the Phoenix on the 15th, then the San Martin for the next two nights, then the Phoenix for three nights. Then start again. I also think alternate nights he should be in the gents at 6 and 7 p.m. Sunday 21st he does one night at the San Martin to restart the cycle. That should confuse any watchers.

'I'll tell him the hotels I'll use in Bahia Blanca, Comodoro Rivadavia and Rio Gallegos. Tell him we'll do the newspaper dead letter drop at six in the morning and I'll find a way to show him my room number the night before. He'll then need to get the information across to Yamauchi as quickly as possible.'

Andy mused, 'Getting information out is always the problem, isn't it? I wonder how many of our agents have obtained fantastic intelligence in the past but we've never known because they were stuck with it. I think your caution is justified and you're correct in assuming they'll shut down communications. Until they actually invade, if they're going to, they won't want to prevent a journalist from North America going into Patagonia, as it'd look too suspicious. So Arthur Dean should still be able to move around and get the information out. Yamauchi was setting up the link with Dean. I'll check the contact arrangements are robust and secure.'

'I've left the most difficult phase till last,' John pointed out. 'I think I can get down to Rio Gallegos and I can get the initial information out by Arthur Dean from there. I'll probably need to establish an OP on the airfield for a day at least to check what's operating from there. I presume the navy is still anxious about the whereabouts of the Dassault Super Etendards with their Exocet carrying capability?'

'Yes, they still believe they represent the biggest threat to any fleet operations around the Falklands.'

'So I do need to hang around there. My best plan, given I have no business reason for being down there, is to quietly dump the hire car at the airport and get Maria to pick me up. The hire company may just assume I took a flight out and didn't bother to tell them. I'll just have to claim I'm a businessman doing a few days sightseeing if questioned. I need a good observation point from which I can do the monitoring.'

'Where will you have your OP?'

'I think I spotted a small hill on the map about three kilometres west of the base so that might do. My problem will be getting out afterwards. I'd thought about Maria taking the RN 40 inland route but it's a very rough road and I think speed will be vital. So we'll try to avoid Rio Galle-gos then cut back onto the coast road, the RN 3, and head directly to Comodoro Rivadavia. We need to check all this on the map. The journey should take the best part of a day.

I can fly out and she can go back. Although I'll try to persuade her to come with me.'

'Are you very concerned for her?' asked Andy.

'I guess so, ' replied John. 'I suspect her husband is an arrogant bastard and we know he's an ultra nationalist. Should he find out she's helped me I don't think he'd listen to any protestations that she was only helping a friend. I have no option however, if we want to get the information I'll have to use her.'

Looking at him Andy saw yet another side of this complex man she loved. He was warm, loving, gentle and caring but if it was necessary he could act coldly and ruthlessly. She realized it might be hard for him but if necessary he would be the same with her. She was surprised to realize this didn't affect her love for him at all.

The briefing continued for most of the day, then Andy returned to her office to set in train the agreed actions, and John prepared faxes setting up his various meetings in Argentina.

Later Andy returned to report that their respective bosses agreed their plan. She had also spoken with Jim Graham at Canadian Intelligence and he would ensure that Arthur Dean was fully briefed and understood the need for extreme caution. They then strolled down to their favourite restaurant, Giovanni's in King Street East, where they spent a quiet evening together enjoying the excellent Italian Milanese cuisine.

The rest of the week passed very quickly for Ridley as he had his Nippon Health personnel work to do as well as making the final preparations for his trip to Argentina: ensuring he had all his travel tickets, the apartment in Esmeralda Suites would be ready for him, and being reassured by the car rental company in Comodoro Rivadavia

227

that they would be able to provide a car for him at short notice should he require one.

Time however didn't pass very quickly for Andy for she had little to do apart from monitor the regular intelligence briefs passing across the desk. She thought, 'I hate the few days before he goes but I hate it far more when he is away and in danger. I must go to see Angie and Ross and the kids this Sunday when he has gone. They'll cheer me up.'

Chapter Fifteen

Buenos Aires March 1982

Monday 8th March there was a further meeting in General Alfredo Coro's office concerning John Ridley. Colonel Johnson reported to the assembled group of military intelligence officers, 'Ridley will be arriving back here on the 15th. He has apparently gained the approval of his company to set up a subsidiary here. He'll be making a formal application to the Ministry of Health and looking for staff. It appears to be a genuine business initiative by this Japanese company.'

Coro glanced sharply at him, 'I still think there's something not quite right about him. I just can't put my finger on it. We'd better keep an eye on him.'

Colonel Lupo of internal security pointed out, 'Sir, we are very stretched watching all the politicos and these Chilean agents. The president wants to avoid any serious demonstration over the next few weeks when the world's media are here. To watch Ridley adequately we'd have to take resources away from monitoring the agitators. We still haven't found any evidence that Ridley is anything other than he claims.'

Coro relented, 'OK but get that Sabato woman to stick with him. He seems to like her even if not enough to bed her. She must report regularly to you. You're right we must focus most of our surveillance on these communists set on bringing Argentina down.'

Monday morning 15th March Ridley had a strong sense of *déjà vu* as he was shown into Señor Roca's office and saw Cristina Sabato sitting at the conference table. She was accompanied this time by some other male officials. She smiled at him warmly and poured him a cup of coffee without asking him, and it would be clear to everyone she knew him well. Roca appeared and they got down to business. Ridley confirmed Nippon Health's wish to establish a subsidiary in Argentina to sell its pharmaceutical products. He outlined the planned organization including using the distributor in Comodoro Rivadavia to cover Patagonia, and the officials seemed pleased about that. He briefly described how the business finances would be managed and the plan to staff the new company with Argentines, apart from the general manager who would be a senior company manager, probably from Mexico. The officials spent some time checking the detail, and then the conclusion of the meeting was that there should be no problem. 'Of course,' explained Roca, 'there are forms to be completed and it would be helpful if the company could make some early commitment.' Ridley reassured them that he planned to take options on leases for offices in Buenos Aires and Bahia Blanca during this visit.

After this fruitful meeting, Señor Roca stated, 'Señor Ridley, I find all this very satisfactory. We'll do our utmost to progress your application as speedily as possible. I'll report favourably to the minister this afternoon. I suggest Señora Sabato should continue to assist you. She can be the link between you and my department and will be able to help you complete the application forms.'

Ridley looked at Cristina and saw her looking very pleased at this. He smiled at her, thinking, 'If one has to have a jailor, then one might as well have such an attractive and pleasant one, who you know is your friend.'

Turning to Señor Roca he thanked him and his staff for the very helpful advice. He said he was confident the outcome would be to the mutual benefit of Argentina and Nippon Health. As he left he found Cristina was at his side indicating he should follow her to her office. Picking up her coat and bag she led him through the warren of corridors to the back of the building, where once again they found her little red Alfa Sud. Placing her coat carefully on the back seat she slipped behind the wheel and quickly left the car park. Once out on the street she sighed, 'John, it's so good to see you again. You look very well. Thank you for agreeing to have me as your assistant. It would've been awkward if you hadn't. Internal security wants me to work with you and report what you do. They might have been suspicious if you had refused.' She smiled at him, 'Anyway, I want to work with you.'

John took a risk, 'Cristina, thank you for letting me know. I don't want you to be involved, but you should know I'm anxious about these rumours about Las Malvinas. I must find out more while I'm here.'

'John, I'm not stupid you know,' she chided. 'I understand what you're trying to do and I think you're very brave. I don't think any war can be good so if you can possibly help prevent one I must support you. Shall we go to your apartment and then we can discuss how I may help you? I'd like to see it anyway. Do we have to assume we can be listened to?'

'I think so Cristina, though if you're to report on what I do then maybe they won't have bugged the apartment. As we can't be sure, assume it is until I can check it.'

At the apartment Cristina prowled around investigating

the rooms and chatting gaily about how nice it all was, as Ridley checked for bugs. He then went into the kitchen, switched on the electric kettle and when it was bubbling he ushered her into the kitchen. Under cover of the noise from the kettle he said, 'Cristina I don't think the apartment's bugged but don't say anything sensitive here. Keep that for your car or out in the open when we think we are alone.'

After making coffee they moved into the sitting room and Cristina curled her legs under herself on the settee and looked at him expectantly. John knew what was expected of him so he crossed to her and holding her shoulders in his hands kissed her long and hard on the mouth. After taking a breath, and looking very much like the cat that has got the cream, she then kissed him back. After that he extricated himself and sat across from her where it was safer.

He explained, 'As I see it I have two clear tasks on this visit which may last for three weeks or more. Firstly, to ensure all the paperwork is completed both here and in Montevideo so that the business start-up application may be progressed speedily by both governments. I can't go forward without these approvals. Secondly, there's the detail of setting up the organisation such as getting the offices and recruiting staff. When will I get the forms to complete?'

Cristina replied, 'I have them in my bag. You'll have to attach copies of supporting papers and we'll need to see a lawyer to have the papers properly attested. We should be able to submit them by the end of the week.'

'That's great. I need to go over to Montevideo tomorrow to get things started over there but I'll be coming back in the evening. I think we should go through the forms now to confirm I have all the information to complete them. Then I'll tell you my plans for the next couple of weeks and perhaps you'd make some arrangements for me while I'm away tomorrow. After that I'll take you out to dinner, if that's allowed?'

She rummaged in her large bag and produced a file of forms and they spent the next hour or so checking through them and looking at his supporting material to check he had everything that was required. Eventually they were satisfied all was in order. She would contact his lawyers there and set up a meeting on the 19th so the papers might be properly certified before submission.

After this he ran through his travel plans. She agreed a day out in Mar del Plata on Sunday would be fine and, yes, she would bring her bikini. She said she would book flights for them to Bahia Blanca on 22nd returning on the morning of 23rd plus a hotel, and to book him an early morning flight to Bahia Blanca on 26th returning early afternoon. Smiling she agreed to have a meal and go dancing afterwards when he got back. She would organize all these things while he was over in Montevideo.

So pleased that everything was in hand and she would be with him, she headed for his bathroom to freshen up. After he had shaved and changed, for although coming into autumn the weather there was very warm, they headed out into the Avenida Pyrredón and arm in arm towards the Palermo district where there were plenty of inexpensive restaurants.

Tuesday 16th Ridley caught the early ferry to Montevideo and went straight to the embassy. Mr Yamauchi quickly appeared and took him to his office. Ridley succinctly briefed him on his plans for the next few weeks and checked whether he would be available that coming weekend in case there was a need to meet. Yamauchi confirmed he would be at his house in Atlántida all weekend.

Collecting the embassy finance man they then set off for the Uruguayan Ministry of Health and the appointment with the minister. This followed a similar pattern to that in Buenos Aires, and Ridley left the meeting with a small set of forms to complete and an assurance that 'There should be no problem'. Bidding farewell to Yamauchi he headed off to see the Uruguayan branch of his company's international lawyers to ensure they would certify the forms he forwarded to them and deliver them promptly to the Ministry of Health. They assured him they would do so and they would demand a receipt for them. You know what these civil servants are like.

Satisfied with progress he caught the early evening ferry across the Rio de la Plata. Wednesday and Thursday he went to the recruitment agency to interview candidates for marketing, sales manager and sales representative positions, but also found time to suggest to Tony Marini they should meet for a drink. Marini sounded pleased and suggested they meet again at the jazz club in San Telmo on the 18th. Getting back to his room early evening he turned on the TV news and there was yet another report of a major demonstration in the Plaza de Mayo. It was a trade union demonstration demanding more jobs and less inflation. A peaceful demonstration but he thought the police reacted very violently to it. Clearly the Junta was under extreme pressure.

Thursday evening he took a taxi over to San Telmo and entered the jazz club at about 10 p.m. just as the band was about to play its first set. Seeing Marini at the bar he went over and greeted him. He was shocked to see how the man had aged over the past six weeks or so. He appeared to have drunk a lot already and the hand holding the cigarette shook. Taking Ridley's arm he led him to a table at the front near the band. The waiter brought Ridley a glass of Malbec and another whiskey for Marini. 'It's good to see you, my friend,' croaked Marini. 'As you see my job is taking its toll,' he remarked drily. 'Is your project going successfully?'

'Yes, that is why I wished to see you,' replied Ridley. 'My board has approved the project. I'm starting the approval process here and I expect to set the company up before the end of the year. I have the information here and it would be good if you would draft a few paragraphs for your business pages.'

Hearing this Marini cackled, 'You'll be lucky! I'll have got my scoop before then, but I doubt whether your company will still decide to invest here. My sources tell me the invasion plan's approved, and it will begin soon. The people will be ecstatic.' Ridley couldn't tell whether Marini was being sarcastic when he went on to say, 'It'll make our country great again.' Marini fell silent and sat sipping his whiskey, listening to the music and eventually fell asleep. Ridley left him to it and headed back to his apartment.

When the band finished, the waiter roused Marini who staggered upright and stumbled to the entrance, and then staggered his way down the street. He passed a car parked without lights but he was too drunk to notice. After he had passed it, the car started up and gathered speed, mounted the pavement by Marini, and struck him a violent blow in his side that threw him high into the air and hard against the wall. The force broke his neck and he lay on the pavement like a broken doll, just another drunk who didn't watch where he was going.

Friday 19th Ridley switched on the morning TV news before Cristina arrived. The programme was making much of a group of fifty Argentines who had landed on the island of South Georgia and were claiming it for Argentina. There was also a small report about the death of Tony Marini, a reporter for La Nación, who was knocked down by a car the previous night in San Telmo. It was understood he was probably drunk at the time.

'Poor Marini,' thought Ridley. 'The poor sod was only trying to get a good story. He was as loyal as they come. Someone obviously reported him. They'll clearly stop at nothing. I'd better watch my back! It does add credence to his information though,' he mused. 'I'd better pass it on to Arthur Dean as soon as possible.

'This South Georgia thing looks like a put up job,' he thought. 'I bet they are marines and this will be used as an excuse for the Argentine Navy to support them. The balloon's about to go up. I had better contact Maria.'

So he rang her college and left a message. A short while later the phone rang and he heard her voice, 'John, what can I do for you?'

'Maria, it's good to hear you. I'm back in BA and will be making a trip south in about ten days' time. Might I stay with you?' Hearing her agreement he went on, 'Perhaps you would pick me up from the airport on 31st March on your way home from work?'

'Yes, John, that will be very convenient. There'll be no problem as Rafael's away and I don't expect him back for many weeks. I usually pass the airport about 4 p.m. so I'll see you then. Bye for now.' Sounding cheerful she rang off.

A little later his doorbell went and Cristina was standing there in a smart green suit with a skirt that could only be described as minimal. 'Latin women instinctively are so much better at showing off their figures,' marvelled John.

'Good morning, Cristina. You are looking even more sexy this morning. How are you?'

'Thank you, John, I am very well,' she replied clearly

236

pleased with his admiring glances. Sitting down on the settee, and showing so much of her thighs that John had to change seats to avoid constantly looking up her skirt, she told him she had made all the arrangements for the next week. She produced the copies of his supporting documents and they set about completing the application forms for the Ministry of Health. He rang down to reception to order a pizza and salad for lunch which arrived with a bottle of white wine just after they had finished. The meeting with the lawyers was not until 3 p.m. so they sat back and relaxed.

She suggested, 'The political situation seems to be getting worse. This South Georgia invasion can't help.'

'No. It's bound to inflame the situation. It should be a warning to the British but I fear they still think they can negotiate with Argentina. I believe it's too late for that. Anyway, no point in worrying about it. Let's go and see the lawyers.'

In her car she told him she had reported regularly that he had just been working on the business project since he arrived. She said she had nothing planned for Saturday, and asked whether she might stay with him for the weekend. She reassured him that she wasn't trying to seduce him and that she would sleep in the spare bedroom. She told him she was a good cook and she would love to cook for him. So he relented, thinking, 'I don't know how I'm going to explain this to Andy.' After they had completed the legal processes they went back to the Ministry of Health and presented the completed application to Roca. She then drove to her flat and collected her bag, already packed, and with a smile headed back out to her car saying, 'A girl has to be optimistic.' Ridley followed laughing and shaking his head, thinking, 'She is good to be with but don't drop your guard my boy.'

True to her word, Cristina proved to be an excellent cook and they had a fun evening. She went to the local *supermercado* and returned with Patagonian trout, lots of vegetables and spices and prepared a fine looking, wonderful smelling and very tasty dish with pasta. They got through a bottle of good Malbec whilst enjoying each other's company. Then true to her word she kissed him goodnight and headed for the spare bedroom.

Saturday 20th March they spent the day exploring the city. John knew the centre quite well now but she was a *porteño* and had lived most of her life in Buenos Aires. She knew every back street and alley and found interesting little shops, cafés and gaily painted houses in the barrios. They went down to La Boca, probably the most colourful, and home to one of the two rival teams in BA, Boca Juniors. They returned to the Florida shopping area for she claimed she needed some new clothes for the autumn season. Given that the temperature here was still quite warm he translated 'the autumn' as code for 'just needing some new things'. Watching her choose the clothes he thought, 'how different she is to Andy. She knows instinctively what will suit her, a bit like French women. But Cristina is much more daring and provocative.'

After shopping she led him north towards the Palermo district to the Parque 3 de Febrero. A wonderful lake in an area called Paseo del Rosedale had grand bridges crossing it. There were people in rowing boats, families picnicking on the banks, bronzed men exercising, 'showing off,' she said disdainfully. There were young couples like confetti on the grass and it seemed babies and young children everywhere.

Ridley exclaimed, 'What a lovely place. It's so nice to see so many people just being happy and enjoying themselves.'

They saw ice-cream vendors who also sold warm peanuts, popcorn and candied apples.

'This park is a thousand hectares and it has fields, woods and lakes. I like it so much,' she replied. Taking his hand she led him through the beautiful park before going on to a small café for a coffee.

Early evening they decided to stroll back and eat at a restaurant in the Microcentro, so John suggested they had a drink in the bar of the Hotel Phoenix as it was on their way. They settled comfortably in the plush seats for a while and enjoyed their drink and the pleasant ambience of the stylish surroundings, and at 7 p.m. he excused himself and headed for the gents. Going in he found Arthur Dean alone and silently handed him the envelope then proceeded to relieve himself as Dean left. Taking his time over washing his hands and combing his hair he returned to Cristina. They finished their drinks then she excused herself and he thought, 'Well, that exchange worked OK. He now knows my itinerary for the next week so hopefully he'll keep up with my movements. There's also some information to pass on, including Marini's comments, so that will test his link with Yamauchi before things get critical.' Cristina returned freshly groomed and they strolled arm in arm to a pleasant little restaurant nearby.

Sunday 21st was a wonderful, sunny day and Cristina was very excited as they had an early breakfast and got ready for their trip to Mar del Plata. She was wearing a cool-looking halter-neck dress and some sandals, but assured him with a bright smile that she had her bikini in her bag. Climbing into her car, the seats already warm from the bright sun, they headed southeast on to the RN 2 ahead of the masses of cars that later on would be going in the same direction. Passing over the low hills behind the town, by late morning they were parking close to Bristol beach. Grabbing their beach things they quickly found a free spot on the beach and Cristina erected a colourful striped umbrella and laid out two bright towels to mark their territory. Saying she was going to change she headed back towards the promenade and the rows of blue-topped permanent tents there. John looked around the beach and noted the piers jutting out from beach, the tall apartment buildings fringing the beach and the serious sun-lovers in skimpy swimsuits already tanning themselves on the beach. Cristina returned in a minimal bright green bikini and informed him that he must change in a tent, not on the beach. She had reserved one for them, number 105. He took his bag and was soon back in the new shorts he had bought on his last trip. He saw her looking at him and smiled nervously.

'Are you wondering if you come up to scratch?' she queried. 'Well, if you are, I'd say you are probably more of a man than nearly everybody on this beach!'

'Thank you, I have to admit that having a woman admire you is a very good feeling,' admitted John.

'Doesn't your fiancée then?'

'Yes, she does in her way. But she isn't as openly vibrant and sexy like you. You're both very different but I think you both love hard and strong.'

He terminated this difficult conversation by running down to the sea and swimming out to one of the floats off the beach, and soon she joined him. They swam around for a while then sat on the float to sunbathe. After a while she suggested, 'Perhaps we should have a light lunch now and then go for a walk.'

'Where would you like to walk to?' he asked.

'I'd like to walk along the Rambla to Cabo Corrientes and

down to the fishing port. We can get a good view of the lighthouse from there.'

'We can also get a good view of the submarine base,' thought John.

So after lunch they put their beach gear in the boot of the car and strolled south along the rocky coast. The Rambla was the fashionable promenade behind the beach where everyone wanted to see and be seen, so it was interesting strolling along it and admiring the beautiful and tanned as they walked by. Opposite the beach there were smart boutiques that would open later in the afternoon. As they reached the rocky cape they found a smart boulevard above the Playa Grande beach, and before long arrived at the fishing port with many red and yellow boats moored for the weekend. They appeared to be all virtually of one design with a square deckhouse, a short mast, flared bow and broad in the beam. 'They look very much like coastal fishing vessels,' thought John. There were a few ocean-going trawlers but these were moored off the jetties. Walking up above the port on the road back into the town he found his observation point from his last visit, and he looked down into the submarine base. This time there were only two in harbour. 'So where are the other two?' he wondered. 'I'll have to report this. Perhaps they delivered the Argentines to South Georgia. There also seems to be quite a lot of activity on the submarine support ship in the base. Quite a lot going on for a Sunday!'

They strolled back through the smart town and found a café for a coffee and a cake, and then Cristina suggested they drove back ahead of the crowds because she planned to cook another meal for him. 'I'd like to spend a quiet evening with you before we go to Bahia Blanca,' she admitted.

Back at the apartment while she was cooking John told

her he must call Andy as he hadn't spoken to her since he left. As she picked up the phone he said, 'Hello, darling, I love you.'

'John, I was just thinking of you as I got my supper,' she replied. How is the trip going?'

'Pretty well I think. Cristina Sabato is helping me and we submitted the application to the Argentine Ministry of Health last Friday. I'm heading to Bahia Blanca tomorrow then I have other meetings here during the week. I've been down to the beach at Mar del Plata today. It's been very warm weather these last two days. I don't know if it will last. Take care my love. I'm missing you lots, Andy.'

Andy whispered down the phone, 'Take great care, my dear man. All my love, bye.'

John rang off thinking, 'At least the message's been passed about the submarines as there's no way I could have met Arthur this evening.'

A little later Cristina came in, saw him sitting pensively and set the dining table without saying anything. John stirred himself and opened a bottle of white wine that had been chilling in the fridge as Cristina brought in the steaming dishes, this time of grilled chicken and lots of vegetables, followed by a dessert of some wonderful chocolate ice cream and a selection of fresh fruit. John put on the percolator and made strong coffee for them both. This machine was one of those scary Italian ones that you screw together and then stand on the heat. He never seemed to get it tightly sealed and it hissed and bubbled as it heated up. Then with a rushing roar the water poured through the coffee grains into the top receptacle producing a surprisingly good expresso.

After they had cleared up they both sat on the settee and listened to some tango music on the radio and she leant into him, his arm around her shoulder. 'John, you're a very good friend. I've enjoyed my weekend with you. I hope I'll be your friend for a long time,' she said.

'Cristina, I'd like that but you'll have to meet Andy and become her friend also. Otherwise it might be difficult for us to handle.'

'Fine, I'd like that,' agreed Cristina. 'Now I'm off to bed because we have a fairly early start. I'll take my car and leave it at the airport.'

About 9 a.m. on 22nd March they were out at the Aeroparque boarding their ninety-minute flight to Bahia Blanca. They had an uneventful flight and as they began finals Ridley looked out of the window as the plane came over the Puerto Belgrano naval base. Although he only had a minute he could see that the aircraft carrier, the cruiser and all the destroyers were still alongside. As they landed and taxied past the military side of the airport he observed more aircraft parked there. Not a lot more but certainly a few more and most seemed to be transport aircraft of one type or another.

As they came out of the terminal and Cristina looked for a taxi, Ridley gazed around and more military uniforms were in evidence. Getting into the taxi they went direct to the Hotel Elizabeth and registered. Yet again she had booked them adjoining rooms. 'At least this time Cristina hasn't booked me a suite,' thought Ridley. After freshening up they decided to have lunch in the hotel restaurant as it had a nice glass-windowed patio restaurant. Today, because it was so warm, the side doors had been opened to allow the gentle breeze to cool the shaded area. They were shown to a table overlooking the sea and Ridley had a good view of the road that led out of town towards the naval base. During lunch he was able to spot a number of small military convoys moving towards the naval base at regular intervals.

After lunch they went to the real estate agents and checked what offices were still available. Two on Ridley's preference list were still available so they visited them and discussed the relative merits of each. Late afternoon they returned to the real estate company offices and Ridley began to negotiate a deal for the lease. This took some time but after some haggling the agent indicated that the owner might accept what Ridley was suggesting, but he would have to refer it to him. Ridley accepted this and agreed that the agent should call him in BA. If a deal could be agreed he would come back on Friday to take an option on the lease pending approval from the Ministry of Health. Ridley thought, 'My luck is in at the moment. A ready made excuse for another check on the fleet base.'

There was no late flight to BA and that was why they had to stay over and get a flight in the morning. Cristina and John went out to find a fish restaurant near the port and decided on one that seemed to be busy. In fact as they were eating John realized some of the diners were naval officers so he listened to the conversation as fragments of it reached their table. It was difficult to pick out but he knew that Cristina was also listening surreptitiously, so he would ask her later. He heard, 'Las Malvinas', 'must be soon', 'special forces', 'April'.

'They look very confident,' he observed.

As they got back to the hotel he invited her to his room for a drink and ordered from room service. 'I think they were naval officers at the other table. They seemed to be having a jolly time,' he remarked.

Just as offhandedly she replied, 'Yes I think they were.' She smiled, 'If you want me to tell you what I heard them saying you'll have to ask me outright. I'll not be pumped covertly.'

John held up his hands in apology, 'Cristina I'm sorry. I'd like to know what you heard.'

'I think I heard, "the Fleet is ready", "will sail soon", and "Las Malvinas",' she reported, 'but they were only fragments.'

John mused, 'We only saw that one group of naval officers. We saw no others as we walked about afterwards and there were no sailors in the bars. That's very strange when there's a big naval base close by.'

'I think it might have been a birthday celebration. Perhaps they were given special permission.'

'I wonder if shore leave has been stopped.' He thought, 'That would indicate the operation is imminent.'

A little later they said goodnight and went to bed.

By lunchtime on Tuesday 23rd they were back in BA and Cristina dropped him off at the Esmeralda Suites saying she would call him later in the week.

Ridley prepared his message, covering all the facts observed in Bahia Blanca, for the courier and sealed it in a blank envelope. Just before 6 p.m. he arrived at the Hotel Phoenix feeling tense, but trying not to show it, for he realized if he was stopped and searched now it would be curtains for him. Heading for the bar he decided to go to the gents first so retraced his steps slightly and pushed open the door. Entering, he quickly passed the envelope to Arthur Dean who was standing at the next urinal. Without a word each finished and after washing their hands they both left the gents, Ridley first to further confuse any surveillance. Dean left the hotel immediately and Ridley went into the bar where he spotted a business acquaintance and spent an hour discussing the parlous state of the Argentine economy before returning to his apartment.

Chapter Sixteen

Chivenor UK Late March 1982

James Sandison strode quickly into the office building at RM Chivenor, knocked on the CO's door then entered and saluted.

'James, there's a bit of a flap on. HQ Royal Marines needs us to up our state of readiness.'

Sandison waited for Major Allen to elaborate on his opening remarks. 'Apparently some hard intelligence has come in from the South Atlantic suggesting the Argentines might make some move against the Falklands quite soon, and CinC Fleet has encouraged the Major General Royal Marines to bring some of his force to immediate readiness. Unfortunately the politicos aren't buying the intelligence message at the moment so we are to be ready in case we're asked to move very quickly.'

'I presume we're talking about an invasion of the Falkland Islands?' queried Sandison. 'They've certainly been going on about it for a while now.'

'That's correct. The view is that the Argentines will invade in the next couple of months. We need to bring all available Special Boat Service teams to immediate readiness in case we have to reinforce the token Royal Marines force down there. I guess you'll have to travel light if speed is vital: weapons and some diving gear. You'll have to leave the rigid raiding craft until later. May have to fly in from Uruguay as I doubt whether Argentina would allow our military aircraft to fly through their airspace.'

'Right, I'll get the guys started on this. We need to improve our knowledge of the Falklands and assess the likely military options.'

'I suggest you try to get maps out of RAF Chivenor or the local library. I don't want any hint of this planning to get to the Ministry of Defence or the Foreign Office in London as I gather they wouldn't support it. If CinC Fleet believes the intelligence is good then I'll go along with it.'

Sandison grinned at his boss, 'It's nice to have the prospect of a bit of soldiering. It had been a bit quiet recently. Mind, if it's genuine and the Argentines get there before us it'd be a major task to dislodge them. It must be almost 8000 miles from here to the Falklands.'

He saluted, turned smartly on his heel and strode out of the building into the early spring North Devon sunshine looking for his sergeant major. Spying him on the far side of the parade ground he walked quickly over to him. Tall, thin and very fit, with fair hair and blue eyes people always thought that James Sandison could have been the model for Action Man, the doll popular with all young boys.

Returning the sergeant major's salute, 'Sarn't Major there's a bit of a flap on that may mean some action for us. We need to do some planning. Delegate your current tasks then join me in my office. Also inform the officers there'll be a meeting in the conference room after lunch.'

Bahia Blanca Late March 1982

Ridley again took the early morning flight to Bahia Blanca on Friday 26th March. He had a window seat and as they came into land he looked out over the Puerto Belgrano naval base. 'Shit,' he thought to himself. 'It's completely empty. Not one ship remains alongside.'

As they landed he saw evidence of the military build up on the airbase. More C130s (Hercules as he knew them) were parked at dispersal and some Mirage 3s that weren't there last Tuesday. As they taxied past he could see more sentries around the tarmac and they were all armed so security was certainly at a high level. At the real estate offices they confirmed the phone call that indicated the owner would accept Ridley's offer. Checking they understood that he could only take out an option on the lease when he received approval to set up the company from the Argentine Government, he signed the document and it was duly witnessed.

To celebrate their agreement a bottle of champagne was produced along with some lunch. He could sense the palpable excitement amongst the people. 'They know what's happening,' he guessed. 'Probably many rumours have been spreading since the Fleet sailed.'

He observed offhandedly, 'The naval base appears to be fairly empty at the moment.'

They looked at each other quickly. One of them replied, 'I think they have sailed for a major exercise,' he said with a smile.

Ridley was due to get a mid-afternoon flight back to BA so he went direct to the airport from the real estate company. There was clearly more military traffic on the roads, and some towing equipment. He was no expert but a couple of the vehicles on an army transporter he passed appeared to be Roland mobile anti-aircraft missile system launchers. There was certainly a lot more security around the airport.

Arriving back in BA he headed quickly to the apartment

and prepared a report for Arthur Dean, and then called Yamauchi to ask whether he might visit him the next day. He also found on his desk a note from reception saying that Cristina had called. Calling the number he was given he learned she wished to invite him out for dinner and dancing that evening, reminding him that he had promised a while ago. So he agreed to meet her at the Hotel San Martin at 7.15 p.m. At 6.45 p.m. he arrived at the hotel and ordered a drink at the bar. Then just before seven he entered the gents and was relieving himself when Arthur Dean entered and stood next to him at the urinals. Again Ridley slipped him the envelope, then zipped himself up, and moved to the wash basins, before returning to the bar to find that Cristina had already arrived and was being stared at by every man in the room. He thought, 'Another pleasant evening ahead. I'm a lucky man – such brilliant cover.'

Saturday 27th saw Ridley on the ferry to Montevideo. In response to his telephone call Yamauchi promised to meet him on arrival at the Darsena Fluvial. Sure enough as Ridley walked off the ferry he saw Yamauchi's Honda Accord with its diplomatic plates in a no parking area nearby. 'Good morning, Yamauchi-san,' he said. 'I see being a diplomat has some advantages.'

'Yes. Foreign governments expect it of us so we mustn't disappoint them,' he quipped. 'I think we should stay at my house at Atlántida this weekend. We shall be away from prying eyes and the building is very secure and regularly checked for listening devices. We can also spend some time at the beach, although I gather you may like a break from females. I believe La Sabato has been looking after you! I doubt if I would have been able to keep my hands off her. You must have iron will-power, Ridley-san.'

249

Yamauchi started the car and headed east in the light traffic along the coast. After about thirty minutes they arrived at the small town beside a wide beach stretching to the horizon along the coast in each direction. Towards the centre he turned north off the coast road and after about 200 metres swung in through wide gates. The drive led around to a low white house partly hidden by palm trees. The garden was mainly laid to lawn with Mediterranean shrubs in beds, was surrounded by a high white wall – extremely private and not overlooked. As they pulled up in front of the house Yamauchi explained, 'I have staff here but they are all Japanese and fully vetted. You'll find the house extremely comfortable. Please consider it your own home on this visit and any others you might make in the future. My woman friend will join us for a meal this evening and will probably stay over.' He smiled, 'So don't worry if we don't surface early tomorrow. By the way, she's also been fully vetted. The staff will be around early tomorrow morning and they'll get you breakfast if you wish. Go for a walk or sunbathe. Just take it easy for a while, my friend.'

As they got out of the car Ridley found the housekeeper and two male staff members waiting for them at the entrance and soon he was being led to a light airy guest room with wide French doors that opened onto the garden. Insisting they would unpack his clothes for him, he was led back to a shaded patio at the rear of the house where Yamauchi was already seated with his daily newspaper. There was a tray of coffee and cups on the table and as Ridley arrived he put down his paper and poured out two cups of coffee.

'I take it, as you are here, that you believe it has started. Arthur Dean passed your reports to me and they have been safely transmitted to SIS so at least your navy will be alerted.'

Ridley replied, 'Their ships have all clearly left apart from two submarines, and I've seen a lot more military activity in the vicinity of their bases. There appear to be more frontline aircraft at the Bahia Blanca airbase. Also more transport aircraft especially C130s. I reckon they're on their way. The only question is when they'll attempt to invade.'

Leaning forward Ridley said forcefully to his friend, 'Yamauchi-san, I want you to send another urgent message to SIS and DNI saying my assessment is that the invasion fleet is now at sea and will probably arrive in the Falklands in a few days' time. Suggest they sail a token task group as it would at least send a warning signal to the Argentines!'

Seeing Ridley's anxiety Yamauchi agreed immediately, 'John, I'll go and send it now. Relax and drink your coffee.'

Soon Yamauchi was back saying, 'The message has been passed with an urgent request for it to be sent immediately to the heads of SIS and DNI. Relax, you cannot do any more at the moment. It's not your fault if the politicians will do nothing.'

On hearing this Ridley shook his head then continued, 'I have no option now. Unless we react quickly the Argentines will invade and then it will be war. I have to break cover and do one swift run down to Rio Gallegos to check the airbases in south Patagonia. If I break my pattern I may keep ahead of them and get out before they catch up with me. Cristina Sabato, my minder who reports daily about my movements, reckons they are not sure of me. She thinks it's something personal though, not any suspicions about my business role. I think they must be fairly relaxed about me however because she is my only surveillance at the moment. Over the past few months we've become firm friends and I trust her not to betray me. I'll have to slip away without her knowing so I don't put her under suspicion.'

'You have some very rare gift Ridley-san,' said Yamauchi admiringly. 'Perhaps it's because you like women, but they are certainly willing to die for you. I wish I had that gift.'

Ridley grimaced, 'Let's not joke like that. I have a premonition about this one. It's going to end in tears for someone just as Admiral Collingwood said some months ago. Yamauchi-san, I'd be grateful if you would personally brief Andy about my plans. Also please reassure her that I shall take as few risks as possible. If she speaks with you and gets to know you better she will be happier that everyone is working hard on my behalf. Give her my love.'

'Of course, John, I'll do this for you, my friend,' reassured Yamauchi. 'It'll be an honour. Now let us put our cares aside for a while. I suggest we take a stroll along the beach before lunch at a little restaurant I know. I need to pep up my libido before my friend arrives this evening.'

Laughing, Ridley chided his friend, 'Yamauchi-san, you are incorrigible. It is good though to see you enjoying life so much. Yes, but tomorrow morning I must take you through my plan before I go back to BA.'

They enjoyed the rest of the day and then Ridley met Yamauchi's lady friend who turned out to be a small but very stylishly dressed Japanese lady in her early forties. Like many Japanese women he had met she was dressed in Italian or French designer outfits. 'It must be the current strength of the yen,' he surmised. Yamauchi introduced her as Miss Aiko Ishihara. He said, 'She is my little love,' and they both laughed. It was clearly their little joke. Seeing Ridley looking questioningly he explained, 'Aiko's name in English means "little love". Aiko, let me introduce you to a good friend of mine, Ridley-san.'

Bowing to her, Ridley formally replied, 'I'm very pleased to meet you, Miss Ishihara. Please call me John if we don't have to remain on completely formal terms.'

Observing his attempt at Japanese gallantry Yamauchi snorted, 'See we have at least managed to instil a little culture into this *geijan*. I'll be watching you both, however, for he appears to have magic about him. All the women he meets fall in love with him.'

Smiling at him, Aiko said, 'Toshiro, don't be stupid. It's you I love and it's time we married. You've been alone for far too long.' Leaving this thought hanging in the air, she led them both to the dining room and became the accomplished Japanese hostess. Ridley could see that Yamauchi was very much in love with her, and Ridley hoped Yamauchi would be able to reach out to her past the memory of his still dearly loved, but dead, wife.

Sunday 28th March Ridley rose early and, as it was another beautiful day, he went down to the beach and walked for miles along the golden-coloured sands. The sea where the fresh water of the Rio de la Plata met the salt water was an unattractive muddy brown that wasn't very enticing for swimming. This early in the morning the beach was the preserve of runners and walkers, although later on people would flood out from Montevideo for the Sunday pastime of sunbathing and playing beach games.

Looking at his watch he decided he should return to Yamauchi's house. He found him sitting on the patio. Clearly Aiko had left discreetly so that the two men might complete their discussions. Ridley went through his plan for the next week. Firstly, he would go down to Comodoro Rivadavia for a business meeting, then, having collected a hire car, he would head down the RN 3 as far as he could get. With any luck he could reach Rio Gallegos and meet

253

up with Maria. He planned to check the airbases at Puerto San Julian and Rio Gallegos and identify OPs at each. Once he had either confirmed where the Super Etendards were, or it became too difficult, he would leave. He described his planned return route and checked the rendezvous point with the Uruguayan fisherman in the delta. He reminded Yamauchi that he would try to persuade Maria to escape, so the fisherman might have two passengers. Finally, he confirmed to Yamauchi that Arthur Dean knew his movements and the courier would shadow him all the way down to Rio Gallegos, travelling by air.

As Ridley ended his monologue Yamauchi confirmed, 'That's all understood, John. I can't see any flaws in your plans other than the obvious one of the Argentine security being very tight down there. That is the risk you've decided to take. Be very careful though, my friend. I will call your Andy this evening and then send a detailed report to her by the secure route.'

Later in the afternoon Yamauchi dropped him at the ferry terminal and with a wave of the hand saw him turn and stride purposely on to the waiting ferry. 'There goes a brave young man,' thought Yamauchi. 'I wish him every success and hope he will return safely.'

As the ferry headed across the estuary Ridley stood on the upper deck in the warm air and watched the sun setting over the delta in the west. It was wonderfully peaceful and even the low throb of the diesel engines was strangely reassuring. 'The lull before the storm,' he thought. 'I need to be on top line from tomorrow,' he reminded himself. 'No second chance if I make a mistake.'

Monday 29th March the taxi picked him up at 5.30 a.m. and took him the short distance to the Aeroparque for the internal flight to Comodoro Rivadavia. By ten o'clock he was stepping into a taxi there and heading for the offices of the pharmaceutical distributor. On the short journey into the city he reviewed what he observed as the plane landed and taxied across to the civilian terminal. Like Bahia Blanca there seemed to be tighter security and what looked like air defence missiles and an AA battery on the airfield perimeter. There was certainly more aircraft, especially transport planes. There were army lorries near a couple of them so he presumed they were being loaded. On the way to the offices they passed the entrance to the commercial port and here again there was evidence of an army on the move. A short convoy of heavily loaded army lorries was entering the port although he couldn't see what they were carrying, and he saw military police at the entrance to the port.

Arriving at the offices he was ushered very politely into the managing director's office where they quickly negotiated a provisional agreement. 'Subject of course,' emphasized Ridley with a smile, 'to the formal approval from your Ministry of Health.' The managing director then offered him a drink to celebrate the deal but he refused claiming it was too early in the day for him. He did however accept some lunch and, while they waited for this to be served, Ridley gazed out the window of the top floor office. He realized he had a good view of the port although he was some distance away. Looking hard he was able to make out the ships there. Most appeared to be commercial vessels including one oil tanker, but closer in there was one dark grey ship that looked very much like a fleet transport. In fact once he had had a second look he was certain it was. So that was where the military convoy was heading. 'Definitely something going on,' he thought. 'The pieces of the jigsaw are fitting together. That ship wasn't here last time.'

Saying farewell to the MD he walked the short distance to the local Argentcar car rental office. Showing his International Driving Licence, and reminding them he had called earlier in the week, they soon provided him with a small Korean 4x4 that was virtually brand new. 'This is ideal,' he thought, 'it shouldn't be conspicuous at all. Any air reconnaissance will think I am a local.'

After checking the petrol tank was full – for there were not many gas stations in this part of Patagonia – he headed south out of the city on the RN 3. 'It's quite a nice day for down here,' he thought as he drove the lonely road. 'If the wind stopped blowing it might be quite warm.' After a while he passed a solitary estancia just off the road. Autumn was well advanced. The leaves on the poplars were turning a warm yellow and the beech trees had a red and yellow mottled hue when seen from a distance set against the enormous sky. 'That is what you remember about Patagonia,' mused John, 'how the sky dominates the flat steppe.' For the first part of the journey he passed oil wells scattered across the landscape recognizable by the nodding donkey oil pumps at the wellheads. The grass looked sparse but the cattle seemed to be thriving on it. After about two hours he reached the broad valley of the Rio Deseado and there was more life here and much of the land by the river was cultivated. Soon however he left it behind and came on to the empty steppe again. The vegetation got even sparser and the only grazing animals were sheep.

After four hours driving he reached the outskirts of Puerto San Julian and headed towards the picturesque port and the small hotel, the Residencia San Julian, the only one the town had to offer. Luckily Argentina did not apply daylight saving so it was still light as he drove in. Passing the San Julian airbase he kept his eyes on the road but couldn't mistake the stringent security at the main gate. Parking by the side of the small hotel and going in, he was pleasantly surprised to find it looked cared for, there was a cheery bar and restaurant and his room, if small, was comfortable and warm. San Julian was a small town so he was hopeful local people might congregate here in the evening. He planned to spend the evening in the bar and the restaurant listening hard. So about 8 p.m. he came down into the bar, ordered a glass of Malbec and talked to the barman. He was surprised no one seemed curious about him and strangely he wasn't asked to show his passport when he arrived. 'If there is no check before I move on I might have covered my tracks successfully,' he hoped. Looking around the bar he thought, 'They're the same the world over. When they're empty of people they are cold and bare but when a lot of people arrive they become warm and friendly.'

About 9 p.m. the bar started to fill up and Ridley ordered another glass of wine and moved into a corner from where he could watch and listen until the restaurant manager summoned him to his table. Some of the new arrivals seemed to be local fishermen, with that weather-beaten look and strong, stocky physiques, but another group was quite different. All of medium height, they had short-cropped hair and looked very fit. It didn't take him long to recognize them as aircrew. 'They look the same the world over,' he thought. 'Even the Japanese.' They were clearly not on operations the next morning or they would not be drinking at all. It seemed it was one of the group's birthday and they were having a celebratory meal. Ridley was elated, 'This is better than my wildest hopes. I'm bound to pick up a lot of information this evening.'

As the evening progressed and they all moved into the

restaurant, Ridley in the perfect position at a small corner table, he learned that the base was at a high state of readiness, the invasion was expected at the end of the week, and they hoped the Brits would dare to come so they could have a go at them. 'Probably Skyhawk pilots,' mused Ridley, 'for I don't think there are any observers here. Therefore they are single seat and that's either Skyhawks or Mirages. They sound more like ground attack. So the Super Etendards may be elsewhere.' He gleaned no more information as the evening progressed and took his time over coffee gazing at the décor. The restaurant had panelled dark wood walls hung with photographs of the local countryside, heavy wooden tables covered in bright cloths, wasn't brightly lit and was very traditional for Argentina. Ridley let the pilots go back into the bar before he left and went to his room. 'I doubt whether they noticed me at all,' he thought.

Tuesday 30th March he had a light breakfast at the Residencia, refuelled the car and then headed quickly south again on the RN 3, musing about what he had discovered the previous evening. Ahead of him was a five-hour drive alongside a rocky sandstone coast with low cliffs and a few sandy bays. It was bleak country with sparse hummocky vegetation, small lakes in the boggy ground in places and occasional solitary flat-topped hills. Everywhere he was conscious of the vast sky just like on the prairies of Canada. He stopped regularly to stretch his legs and relieve the boredom. He was surprised he hadn't come across any security checks – perhaps because there was nothing out there in the vast wastes of Patagonia. During one of his stops near the wide inlet at Puerto Santa Cruz where the Rio Chico reached the sea, he saw a four-engine plane offshore and he presumed this was maritime reconnaissance, and later on he saw a helicopter in the distance but it did not divert to investigate him. There was little human habitation visible and he saw no one. No cars passed him and apart from one estancia inland on a hill he didn't spot any buildings along this part of the route. It appeared to be completely empty. There were plenty of sheep, however, especially as he neared Rio Gallegos. By mid-afternoon he was parking the car near the port having made very good time. Feeling famished he went into a small café nearby for a coffee and a sandwich. From this vantage point, and sheltered from the inevitable strong wind, he is able to look out over the small port. 'No action of any sort here,' he observed. There were only a few fishing boats in, so most were probably out fishing. The fishery protection patrol craft was still moored along the jetty so presumably it was business as usual. A loud roar broke through his reverie and looking out he saw a delta-wing fighter roar towards the horizon. 'Well, now we have a definite sighting of a Mirage 3.'

Getting back in the car he headed for the hotel and a brief sleep before dinner, for he found the long drive, the cold outdoors and then the warmth of the café had made him sleepy. The Hotel Comercio, where he had stayed before, was a modern three-star business hotel with plush sofas in the lobby and an efficient girl receptionist who asked for his passport and the registration number of his car. There was a group of people milling around in the lobby with their bags that he took to be tourists. 'I might not stand out too much then,' he hoped optimistically. When asked the purpose of his visit he replied, 'A mixture of business and pleasure.'

He found he was on the third floor in a corner room (309) with a partially restricted view towards the harbour. The room had twin beds and its own bathroom so he should be quite comfortable for one night. He hoped the flight from

BA had got in, and Arthur Dean was on it, because he had a lot of information to pass to him. Deciding to sleep for a couple of hours he booked a table in the restaurant for 9 p.m., set his alarm clock for 8 p.m. and went to sleep. Waking sharply as his alarm rang, he showered, shaved and dressed for dinner then sat down at the desk to draft the brief report that he would pass to Arthur Dean the next morning covering the situation in Comodoro Rivadavia and San Julian, and suggesting a possible OP on the coast near Puerto San Julian from which to watch operations at the airbase. It would be possible for an SAS or SBS team to slip in unobserved and pass on early warnings of air strikes. He confirmed there was at least one squadron of McDonnell Douglas A4 Skyhawks at San Julian. Placing this in a plain envelope he had brought with him he slipped it into his inside pocket and then went down to the bar for a drink before dinner. Walking up to the bar he noted that Dean was sitting quietly at the far end. When the barman served him Ridley asked for it to be charged to his room bill and when he was asked for the room number he said loudly, 'Mr Ridley room 309.' As it wasn't very busy in the bar yet he knew Dean would have heard the room number and would come for the dead letter drop tomorrow morning.

Ridley moved away from the bar to sit at a small table, and looked at the TV that was showing a news programme. A man nearby shook his head and commented, 'Things are going to the dogs,' as the programme showed scenes of violent demonstrations in Buenos Aires. Ridley observed that Dean had been joined by an acquaintance and by the sound of the conversation he was another journalist. 'That's clever,' judged Ridley. 'He can't be accused of wandering off on his own.' He settled down to listen to the conversation as the bar filled up but he didn't hear anything of interest.

It was the same as he quietly had his dinner so he decided to turn in early as the switch was at 6 a.m.

Wednesday 31st March he was up quietly at 5.45 a.m. and prepared the newspaper. Yesterday he bought a local daily paper. He put the envelope in the centre, folded the paper carefully so the envelope would not fall out and turned the paper so that the top page would not reveal it was a day old. One minute before six he partially slid it under the door so about one-third stuck out into the corridor. Just after six he sensed someone on the other side of the door and the paper disappeared into the corridor. Ridley prayed that it was Arthur Dean who had collected it, and not a member of Argentine Internal Security. 'If it is the latter I shall know soon enough.' Having completed the drop successfully, he hoped, he returned to bed and slept for a few more hours. He rose late and watched the news on TV for he wanted to let Dean get clear. He then went down for a late breakfast and idled away the morning before checking out just before noon. Leaving the car in the hotel car park he wandered into town and had the staple Argentine meal of *parrillas* and vegetables in a packed and steamy restaurant in the centre of the town. After lunch he drove out to the airport and enquired about flights to Tierra del Fuego and return flights to BA. He observed heightened security but from the civilian terminal he couldn't see anything of the military airfield. He decided to go to the airport café. Having sat down with his coffee he became conscious of a stocky man sitting in the corner and scrutinizing him intently. 'He has the look of security,' guessed Ridley. Just after this the man wandered over and struck up a conversation with him. Ridley invited him to join him.

Before the security man could take the lead Ridley

offered, 'I'm over here on business and I thought I should see Patagonia. I've just been enquiring about flights to Ushuaia but I can't make my mind up whether I'd prefer to go inland to Rio Turbio. It sounds very interesting. It's a pity about the weather. Is it always so windy down here? Anyway, the airline's checking if there are any seats on the flight tomorrow to Ushuaia. Are you waiting for a flight?'

The chap nodded and didn't say anything so Ridley continued feeding him information to reassure him. 'I really do need to get back to Buenos Aires this Friday.' Appearing satisfied with this information the man got up, wished Ridley 'A good trip' and wandered off to check other passengers. 'Low level security surveillance,' thought Ridley. 'Just a routine check and not occasioned by a specific security alert. I don't think they're looking for me yet.'

Finishing his coffee Ridley went out to the car and drove back into town. A little later he came back and parked the car in the parking area reserved for returned rental cars, leaving the doors unlocked and the ignition key under the driver's seat. 'Hopefully they'll assume I was late for my flight and just dumped the car.' He went in to check whether there were any seats on the next day's flight down to Ushuaia and acted disappointed when the girl informed him it was fully booked. Then he took a seat in the airport foyer and watched for Maria to arrive. Just after 4 p.m. he saw a large 4x4 drive up and Maria got out. Ridley grabbed his small bag and made for the entrance meeting Maria just as she was about to enter. Taking her arm he steered her to the car explaining, 'We can talk as you drive.'

Smiling delightedly at him, she put the big Toyota Landcruiser into gear and left the airport, turning west on to the road that ran past the airport entrance. After about fifteen kilometres she turned right off this road on to a track and after crossing the Rio Gallegos took the left fork that headed uphill. After a couple of miles of rough track he saw lights ahead and he could see her smiling in the glow from the car instrument panel. 'That is El Indio estancia. Welcome to my home.' She drove into the centre of a group of buildings. In the gloom he saw a single-storey stone building with tall chimneys, resembling a large bungalow. Spread around it he could make out a number of low farm buildings around the main house. The house was sheltered from the persistent west wind by a low hill and some trees and a dense patch of scrub. There appeared to be lights in another low ranch-style building. 'That's where the staff live. The ranch manager lives in another house nearby but he's away tonight. Let's go in.'

They climbed up some steps and Maria opened the main door, calling to her housekeeper, 'Rosa, we have a guest to stay. Please make up the guest room for him. I hope we have enough to eat.'

A wrinkled older woman appeared from another door in the hall and, as she was accompanied by a wonderful smell of cooking, Ridley presumed it was the kitchen. Bobbing a curtsy to him she asked him to follow her and she led him to a guest bedroom on the first floor. He could see the curiosity written all over her face and felt sure Maria would be grilled about him as soon as she got downstairs again. She told him she re-made the bed regularly so the sheets were fresh, so all she needed to get was some towels for him. Soon she was back with them and then she rushed out of the door again, and he heard the patter of her heels on the stairs as she rushed down to speak to her mistress.

Ridley freshened up then returned downstairs. From outside he thought the building was a single storey but in fact it was a sort of large dormer bungalow with bedrooms upstairs. Like many Argentine interiors there was plenty of wood in evidence making the inside of the house seem very warm and cosy. 'Just what you need with this incessant wind,' he supposed. The living room and the dining room both had blazing fires going even though the evening didn't seem that cold. Unlike other rooms in the house they weren't panelled but painted in a plush creamy-yellow colour. The furniture was a mixture of modern and Spanish traditional, as were the ceiling and wall lights. So the effect made both these rooms stylish but also warm and comfortable. The hall and staircase were panelled in dark wood and looked quite grand as befitted the owner's house. He supposed you would find the same thing on a big ranch in the United States Midwest.

He found Maria sitting in the living room with her feet up on a long settee. Seeing him she rose and greeted him, 'John it's so good to see you again. I was very pleased to get your call. I hoped you hadn't forgotten me.'

'No, Maria,' replied John, 'I could never forget you. I just wish we'd met again in better times. I fear I may put you in danger and if I could've found a way to avoid that I would've done so. But things are happening and I have to find out what's going on at the airbase. Then I must try to get to Uruguay.'

Looking at him very seriously, Maria reminded him, 'I said I'd help you whatever the cost because you're my big brother and I know you'll care for me if you can. I felt that during our last meeting – it was so good to have you helping me. Anyway, I'm sure no harm will come to me.'

He then explained to her his task. 'There's a small hill from which I can observe the airbase. The hill's not far off the road you take to work and about three kilometres from the base. I'd like you to drop me off on the road as it gets light and pick me up there on your way home. If I'm not there when you come past don't wait more than five minutes, as I don't want you drawing attention to yourself. Does Rafael have an anorak and possibly some binoculars?'

Maria nodded, 'That shouldn't be difficult. I think I know where you mean. There's a sign around there indicating the road ahead is rough. I usually leave about 7 a.m. because I have breakfast in town, but it wouldn't seem unusual for us to leave at 6 a.m. I'll get some food for you once Rosa's gone to bed. Rafael has a green anorak hanging in his dressing room and I think there may also be a pair of waterproof trousers. You'd better take a pair of his boots otherwise your shoes will be ruined. I think you're both a similar size. You can take my binoculars, they are quite powerful.'

Anxious to protect her he reminded her, 'If anyone questions you, you must say I'm keen on bird watching, and that I said I wanted to go out early to get in a good position from which to observe the birds as the sun rose. You knew me in Spain when you were young and you think I am a businessman now. Whatever happens stick to that simple story.'

Smiling she reassured him, 'Don't worry, I'll tell the correct story. You're being my big brother again. It's nice. Let's have a happy evening together.' She went over to a desk and withdrew a photo. 'Look what I found the other day.' She showed him a photo of both of them taken on La Toja when they were much younger. 'I want you to have it to remind you of me until we next meet. I have plenty of other photos of you.' So he put it safely into his wallet. He thought, 'I hope Argentine Security don't get their hands on her photos until I am out of the country!'

265

Rosa called them to the dining room and they spent a happy dinner reminiscing. After they had had coffee and moved back into her living room she turned serious again. 'Is it going to be war between Britain and Argentina? I have heard rumours in Rio Gallegos that they are going to invade Las Islas Malvinas.'

'I hope not,' John exclaimed, 'I am doing my best to prevent it but unfortunately the British Government isn't listening to the warnings. Perhaps we can persuade the USA and the UN to put pressure on the Argentines to draw back before it is too late. I fear that if they do invade they won't back down. I have been surprised how strongly the Argentine people feel the injustice of Britain retaining sovereignty over these islands. They will support the Junta if they do invade. If we decide to retake the islands then there will be bloodshed on both sides.'

Maria sighed, 'It's a black time for Argentina. This country has so much going for it yet it never seems able to exist as a democracy. As I told you before, I despair for them and I don't feel like one of them.'

'Then why don't you come with me when I leave Argentina?' pleaded John. 'You could go back to Spain. I'm sure your family would forgive you and welcome you home.'

Shaking her head vigorously Maria stated firmly, 'No. I have made my bed and I must lie in it. To leave Rafael would bring dishonour on my family. I must make the best of it here. If I feel Argentina has to change then I must work to help it do so. Not walk away from it. Through my courses at the college at least I can help the young people understand what democracy is. Perhaps they'll demand better government when they are older. Perhaps later I'll try to get a job at the university in BA. Now I'll get you those things and then we should go to bed. I'll call you at five-thirty.'

April 1982 Patagonia

Just after 6 a.m. on April 1st, while it was still dark, they left the estancia quietly. In a small bag Ridley had some food and the binoculars, and he was dressed in Rafael Gomez's trousers, anorak and boots. A few kilometres down the road he saw the low hill in the gloom to the north of the road and a road sign opposite. He slipped quickly out of the car telling her he would be waiting in the scrub by the road sign at four o'clock that afternoon. She headed into town and he began the slow careful walk towards the low hill situated between the Gallegos and Coyle rivers. Luckily there were quite a few crossing places, put there he presumed by shepherds to save their legs. Crossing the Rio Gallegos he followed a winding sheep path through the hummocky grass that seemed to go in the right direction, but when it began to turn east back down into the valley, he had to strike off through the rough scrub. Luckily it wasn't too dense and as daylight came he could see a clear way up to the hill. Spotting a large flock of sheep ahead he had to make a long detour, for he didn't want a casual observer down below to wonder what had startled the sheep. Getting clear of the sheep he aimed for a thicket about half way up the slope on the eastern side of the hill that he judged should have a good view down on to the base. If the thicket was dense enough, he should be able sit deep in it and use the binoculars without any risk of a reflective flash being picked up by anyone down below.

Reaching the thicket he checked around the back, and then lying down he slid around the edge and peered down towards the east. Clearly in view were the runway lights – it was a good position. Sliding backwards away from the edge, he found a way in through the back of the thicket and moved forward until he reached a hollow near the front with a wide field of view, where he could sit looking through a screen of branches. So even if the sun was bright it would not reflect off the lenses. For he would be looking east which meant, unfortunately, for much of the day the sun would be coming directly at him. He searched around to find enough branches to make a comfortable seat for himself and settled down for his day's surveillance.

He began his search by systematically checking each part of his field of view. He wasn't bothered about the civil terminal but used it as a reference point for the other buildings on the airfield. Working steadily northwards across the area until his view reached the hangars and the concrete aprons in front of them. As he finished his initial scrutiny the base was beginning to come to life for he could see lights as a hangar door opened. They were going to manoeuvre out some aircraft for sorties. As the morning moved on he noted Mirage 3s and Skyhawks taking off and landing but no Super Etendards. A Tracker A/S aircraft took off and flew out over the sea, followed a little later by a Neptune maritime reconnaissance aircraft that headed off in the same direction. A C130 landed, unloaded some equipment and then took off again heading in a northerly direction. Otherwise everything was fairly quiet and if you didn't know there was usually only limited flying from here you wouldn't think much of today's air activity.

He began to scrutinize the airfield perimeter. At the western end of the airfield nearest to him there was some sort of outpost. As the sun came around and threw the shadows in a different direction he recognized it as a vehicle carrying a Short Tigercat AA missile quad launcher. Near the hangars he spotted two Panhard AML90 Armoured Cars that were clearly being used for airfield defence. He made a mental note 'I think these are new.'

The sun reached its zenith and it was getting quite warm in his thicket. He removed the anorak, moved deeper into the thicket and found the food in the bag. He was eating one of the sandwiches Maria prepared for him when suddenly he heard the beat of rotor blades coming towards him. Staying very still he listened carefully as the sound seemed to reverberate all around him. Eventually he spotted it a little below him crossing his sightline, moving from right to left until the engine noise faded. A little later he saw it to the north of the base and then it flew south before coming past him again and landing in the base. He guessed that they were checking the perimeter of the base; not looking for any spotters. 'Yet another pointer to some action coming off soon,' he thought. 'But where are these Super Etendards? I felt sure they'd operate from here, not Esposa at Bahia Blanca. It's too far away from the Falklands for them to be effective from there.'

Three o'clock passed and he was just thinking he would have to slip away soon when he heard a roar above his head and there was a Super Etendard on finals. It landed and was quickly followed by five others. They rapidly taxied to the hardened hangars. All six were parked in one of them and the doors closed fast. 'Well, that was very slickly done,' he thought. 'Most people wouldn't know anything special had happened. If they are bringing them in like that, they certainly intend to use them from here. They're not passing through to Rio Grande airfield on Tierra del Fuego.' He ran his mind over other air movements today and wondered if the C130 had brought the spare Exocet missiles for the Super Etendards that had just landed so slickly.

He realized he should leave so he spread out the branches

he collected and roughened the area he used and checked he wasn't leaving anything behind. He backed out of the thicket and then slipped back down the hill, keeping well clear of the flocks of sheep, going carefully through the scrub and out along the sheep track again. In the gathering gloom he had a little difficulty finding one of the rickety bridges across the Rio Gallegos, but eventually he was resting in the scrub by the road sign. Looking at his watch he saw it was just before four. Whilst he was waiting a couple of civilian vehicles went by, one in each direction and he thought, 'I'd better be quick when Maria comes. I don't want her to be seen picking someone up here!' After about five minutes he saw another set of headlights in the distance and soon Maria's Toyota had stopped and he quickly climbed up into the cabin. 'OK?' she asked.

John replied, 'Yes. No one saw me and I got what I wanted. Let's get back to your place.'

Back safely in the estancia ranch house she put the TV on for the evening news and they heard that the airport has been closed indefinitely because of problems with the approach radar. 'Nothing wrong with it this afternoon. That's the normal ruse if you wish to stop civil aircraft operations,' explained John. 'This means it's about to start. I'd better leave tomorrow. Will you drive me to Comodoro Rivadavia?

Looking sad but smiling bravely she walked across and gripped his arms, 'Of course, John.' He put his arms tightly around her, and the surrogate brother and sister stood together like a Henry Moore statue. John then rang Cristina and without explaining asked her to meet him at the Aeroparque on 3rd April. He would call just before he took off.

Friday 2nd April was a fateful day in the history of Argentina. While Maria and John slept Argentine Special Forces landed from the destroyer Santisima Trinidad at Mullet Creek on East Falkland and took Government House at Stanley. Once the Royal Marine force was captured, two companies of Argentine Marines landed in amphibious personnel carriers. The recapture of Las Islas Malvinas had begun.

By the time Maria and John got up the news had spread and a huge flag-waving crowd had gathered in the Plaza de Mayo in Buenos Aires. At breakfast Maria turned on the radio news and they listened silently as the announcer described the recapture of the islands. 'So it has started,' she whispered, 'where will it end?'

'I certainly need to get out quickly now,' said John, 'but I can't put you at risk. Let me take the car. You can pick it up later.'

'No, I want to help you. You must let me. I know some of the back roads.'

Relenting, John argued, 'Well, at least bring your passport so you can leave with me.'

'All right, I'll bring it to please you but I have no intention of leaving here. I'll be OK.'

Gas stations are far spread out down in Patagonia so people always fill up when they pass a gas station. So her car had plenty of fuel but they realized they would need to refuel once on the way so they couldn't avoid civilization completely. After a quick breakfast, they piled food into the car telling Rosa they were going out for a long drive and a picnic. From her face they knew she didn't believe them, but nothing was said and she just hugged Maria tightly then turned away into the house. They avoided going into town, taking a more circuitous route. Turning left at the fork before the road, they slowly followed a very rough, potholed, dusty track through low hills to the west. As they reached the low buildings of another estancia, Ridley heard the thump of rotor blades and looked up to see a helicopter flying towards them. It appeared to have military markings and was similar to the one he saw during his observation at the airfield. 'Maria, smile and wave at them happily,' Ridley ordered. As it passed them slowly they slowed down and both looked up and waved delightedly at the crew, like holidaymakers on the beach as the rescue helicopter passed. After giving the vehicle a good scrutiny it banked to starboard and resumed its flight back to the airfield and they continued on their way along the track. As they began to relax after this incident they passed another estancia before coming on to the RN 3 well to the north of the town. Turning north they drove as fast as they could, praying there wouldn't be roadblocks near San Julian. Ridley remarked casually while smiling reassuringly at Maria, 'Well, they are clearly not looking specifically for you or me. They've just tightened airfield security and are keeping an eye on anything moving around the perimeter. We should be OK now.'

Chapter Seventeen

2nd April Buenos Aires

Just before lunch Colonel Johnson strodes into General Alfredo Coro's office. 'Sir, I've just received a report from Gomez's ranch manager to say Maria Gomez is entertaining a man at the ranch near Rio Gallegos. From the rough description given I think it might be Ridley. We didn't know he'd gone down there. Señora Sabato informed us he was going down to Comodoro Rivadavia for a business negotiation. He must've gone on by road. This report came in last night but with all the action going on the collators didn't get to it until a few minutes ago.'

'Bloody typical,' growled Coro. 'Get Gomez to come over here immediately. We'd better see if he knows anything about Ridley. Let's meet after lunch. I've been summoned to the Casa Rosado for lunch to celebrate this glorious day in our history.' Johnson wasn't sure whether he was being genuine or sarcastic so to be safe he stayed quiet, saluted and left to find Gomez.

About 3 p.m. Gomez and Johnson had been waiting for a good half hour when Coro strode into his office. 'Have you shown him the photo we took?'

'No, I thought it best to wait for you,' replied Johnson. He showed Gomez the photo taken outside Esmeralda Suites.

'Is this man fucking my wife?' was the first thing Gomez wanted to know.

'No, we don't think so,' replied Johnson. 'We think they

are friends. In fact, the receptionist there said they were more like brother and sister.'

Gomez frowned and looked again at the photo. 'I think I remember. It was in Madrid before I got engaged to Maria. She introduced me to this Englishman who was studying Spanish. He'd spent time with her family practising the language and they became friends. She said she thought of him as her big brother.'

Coro barked, 'You say he is English? He now claims to be Canadian. Think hard, man? What else can you remember? It may be important.'

Gomez looked again at the photo and strolled over to the window, then turned and looked back at the other two men. 'I think he was in the British Navy.'

Coro looked grim, 'If you are correct then we have a dangerous spy in our midst. However, I don't want to cause a diplomatic incident with the Canadians or the Japanese at this juncture so we must proceed carefully. I told you I had a nagging doubt about him. I think my father may have said something in the past. It's possible he might provide the clue. I'm seeing him later this afternoon. So I'll put a couple of questions to him and if I get the answer I suspect it will confirm that Ridley is a British spy. Johnson, request a Learjet flight to Rio Gallegos tomorrow morning. We should be able to catch them at the estancia.' Turning to Gomez, he said, 'Keep quiet about this. You'd better come with us tomorrow as we may want you to confront him.'

Later Coro ordered his driver to take him to his father's grand house in Recoleta. When he got there he showed him the photo of Ridley. His son knew he had remembered as soon as he saw his father's face. 'Who is he, father?'

Gustavo Coro said, 'It's like seeing a ghost. If I hadn't

seen his dead body I would have said it was John Ridley who we disposed of in 1951. His son survived the crash that killed his parents. I think the baby was looked after by two of their friends in the intelligence fraternity, one of whom was Andrew Collingwood.'

'What,' exclaimed his son, 'the Director of British Naval Intelligence? Then he must be a British spy and it'll be a great coup to capture him. He's on a ranch near Rio Gallegos and we'll go to arrest him tomorrow. May I use your phone?' He then called Colonel Johnson and confirmed the trip for tomorrow, warning him to keep the information confidential so this would be their triumph.

Patagonia 2nd April

Unaware of the commotion in the intelligence service in BA, Maria and John made good progress northwards and couldn't believe their luck – they had not met any roadblocks. They saw very little traffic going in either direction and only once did they became nervous as they saw a small military convoy coming towards them north of San Julian, but it drove steadily on past them. On the long journey north across the featureless steppe, Ridley tried a number of times to persuade her to come with him but she just smiled and shook her head, telling him, 'I'll be OK.'

By 8 p.m. they reached the outskirts of Comodoro Rivadavia and saw a small motel where they decided to stop for the night. John went in search of a public phone booth and rang the airport to book a flight to BA. There was no problem, apparently few people were flying, and his American Express charge card quickly secured him a seat on the 8a.m. flight. He then rang Cristina's telephone number. As he waited for her to answer he glanced out of the kiosk and tensed as a police car drove up and parked outside a bar just down the street. One of the policemen got out and walked into the bar. 'I hope he's just getting some cigarettes,' Ridley thought optimistically. He was more worried by the other policeman who remained sitting in the car and appeared to be staring directly and persistently at him. 'Hopefully he's listening to the radio and dreaming.' Then Cristina picked up the phone and Ridley told her he would be arriving at around 9.30 a.m. tomorrow and she confirmed she would pick him up. As Ridley replaced the receiver he saw the other policeman return to the car and as he climbed in the car began to move off, so John loitered in the kiosk for a few moments to let the car get clear away. 'Phew, I am getting too old for this,' he thought.

Maria and John found a small pizzeria and had a simple meal and some wine before making their way back to the room. Stripping down to their underwear, for neither of them had any pyjamas, they got into bed together and gently hugged each other before falling asleep in each other's arms. As John woke in the morning to find himself still entangled with Maria he thought, 'Just like the babes in the wood.' Rousing her they dressed quickly and said their farewells before getting into the car and driving to the airport. As she halted in front of the terminal building he leant over and kissed her on the mouth and said, 'Remember to stick to the simple story. I love you, take great care, Maria. Bye!' He grabbed his bag, got out of the car and with a friendly final wave went into the terminal.

Maria, with a heart-wrenching sob, put the car into gear and drove into the city to find a hotel in which to freshen up and have breakfast before the long journey back. 'I wonder when I'll next see him,' she thought. 'I'm really glad I met him again and it makes me happy to know he still loves me. He really is my only family now. I hope he'll get out safely. I have no regrets about helping him for this madness must be stopped somehow.'

Ridley walked up to the check in desk, collected his boarding pass and as he turned away towards the departure gate he heard an official voice ask him, *'Perdóname, Señor, documentos personales por favor.'* Turning he saw a tall, smartly dressed man standing next to him. Smiling at him, Ridley handed him his passport thinking, 'Is this where it all ends? I'm so close to getting out. Stay calm.'

Scrutinizing the passport carefully, the security man asked, 'Señor Ridley, what have you been doing down here?'

'I've been conducting business with a company here. I'm setting up a pharmaceutical company with the approval of your Ministry of Health. I'm now returning to BA where I have an apartment.'

'May I ask who you were meeting?' questioned the man.

'The pharmaceutical distribution company here. I hope to be able to give them some business,' replied Ridley.

'How long have you been here on this trip?'

'I flew down from BA on the 29th March but I managed a couple of days sightseeing,' he answered. 'The petrified forests just outside Sarmiento are fantastic.'

'Are you intending to remain in BA for some time Señor?' queried the man.

'No, I think I shall return to Canada for a while until the present troubles are over. Everyone seems delighted you have retaken Las Islas Malvinas.'

Hearing Ridley use the Argentine name for the islands and appear supportive, he seemed less suspicious now and, after checking the name of Ridley's company, he handed the passport back and wished him a pleasant flight to BA.

'Blimey,' thought Ridley, 'that was a close shave. Clearly there isn't a country-wide alert out for me yet. Perhaps they haven't realized I've gone AWOL. It was just a general security trawl like the one at Rio Gallegos.'

Without further incident, Ridley arrived in BA on 3rd April, got his bag without any difficulty, and coming out of the Aeroparque terminal suddenly found Cristina beside him. Without speaking she took his arm and steered him past the soldiers guarding the front of the terminal building to a battered, dirty old Volkswagen Beetle of indeterminate colour. Driving off sedately, she headed north in the direction of Tigre and soon they were north of the suburb.

Ridley noticed she kept looking in her rear view mirror so he queried, 'Cristina what is it?'

'There's a police car following us,' she replied anxiously. It's been behind us for about five minutes.'

'OK, relax. Do you see that gas station ahead? Well, pull in there and fill up. We'll see whether they follow us or just drive on.' As Cristina turned in Ridley gazed out surreptitiously through the side window and saw the police car continue its untroubled drive north. After they got going again she turned off the main road, and then took a number of thickly tree-lined side roads that twisted and turned alongside narrow water channels, before pulling up by a smart house with a large garage attached. She got out, opened the garage door and quickly drove the car in. Getting their bags out of the car she shut the garage door and swiftly opened the front door and they went inside.

'Are you OK? That was very smartly done,' he commented.

'I've obviously been watching too many spy films,' she

joked. Looking closely at him she asked, 'More importantly, how are you?'

'OK. I don't think they're on to me yet, but I had to get away from Rio Gallegos quickly when they recaptured Las Islas Malvinas,' explained John. 'I had a bit of a scare at the airport in Comodoro Rivadavia when I was stopped by a security man but he wasn't suspicious. It was just a routine check on someone who wasn't an Argentine. I hope to get out tonight but I need to make a phone call to Montevideo. Is there a phone here?'

'Yes. It is connected but I had better make the call. Is it to your Japanese friend?' Ridley looked at her in surprise. 'I'm not stupid you know. Like you I can do jigsaws.'

John looked closely at her. She had dressed drably today, not her usual smart, very chic clothes and she wasn't wearing any make-up. She clearly had tried hard to be anonymous. He mused, 'There is more to this woman than meets the eye.'

John assented that the call was to Yamauchi to ask for the 'package' to be collected that evening. He told her the number and that Yamauchi knew who she was. She picked up the phone and called the embassy in Montevideo and, giving her name, asked to be put through to Mr Yamauchi. Yamauchi quickly answered and they held a polite conversation in case the call was being monitored. Then she asked whether the package for London could be collected that evening by one of his staff. Yamauchi assured her that would be satisfactory and rang off.

Cristina turned to him, 'Is that OK?'

'Very much so, 'answered John, 'but it isn't the first time you have done something like this, is it?'

'Before I answer that question,' she said, 'I'd like you to answer one for me. I feel we've reached a point in our relationship when we should be honest with each other. Are you a spy?'

It didn't take John long to decide what to say for he believed his cover would be blown very soon. 'I am a British Intelligence Officer and I've been trying to prevent a war between our two countries. It seems I have probably failed. The information I wish to get back to my people might save lives on both sides if it does come to war. I can assure you I haven't been collecting information to help the British invade or bomb Argentina.'

'Thank you for being so honest and for trusting me, and, if it's in my power, I will never let you down. Of course I'll continue to help you because I think my country is taking the wrong path and also because I love and respect you. As for your question, yes, a few years ago I worked in the intelligence assessment department in the Foreign Ministry and one learned some of the tricks of the trade but I have never been a spy.

'Now we need to consider the practicalities,' suggested Cristina. 'I saw you looking at my clothes before. I plan to change into something smarter. Anyone around here would think my present garb very strange.' She smiled, 'Anyway, I think you enjoy seeing me in smart and sexy clothes. Then I need to get us some supplies. There is a small *supermercado* just a kilometre down the road so I'll walk down and get us some food and drink for the day. I'll also get some wine. I presume you'll want to go after an evening meal.'

'Yes, the pick up is at 11p.m. near a small settlement called Dorada that shouldn't be too far away from here. The boatman will slip over from Uruguay.'

'I think I've heard of it. Actually, I think it might be near the *supermercado* so I'll ask when I'm getting the food. Would you like a newspaper?'

She gave him a brief kiss and taking her bag went into a bedroom to change and John slipped off his tie and stretched out on the settee. She was quickly back looking smart and chic in a short blue dress with large white buttons down the front, and blue high heel shoes. Kissing him on the top of his head she picked up her shoulder bag saying, 'Don't answer the door or go off with any strange men or women.'

After she had gone Ridley quickly went into the bedroom she used and checked carefully through her overnight bag but didn't find anything incriminating. 'If she's going to betray me it'll be now,' he thought, 'so if I'm not arrested in the next hour or so I am probably in the clear. However, I'm sure I can trust her with my life.' He then stripped off and had a shower and shave before dressing again in the same clothes – he had been travelling very light.

Buenos Aires/Rio Gallegos 3rd April 1982

At about the same time as Ridley left the Aeroparque terminal with Cristina heading for Tigre, the Learjet carrying Coro and the others to Rio Gallegos took off on the four-hour flight. Arriving they requisitioned an army jeep and quickly drove out to the estancia El Indio. Rafael Gomez leapt out of the car and rushed into his house but couldn't find either Maria or Ridley. Hearing the commotion Rosa appeared from the kitchen. Under questioning from Gomez and Coro she explained that a foreigner had stayed and on 2nd April they went out for a drive and a picnic. They did not return and she thought they probably wanted somewhere private for the night. Shrugging and looking defiantly at Gomez, she suggested they were probably lovers.

Gomez summoned the ranch manager and they questioned him. It became apparent that a fatal delay occurred in the passing of the information and that Ridley had probably escaped. General Coro ordered, 'In case he is still in the country I want his description passed to all the border crossings immediately and Ezeiza in case he tries to slip out by air. Where is your wife, Gomez? Is there someone here she would go to for help?'

Gomez shrugged, 'No one I know, but I haven't been down here much recently so I don't know what she's been doing. We could check with the college where she works, I suppose.'

Coro nodded at Colonel Johnson who picked up the phone and checked with Rio Gallegos College. Turning to Coro he reported, 'She's been absent without leave for two days and they haven't heard from her.'

Coro decided to head for the airbase to coordinate the search and ordered Gomez to stay at the Ranch in case she returned.

Meanwhile Maria was driving steadily down the RN3 listening to popular music interspersed with news reports about Las Malvinas. She stopped briefly at Puerto San Julian for some food and then drove on down to Rio Gallegos. Ahead of her the weather looked very grey and she guessed that autumn was coming to an end and soon the bleak winter weather would arrive. She was totally unaware of the fate awaiting her on her return home.

The Delta lunchtime 3rd April

Cristina returned laden with food and drink that she quickly put in the fridge. Then she came into the living room and sat opposite him and scrutinized him intently. 'I know you quite well after all this time, John Ridley, if that is your real name. I think you're very tired and mentally exhausted but there's something else beneath all that. Some sadness. Do you want to tell me?' As she said this she moved onto the settee next to him and enfolded him in her arms.

John settled in a comfortable position and then said quietly, 'I think I may have sacrificed someone very dear to me so I could make my escape.' Seeing her surprised look he added quickly, 'I don't mean you, Cristina.' He told her all about Maria. 'I tried to persuade her to leave with me on a number of occasions but she refused. I fear she may get into serious trouble.'

'Ah, now I see,' sympathized Cristina holding him tight and stroking the top of his head gently as a mother does to her baby. 'Of course you feel guilty, but you are a mature person able to live with the consequences of your actions. You did try to persuade her to come with you. It was her decision to stay. I don't think you do anything lightly or without thinking deeply about it. We must hope her involvement isn't discovered and pray for her.'

Trying to lift the mood she suggested, 'It is time you had something to eat and drink. I managed to get some salad and decent bread and the Malbec wine you like. Shall I prepare some lunch?'

Smiling his thanks he kissed her gently on her cheek thinking, 'She really is a very special person. I've grown very fond of her. I hope she and Andy can become friends.'

Over lunch they discussed the developing situation in Argentina and Cristina surprised him by telling him that Señor Roca had some links with the more liberal members of the Junta, and some socialist politicians. She said she didn't like what was happening in Argentina and some of the people of influence she knew felt the same. They could do nothing at the moment but if the Junta lost credibility by its actions, a time might come when they could act. She told him she agreed with this view. If she could help him in any way, she would.

They sat quietly together on the settee drinking coffee for a while, then she turned to him with eyes shiny with tears, 'We have so little time left together. It may be a long time before we see each other again. You know I love you and ache for you. Would you please make love to me this once before you go?'

John didn't answer her but continued to look at her beside him seeing the dark hair, her dark eyes and remembering her body on the beach at the cove near Bahia Blanca. Saying a little prayer, 'Andy, please forgive me,' he took her arm and led her into the bedroom. She turned down the covers then took off her dress in that fluid movement women have, removed her underwear and quickly slipped between the sheets. Smiling, she watched him as he slowly stripped off and got in the other side of the bed. 'This is going to be loving, not lust,' he thought. 'That is good.'

They lay facing each other for a while as the afternoon sun shone in through the closed curtains, just examining each other and occasionally kissing gently. Both were savouring the anticipation of the act to follow. Then he reached out to her and began to caress her breasts, her back and bottom, and as she became fully aroused he entered her and loved her until she reached her climax, and they both lay spent in each other's arms. She gave a satisfied, 'Mm,' and promptly fell asleep.

John lay on his back with his arm about her and thought back over all that had happened on this trip. He thought about Cristina, 'She's a wonderful woman and I'm very fond of her as a friend, but I don't love her. I love Andy and I want her to have our children. Cristina is the sexy woman friend who comes to visit regularly and we all have a fantastic time but we all know it works because we don't live together all the time. If I get out safely I must help her to get a good man because she certainly likes being with men.'

John drifted off to sleep and awoke to find he was in Cristina's arms and she was looking down at him. She kissed him and said, 'Thank you John. I shall remember this forever. When I see you I'll remember how I was loved. I don't think I've ever been loved so gently by a man or felt so pleasured,' and she smiled contentedly. 'Don't worry, I know you're fond of me but don't love me. You love your Andy and I hope I may meet her one of these days. I remember my promise to you and I shall never again ask you to sleep with me.' They spent the remainder of the afternoon lying in each other's arms then she roused herself and went off to shower.

Later as it began to get dark she prepared a simple meal of pasta and some grilled pork and they finished the bottle of wine. Then they tidied up the house, and packed their bags making sure they were leaving nothing behind. Taking the wine bottle and the rest of the trash Cristina walked down the road and deposited it in the communal bin so it couldn't be traced back to them.

3rd April Early Evening El Indio Estancia

As it got dark Maria arrived back tired at the ranch after her long drive from Comodoro Rivadavia. Entering and calling to Rosa she was surprised to find Rafael coming into the hall. 'So you are back, you bitch,' he snarled. 'Have you been having sex with another man? Or are you just helping him to betray my country?'

A cold fear gripped her heart as she realized he knew all about Ridley. Turning from her he called the airbase and asked to speak to General Coro. After putting the phone down he told her, 'You had better sit down. Argentine Security will be here soon to interview you. I cannot protect you any more, Maria. You have besmirched my honour and put at risk my position with the Junta. I know you knew him in Spain but I would have thought you would have had more sense than to get involved with him again.'

She sat down in a chair, clasping her arms about her and feeling utterly terrified. She tried to fasten her thoughts on John and how he was probably now on his way to safety, and her love for him and his love for her, but the thoughts were constantly driven away by her fear. A little while later she heard a car engine and then footsteps in the hall as General Coro and his people strode into the living room. She stood up as he stopped directly in front of her and asked, 'Where is he?'

Maria replied clearly, 'He asked me to drive him to Comodoro Rivadavia yesterday as the airport here was closed. He caught a flight from there to BA this morning.'

Coro started to interrogate her, 'What was he doing here?'

'He came to see me. I knew him in Spain many years ago and we met again here on one of his business visits. He is a Canadian working down here at the moment.' Looking at her husband she added, 'We are friends not lovers. He went bird watching one day then we heard the airport was closed and Argentina had invaded the Las Islas Malvinas. He decided he must leave quickly.'

'I bet he did,' said Coro, looking at Colonel Johnson. 'He was probably checking out the airbase and you helped him'

Coro suggested. 'Did you know he still worked for the British?'

Seeing her shake her head he commented, 'Your denial is not very convincing my dear. Where did he go yesterday?'

Maria tried to explain, 'He's just an old friend. I dropped him off on the way to work and he went walking and bird watching. I picked him up on the way back.'

'When did you leave him at the airport?' he demanded.

Sobbing Maria said, 'He caught the first flight from Comodoro Rivadavia this morning and I think he was planning to go straight on to Canada.'

Coro shouted angrily at her, 'I bet he was. You are a closet communist. I believe you knew what he was doing and you helped him willingly. That is treason in my book and I shall have to arrest you and take you for further interrogation in BA. Go and pack a bag – you'll be away for quite a while! Go with her,' he ordered the woman security officer, 'make sure she doesn't try to do anything stupid.' As she left the room he advised Gomez, 'It is best if you forget her. Get on with your job and support the Junta to the best of your ability, and maybe this incident might not count against you.'

Then Maria was taken away in the vehicle and disappeared.

The Delta Late Evening 3rd April 1982

Cristina had discovered that John's pick up point was only about fifteen minutes from the house, so allowing for not finding the spot immediately they left just after 10.30 p.m. Cristina drove carefully along the track by the waterway past the *supermercado* building, and as a small track appeared on the right she turned slowly down it and ran along this between the trees until they reached a small jetty that pushed out into a slightly wider channel. Turning to him she said, 'I think this is it. We have only a few minutes. Please hold me before you go.'

'Cristina, thank you for all you have done. When this madness is over you must come and visit us in Canada or UK or wherever we are. You still have my address and telephone number?'

Smiling through her tears she sobbed, 'Yes, I have them. I love you and I'll never forget you. Please take care my love,' and with a final kiss she tore herself away from him and pushed him out of the car. Grabbing his bag he walked to the end of the jetty and just then he heard the soft phut phut of a small diesel engine and saw a dark shape coming down the channel. Crouching down in case it was a police launch he waited until the boat came alongside and a voice called up, 'Señor Ridley, are you there? Mr Yamauchi sent me.' Turning with a final wave to Cristina and slinging his bag over his shoulder, he climbed down the straight ladder into the small boat. The fisherman turned the craft and headed back down the waterway without speaking. Looking back Ridley saw the headlights of Cristina's car turn and move off.

It was a dark moonless night and Ridley couldn't work out how the fisherman found his way without running aground. 'Perhaps not so difficult in the narrower channels where you can distinguish both banks, but how does he avoid running aground in other places? The dense vegetation prevents any light coming in from the stars above.' Anyway the fisherman knew the route well for eventually they came very carefully to the mouth of a channel, where he cut the engine, and the boat glided silently along in the dark while he listened intently. Not hearing any other craft nearby he restarted the engine, and they ran northwest along the mouth of the delta past the Isla Martin Garcia. Abreast the mouth of the Rio Paraná Guazú they turned to starboard and headed for the Uruguayan shore and the lights of the small town of Carmelo. When they could see them very clearly the fisherman turned to Ridley and told him with a smile that they were now in Uruguay. Ridley thanked him and shook his hand. Soon they were slipping into the small fishing harbour near the marina, and John made out Yamauchi waiting near the slipway. Saying farewell to the fisherman he walked over to Yamauchi and gripped him by both arms in a friendly hug. 'Thank you, Yamauchi-san, the arrangements worked perfectly.'

Slapping him on his shoulder in a brotherly fashion Yamauchi turned and led him along a cobbled street between old stone houses until they reached his car. It was parked very discreetly down a side street and Ridley noticed the CD plates are covered up. Yamauchi set off. On the outskirts of the town he stopped and removed the covers from the car's registration plates. Getting in he smiled at his friend and said, 'There, we are legal again. It's better not to leave any traces behind us. I'm taking you to my house in Atlántida where you must rest. Tomorrow morning I'll debrief you so I get your raw information as quickly as possible. You won't be surprised to hear that your government wants to take action now it is too late. Don't worry, when we get to the house I'll call Andy to tell her you're safe. I need you rested so I can't let you talk to her tonight. Rest now because I have a long drive ahead and the first part of this road isn't very good.'

Chapter Eighteen

Sunday 4th April Atlántida, Uruguay

Ridley woke with a start in the strange room and for a minute feared he was still in Argentina. Then he relaxed as his memory reassured him that he had arrived in Uruguay the night before and he was safe with Yamauchi. Turning over he looked at his watch and finding it was eight o'clock he got up and showered. Going over to his clothes he found that somehow his suit was pressed and a shirt had been washed, dried and pressed while he slept. So he looked moderately presentable as he descended to the patio to find Yamauchi having breakfast and reading the national newspaper.

'Good morning, John, I trust you are feeling rested. Let's have some breakfast and then we must get started because London has already been on demanding your information. There's a final briefing later this afternoon at your fleet headquarters at Northwood before the first ships sail tomorrow, so they want your information before that.'

So after breakfast they went into Yamauchi's study and John reported his observations. 'There are definitely A4 Skyhawks at San Julian at a high state of readiness and the pilots seem very confident. Maritime reconnaissance aircraft are patrolling the Atlantic coastline and there's a lot of air transport activity. I didn't know they had so many C130s! Rio Gallegos has a squadron of Mirage 3 and also a squadron of A4s. Late afternoon on the first of April six Dassault Super Etendards arrived and it looks as though they'll operate from there. I think a C130 arrived with a consignment of Exocet missiles for them but I can't be sure. The aircraft were immediately hidden away from prying eyes in one of the hardened hangars. The airfield defences have also been strengthened. There's at least one quadruple Tigercat launcher and there may be more. They also have some of their Panhard armoured cars patrolling the perimeter. The OP I established would be a good position from which an SBS or SAS team could provide flash warnings to the fleet. I don't have the map coordinates but it's the low hill about three kilometres due west of the airfield. If you can get a large scale map of the area I will provide the coordinates.'

Ridley continued, 'There were a lot of military convoys on the road. I think they are using the commercial port at Comodoro Rivadavia as it is closer than Puerto Belgrano. I certainly saw one fleet transport in there and there was a military convoy going in at the time. By the way, there were also military police guarding the main gate.'

John paused and looked chastened, 'You know when one tells it baldly, as now, it never seems very significant.'

Yamauchi responded, 'Let us be the judge of that. You're just suffering a bit of post-operation depression. I just want to check a few points that you glossed over.' Yamauchi took him through most of his report skilfully drawing more facts from him to support his conclusions. Eventually Yamauchi felt he had got everything he could out of John and relented. 'Right John, that is everything. I must now prepare the report and get it sent off. I'll send one of my aides in with a chilled bottle of Pauligny Montrachet 1977 that I've been saving for just such an occasion. I suggest you sit here in the sun and enjoy a couple of glasses and congratulate yourself on a job well done. After lunch

Andy will call and I suggest you use my study, as it's nice and private.'

So, John sat in the sun thinking about the three brave women who had been at the centre of his life for more than six months, and sipping the wonderful light-golden wine from Burgundy. Around him the madness continued, the Argentines whipped up national fervour and consolidated their hold on Las Islas Malvinas, and the British as was their way, coolly and calmly decided they would re-take the Falkland Islands at the other end of the earth during the winter season.

Yamauchi appeared, told him the report had been passed and then they had lunch. As they finished one of the staff announced the call from Andy and John quickly moved through to the study to take it. Hearing his voice she cried, 'You're safe, thank God. I love you so much, my darling. When I heard there was a full alert out for you, and I didn't know whether you had escaped, I felt I was going to die. At least now your cover is blown you can't go back. I know that's selfish but that's how I feel,' she added defensively. 'Anyway, I should be asking about you. How are you?'

'Darling, it's really good to hear your voice. What kept me going was the thought that I must get back to you. I feel a bit tired but that's just a reaction. Yamauchi has sent my report to the UK but you probably haven't seen it yet.'

'No, but I'll have to ring off soon because they'll be calling me to brief me. I just wanted to hear your voice to be sure you're safe. I have to catch the evening British Airways flight to Heathrow and you'll be leaving tomorrow. Yamauchi is going to send you from that airport near where you are – Maldonado isn't it? – to Sao Paulo and you will then catch the British Airways flight to Heathrow. I'm afraid you'll have to undergo a full debriefing by SIS and

DNI. I'll be at the airport to meet you but they won't let me attend your debrief. Apparently the politicians are now looking for scapegoats so we both have to undergo formal debriefings. Take care, my love. It won't be long now.' She rang off.

Ridley wandered out into the garden and saw Aiko Ishihara sitting with Yamauchi in the shade. 'Of course, it's Sunday,' he remembered. He thought how good they looked together so for the first time with his friend he breached Japanese etiquette as he approached them. 'Forgive me, my friend, but seeing you and Aiko together I have to ask you why you refuse to acknowledge your love for her. I think you should get married before you get too old.' Smiling at Yamauchi he attempted to soften the impoliteness 'Anyway, I now need an excuse to visit Japan as I'm sure Nippon Health will regard me as *persona non grata*. Coming to your wedding would do. You will both of course be invited to mine.'

Grinning happily at Ridley Yamauchi took hold of Aiko's left hand and showed him the gleaming solitaire engagement ring. 'Ridley-san, realizing how happy Andy and you are, I decided to act without delay. We shall marry soon, probably in Tokyo, and of course you and Andy will be our special guests. I thought we should have a celebratory dinner this evening before you leave us, so I've booked a table at the best restaurant in Punta del Este. It's time to thumb our noses at the Argentines staying there.'

Monday 5th April: Uruguay/Brazil/London

After lunch Yamauchi drove Ridley to Maldonado airport where he caught the commuter flight to Sao Paulo. He found he was booked in first class for the flight to Heathrow although after the excellent meal and a couple of glasses of champagne he was soon asleep in the comfortable wide seat. He arrived in Heathrow as dawn broke, and found he was asked to leave the plane first and was put in a car that whisked him away to the VIP lounge. There a waiting immigration official checked his passport and he was directed to a side room and Andy. After hugging him tightly and scrutinizing him to check he was OK she whispered to him, 'You'd better make sure you are fighting fit for tonight because I'll see you don't get much sleep.' Escorting him to a waiting black limousine they travelled into central London as the city woke up to a lovely spring morning. All she would tell him was that she had been debriefed, and she would wait for him to complete his debriefing.

Ridley's debriefing on 6th April was long but not too tricky. As well as the usual SIS and DNI senior personnel, there were JIC members and two junior ministers present, one from the Foreign Office and one from the Ministry of Defence. 'There's clearly a damage limitation exercise going on,' he observed. As they came to the end of the summing up, Andrew Collingwood turned to the assembled company and checked everyone was satisfied with Ridley's answers. 'In that case,' he said, 'I must thank Ridley for his work in Argentina at some personal risk I must add. It can't be his fault that the information he got back to us was not acted upon.' As one of the politicians was about to object he held up his hand and added, 'I don't think we should have any recriminations. With hindsight, the judgement made was wrong, and now we have to concentrate on recovering the Falklands. Ridley's recent information will be very helpful.'

Turning to him he said, 'Off you go now. Report to me

tomorrow at 12 noon. After I have seen you I want you to go away for two weeks' leave.' Turning to the Head of SIS he suggested, 'I think Miss James deserves some leave also.' Smiling and muttering something about him being an old romantic, her boss agreed.

Ridley left the conference room and met Andy, looking very anxious, in the anteroom where she had been waiting. Holding his hands she kissed him and asked, 'Was it OK?'

Smiling to reassure her he replied, 'Yes, they were searching questions but very fair. Our bosses are sending us off on two weeks' leave but I have to see Admiral Collingwood at 12 noon tomorrow. Until then though I am yours.' Trying to keep the tone light, he was terrified of what her reaction would be to his confession about Cristina.

She took him to their discreet hotel in Knightsbridge and when they were in their bedroom John said, 'Andy, before we go any further I have a confession to make. When I was with Cristina in the safe house in the delta she asked me to make love to her before I left, as we might never meet again. I'm ashamed to say I did and that I enjoyed it. All the time, however, I was thinking of you. I know I love you, not her, and she knows it too. But if you feel you don't want me anymore I'll understand.'

Realizing this was a critical moment in their relationship she treated it very seriously after looking at his strained expression. She admitted to herself that she wasn't surprised: not because John was a philanderer but she knew how close men and women could become when they are thrown together in dangerous situations and their lives were at risk. 'I can't say I'm not jealous of Cristina Sabato as I don't want to share you with any woman. I'd have preferred it not to have happened. However, I can't begrudge her some comfort and pleasure in the risky situation you were both in. She was risking her life for you. She's very brave, as is Maria Gomez. I doubt you'd have evaded capture without the help of both of them. So I'll forgive you this one and only time,' and then she wagged her finger at him like a teacher, 'but don't expect any forgiveness if it happens again.'

John promised, 'It will never happen again because I'll be married to you soon and I'd never betray you. Also I'll be telling Admiral Collingwood I want to give up my front-line role. Somehow I also need to help Nippon Health sort out the problem I've caused them. Over the years they've been good to me. Now take me to bed and love me like you promised.'

Andy made love to him with a vigour and tenderness he had never quite experienced from her before, and she succeeded in completely superimposing the sensation of her loving over that of Cristina Sabato in John's memory. As they lay together afterwards savouring the moment she thought thankfully, 'There can be no doubt now it is me he loves and wants.'

Later lying cosily in bed they planned their leave. They decided they must visit her parents at West Stoke in Sussex, and then they would go up to Hexham for a few days so he could show her the Northumbrian countryside. Andy reported she contacted his friend James Sandison and he was now at Eastney Barracks near Portsmouth with his SBS team. He would like to meet up before he headed south. After that they wanted to go home. They were both surprised as they realized they meant Toronto!

Before breakfast on the 7th April, the bedroom phone rang and it was Andrew Collingwood's assistant ringing to clarify that they were both expected at 12 noon. After

John relayed this information to Andy they both looked pensive. Looking across to Andy, John wondered, 'What is the old bugger up to? His assistant said that as you are on leave you should come along as well. Did he mean he didn't therefore need to clear it with your boss?'

Promptly at 12 noon they were shown into Collingwood's office to find he had another visitor. Jim Graham of Canadian Intelligence was sitting in a large leather chair clutching a glass of whisky. 'You both prefer wine I think,' remarked Collingwood, pouring out two large glasses of white wine. 'You remember Jim Graham? I'm afraid we have something very important and serious to tell you. It's something about your past, John, that I should have told you about before, but my courage has always failed me when I tried. Jim is here to give me moral support on this occasion.'

Launching straight in Collingwood began to explain. 'It's about your parents, John. Your father, also called John Ridley, was a naval intelligence officer based in Argentina in 1951. He was trying to find out information about the black deeds being perpetrated by Peron and his supporters before the election due that year. He and your mother, Paula, and their one-year-old baby – that's you – were in a car travelling back from a meeting with some liberal politicians and trade unionists in the delta.' As he explained this he heard Andy's sharp intake of breath and looking up saw her looking shocked with one clenched fist to her mouth and gripping John's tightly with her other hand. 'We don't know whether he got the information he sought that day, but on the road back from Tigre the car was in collision with a lorry that drove off quickly after side-swiping their car into the ditch. Purely by chance a police car was close by, and they saved you but they couldn't save your parents.

297

Jim and I were both attached to our respective embassies and your father worked for me although we were of a similar age. As we told you in Ottawa at Christmas we decided we'd look after you but for a multitude of reasons neither of us felt we should adopt you. That is why I'm your guardian and Jim and his wife are your godparents.

'Over the years we continued to investigate your parents' death and the file we have compiled is pretty conclusive. We believe there's a very high probability the killing was carried out by a secret military organisation with strong fascist leanings that helped overthrow a previous president in 1943. We believe they feared that the president's re-election might be jeopardized by the information your father was seeking or had obtained. We know at the time this organization was led by General Gustavo Coro. He is still very much alive. You met his son, General Alfredo Coro at that dinner you hosted for the Minister of Health. The son is currently head of Argentine Military Intelligence and we believe he's deeply involved in the strategy of the Disappeared. I'm sorry I've given this information to you so starkly and coldly but I've agonized for years about how you tell you. I have arranged for lunch to be served in private here a little later so we can talk it through.

'I do have one other related topic I must cover. It wouldn't be fair to avoid it. I wouldn't ask you to do it if I didn't think you were the only person who might pull it off. I have to order you to go back into Argentina, probably in early June but the timing depends on the success of our operation in the Falklands. Our embassy will have to pull back to Montevideo now so they won't be able to meet with the key opposition personalities. You'll enter covertly and meet some liberal members of the Junta, opposition politicians and trade unionists and present the British negotiating position to them. You'll also give them a copy of our file on this secret military organisation and Gustavo Coro and ask them to act upon it. I expect you'll go over one night, meet the people during the day and return the next night. We think we might use your safe house in the delta if it is available.'

Andy protested, 'You'll be putting John into exactly the same position as his father. Why can't you send someone else?'

Seeing her terrible fear for John's safety Collingwood felt sorry for her. Crouching down before her he took her hand and replied gently, 'Not quite the same, Andy, but I admit the plan has a certain irony. I'm afraid there's no one else. John is known and trusted already by some of the people he may meet. I can't tell you who they are, but be assured I wouldn't use him if I thought I could do it with someone else. I want you to go off on your leave and return here on Monday 26th April as we can do nothing until our troops land in the Falklands and that won't be for a while yet.'

London 26th April 1982

Arriving at Heathrow from Toronto Ridley discovered that the first part of the British plan had been completed. The islands of South Georgia had been recaptured and one of the Argentines' four precious submarines had been badly damaged there. It was a small victory but it gave the British public growing confidence. 'People are naïve,' thought John. 'They have no idea of the severe challenge to mount an amphibious landing more than 8000 miles from the UK in winter.'

Going direct to the Admiralty Building he was shown

into Andrew Collingwood's office. 'My boy, you are looking well,' he said. 'Andy is certainly good for you. She's well, I trust, and not worrying too much about you?'

'I'm fine, Andrew, thank you. Much refreshed and ready to go when you need me.'

'I'm relieved to hear that,' replied Collingwood. 'If you'd said you didn't want to go, I had resolved that I wouldn't order you, and SIS agreed with that view. We didn't feel you should be put further at risk because our politicians managed to do a good imitation of fiddling while Rome burns.'

He went on, 'The time isn't right for any meetings with the opposition. The Junta still has the support of the people. In a few days we'll declare a total exclusion zone around the Falklands and will then be free to attack anything attempting to get there, and also the occupying forces in the islands themselves. It will, however, be some weeks before we attempt a landing, as the diplomatic niceties have to be followed. There's also the vexed question of the United States' support. They belong to NATO but see South America as being very much in their sphere of influence. We need their support because we'll need many more air-to-air missiles if we get into serious combat down there.

'Only when the Junta is weakened by reverses in the Falklands will the opposition feel it is sensible to begin to challenge them. That's when you'll go in. Before then I think you should operate from Uruguay and Yamauchi's been asked to find a small house for you in Atlántida.' With a broad grin he added, 'It's also been agreed that Miss James should operate from there to keep an eye on you. She can provide the link with the embassy and the Foreign Office.

'We would like you to be down there by 24th May so you have time to get everything set up before we need you to go across. You have a seat booked on the Air Canada flight to Toronto tomorrow morning. For the rest of today I want you to see a number of people in the Foreign Office and SIS, for they will all be relying on you and they must have absolute confidence in you. This evening we are dining with two junior ministers from the Foreign Office and MOD, and their permanent secretaries, and they'll provide you with a very honest political briefing. I hardly need to stress, John, that this will carry the highest possible security classification. It's the stuff that never gets released to the public, not even after thirty years.'

Chapter Nineteen

San Carlos Water, Falklands 21st May 1982

It was 4 a.m. and still dark as the County class destroyer heaved to about one mile north of Fanning Head on East Falkland Island. Captain James Sandison, Royal Marines, quietly gave the order to embark and his Special Boat Service unit slipped agilely into the rigid raiding craft secured alongside. These were the cream of the Royal Marine Commandos, skilled parachutists and divers and the toughest soldiers in the navy. When everyone was onboard they moved slowly away from the ship and headed in line astern towards the dark smudge of their target on the horizon. Before sunrise the task force would steam into San Carlos Water to begin landing the British troops of the invasion force, and Sandison's team must neutralize the twenty or more Argentine troops and their artillery at Fanning Head before then. After this they must move on to their second target and take Port San Carlos where there were thought to be around 40 troops billeted.

As their boats slid gently on to the sand of a small cove just inside the wide bay they quickly leapt out and fanned out across the beach. Stepping ashore, Sandison thinks, 'I'm the first British Officer to return to the Falklands since the Argentine invasion.'

Crouching low on the pebble and sand beach they checked for movement around them. Confident there were no sentries out on this side of the point Sandison raised his hand in a sweeping motion and they formed up and climbed the gentle hill in platoon formation towards the Argentines' position. Moving cautiously once they reached the brow of the hill they checked for sentries and booby traps. Confident they had reached the perimeter of the artillery position he deployed his men across the point then instructed the interpreter to use the loudhailer to call on the Argentines to surrender.

After the call there was silence as the startled sentry no doubt alerted someone more senior. 'Call them again,' Sandison ordered. 'Let's try to do this without bloodshed.'

But the second loudhailer message was greeted with machine-gun fire in their general direction. Reluctantly he ordered his men to return fire and they fired very deliberately at the muzzle flashes of the enemy's weapons. After two or three volleys they moved forward into even closer positions. From aerial reconnaissance they knew there were no strong points, just a couple of hurriedly erected huts. After about fifteen minutes he was sure the Argentines had taken some casualties so he ordered a ceasefire then called upon them again to surrender. This time there was a reply in Spanish.

'Tell them the ship to seaward will begin bombarding their position if they don't surrender immediately.'

That did the trick and the interpreter reported that they would surrender. They told them to walk towards the torchlight that was being shown and soon they could just make out the Argentine artillerymen walking out towards them with their hands in the air. An SBS soldier checked them with another torch as they passed him. When they were well clear of their base the Marines ordered them to lie down on their fronts and they were carefully searched before being marched off down to the bay and into captivity.

'Right. Immobilize the guns then it's time to move on. We're just about on schedule but it may take us longer at Port San Carlos. Hopefully this fire-fight wasn't heard down there.'

They quickly march the three miles to the next small settlement. However, as the SBS men moved cautiously up to the outskirts they saw a white flag being waved in their direction and soon it was confirmed that the garrison here wished to surrender. Clearly the small garrison had heard the firing but instead of preparing to resist they had decided to lay down their arms without a fight. They were all conscripts not regulars. As the surrendering Argentines were being searched the first elements of 40 Commando and 2 Para sailed up San Carlos Water past them heading for their disembarkation point at San Carlos Settlement.

His task completed Sandison looked east across the Island to the lightening sky as dawn broke thinking, 'Well, that's the first phase completed and thank God the weather seems to be holding. If we can just get most of the troops and stores ashore today before the Argentines can respond with heavy air raids, then we should be OK.'

Looking across at the sorry lot of prisoners sitting under guard by the water's edge, he thought 'So far not a very determined enemy, just young conscripts with a few regulars to lead them. Not much of a match for our professionals. Let's hope we can keep the Argentine Navy and Air Force away, then it'll be just a matter of time, grit and determination.'

Quickly the British troops secured the surrounding hills and then the twelve troop and supply ships entered the Sound to unload further troops, ammunition and food. 45 Commando and 3 Para landed and soon after dawn the first 105mm guns and Rapier anti-aircraft systems were airlifted ashore. Unfortunately the last of these were not set up before the air raids began a couple of hours after dawn.

Watching the attack from Fanning Head, Sandison marvelled at the Argentine Skyhawks skidding low across the sea towards the supply ships, the gun-line of warships out in Falkland Sound and San Carlos Water firing their 4.5 inch guns and Seacat missiles at them, whilst manoeuvring with restricted sea-room occasionally veiled from his sight as rain squalls drifted across. Rapier missiles from the surrounding hills chased them as they sped towards the supply ships. Looking down on to the Sound he found it black with craft busily disembarking all the vital resources for an invasion force despite the mayhem going on about them. This first attack was clearly surprised by the violence of the defence, and failed to reach the supply ships that were their main target before calling off the attack. Sandison thought, 'You cannot doubt the bravery and determination of the Argentine pilots. One plane's been shot down by a Rapier missile. Another's claimed downed by a Seacat from one of the frigates. One left the scene trailing smoke. It's unlikely to make it back to its mainland base. They will be back.'

Just then his signalman reported his troop was ordered to move from San Carlos eastwards to reconnoitre the route that the main force would take in a few days when the beachhead was consolidated. Calling them all together he led them away from the busy beachhead.

Atlántida, Uruguay, May 1982

Monday 24th May, Andy and John walked into the little house accompanied by Yamauchi. 'This is so pretty,' exclaimed Andy. 'It'll do nicely.'

'You should remember, woman, we are here to do some work,' said John, attempting to sound gruff.

'I see you had to get married quickly,' quipped Yamauchi, referring to the wedding rings they were both wearing. He explained their cover story, 'This house is being rented in the name of Mr and Mrs John and Adrienne Cunningham. They are Canadians and he is a writer researching his next book to be set in Uruguay, Argentina and Brazil. For the moment they're keeping away from Argentina because of the present troubles. John,' he ordered, 'you must definitely keep away from Montevideo, as we believe the Argentines are watching the British Embassy there now there's no British representation in BA. Andy will be your contact as the Argentines don't know her. I'll leave you to settle in now but please come to dinner tonight as I want Andy to meet Aiko. My house is only a short walk from here.' After giving them directions he began to leave, then tapped his head and turned back to them.

'I nearly forgot,' shaking his head, 'it must be early senility. I have a message for you from the chairman of Nippon Health. Apparently the British Ambassador in Tokyo briefed my Foreign Minister and he has spoken to your chairman. The message is, 'They believe you have acted with honour. They recognize that you cannot continue to work for them and they will appoint a Japanese Section Head to replace you. However, when the troubles here are over they would like you to act as consultant on the project until the subsidiary company is established. They plan to go ahead because it is an excellent business opportunity.' He laughed, 'They suggested you might be based in Uruguay as it might be difficult for you to visit Argentina for some time.'

'How wonderful,' commented Andy, 'Yamauchi-san,

your people are so generous. Most western companies would be suing John for potential loss of business. John has told me about Aiko and I'm very happy for you both.'

As the sun began to drop towards the water of the Rio de la Plata, Andy and John walked hand in hand down the narrow lane to the waterfront and wandered along the empty sandy beach. It was a beautiful late autumn evening and they enjoyed the warm breeze on their faces, but as twilight set they turned inland up another lane nearby to Yamauchi's house. Yamauchi quickly opened the front door and ushered them into the sitting room. John wondered at the change that had occurred in his friend. Aiko was clearly very westernized and Yamauchi was comfortable with that. Soon Aiko appeared, in an apron, and took Andy off with her to the kitchen leaving the men to chat over a glass of Chablis as the meal was prepared.

'Yamauchi-san, you and Aiko are clearly very happy. I'm very glad for you both,' said John.

'Thank you, Ridley-san. Now you see how westernized I have become perhaps we should use western forms of address. Please call me Toshiro and I'll call you John. Tomorrow we must start planning for your meetings now your forces are on East Falkland. I think we should have a joint session with Andy first so you can give us your views. Then I'm afraid you must leave Andy and me to organize things. I would like you to get to know Aiko better, so I've arranged for her to show you some of eastern Uruguay for a couple of days while Andy and I are busy. I hope that is OK?'

'Toshiro, that's sensible. It's important there's clear, rational thinking about the plans and I'm too involved to do that. That's the potential disadvantage of Andy and I being together here. We must be disciplined about this – it's still a dangerous situation over there. I'll certainly leave you both to sort things out. Then I can concentrate on how to influence the liberal element I'm meeting. I'll enjoy being with Aiko if she can spare the time.'

As they reached this understanding the two women arrived and they took their drinks on to the patio in the cool autumn air talking about life in Uruguay, before retiring indoors for a wonderful Japanese meal directed by Aiko.

Tuesday 25th May Yamauchi arrived after breakfast but before they started he handed Andy a message. After reading it she told John, 'They're just letting you know that the observation points you found are working well, especially the ones at San Julian and Rio Gallegos which are providing good early air raid warnings for the fleet. They tried to do the same at Rio Grande but the Sea King developed engine trouble and had to divert to Chile.'

After this they spent the day going over all aspects of the quick visits to Argentina, getting every thought and opinion of Ridley's on the table so that it could be assessed.

Andy and Yamuchi suggested that as the British forces had established a beachhead on East Falkland at San Carlos Water it was likely that Ridley might have to visit Argentina early in June. For about an hour they discussed whether they should use the house in the delta. Was it easy to get to covertly? Was it easy for the security services to monitor activities? How easy was it for the key people to get there covertly? They eventually concluded it was the best, if not the only, option, and they needed to contact Cristina Sabato as John didn't know who owned the house. They decided it was important to protect Cristina so how they contacted her was critical. Eventually they decided to use Arthur Dean. Incredibly he had not been linked to Ridley and his journalist credentials would allow him to contact her. They decided he should approach her and reveal his friendship with Ridley, then ask about the house and whether it could be used again, stressing that they were all working to bring peace to the troubled relations between Argentina and UK.

They also decided the best entry and exit route had to be via Carmelo. By the end of the day they expressed satisfaction with progress, and Toshiro and Andy told Ridley to go off and enjoy himself with Aiko for a couple of days.

Uruguay/Argentina June 1982

Tuesday 1st June, Andy and John learnt from the BBC World Service news report that the British 5th Infantry Brigade had landed at San Carlos Water beachhead on East Falkland so the British reinforcements should speed up the advance across the island. Later in the day Andy received confirmation that an opposition representative would meet Ridley at the safe house tomorrow so she activated all the transport arrangements. About eight o'clock in the evening Yamauchi drove him through Montevideo and on to the small port of Carmelo. Ridley quickly walked through the cobbled streets and shaking hands with the fisherman stepped into his boat. Without undue delay he got underway and followed the reverse course to Ridley's previous trip. The night was as dark as on the last trip but the fisherman found his way surely like a blind man. As they came alongside the small jetty at Dorada, Ridley grasped the ladder and climbed quickly to the top, as the fisherman went astern and then disappeared slowly down the waterway. As he got to the top of the ladder he saw a small figure just to one side. He experienced a quick burst of adrenalin until he heard, 'John, it is Cristina.' Then she was in his arms and kissing him. Holding him by his hand she led him through the dark to a small car. He could tell it was a different car from last time so she was taking sensible precautions.

Turning the car around on sidelights she drove carefully back on to the road and before long they were at the house and she was hiding the car in the garage. Opening the front door they moved inside without putting on the lights. 'I think we should leave the lights off then no one will see we are still up,' she suggested.

'Yes,' agreed Ridley, 'that makes a lot of sense as we will probably have to use it again. We don't want to lead the opposition into a security trap. Cristina, I didn't realize this house belonged to Señor Roca.'

'Well, I didn't want you to think I just came here with him. I stay here with friends sometimes. I've been here with him, and yes I've slept with him here, but usually I'm his hostess when he brings other friends,' she added defiantly. 'He's opposed to the Junta, although like many he hasn't yet voiced his opposition. He knows his house is being used for contacts but he doesn't know the details. We've just agreed he won't use it for the next two months. Now I think we should get some sleep. Your contact will be here about ten o'clock. I've brought some food with me.'

So they went upstairs to the bedroom without switching on the lights. Cristina turned back the bedclothes and they both stripped off and slipped between the sheets. Then like regular lovers they kissed and cuddled briefly then turned over and were soon fast asleep. They just felt very safe together. With the dawn they woke and talked about what had been happening to each of them since April. Ridley was surprised and delighted to find that Cristina and Arthur Dean had become friendly. She, rather shyly for her, admitted she really liked him. She also thought he liked her and they had been out together quite a few times. Smiling at him she told him they both liked dancing. Ridley told her about Andy and also Yamauchi-san and his girl.

About ten thirty on 3rd June a car parked in front of the garage and as Cristina opened the door a woman slipped in. Ridley was surprised to see it was Señora Mantovani from the Foreign Ministry. '*Buenas dias* Señor Ridley. From the look on your face I see you didn't know who your contact would be. I am somewhat reassured by that. Cristina tells me you're to be trusted, you're honourable, and you tried to prevent conflict between our two countries. I'm here as the representative of a group very concerned, shall we say, at where the Junta is taking us. We'd like to hear what the British have to say.'

They moved into the sitting room and Cristina served coffee then left the two of them to talk. 'Señora Mantovani,' he started but stopped when she held up her hand.

'As we're risking our lives here we can be more informal. I understand from Cristina that your given name is John, and mine is Elena so let's use them.'

'Very well, Elena,' smiled John. 'I'm here as the representative of the British Foreign Office. If circumstances were different then I imagine you'd be having this discussion with the ambassador. My government's position is that, following Argentina's armed aggression and your government's rejection of the British proposals at the UN, the only position acceptable is a full withdrawal by your armed forces. If they withdraw, Britain wouldn't seek any reparations from Argentina. If your forces don't withdraw then British forces in the Falkland Islands will eject them, and we'll go to the UN to seek ongoing sanctions against your country. However, should your country decide to return to being a full democracy, we'll welcome you back into the international community as a full member. My country, and we believe the US also, will be prepared to encourage the International Monetary Fund and the World Bank to help Argentina through its current economic difficulties.'

'John,' replied Elena, 'you should become a diplomat. That was a good diplomatic statement: a good balance of steel within the velvet glove. But unfortunately, as we see it, it isn't quite as simple as you describe. Some of us in government, as I indicated to you, became very concerned at the Junta's military adventurism but we were marginalized or eliminated so were unable to mount an effective opposition. There are a number of senior civil servants at my level who oppose the Junta, and I'm authorized to mention Andres Roca as a gesture of good faith. Also a number of middle ranking Junta officers, and some Air Force generals, who believe the Junta should return the country to the people.'

'Argentina's actions have lost it the support of the United States,' riposted Ridley.

'Yes, but they haven't told the Junta. They still believe the USA will support them as a bulwark against communism and socialism in South America. The other problem is that the senior members of the Junta would consider it dishonourable to retreat or surrender.'

'So how do we move forward?'

'We can't move yet, but if the British seem likely to defeat our forces in Islas Malvinas then we believe we'll be able to force the Junta from power. Unfortunately we can do nothing before then, so more British and Argentine soldiers will sadly lose their lives before it's over. If the Junta falls we'll of course strive to replace it with a democratically elected government. It's what Argentina needs.'

After this positive and realistic statement she asked a number of searching questions about Britain's position on the sovereignty of Las Islas Malvinas as she insisted on calling them. Ridley did his best to answer them using his London briefings and excellent memory to good effect. Eventually she indicated that all her queries had been dealt with. 'John,' she confirmed, 'I'll pass on your comments to my friends and if you continue to make military progress let me know through Cristina and I'll arrange a further meeting.'

After lunch Elena slipped out and quickly drove off. 'Have you known her for long?' asked Ridley.

'Yes, for quite a while,' smiled Cristina, 'she is one of my aunts. You can trust her. I wouldn't have let her come to see you if I didn't think she was safe. She's never been happy with a military government and believes that democracy is the only way. She likes you by the way. When we were setting this up she said when she met you before she felt she could trust you. I don't know what it is you have John Ridley, but women just seem to drop their defences when you are around.'

'I don't think I will ever get to the bottom of the web of friendships and family relationships you Latins weave.'

Sitting down in a chair opposite him she told him, 'Now let's change the subject. Before I prepare dinner I want to know all about Canada.' Seeing his knowing look she blushed very prettily and protested, 'I'm just interested. I've never been there and I've heard so much about it.'

The evening passed quickly as they chatted over a simple meal of pasta and all too soon it was time for him to go. They went through the routine of cleaning the house thoroughly then she drove him once more to the jetty near Dorada. As they heard the boat coming she kissed him and drove swiftly away. For Ridley the journey through the waterways of the delta was fascinating. He loved being on the water in the dark, and this surreptitious movement seemed like the stories he read as a child of navy operations on the rocky Brittany shore, dropping and retrieving British agents on moonless nights: pinpoint navigation based on experience and dead reckoning, just like this fisherman skilfully steering his boat back to safety in Carmelo. As they came into the small fishing harbour Ridley spotted Yamauchi standing in the shadows and after thanking the fisherman he walked with Yamauchi back to his car. On the way to Atlántida he recorded his initial report into a small Dictaphone. Yamauchi would bring this with him in the morning when they prepared the report for SIS.

Late morning 4th June John, Andy and Toshiro met to prepare the report to SIS. They learnt from the radio news that British forces were making good progress across East Falkland Island and Stanley airfield had been bombed again. The detailed report was sent off and they heard no more. Andy visited the embassy on a couple of occasions but the world seemed to be passing them by in their little house in Atlántida.

As June progressed the British marched eastwards across the island and by the 11th they were ready to assault Mounts Harriet and Longdon, and Two Sisters, three hills close to Stanley town and airfield, and if the Argentine forces were dislodged from all three, their positions around Stanley would be threatened.

On the 11th Ridley received orders to return for a meeting with the Argentine opposition. Two dossiers also arrived by courier. They contained all the information collected about the killing of John's parents by the fascist military organization, and what was known about General Alfredo Coro's role with the Disappeared. That evening he again followed the well-tried route to the safe house and arrived there safely, and was met by Cristina in a different vehicle yet again.

The meeting was arranged for lunchtime on the 12th so Ridley had time to prepare. Shortly after noon the first visitors arrived and by one o'clock Elena Mantovani reported everyone was present and Cristina served lunch. Before lunch Elena formally introduced Ridley and then all the Argentines present. Representing the more liberal Junta members were Air Force General Guiseppe Monti and Army Colonel Gianni Gayoso. Amongst the civilians present were Jorge Domingo of the Democratic Alliance Party, Alberto Alonso of the Argentine Trade Union Federation, Andres Roca of Ministry of Health, and of course Elena Mantovani from the Foreign Ministry.

After the lunch was cleared away, Ridley presented the British Government's ultimatum. He told them that the British forces expected to take Stanley by the 16th. There was nothing to stop them achieving their objective. He pointed out that the Junta was completely discredited both militarily and economically, and had no international respect or reputation left at the UN. The only course for Argentina now was to overthrow the Junta and return to civilian government and full democracy. If this was achieved quickly then Britain and the US would support Argentina through the UN, International Monetary Fund and the World Bank. Ridley stressed, 'It will be seen as an important signal when the president resigns.'

Seeing that this had hit home he asked them what they were prepared to do. After much discussion amongst themselves they authorized him to reassure the British government that they would begin to take action against the hard line Junta members immediately. They believed the balance of power had now swung against the hardliners. Looking at their serious demeanours he did not doubt their commitment or underestimate the risks they faced. Wryly he thought, 'I know exactly how they're feeling at the moment.'

As they began to fidget and consider leaving, he asked for their forbearance for a few more minutes. 'I have another serious matter to report to you and it's one that involves me personally. I have here two dossiers prepared by British Intelligence. Once refers to an incident in 1951 and the other refers to the Dirty War and the Disappeared. Dealing with the Dirty War first, we have evidence that implicates the present Head of Argentine Intelligence, General Alfredo Coro, and we wish him to be suspended immediately and the evidence seriously investigated.

'The second dossier concerns the deaths in 1951 of John and Paula Ridley, my parents.' As he said this, a deathly stillness settled around the room and glancing across at Cristina he saw how startled she was. 'In 1951 my father was an officer with British Naval Intelligence attached to the embassy here. On the way back from a meeting with opposition politicians in the delta his car was knocked off the road by a lorry that did not stop. I was rescued from the wreckage but both my parents were killed. The evidence points to the killing being ordered by General Gustavo Coro, then Head of Intelligence, and carried out by a fascist secret military organisation. I'm sure you know the one I am referring to. I understand Gustavo Coro is still alive. I'm instructed by my government to hand over these dossiers to you with the request that they be investigated

316

at the earliest opportunity. If no action is taken within one month of the fall of the Junta the dossiers will be made public at the UN.'

Elena Mantovani responded on behalf of the assembled group, 'John, thank you for your words. The support of the British and the Americans gives us hope and we'll do our best to achieve a democratic government quickly. I'll take these dossiers and will ensure the new government investigates the allegations rigorously. I give you my promise. I also give you my heartfelt apology for what my people did to your family.' Then she came across to him and hugged him and kissed him on both cheeks. 'Gentlemen, I think we should phase our departure. I'm intending to go on to Rosario for the remainder of the weekend so if you don't mind I'll leave first. I'll contact you all on Monday.'

After they had all left, Cristina and John whiled away the time until he was to leave, talking about plans for the future, and he gently probed her relationship with Arthur Dean. Realizing she was being interrogated she challenged him, 'You sound like a possessive father quizzing his daughter about her first boy.'

'No I'm not. I'm just like one of your girlfriends wanting to know all the details. After all I am a very close friend.'

Smiling at that Cristina admitted, 'If you must know I think he might be the one. I enjoy being with you but it's so very different when I'm with him. He's about my age and we enjoy similar things, and I know he really fancies me and wants me. You know what? We haven't made love yet. It's as though we know it's special and we want it all to happen properly. I know this sounds very old-fashioned but it feels right for us. If our luck holds I think I might move with him to Canada and then divorce my husband.'

'When this is over I'm sure Arthur will be given some

leave so you must persuade him to bring you to Toronto for a visit. You can stay with us.'

She smiled happily at him and got up to prepare dinner brushing the top of his hair with her fingers as she passed. John relaxed listening to her working in the small kitchen and concluded, 'This trip would be far more stressful without Cristina's support and company.' All too soon it was time to leave and they followed the same routine as previously. At the small jetty near Dorada, John hugged Cristina tightly, 'Cristina thank you for all your love and support. I realized earlier this evening that the reason I am feeling so relaxed is because you're here with me. I hope this will be the last trip here for both your sake and Andy's. When it's all over please come and see us in Canada. Good luck with Arthur.'

As he finished saying this he stiffened. 'What is it?' whispered Cristina. 'The boat I can hear, the engine doesn't sound the same. This sounds deeper. It may be twin diesels. It could be a small patrol boat. We'd better hide in the trees.' Luckily they had hidden the car a short way down the track in the trees so when the patrol boat played a small searchlight around the jetty nothing excited the interest of the authorities whoever they are. Cristina and John stayed still for a while as the sound of the engines faded into the distance. After about thirty minutes they heard another engine and listened carefully, then John relaxed, 'I think it's my fisherman.' Sure enough the same man soon appeared at the jetty and John climbed down the ladder into the boat. Informing him about the patrol boat the fisherman grinned and indicated he had spotted it and hid up a small channel before it passed. He reassured Ridley that if it followed the same routine they wouldn't see it again. Ridley hoped he was correct in his assumption because it would be sad if the operation struck rocks at the eleventh hour.

As they arrived in Carmelo harbour Ridley felt a strong sense of relief that the operation was over. Greeting Yamauchi he said, 'Hello Toshiro. The meeting went successfully. They informed me they would act against the hardliners in the Junta and make sure the two Coros are investigated. Now it's over do you mind if we just sit here for a while? It's a beautiful still night.'

'I thought you might feel like that,' said his friend. 'I've brought a bottle of Chablis with me packed in some ice and it's stayed quite cool in this cold air. Let's sit and enjoy it in peace.' So the two men sat on the harbour wall looking out on the broad Rio de la Plata, drinking their wine, enjoying their companionship and the satisfaction of a job well done. But for Ridley there was the perfectionist's nagging doubt. 'If I'd found out the information sooner or if it'd been more convincing might the war have been prevented?' Looking down the broad expanse of the Rio de la Plata he thought, 'Out there are brave men, Argentines and British, still losing their lives for what they have been told is right.'

Feeling the cold begin to get to them they roused themselves and regaining the car headed back for Atlántida where John was soon in Andy's arms, and Toshiro no doubt in Aiko's.

Chapter Twenty

Two Sisters 11th June 1982

As dusk fell James Sandison and his SBS troop moved up to the designated start line on the left flank of 45 Commando. Their objective was the flat-topped peak of Two Sisters Mountain: a strategic objective. It was the first mountain before Mount Kent that overlooked the valley leading down to Stanley. Other British forces would be attacking Mounts Longdon and Harriet that night, and the timing of all the assaults was critical, for the Argentine forces on each peak could provide mutual fire support.

Along with two troops of 45 Commando they were allocated to attack the main peak of Two Sisters but must wait until the other troops had taken the subsidiary peak so they could provide fire support for the main attack.

Everyone stood quietly by their heavy packs as they waited for the radio order to commence the attack. His team were all very experienced professionals and had been through many situations like this before. They didn't talk or fidget with their weapons. They just watched the sky and thought about life and perhaps death: but not fearfully. Sandison looked up the mountain and could just make out the top with its mast silhouetted against the starry sky for it was a clear night for once. At 1070 feet it was not that high but it would still be a difficult climb with those heavy packs over broken jagged rock. In the previous 24 hours there had been a lot of patrol activity around their objective, as well as aerial reconnaissance, and they believed they knew most of the enemy's positions on the mountain. British patrols had fought some running battles with Argentine patrols and knew these were professional troops, probably commandos, brought in from the mainland to strengthen the defences. They weren't as well dug in here as on the other mountains as they had had less time to prepare. 'So it should be a piece of cake,' he hoped.

The radio operator called quietly to Sandison, and going over to him he learnt that the other attack had been delayed and both attacks would have to be simultaneous. 'Start time 30 minutes.'

He walked carefully across to the other troops for the grass here was very hummocky and it would be very easy to turn an ankle. Passing the information to the two lieutenants leading them he confirmed the lines of approach and attack, for it would be carried out in the dark unless an Argentine set off a flare.

Exactly to the minute the radio crackled with the move forward order and the troops began the steady walk up the hill. The attack on the subsidiary peak should meet the enemy first and hopefully the fire-fight there might distract the defenders of the main peak. Sure enough rifle fire began from up the slope to their right and the Royal Marines returned fire as they climbed. There was some mortar fire but it seemed to be overshooting and it looked as though the Marines were making it to their objective without too much problem.

Just then a flare exploded above them fired from the main peak and they all froze in their positions as the light drifted gently away to the north. But they had been spotted, for someone fired a rifle in their direction.

'Spread out. Make for that col,' he ordered pointing

slightly away to his left. This would split the fire of the defenders and they should find it difficult to fire down on them without exposing themselves. His men moved quickly up the slope, resisting the urge to return fire for it would just confirm their positions to the defenders. His troop made it safely to the col and slumped down in defensive positions as he reassessed the situation.

'1 Section continue straight up from here to just under the crest. 2 Section to move with me slightly to the right up to the crest. When we have both reached these positions we'll go over the crest and engage the enemy. Keep your heads down. Good luck.'

Both groups moved forward carefully but soon the defenders spotted them and there was firing in their direction, a mortar round exploded to the rear of 1 Section and the ensuing splinters slightly wounded one of his men who slumped to the ground. The rest made it safely to their positions as other mortar rounds exploded behind them and splinters flew through the air but missed them all.

Sandison peered carefully over the crest and observed the disposition of the enemy as marked by the muzzle flashes of their weapons. There were mortars somewhere beyond the crest on the other side and a couple of heavy machine guns for he could hear them, but on the peak the troops seemed to be lightly armed, which was strange. He would have expected the mortars to be up there. He slipped back down to his men as another flare exploded overhead.

'The mortars and heavy machine guns seem to be down the other slope. The defenders up here are lightly armed. If we can pick them off and take the peak we should be able to fire down on the mortars and the machine guns before they can zero in on us. 1 Section spread out left and 2 Section to the right and engage on my order.'

The Marines slipped away as ordered and took up their positions in the darkness and on his order began to fire steadily at the muzzle flashes of the enemy's weapons. The Argentines begin to take casualties and the number of weapons returning fire reduced. The other troops had also gained the peak so there was fire coming in from two sides, and the troops on the lower peak had 66mm mortars in action against the mortars and heavy machine guns on the eastern slope. The Argentine fire seemed to have lessened so the British put up a flare, and they saw the Argentine soldiers slipping quickly down the eastern slope and disappearing into the darkness of the lower slope.

Sandison ordered his men to cease firing and they set up defensive positions in case there was a counter attack. He sent a team down the east slope to secure the heavy weapons so they couldn't be used again in any counter-attack. But as dawn broke they found the country below them empty of the enemy who had all fled back to the next defensive position on Mount Kent, leaving behind ten dead and four badly wounded conscripts. The Marines had lost three killed and three wounded, all as a result of mortar fire.

Sandison went around his men, telling them, 'Well done, lads. Won't be long until we are in Stanley. There really isn't anywhere for them to go. Mount Harriet and Longdon are also ours so we're now ready for the final push.'

Atlántida 13th June 1982

After breakfast on Sunday 13th June, Toshiro, John and Andy met for the formal debrief, not that it took very long, and then Toshiro and Andy called London. She then travelled in to Montevideo with Yamauchi and spent the remainder of the day at the British Embassy while he caught up on his work at the Japanese Embassy. Ridley spent the day unwinding after the tensions of the past six weeks. Over lunch he listened to the radio news and learnt that the British forces had taken Two Sisters, Mounts Harriet and Longdon and the battle had commenced for Mount Tumbledown. 'When that is taken the war will be over,' he thought. Later he took a long walk along the beach. Walking fast in the cool air, on a warship grey day, with a hint of rain coming in from the southeast across the sea, down from where the battle was raging and the ships were tossing in the stormy seas, maintaining the exclusion zone patrols around the islands.

Andy returned to say London and the embassy were very pleased with his work. She had to go back the next day for a review meeting but it was likely they would be recalled soon. They then walked down to Yamauchi's for a companionable evening with Toshiro and Aiko.

Dawn, 14th June on Sapper Hill overlooking Stanley, Falkland Islands

James Sandison stood with a group of officers from 40 Commando and the Welsh Guards looking down on Stanley town. On Mount William, Mount Tumbledown, Wireless Ridge and the other mountains surrounding Stanley similar groups of British officers also kept watch over the Argentine forces now penned into the area of the town and Cape Pembroke to the east. They had nowhere to go and no expectation of relief from the sea for the British Task Force had a stranglehold on the waters surrounding the islands.

Every day since they landed they had been subjected to air attacks either from the mainland or Stanley airfield itself. So far that morning no air attacks: it was easy for the Task Force to achieve air superiority now most of the British forces were circling Stanley and the airfield there was now threatened by the British artillery. But as late as the night before they heard an Argentine C130 had landed presumably with supplies and then quickly taken off again.

Sandison and his SBS Troop were airlifted off Two Sisters to augment a scratch force of the remainder of the surviving Welsh Guards and 40 Commando. They had just driven the Argentines off Sapper Hill, back towards the town and were preparing to move into the town from the south when the 'hold' signal was received.

Sandison turned to the CO 40 Commando, 'Looks as though we may have done it, Sir.'

Colonel Adams nodded, 'Yes, our yomp across the centre of the island certainly outsmarted them. They weren't prepared to defend the area to the west of Stanley although their commandos did make things a bit hot for us at times around Two Sisters and Mount Kent. It certainly made it easier for us and probably saved many lives.'

They heard that 2 Para were moving down off Wireless Ridge into the outskirts of Stanley and soon there was a report that the Argentine defenders wished a ceasefire whilst a surrender document was negotiated. So it was really over.

Atlántida 14th June 1982

Monday 14th June they learnt that the Argentine General Menendez had formally surrendered his forces to the British. It was reported there was great unrest in Argentina but at present the wrath of the people was focused on the British. Yet again the British had stolen their birthright.

Andy learnt that a report from Elena Mantovani, passed to Cristina and then via Arthur Dean, confirmed that liberal senior officers, and the mass of middle-ranking officers in the army and the air force were putting pressure on leading senior Junta members to resign. Although it seemed the navy, always very right wing, was unswerving in its allegiance to the Junta. Andy reported they had to remain in Uruguay for a few more days in case Ridley was needed to go over again to underline the British threats. The United States was now exerting considerable pressure on the Junta. Their line now was that a civilian democratic government was the only acceptable solution. 'Better late than never,' suggested John cynically.

Tuesday 15th a message was received from Elena Mantovani indicating that the senior Junta members had accepted they must resign and that the president would announce his resignation on the 17th. Liberal senior officers would take over as a transitional government until fresh civilian elections could be organized. She understood that both Gustavo Coro and Alfredo Coro had been suspended and were in custody pending the investigation of the facts contained in the dossiers. In the afternoon the embassy called to tell her they were recalled. Seats had been booked on the flight to London on the morning of the 17th.

Wednesday 16th was their last day in Uruguay and they spent it quietly. They went into Montevideo with Yamauchi and explored the city before and after an excellent lunch with Yamauchi and Mr Tanaka, the First Secretary. Motoring back with Yamauchi they hosted a farewell dinner for Toshiro and Aiko at the best restaurant (the only one) in Atlántida. After a wonderful evening the four friends began the Japanese ritual of toasts and to the echoes of 'Kampai' they wished each other long life and Aiko made Andy blush by wishing her many children.

Thursday 17th June as the president announced his resignation, and it seemed a brighter future dawned for Argentina, Andy and John's plane lifted off from Aeropuerto Carrasco on the first leg of their flight to London Heathrow.

Friday 18th June Andy and John were ushered into the office of the Head of SIS. Andrew Collingwood and Jim Graham were also present. Seeking permission from the Head of SIS, Andrew Collingwood remarked, 'We think you have both performed outstandingly and it's been a highly successful operation. After the downfall of right wing Junta members, and now that the majority of army and air force officers are supporting a return to a civilian government, we feel confident Argentina will remain on a democratic course. It's a pity we had to fight a war but at least some good has come out of it. The United States now realizes that democracy is preferable in South America to military dictatorships even if they promise to be anti-communist, and the Junta will be replaced by a democratic government.'

Looking at Jim Graham he went on, 'I am afraid I have one bit of bad news though. We had a report yesterday from Arthur Dean to say there's no trace of Maria Gomez. We asked him to do some quiet checking. It seems she was arrested on the 3rd April when she returned to the ranch. Dean thinks they were chasing you but were too late to catch you there. She was taken to Rio Gallegos airbase and put on a plane to Buenos Aires but as far as he can tell she never arrived. We're afraid she has become one of the Disappeared.'

327

'*Desaparecidos,*' whispered John. He reached into his inside suit pocket and brought out the photo of Maria and him smiling happily at the camera on La Toja. Pushing it at Andrew Collingwood he laughed disgustedly. 'You all make me sick. I struggled to get all the information you needed to prevent the invasion and what was the result? No one took a blind bit of notice. I end up sacrificing the one person who befriended me when I was young, and for what? So that Argentina could regain democracy. That's it, you shall have my resignation before I leave.'

'John, I am so very sorry. We all here feel we have let you down,' confessed Collingwood. 'We did work very hard to convince the government there was a real threat. Your information should have been influential but it wasn't. Our politicians remained blind and were too trusting of their American allies. We fully understand how you feel and I'm sure we'd feel the same in your shoes. Andy, he's exhausted, please take him back to Canada and pick up your lives together again. Jim Graham will contact you when you get back.'

'Come on, my love,' said Andy, 'there is nothing more to be gained here.' With her arm protectively around him she steered him out of the room. 'I think the best thing we can do is go down to my parents at West Stoke near Chichester until we can organize flights back to Toronto. I'm so very sorry, my love, but we will work it out. I love you so much,' she said holding him very protectively.

Postscript

July is a good month for weddings and this was especially so in 1982. In mid July, Andy and John were married by special licence in the Saxon church at Bosham, West Sussex, beside Chichester harbour on a lovely sunny afternoon. His best man was Captain James Sandison DSC, freshly decorated for his outstanding service during the Falklands campaign, and important guests included Toshiro Yamauchi and Aiko Ishihara. Also present was Arthur Dean with Cristina Sabato very much on his arm and, of course, Andrew Collingwood and the Grahams. The Ridleys were giving up their apartments and buying a house in East Toronto, and they were also negotiating the purchase of a cottage by Lake Simcoe that Andy had fallen in love with.

At the end of the month, Toshiro and Aiko were married in Tokyo much to the delight of the Ridleys, and they were also delighted to hear that Cristina and Arthur were engaged and would be based in Ottawa after they were married. Cristina was suing for divorce from her estranged husband and they hoped they wouldn't have to wait too long. (It appeared that Andy and Cristina had a clear and friendly understanding about their men, that Cristina was allowed to look at but not touch John any more.)

During July the ships of the task force began to come home as did many of the troops who fought in that inhospitable place more than 8000 miles from their home.

Argentina had started on the path back to democracy and a human rights commission was being set up to investigate the Dirty War and the cases of the Disappeared. Gustavo and Alfredo Coro had both been charged with kidnapping, torture and murder and were expected to be given life sentences if found guilty. The body of Maria Gomez was never found. She became one of the thousands of the Disappeared.

John had stuck to his promise and resigned from DNI. This meant he could no longer use his Canadian passport and might have to leave Canada. They had visited Jim Graham and his wife when they returned to Canada, and to their surprise Jim offered them formal Canadian citizenship on the grounds that they had experience very useful to Canada. He offered them both jobs as intelligence analysts in Canadian Intelligence. Smiling at Andy he promised, 'You will both have desk jobs!'

In June 1983 Nippon Farma Argentina was formally constituted with its head office in Buenos Aires, and not long after the Ridleys received a large package from Japan. When they opened it they found it was a model of a Samurai warrior in full ceremonial dress. With the gift was a wonderful testimonial to John from the board of Nippon Health. That gift had pride of place in the entrance hall of their new house, along with a certain glowing red lacquer vase they received as an engagement present.

It was reported in 1984 that Rafael Gomez had been shot dead in Buenos Aires by the jealous husband of another of his mistresses, and consequently El Indo ranch was to be sold.